DEAR FAIRYLOOT READER,

Oftentimes, I'll get a spark of an idea and I'll type a few notes then store them in a file for later. Sometimes, the story idea won't leave me alone.

Approximately nine years ago, I was contemplating Ancient Rome and imagined what it might've been like if Romans were touched by the gods with the ability to shift into dragons—if this was what gave them the power to invade and conquer their way across the world. At the time, I was working on several projects, so I did as I always do and put the idea aside for another day.

But not long after, Malina popped into my mind—a beautiful, Dacian dancer who loved her family more than anything. And her fateful meeting with a Roman centurion—a dragon. My muse pestered me so much that I couldn't stop thinking about them. So I decided to at least write the prologue—the first meeting between Malina Bihari and Julianus Dakkia. Instantly, I fell deeply in love with these two and the world I'd only briefly imagined.

But other books were in line to be written so again I set it aside. Over the years, I would think about Malina and Julian on occasion, but it never seemed to be the right time to bring them out of the vault. I loved the idea of this world so much that I wanted to write and release it in a special way. I envisioned a beautiful cover that would reflect my imagination—fire, beauty, the toppling of a tyrannical Rome with a mystical woman and her dragon lover at the helm.

Then, not so long ago, the stars surprised me and aligned perfectly. It was finally time to bring my Roman dragons to life.

As most authors do, I always have little doubts and anxieties about my writing. That never goes away. But when I finally let Malina and Julian take control of their story—*oh, my*—the story poured onto the page. So fast and so richly that I thought perhaps they were asking, *what took you so long?*

All I know is, they've waited long enough, and I wholeheartedly believe that now is the time for the Bihari sisters and their dragon mates to meet the world of romantasy lovers.

Thank you to everyone who picks up this book and joins their journey with me. I hope you'll enjoy *Firebird*—book one in this saga where dragons rule Rome, but *she* rules his heart.

Gratefully yours,

Juliette Cross

FIREBIRD

A FairyLoot Exclusive Edition of

FIREBIRD

Signed by the author

Juliette Cross

THIS EDITION PUBLISHED BY
BRAMBLE IN COLLABORATION WITH FAIRYLOOT

BRAMBLE

FairyLoot

A FairyLoot Exclusive Edition of

FIREBIRD

JULIETTE CROSS

BRAMBLE   FairyLoot

PUBLISHED BY TOR BRAMBLE AND FAIRYLOOT

First published 2025 by Tom Doherty Associates / Tor Publishing Group

First published in the UK 2025 by Tor Bramble
an imprint of Pan Macmillan
The Smithson, 6 Briset Street, London EC1M 5NR
EU representative: Macmillan Publishers Ireland Ltd, 1st Floor,
The Liffey Trust Centre, 117–126 Sheriff Street Upper,
Dublin 1, D01 YC43
Associated companies throughout the world
www.panmacmillan.com

ISBN 978-1-0350-5244-8 HB
ISBN 978-1-0350-5245-5 TPB

1 3 5 7 9 8 6 4 2

A CIP catalogue record for this book is available from the British Library.

Printed and bound by CPI Group (UK) Ltd, Croydon, CR0 4YY

Visit **www.panmacmillan.com** to read more about all our books
and to buy them. You will also find features, author interviews and
news of any author events, and you can sign up for e-newsletters
so that you're always first to hear about our new releases.

For my beloved husband

AUTHOR'S NOTE

The cultured yet brutal civilization of ancient Rome served as inspiration for this fantasy world. However, it is meant to be a reimagining of the Roman Empire, not one of historical accuracy. I used creative license frequently to serve the story.

One example is that Malina Bihari and her family are from the ancient territory of Dacia, which is modern-day Romania. However, in the book, they speak Romanian, not Dacian. This is because Dacian is an extinct language and was not recorded. I chose to use the language of the people who live there today.

I've also reinvented some of the gods, goddesses, and mythology of Rome. In this world, pureblood Romans share ancestry with ancient titans—dragons—and the gods themselves. Their power is divine. Like the historical Rome, they use their power and strength to conquer and burn and enslave. And as history proves, there will always be rebellion and revolution in the face of oppression and tyranny.

THE DRAGON HOUSES

Listed in order of their hierarchy, prestige, and power in Rome.

* **Ignis**—Fire-red line

  Descended from Romulus, one of the two brothers suckled by a she-dragon and given the power of transformation. Romulus slayed his brother Remus and founded Rome as its first emperor. The Ignis line has always held more dominance and power in ruling Rome.

* **Media Nocte**—Midnight-black line

  Descended from Remus, one of the two first dragon brothers. They were both given the power of transformation through their dragon mother, a powerful titan of the ancient world covered in red and black scales.

* **Sapphirus**—Sapphire-blue line

  The first dragon line to be born after the Ignis and Media Nocte. This line was born from a coupling between the god Neptune and the eldest daughter of Romulus.

* **Amethystus**—Amethyst-purple line

  Descended from a girl child of Pluto and Proserpina. When their daughter begged to fly freely in the open skies rather than live only in the depths of the underworld, her parents sent her into the mortal realm to live among them.

* **Chrysocolla**—Malachite-green line

   Blessed into existence by the goddess Diana, whose arrow struck the heart of a Sapphirus dragon while it mated with her nymph Egeria. When he was struck by the arrow, he instantly shed his blue coloring for the shade of the meadow where they made love and gave that hue to their offspring.

* **Griseo**—Gray line

   The lowest caste of dragons, who have no known ancestry. Because of their lack of hierarchy, they are often used in the gladiator arenas.

* **Vicus**—White dragon

   An anomaly of only female dragons who can be born of any house. They are considered to be chosen by the gods to serve as priestesses in their temples. It is a prestigious honor to be born a Vicus.

* **Chrysos**—Gold dragon

   A legendary line with extraordinary fire power, who are extinct. No known origin, though believed to be touched by the god Jupiter himself.

THE MYTH OF MEDUSA

Medusa was born a white dragon. She was a lovely babe who grew into a pretty girl who grew into a beautiful woman. She had one, and only one, dream for her life: to worship and serve the gods.

She was overjoyed to be selected to serve as priestess by the Temple of Minerva. The goddess of war and wisdom was the pinnacle of feminine strength and intelligence.

She praised the gods for granting her a quiet life of service, for that is all she ever desired. She reveled in helping others and devoted herself to keeping the temple and altar a sacred place for Romans to worship and beg the goddess for favors.

Her life was good. She was happy. She was blessed.

Until one day, the god Neptune spied Medusa walking along the seashore where she meditated one afternoon each week.

Neptune became instantly entranced by her glossy locks of pale blond hair and her voluptuous body. When she left the seashore, he followed her. He trailed her into the temple, where she went to work cleaning the altar.

Overcome with lust, he violated Medusa on the altar, stealing her virginity with a groan and satisfying release. He walked away without a glance, leaving her in despair and blood and tears.

Her two sisters found her and wept with her for all she had lost, for all that was stolen. Without her virginity, she would be cast out from the temple, her role as priestess stripped from her. To Medusa, that was a fate worse than death.

The goddess Minerva heard her and her sisters weeping and whispered prayers for help. She descended on a cloud of silver, spreading her dragon wings wide.

"Cry not, my child," she told Medusa.

"But I am soiled and ruined. I cannot serve you anymore."

"Yes, you can, my dear. And you will. So will your sisters."

The goddess drew herself up to her full height, her dragon horns curling more out of her skull, her white tail lashing the air.

Medusa and her sisters stared up in wonder at the powerful goddess, her purple eyes sparking.

"How?" asked Medusa, tears streaking her beautiful face.

Minerva placed a palm upon Medusa's head. "Neptune saw you and was overcome with his own desire. I will give you power over men so that they cannot do this again. And I will give you more." Her fingers glowed white where she clutched Medusa's skull. "I bestow upon you the gift of a sorceress. Like a snake to its prey, you will latch onto any man you choose and pour malice into their hearts. You will be able to force your enemies to feel despair, pain, and loss. You will control them with the magic you hold."

Medusa gasped as she felt the power bleed into her veins.

Minerva then placed her hand upon the sister at her right side.

"I bestow upon you the gift of the siren. Any man whose blood you taste will fall at your feet and do your will. Even if you command him to die, he will do so."

Her sister crumbled as the goddess's power filled her body and blood.

Minerva gripped the head of the third sister, eyes glowing white with ethereal power.

"I bestow upon you the power of Charon's kiss. Your lips will breathe death into the mouths of corrupt men. Their spirits will suffer for all their transgressions."

The third sister cried out as the magic wove into her soul.

The goddess stood tall and straight, stretching her wings wide.

"Neptune has done you wrong, my child. For his crime, men will suffer. But none who do not deserve it. You and your sisters will go forth and serve me well. You will punish evil men and damn them."

Medusa, no longer smothered in dark despair, lifted her face to the goddess. "When will we be done? When is our job finished?"

Minerva smiled, her teeth razor-sharp. "When evil men no longer roam this world."

So the three sisters went out into the world to do their sacred work. But when they were old and on Pluto's doorstep, he took their sweet souls, but not Minerva's gifts. Those powers had no place in the underworld. He sent them back to the mortal realm where they've been passed to worthy women again and again, century after century.

Some say that Minerva's mystical gifts have been seeking the right sisters, the ones to right all of mankind's wrongs once and for all.

PROLOGUE

Dacia, 53 BCE

MALINA

"Malina," hissed my sister. *"Vino aici."*

I ignored her summons again, continuing to peer out through the tent flap.

The crowd thickened close to the stage where Hanzi tipped his head back and slid a sword down his throat. An eruption of awe swept up with applause.

"Malina."

I finally snapped the tent flap shut. Lela removed her headscarf, black waves of hair tumbling down her shoulders. Plopping myself down on the wooden stool, I watched her with undisguised envy. Our bunica, our grandmother, gave her the colorful basma on her betrothal day last month. It still made my heart clench with envy.

"What is that look, *bebeluş*?" she asked.

"I wish you'd stop calling me baby."

Lela tilted her head and smiled in her maternal way, then picked up the stick of kohl.

"Close your eyes."

I did, sighing as Lela lined my left lid first.

"Are you going to tell me what the sighs are for? You always love to dance for the crowd." I could hear the smile in her voice. "And the crowd adores you."

"It's not that. It's just . . . I miss Mama and Papa. I miss home." And I didn't want anything to change. Everything would change when she married Jardani.

Usually, our parents would have come with us. Most of our clan was with our caravan. But winter approached. There was much to do and prepare before the snows began to fall. Our parents and a few selected elders of each *familie* in the clan remained behind. Our caravan had made a small circle through the valley beneath the southern range of the Carpathian Mountains. This last bit of coin would serve us well through the winter months.

As she'd done many times before, Lela smeared the kohl to thicken the shading along the outer edges of my eyes. "This is the last village. We'll break camp in the morning and start the journey home." She laughed in her throat. "But you don't fool me. You'll miss this."

Lela finished dabbing the kohl and brushed out my hair the way she used to before she fell in love and spent all her time with Jardani.

My gaze fell to my lap where I traced the intricate design in golden thread on my red *fustă*. The gold and silver medallions of jewelry sewn into the vibrant fabric winked by the lantern light. Bunica had made the richly adorned woolen skirt in a way that flared in perfect little arcs when I spun on stage.

I stood and smoothed my white blouse, the gold star-shaped embroidery sweeping in gentle curves down to where it met my fustă, creating a continuous design that flattered my figure.

"What do you mean?"

"You're an adventurer, Mina. And too curious for your own good."

I shrugged. "The world is an interesting place."

"And dangerous. Especially for a wild seventeen-year-old girl." Her dark eyes trailed down my body, a frown pinching her brow. "And one who appears much older."

It was true I'd inherited more curves from our mother than Lela. We were polar opposites, the two of us. Lela was all sweetness and gentle ways like our father. I had the boldness and short temper of our mother.

"I'm nearly eighteen," I argued.

"And unmarried and unprotected."

I hated that reminder. She'd be married soon, and Mother was already hinting it was my turn next. All I wanted was for everything to stay the same, but that seemed impossible.

The tent flap whipped open with a thwack. Jardani filled up the entrance, stormy scowl darkening his features, broad shoulders tense with readiness.

Lela straightened. "What is it?"

"Romans."

My throat went dry, fear tripping my pulse faster. "Are any of them—" I swallowed hard, unable to finish the question. But Jardani knew.

"Yes," he growled. "One is a centurion."

The tent flap popped open again. Kizzy and Kostanya swept from behind Jardani's imposing figure.

"Romans are here," whispered Kizzy.

"To watch the show," finished Kostanya.

Our twin sisters, one year younger than me.

"Where did they come from?" Lela's pretty eyes were wide and glittering. "There's been no word of an uprising."

No. This region had been faithful subjects to Caesar. Honor Emperor Igniculus with tribute, and the Romans left us alone. We weren't fools.

Jardani shook his head. "There's a Roman province across the Danube thirty leagues from here. Could be a scouting party from there."

"How many?" I asked.

"Only four," Jardani added. "But that centurion." He shook his head, lowering his voice to a hoarse whisper. "If he wanted, he could kill us all."

I pushed past Jardani and the twins, peering out through the sliver of tent opening. I spotted them strolling through the crowd toward the front. The three soldiers laughed, seemingly entertained by Hanzi's juggling act, but the centurion who followed slowly in their wake did not. His red cape denoted his higher station. He stood taller than Jardani. The baldric crossing his chest held his gladius, the hilt glinting with fine craftsmanship.

His movements were fluid, lithe, a hunter's steady progress toward the awaiting prey. His face was steeped in shadow till they passed a torch. I sucked in a staccato breath.

His face was too hard, too sharp, too arresting. His maker had cut him with an unforgiving blade, molding him into a beast of unquestionable dominance and terrible beauty. He stood off to the side of the front row, his dark gaze sweeping the audience. The gusting torch flame licked along his features, caressing into the shadows like a lover. Then it happened. Flickering flame caught the golden deep of his irises, touching the supernatural doors to his soul. If he had one.

I exhaled the breath I'd been holding, knowing I looked upon the beast of legend. The one who filled our people with fiery nightmares, who stormed across the world and took whatever and whoever he wanted.

"Dragon," I whispered.

Kizzy squeaked behind me.

"What should we do?" whimpered Kostanya.

Jardani gestured toward the north. "Slip off to last night's encampment. Wait for me there."

"No." I followed my instincts, measuring the situation in a blink. "It is known and expected that the Bihari sisters close the show. Every show. That crowd out there is expecting us. If we run and hide, it will only anger them and alert the Romans that something is amiss."

"But, Malina." Kizzy's chin trembled. "He's a—a—"

"Yes. I know. And how far do you think we'd get if we ran and hid in the woods like thieves in the night? If we close the show without the final act, those villagers will want their coin back and cause a riot."

I leveled on Jardani, who stared back, contemplating quietly. Finally, he cursed under his breath, then hung his head, hands on hips.

Lela stepped forward, her expression tight. "What do you *feel*?" Besides Bunica, she was the only one who ever outright spoke of my gift. And they would never mention it outside family. To be an empath like me held its own dangers.

I turned my face back toward the tent opening, closing my eyes. Finding the quiet within, I reached out into the boisterous crowd, touching the life-light of every person. My gift allowed me to read the unique essence emanating from within a person.

When I found the centurion, knowing it was him by the stark potency of his life force, my empathic sense shuddered. I probed deeper, a feverish sweat sweeping over my skin, a vibrant cord of power pulsing through our connection. No anger, animosity, or violence trembled along the invisible thread I tethered to him. It was difficult to gauge from this distance, but odds were in our favor.

I opened my eyes and spun to them, shaking my head. "No aggression."

Jardani gave a stiff nod, then moved closer to Lela. "Keep the dance short and keep your distance." He cupped Lela's face, his brutish hands gentle, tilting her face up to look at him. "Be careful, *iubirea mea*."

I turned away from the intimate gesture. Jardani was a good man, and he adored my sister. Eventually, I'd forgive him for taking her away from me. Right now, my focus was on the crowd beyond the tent, roaring with applause. Peeking out, I caught Hanzi finishing with his flourishing juggle of flaming torches.

"It's time," I called over my shoulder.

The twins nodded and snatched metal zills from a basket on the shelf and fitted them onto their thumbs and middle fingers. I didn't, as I needed my hands free for my part of the act.

"Right," Lela snapped in her maternal tone. "Go, girls."

On cue, the first lilting strains of Yoska's lute carried from the stage. Then Rukeli's soft rhythm, his hands sweeping on the tympanum, silenced the crowd. The hypnotic beat of the drum and the magnetic rise and fall of the lute riveted everyone's attention to the stage. The four of us slipped into the shadow behind the stage.

Hanzi was there, sweat-drenched from his performance, but wearing his ever-present bright smile for us. A brighter one for me.

The twins leaped onto the stage before me and Lela, clacking their finger cymbals in rhythm with Yoska and Rukeli's melody.

"*Baftă!*" called Hanzi with a wink, placing a firm hand on my shoulder and giving me a squeeze.

"I don't need luck," I answered with a smile before sweeping past him and up the steps.

Chin raised, body poised with straight back, one shoulder dipping lower, I glided onto the stage in bare feet, despite the chill in the air. Lela spun in a rhythmic circle down the center of the stage, her bejeweled blue skirt curving in arcs like a glittering ocean wave. Her

12

breathless beauty drew all eyes, while Kizzy and Kostanya mirrored her movements. A mesmerizing scene.

I smiled and kept to the back, swaying gently and clapping my hands in tune to the beat, trying to remain invisible while Lela danced her part, captivating her audience with each swing of her hair and swirl of her skirts.

Then . . . I felt him. His eyes were on me. My skin prickled with awareness. It was too much to withstand, to ignore. Cutting my gaze to the left, I faltered, my hands holding on a single clap.

Watching him from afar was entirely different than seeing him this close. He leaned against a wooden post, arms crossed in casual repose, expression blank. But his fire-gold eyes. They told me another story. One of heat and mystery and unmistakable interest. Caught in his gaze, like a hare in the wolf's claws, I almost missed the shift in the music that was my cue.

Rukeli beat louder on the tympanum with one beat of his hand, then silence. Breaking from the centurion with a snap of my head, I took my first step forward.

The defiant spirit that had buoyed me up so many times before rejected the fear that a dragon among us conveyed. Yet, the tether I still held through my empathic link didn't scream of the fear I was told a dragon would. His essence was alluring. Exciting. That inner fire burned through my limbs, guiding my dance like never before.

With slow, precise steps I advanced to the stage dead center, swayed my hips, rose my arms heavenward. Rukeli pounded out another single drumbeat in unison to the stomp of my feet. My sisters clacked their finger cymbals slowly as I slid one foot forward and rolled my body.

Spinning to face the back of the stage and my sisters, I ignored Lela's shake of the head warning me not to do it. There was one daring move I reserved for certain audiences. Not one with a Roman dragon standing in watchful attendance.

Best not to dazzle too brightly in the presence of one of them. They liked treasure. But the witch inside me defied the interloper in our midst. I ignored my sister's silent protests as the music rose seductively.

I repeated the roll of my body from the ground up in slow repetition. With each wave, I arched my back farther and farther, bending my spine, my arms reaching and waving suggestively to the crowd appearing in my vision upside down.

My long hair brushed the stage as I bent, my blouse pulled tight over my upthrust breasts, one sleeve baring a shoulder. And still I contorted my body into an impossible arch.

When my head nearly brushed the floor, I straightened with a whip of my body to the beat of the drum. Rather than simply spin away, I gathered momentum and outstretched my arms, tumbling in a back flip where I stood. The audience gasped, then applause erupted.

The edge of my underskirt and fustă caught on my hip, baring the length of one bronze leg. The centurion's gaze dropped, his phantom touch catapulting my pulse faster. I gripped the skirts in one hand and began to spin with swift, stomping footwork before I leaped boldly to the teetering end of the stage where he stood. The music was now a maddening frenzy, the audience clapping to the beat of the drum.

Angling my chin down over my bare shoulder, I locked my gaze onto the centurion, the black waves of my hair swaying with the melody. His dragon eyes simmered an otherworldly gold, reflecting the internal fire within. When his mouth ticked up on one side in a smoldering half smile, I faced forward and launched into a series of front tumbles, flipping so fast my skirts whirled in tandem.

Yoska and Rukeli played wild and fast, spinning me and my sisters into a whirl of skirts and flourishing moves. The music sped higher and faster into a sudden, dramatic stop where we each froze into a goddess-like pose, legs and arms intertwined, bodies curved, necks arched, and eyes shining bright.

Leaping from their seats, the villagers cheered. Small coins plinked and rolled onto the stage. As was tradition, our finale dance was showered with pennyweight coins. Hanzi scurried onstage to collect them while we bowed and smiled, waving to the crowd.

I tried to keep from looking but my gaze cut to the centurion anyway. He was smiling. For a moment, I was caught by his welcome and attractive expression. He reached inside a pocket on his belt, then held up a coin to me. It looked bigger than the ones being tossed onto the stage. I held out my cupped hands and he tossed it. I caught it with a laugh, then Lela pushed me roughly toward the steps.

"Malina," she hissed, as we stumbled behind the stage. "What do you think you were doing?"

"Giving the customers what they came for."

"You know what I'm talking about. That was too . . . too—"

"It was nothing."

"It was *reckless*. As you always are."

"Stop worrying, Lela. Go and pack. Jardani will want to leave tonight."

Trembling from the performance, I stormed off before Lela could scold me further. The crowd still buzzed. Yoska and Rukeli played on. Jardani ushered them over for ale and watered-down wine. A few extra coins before the villagers wandered home.

Lela was right. I'd never displayed myself quite so provocatively. Why would I do it for him? I hated Romans. Hated their superiority. Their conquering and burning of the whole world, simply because they could. Because no one could defeat dragons.

Perhaps that was why. I wanted to flaunt my fearlessness in front of him. Show him I was not afraid, no matter what beast stared back at me, but my inner witch whispered, *no, that's not the reason.*

Cutting through two wagons and behind the horse pen—the foul-tempered gelding chuffed and whickered at me—I rounded another wagon and peeked from behind. Jardani's makeshift tavern, nothing

15

more than a weathered canvas top and two casks propped on stools, lured the audience in well enough. Yoska and Rukeli played a lively tune, while Hanzi served drinks and collected more coin.

Slipping past and clutching the centurion's coin in my palm, I grabbed a torch and ran along the path into the woods toward our encampment. But rather than go directly to our tent, I cut into the little meadow where we let the horses graze during the day, so I could observe my coin without my sisters fussing or asking questions.

Stepping into the open under the bright moonlight, I raised my palm and the torch so I could get a better look.

"Bendis above," I whispered.

It was gold. Or at least it looked like gold. I'd never actually held the precious metal in my hands. One side depicted a temple, the edges soft and well-worn. The other was a woman, a goddess sitting on a throne, an upside-down crescent over her head, a cornucopia held in both hands.

"She is Lady Fortuna."

I froze. The voice was a deep, melodious rumble, like thunder over the mountain. Like danger in the distance, drawing ever closer.

Stars save me. It could only be one man.

Spinning, I stared a mere few feet away at marble-like features cut into slashes of shadow by the moonlight. The centurion. And the dragon.

I glanced to the right, preparing to flee, wondering if I could actually outrun him. Panic gripped me. I certainly wasn't fearless now.

"No, wait." He held up both palms in a disarming fashion, then took a step backward. "I won't harm you."

But it was impossible for a man of his height and breadth and birth to appear harmless. He was a noble-born Roman with ancient magic—and a monster—firing through his blood.

My pulse raced, and I realized we were alone. If he wanted to hurt me, he could quite easily do so before anyone would come and help me. *If* they could help me.

16

Still holding his palms out in a placating manner, he nodded to my hand where I still held the coin. "That aureus is special."

It *was* gold. My arm holding the torch shook, a flame gusting as I exhaled a trembling breath.

I was terrified, but I lifted my chin with all the confidence I could muster, realizing he must've given me the coin for nefarious reasons.

"Why would you give me a piece of gold?" I snapped, though my voice quivered.

Everything about him screamed for me to run. Except my empathic sense, which was still annoyingly quiet as a calm sea. My witch told me to keep still. So I did.

"You're a gifted dancer," he stated with calm and poise, lowering his arms to clasp his hands behind his back, still trying to appear harmless. It did ease my panic a little, though my body remained poised for flight.

"I'm the best of my sisters," I finally replied, using bravado to cover my quaking fear.

He smiled. My gaze automatically dropped to his mouth. That's where I realized what gave him some semblance of softness. Where his jaw, chin, nose, and brow were all sharp angles, his wide mouth seemed soft.

"You are," he agreed. "I witnessed the proof of it just now."

"Why would you give me a gold coin for a dance?" I snapped again, my fear morphing into ire. "You will not get anything else for it."

Still poised, even at my assumption, possibly an insult, that he'd been trying to buy something else from me that I wasn't prepared to part with, he replied steadily, "I do not want anything else."

A cloud billowed above us across the moon, the shadows hiding his face. Even so, his dragon eyes glowed in the dark. It reminded me of the wolves back home in the Carpathian Mountains, when the winter grew harsh and they came looking for easy prey around our village. Strangely, this Roman didn't incite fear in me with his gleaming dragon eyes.

I stepped forward and raised my torch so that I could see his face more clearly. He remained unnaturally still. I knew he was trying to assuage my fear. We both knew that if he wanted to harm me, he could. Only noble-born Romans with the blood of the dragon coursing through their veins could be centurions.

His eyes. Bright as a burning star, they watched me. "This coin is special," he told me. "It's worth more than the gold it was forged from."

"Why is that?"

"Fortuna is the goddess who guides our path through life. She bestows good fortune to those who give her tribute, who pray and listen to her."

"I do not believe in your gods," I told him boldly.

"That does not matter." He took a small step forward.

I braced to run, but he stopped at that one step, seeming to want a better look at me.

"We all have our own gods," he added, clasping his hands in front of him now, very large hands to equal the rest of his towering physique. He was far taller than any man I'd ever seen. I'd been told that before about dragons, that they were larger than human men. Still, it was astounding to behold with my own eyes. "But Fortuna loves all people of all provinces and all regions."

His words were confusing to me. We had our own gods who we prayed and sacrificed to. Why would a goddess I didn't worship care about me?

"Not only is Fortuna a special goddess to me," he went on, "but this aureus was given to me by my mother, the gold minted by my own father when they married. A wedding gift. I've carried this aureus on me for many years."

"Which again makes me wonder why you would give something so precious away to a stranger."

The fear was sinking its claws in again, but then he said, "Fortuna speaks to me sometimes." He paused. "Do you believe that?"

Of course I believed the gods and powers unknown spoke to us. I was one of a long line of mystical women who wielded gifts not of this world. My inner spirit spoke to me often. I merely nodded.

He graced me with another smile. "She spoke to me tonight. And I knew you'd need the coin for good fortune one day."

I peered down at the image of Fortuna in my palm, the torchlight glittering on the gold piece. Then I gazed at the centurion.

"We could all use the favor of the gods. I will not shun such a gift if Fortuna has selected me for her favor."

"Indeed." He dipped his chin. "You are wise as you are beautiful, little firebird."

I frowned at his familiarity and the moniker. I didn't know what a firebird was. But before I could ask, he had taken a step back and then did something rather shocking. He bowed, a gesture saved for nobility alone.

"Farewell," he crooned softly. "May Fortuna guide your path."

Then he spun away, his red cloak rippling, stalked into the shadows, and disappeared.

Clutching the aureus to my chest, I fled back to our family tent, knowing I'd keep my small treasure a secret. After all, Fortuna had chosen me for her good grace. I would cherish the centurion's coin, no matter that it was delivered by the enemy, a dragon.

I

Four years later—Eastern border of Gaul

JULIAN

Standing atop the hill, I looked down on the bloodstained field and charred bodies still smoking after the battle. Little remained of the Celtic horde, which was no surprise against a Roman legion. Though this particular clan of Celts had resisted defeat quite a few times before. I was glad their king had died on the field so that I wasn't forced to bring him back to appease my uncle. He so enjoyed a gory public execution. The thought turned my innards to roiling acid.

The cohort of deathriders circled above—giant winged shadows in the moonlit night sky, their fires still burning the perimeter so the Celts had no escape route. Pillars of smoke billowed upward and wafted on the wind. The deathriders would remain vigilant and on guard until I sent a messenger into the skies to let them know they could return to our base camp.

Cries erupted from the Celtic encampment in the woods where my men were now rounding up survivors for the slave market.

My most trusted tribune, Trajan, marched up the hill still in half-skin, wearing only a baldric across his chest for his gladius as was our tradition in battle for officers—the noble-born.

Triple his normal size in human form, Trajan's dark blue-scaled skin appeared black under the cover of night. His arms bulged with muscle, hands tipped with finger-long black claws. Midnight leathery wings jutted from his back. He met my gaze with pale blue reptilian eyes, his snout jutting too far to be human, jagged teeth lining his wide dragon mouth, his thick tail lashing.

"All secure, Legatus."

His speech was more understandable than most in half-skin. Some men couldn't even speak at all, the dragon too willful and dominant. Powerful dragons could speak clearly in half-skin, even if his or her voice sounded rough and guttural.

He stood next to me, looking below.

As commander of this invasion, I'd remained in human form, fully clothed in regalia fitting my station. Generals no longer needed to shift into half-skin and get bloody on the battlefield. We'd earned our right to keep our hands and uniforms clean. It was a sign of power when you ordered commands for battle without ever letting your dragon loose.

But each soldier knew that I could shift in a blink and take their head off if they stepped out of line. Our beasts gave us dominance over every battlefield, but when released, they were also predatory, single-minded monsters. If the officers didn't know without a doubt that their general was the most dominant beast among them, then their dragons would never submit to his command.

I'd earned my right to stand on this hill and command from afar—no matter who my uncle was. Every soldier in my legions knew it.

"No bands of Celts beyond the fire line?" I asked.

"None."

The Celts were vicious and cunning. They often held back a band of warriors to catch Romans unaware with archers and spear-wielders who'd tipped their arrows with poison. This particular region of Celts had bested my predecessor, Legatus Bastius, three times. Allegedly, they had some sort of sorceress who aided somehow, but that was still a mystery.

My uncle, the emperor, finally invited Legatus Bastius to dinner at his palace in Rome after his third defeat. They'd grown up together. Bastius was nervous nonetheless. My heightened dragon senses detected the sweat he reeked and his increased heart rate as Bastius took his seat on a cushioned chaise across from me for our meal.

He was told the emperor would discuss strategy for his next invasion. Instead, my uncle fed him a grand feast, let him fuck one of his slaves during dinner, and laughed over their old conquests in Germania. Right as Bastius was regaling us with a story of one of his bloodier kills, my uncle staked him to the wall with his own gladius through the throat, then gutted and beheaded him.

When he was done, Bastius's beheaded carcass bleeding on his marble floor, Uncle Igniculus stalked across the deadly silent room, still full of his party guests. He stopped and stood in front of me in half-skin, speckled in his former friend's blood.

"Congratulations, nephew." He'd pressed his bloody palm flat to my chest, yellow eyes glittering with his dragon. "Or should I say, Legatus Julianus *Ignis Dakkia*." He always liked to emphasize the names we shared in common.

That's how I received my promotion. That's why I was standing here now, ensuring this Celtic tribe didn't escape yet again.

"Be sure to get their king's head. Uncle will want it for his Wall of Victory."

"It will be done," agreed Trajan.

A female shout echoed from the distant encampment, followed by growling and laughter, drawing my attention.

Though I couldn't admit it to anyone but Trajan, I didn't want senseless murder taking place under my command. Bastius had been a sloppy general, letting his soldiers become undisciplined with his lack of leadership. I wouldn't have my men murdering women and children for fun when the battle was over. I'd heard about how they'd raped and pillaged and destroyed an entire village in Thrace before burning it to the ground.

Since I'd inherited this defiant rabble, I'd been forced to harshly discipline a number of soldiers. Some had nearly died from my punishments. But strength was power and the only way to control them was through brutal force.

A woman's scream echoed up to us again.

"They aren't killing the prisoners, are they? I want a large haul for the market."

"Not killing, Legatus," answered Trajan. "They found the Celtic witch. Just having a little fun with her."

I cut a hard look to him. He recognized I wanted a full explanation without me even asking. We'd been friends before I'd become his superior, and he knew me better than any other.

"The sorceress who's been helping the Celts defeat us so many times before. They cornered her. Going to take turns with her before they hand her over to the *mangones*."

"In half-skin?" I demanded to know.

"Only Silvanus is in half-skin."

Ire flamed at the thought of the savagery these men had bestowed on too many already. It would *not* happen under my command.

"There will be nothing left to give the slave master when he's done."
Marching forward, I commanded, "Follow me."

My dragon pulsed a hard beat behind my breast, burning to cut
loose and show Silvanus and his lackeys what terror truly felt like, the
kind of terror they were bestowing on the witch below. I didn't care if
she mystically aided the Celts. This was vengeance because a woman
bruised their egos.

I knew how brutal Silvanus could be without any cause at all.
They'd kill her for sure if they violated her in half-skin. Above all else,
he was defying my orders. And *that* could not be tolerated.

Officers towering above me in half-skin, along with human
soldiers—common-born Romans—turned as I crossed the battlefield.
They stepped back, clenched their right fists, and struck them over
their hearts in salute and submission, eyes straight as I passed. The reek
of burning bodies filled the air, the smell of victory.

Trajan trailed a step behind me and to my left as was proper of a
general's second. The raucous laughter lilted closer as I stepped into the
line of trees. The *mangones* loaded his newly acquired property into carrying nets—women, children, and the few men who survived the battle.
Though there were also female warriors among the Celtic men. They'd
catch the finest price at market.

A feminine cry reached me through the trees.

"Fucking whore!" growled Silvanus in his garbled half-skin speech.

More laughter.

"She got you good that time," said one of his comrades. Sounded
like Zeno.

I stepped into a small clearing where three tents burned off to the
left, lighting the scene. Silvanus towered above everyone, rippling with
gray scales over his bulging form.

Perhaps his fate as one of the Griseo line, his dissatisfaction as the
lowest caste of dragon, propelled his cruelty. As if he could pound and
fight his way up the ladder of nobility. Seeing this display only verified

that the fates had it right. He belonged beneath the rest of us. Not because of his birth, but because of his own brutality.

He gripped his cock and stroked it, stalking closer to the disheveled woman holding a dagger where she crouched in front of a wide tree, the trunk shielding her back.

Zeno and two others watched with feverish glee. They were now in human form, naked and hard, the adrenaline of battle pumping their bodies into a frenzy. Violating a helpless woman with their large, formidable bodies as men wouldn't harm her nearly as much as Silvanus planned to. She might survive the men, but not a dragon in half-skin.

Silvanus stepped closer. "You've never had the likes of me, witch."

The woman tensed, readying to defend herself. The knife cut on his thigh proved her a warrior. Or at the very least, a woman ready to die fighting rather than submit to the monster coming for her.

I could smell his blood. Or maybe it was hers. Her dark hair was wild and mussed, covering most of her face, her handspun tunic soiled and torn at the neck. She hadn't seen me, her head turned toward the predator stalking closer.

None of them had seen me where I stood in the shadows. It wasn't until Trajan stepped forward, partially into the light, taking his place at my side, that Zeno's gaze found us. Then the other two looked my way.

My entire focus was on Silvanus terrifying this Celtic witch. Whatever her offenses, they were mine to judge and punish. Not his.

"I'm gonna stuff you till you bleed," growled Silvanus.

"No. You will not."

Immediate silence fell following my curt reply. Others outside our circle froze where they were and watched the scene. Good. Let them all watch and see.

Silvanus stiffened in place, his muscles bunching. The three others stood to attention, saluting me with fists over hearts that raced faster when I took three long, even steps into the firelight. Silvanus swiveled, still holding his cockstand with vulgar display.

"Legatus," he drawled in greeting, not saluting me, his maddened eyes full of the beast, little sign of the man.

For a long moment, all I heard was the crackling fire of the tents and the birdlike, fluttering pulse of the woman cowering behind Silvanus. Finally, I spoke.

"What was my command regarding the prisoners?"

He held my gaze defiantly. He seemed to be calculating if he could attack and kill me before I shifted. I narrowed my gaze, willing him to try.

He grunted and let go of his cock, which bobbed perversely between his legs. "She isn't a regular prisoner, Legatus," he said with mock obedience. "She's the fucking witch who helped the Celts."

I waited and said nothing, the snapping fires and stillness stretching the tension.

"*What* was my command regarding the prisoners?" I repeated, letting my dragon dip into my voice.

Silvanus huffed, opening his wings in a dominant display before replying, "You commanded that all prisoners were to be handed over to the slave trader."

"And?" I prompted in an icy tone.

"Unspoiled," he added begrudgingly.

"That is correct." I lifted my voice for all to hear. "As I have informed you all before, you have had your fun under Bastius. It is not your fault that you were misguided by your former, undisciplined general. He was weak. Because of his failures, his head rots on the Wall of Traitors."

The skulls on pikes along the Wall of Traitors was double the number along the Wall of Victory. Every soldier here knew it.

"If you think that I would let you become the ignoble degenerates that you were under Bastius, you are soundly mistaken."

I paused, letting my words sink in as I turned my gaze back to Silvanus.

"We are not barbarians. We do not spoil and mar the property of Emperor Igniculus. Every prisoner you beat, every woman you rape and damage, brings less coin at the slave market. Less coin in the emperor's coffer. And less coin in reward that you will receive as victors of the battlefield."

Silvanus flexed his muscles and stretched his wings, readying for his punishment. I'd considered killing him in front of his lackeys and my men. But decided a good beating in half-skin should do the trick. Bearing him back to Rome in chains in one of his soldier brother's nets would be the perfect humiliation before putting him on trial. Public execution or lashing would be best to prove my point and send the message that my orders were to be obeyed to the letter.

"Trajan."

"Yes, Legatus."

"Shackle Silvanus."

The woman, who'd remained in a crouch the entire time, finally stood from behind Silvanus and stepped away. Her chin lifted, she swiped a lock of bedraggled hair away from her face with the hand not holding her dagger. Then her gaze caught mine.

Jade-green eyes as clear as glass struck me straight to the heart with a piercing sting.

"Firebird," I whispered in utter shock, remembering the young girl I'd spoken to in a meadow under the moonlight, long ago. The one Fortuna had singled out as special. But not only Fortuna. My dragon as well.

Suddenly, my dragon recognized her and *roared* to the surface. Pain lanced through my flesh and seared through my veins, pushing me out with savage force. His fury that she was nearly another victim of Silvanus's blazed through my blood.

"Son of Dis," I growled, knowing I couldn't fight him.

With earth-shattering violence and terrible swiftness, my bones broke and realigned, wings sprouted beneath my skin, fire burned in my belly. The beast rose out of me so fast my thoughts splintered and . . .

Treasure.

Slicing into the world, I roar. The gray half man shakes with fear. As he should. He is no dragon. Nor man. He is a vile creature who planned to defile my treasure. He must bleed. He must die.

I open my jaws and snap him in two where he stands, then fling his carcass into the trees. His blood wets my tongue. So sweet. So just.

My female. Her skin is splattered with the blood of the enemy. Pleasure throbs up my throat as I gaze upon her. She stands. A fierce treasure, I have. She wants me to take her away.

Opening my wings, I wrap her in my talons, lift into the sky, and carry her toward my lair. Where she belongs.

MALINA

My scream died in my throat as the monstrous red dragon, the general, carried me away. I lost my breath from his claw pressing on my chest and stomach.

He'd snapped my attacker in half with his giant jaws.

The general.

I had stood there in awe, recognizing the centurion of long ago. He'd changed, grown even bigger, his hair short and militant, his golden eyes cold. But it was him.

Then his dragon ripped out of his body, changing into the beast in less than three seconds. A man behind him screamed when he was thrown by his thrashing tail. A red-scaled dragon with black-rimmed eyes and black-edged wings towered above me, his head even with the top of the tree line. But his height and girth didn't make him slow. He killed that disgusting monster who attacked me with gruesome speed.

Then I found my voice, screaming as he loomed over me with blood dripping from his finger-long teeth, seemingly proud of his kill. He lowered his gargantuan head, his serpentine, gold eyes narrowing. I had no breath to scream once he gripped me around the waist and carried me into the sky.

My stomach fluttered and twisted into a knot as the ground fell farther and farther away, my legs dangling in mid-air.

Bendis, save me.

I was going to die. He was going to take me high into the air and drop me, letting me fall to my death. I was, after all, the witch who'd kept them at bay three times before.

All for naught. My clan was dead and enslaved anyway. I saw Enid being herded toward the carrying nets. The kind older woman who'd become my savior, who'd convinced her clan to take me in, who'd cared for me as any mother would. Because of my failure, she was going back to Rome and to the slave market, her people dead and scattered. Just like my own.

Bunica was wrong.

My gift wasn't strong enough. I hadn't turned the tide of any war. I'd only stopped an incompetent general and his men until a better one came along.

The centurion.

The gold aureus around my neck dangled freely in space. I reached up and clutched it, somehow still not wanting to lose the one treasure of my old life that I still had.

Tears welled at my sad reality.

Since that night I'd been given the coin, I'd worn it secretly on a leather thong around my neck, underneath my blouse. Whenever I began to sink into despair, I remembered that Fortuna had singled me out for her favor. I never prayed to the Roman goddess, but some part of me wished that she might somehow help me succeed.

The night the Romans attacked our village three years ago, the night of my sister Lela's wedding to Jardani, it was the only possession of value I managed to escape with. Everything else—the brush Papa had carved for me, the red fustă from Bunica, the quilt Mama had made, and the embroidered blouse from Lela—all were gone. Likely burned in the fires with our village. I didn't know because I escaped during the attack. I ran and kept running until I collapsed with exhaustion miles from my home, alone in the cold and the dark.

Pathetic girl, I chastised myself.

Running from her family. Leaving them behind. And still holding on to this aureus like Fortuna actually cared about me. Look where she led me now, clutched in the talons of an enemy. I wanted to laugh at the coincidence that it was the Roman who'd given me hope in this small shining coin who had finally defeated and destroyed my Celtic clan, my adopted family.

I tried to yank it from my neck so I could throw it into oblivion, but one of his claws had my elbow pinned. With the other hand, I gripped the curve of one talon, unable to pry my fingers loose, too afraid he might suddenly drop me.

The fires and smoke of the burning Celtic encampment and battlefield grew distant. We rose into the clouds, and I wondered if a death from this height might be better. Closer to the stars, I wished I could keep going higher and disappear into the night sky.

"I'm sorry, Bunica," I whispered into the dark, sniffling at her loss yet again.

I'd lost them all—Mama, Papa, my sisters. The last thing I remembered was a soldier grabbing Lela while another bashed Jardani over the head, my sisters Kizzy and Kostanya screaming. My father threw me behind him, then turned terrified eyes on me. "Run, Malina," he'd ordered gruffly.

I obeyed. Fear spurred me deep into the woodlands in the dark until the screams and cries vanished like a dream. A nightmare.

The only thing that had kept me from taking my own life to join my family in the afterworld was Bunica's foretelling, "You will save us all."

But she was wrong. I'd become a slave like everyone else. Perhaps death would be better.

What would this dragon do with me now?

He'd caught the Celtic clan's witch. He'd punish me accordingly, likely a public execution or torture. Rumors of the brutality in the capital city of Rome were legendary. It was said the Romans kept the corpses of their enemies on display in their forum, that they drank from the skulls of defeated kings, that they used their slaves abominably.

I shivered at the dreadful future in store for me, even if it was short-lived.

Then we started to descend, his great wings beating more swiftly as he angled down out of the clouds. In the near distance, torchlight from many homes and buildings dotted the city of Rome.

I gasped, having never seen so many lights together before. I could even make out the circular curve of the Colosseum under the moonlight. But he banked in the opposite direction toward the edge of the city, a green hillside where large, white-stone buildings jutted out of the earth.

He slowed his descent, obviously aiming for a wide terrace to one home in particular. The general was wealthy.

But of course he was. I'd known it that night we met by moonlight. He reeked of noble blood. I'd been fascinated. Now, I was simply terrified. But I wouldn't let him know.

Lowering slowly over the terrace, he beat his wings rapidly until I was only a foot off the ground and then he let me go. I caught myself and watched as he landed on the terrace beside me, a painful groan rippling through him at the same time, the sickening cracking of his bones and revolting morphing of his body shrinking him down to a man. A naked man. I stared in sheer shock, but he didn't even glance my way. He walked directly into the arched entrance of his home without saying a word to me.

I couldn't help but stare at the magnificent man he'd become—physically anyway. Over seven feet tall, his body thick with muscle, his manhood hanging long and heavy between his legs as he marched inside.

I was panting in fear. When I finally realized that I was just lying there on the cold terrace, I stood and looked around, wondering if I could make a run for it.

"Don't try it, girl," came a harsh voice.

I snapped my eyes to the arched entrance as an older man walked toward me, a limp in his gait.

"You'll be picked up by patrolling centurions and brought back here." He had a dark complexion and gray-speckled hair. "Or worse. You'll be brought somewhere else," he warned. "Come with me."

"Where am I going?" I asked as he turned and marched back toward the archway, expecting me to follow.

"To your new room, of course. You'll get cleaned up." He looked at my clothes over his shoulder and sneered. "And change clothes."

"Then what?"

"Then the master will want to see you."

The master. *My* master.

I gulped hard at my new reality. My centurion from long ago, the man who'd given me a gold coin and hope and dreams of a better future, was now my new nightmare, my new master.

MALINA

I followed the lame man into the villa, noting that the doorways and ceilings were overly wide and spacious. I wondered if it was because the general and his fellow Romans often walked around in half-skin.

A shiver trickled icily down my spine remembering the half-skin soldiers clawing, killing, and burning the Celtic clan who'd adopted me. The suffocating sensation of smoke and being penned in by fire had me squeezing my eyes shut for a moment, wishing away that horrific sight of only a few hours ago. And the screams.

It had taken all of one brief battle for this general and his army to cut them all down. They'd moved in by stealth. By the time we realized what was happening and had rallied, it was too late to use my gift to help them. Panic had gripped me hard, and I couldn't save them. I wondered where poor Enid was now, the woman who'd taken me into her home, who'd treated me like her own.

I swallowed the pang of grief as the man wound around an atrium set in the middle of the house, a fountain trickling into a pretty pool bordered by blue inlaid tiles. The fountain was surrounded by all manner of leafy plants and vines, a dome above it open to the night sky.

I nearly snorted with derision. The wealth these Romans had, and yet, it was never enough. They took and took and took. They always wanted more. More land, more goods, more slaves.

Blinking back the tears of anger, I continued to follow the older man through the huge house, down a winding hallway, the many torches in sconces keeping the house well lit even at this hour of night.

"Are you Greek?" I asked, having noted his accent.

"Thracian," he said without stopping or looking over his shoulder.

"Did the master steal you from your home as well?" I asked bitterly.

He didn't answer as he stopped at an open door and turned, his expression hard and unreadable. "This will be your room. There should be a clean tunic in the trunk. Clean up and get dressed. I will return shortly."

"What is your name?" I asked.

"Ruskus."

Then he walked away, leaving me staring into the darkened room. Taking a torch from the sconce at the entrance, I entered and shut the door, not sure what to expect. It was rather large and clean, a bed set in the corner, a trunk at the foot. To one side was a changing screen with an embroidered red dragon flying straight up and breathing fire.

I bit my lip at the thought of the red dragon who'd just taken me in the air in his claws. I pressed a palm to my stomach where the tip of one of his claws had pressed and torn through my shirt. Though he hadn't cut through my skin, there would be a bruise. At least I was whole and unsullied. I should be grateful the red dragon's sudden—yet gory—slaying of my attacker had saved me from a worse fate.

Sighing, I took in the rest of the room. There was a table next to the bed, a small shelf set above it lined with three books. Books? What slave needs or has time to read? Bound books were rare and expensive. Why on earth would there be any in a slave's quarters at all?

I wandered closer, expecting some drivel by the famous Roman historians or scholars. But no, these books were all Greek. I could read a little. My bunica had taught me and my sisters, telling us once, "The Greeks use their brains more than their swords. You should know their words."

When I'd asked why we had to learn Latin as well, she'd replied, "Survival. You must know what your enemy is saying."

I lifted out one of the books, marveling at the leather binding and the neat script copied inside. It was by one of the famous Greek philosophers on human nature and morality.

"What in the world is this doing here?" I muttered to myself.

The second was of a similar topic. The third was a collection of stories of adventurous heroes. Perhaps I was put in a guest room. The master had literally dropped me on his terrace without warning the household. Maybe Ruskus had nowhere else to put me.

Glancing around the room, I realized that couldn't be true either. While the room was more spacious and well-furnished than I'd expect for a slave, it wasn't elegant enough for a Roman guest. Not a patrician anyway. What other kind of guest would a general in the emperor's army have at his home?

Realizing I had little time to gawk at my new prison, I hurried toward the trunk and pulled out a tunic. It wasn't of the fine material that Romans wore, but a soft linen, well-made, in a pretty pale green. There was a small washbasin, only big enough to stand in for washing, and a bucket of steaming water set next to it.

Ruskus had worked quickly. I'd barely been outside a few minutes before he'd appeared and shown me to this room. And to be given heated water was unusual.

Confused, but well aware that my time was running out, I hurriedly stripped the soiled and torn clothing that Enid had so carefully made for me and stepped into the stone basin. Using a cloth set there as well, I washed the dirt and blood from my body. The blood of that creature. But also of a friend.

Another memory flashed across my mind, when a Roman in half-skin had brutally clawed out the throat of Aodhan, a Celtic warrior and friend, who'd been trying to protect me. I had thought we might become more than that if the fighting had ever ended. He'd been kind to me when most of the clan was wary. Though they appreciated how I'd managed to manipulate the Romans who'd attacked them twice before, they didn't understand my gift and stayed clear of me.

But not Aodhan. He'd smiled kindly, spoken softly. He'd brought me and Enid an extra hare when they went hunting, or a shoulder of deer for our larder. I sniffed back the tears but they came anyway, slipping freely as I wiped his blood spatter from my face and neck and the dirt from my body.

I kept glancing above the screen, expecting the master to burst through the door to finish what his soldiers had started back in Gaul. But the door remained blessedly closed while I finished washing.

There was a bottle of scented oil next to the bucket. Though it was impossible to wash my hair properly as I would've in the stream near the hut I'd shared with Enid, I did my best to use the oil and warm water to untangle the knots in it. I used the last bit of water to douse my head, the dirty water pooling around my ankles in the basin.

Quickly, I dried with a scrap of toweling, combed out my damp hair, and slipped on the green tunic, which hung loosely around my thin frame. It was made for someone larger, but it was clean and soft, and for the first time since we'd heard the roar of deathriders overhead, I exhaled a breath of calm and sat on the bed.

Ridding myself of the remnants of the battle and scrubbing my skin clean had somehow eased my trembling body, even while I waited to meet him. Again.

A knock came at the door. I jumped to my feet. There was a brief pause, then Ruskus opened the door. "Follow me, girl."

I walked out behind him. For someone with a limp gait, he moved rather briskly.

"My name is Malina. Not *girl*."

He grunted as if he didn't much care. Perhaps there was no need to make my acquaintance. The general might be preparing to sell me at the market. A surge of new fear washed through me, pumping my heart faster. I might be sold to a harder master. Or a brothel.

Squeezing my hands into tight fists, I tried to find that calm of the moment before, using my empathic gift to cool my thoughts. I took deep breaths in and out as Ruskus led me through the home.

We walked across a giant entranceway where the floor was inlaid with yet another red dragon, flying upward and blowing a stream of flame. I supposed this must be my master's family sigil. The mosaic was intricate and colorful and must've taken an eternity to create by a talented artisan. Still, it spiked my anger.

Wherever I went in the home, there were constant reminders that I was in the lair of a dragon. A powerful creature who took what he wanted and ruled with fear and violence. But I couldn't wear that fury on my face when I met my master. I needed to play the obedient slave so that I could discover the best way to escape.

Down yet another corridor on the opposite side of this home of endless hallways and rooms, Ruskus finally came to a stop outside a large arched doorway. He gestured for me to enter so I did. Ruskus stood at attention inside the double-door entry, his hands clasped in front of him.

I walked into a vast room with more arched doorways decorated with ornate columns leading to another terrace, though I was sure this was on the opposite side of the house from where the dragon dropped me. Beyond the veranda, lights dappled the city below. Rome.

"Have you ever been to Rome?"

I startled at the deep voice to my right. He stood mostly in shadow, but the dim light still revealed his bedchamber behind him. My instinct to flee gripped me hard, my pulse racing at what Fortuna had in store for me now.

"There is nowhere to run, Malina."

I froze at the sound of my name on his lips. My heart skittered even faster. "I wasn't planning to run." Not yet.

He arched a brow at my obvious lie. "You may go, Ruskus," he called across the room.

I turned my head to see the Thracian frown, pausing only briefly before he left the room and closed the doors behind him, leaving me alone with the master.

His gaze was cool and steady on me when I turned back to him. It was obvious Ruskus found it unusual to be dismissed, but that wasn't the question poised on my lips.

"How do you know my name?"

"I've always known it." He stepped farther out of the shadows, the glow of the oil lamps set upon shelves lining the walls illuminating his face. "Since that day I met you. I heard your older sister speak it."

Lela. My heart twisted in acute pain. I refused to think of her now, the last moment I saw her. I wanted to stretch out my hand and yank my name from his mouth. He had no right to speak it. And yet, I couldn't say a word, a new shudder rippling through my body, though I couldn't exactly pinpoint why.

I wasn't afraid of him—as I should be. So what was this new emotion shivering down to my bones?

"I have never been to Rome," I stated coldly, finally answering his question. As if I would ever have reason to come to this ghastly place.

Those golden dragon eyes glowed in the dark, like it wasn't simply the man who examined me with such fierce scrutiny. His dragon watched me as well. He was dressed—thank the gods—in a silken red tunic that stopped at his knees. And still, I could barely repress the image of him walking tall and proud and naked into his home less than an hour ago.

"I am Julian," he stated simply.

Why did he tell me his name? It wasn't as if a slave was permitted to call her master anything but dominus. Perhaps he simply wanted me to know his name in case I got lost in the city or escaped and, gods forbid, was captured and needed to be returned to him.

"Sit," he commanded coolly, gesturing to a long cushioned bench with an intricate wooden base that was painted gold. There was no point in being defiant—not now—so I did.

He took a seat opposite me on a fancy sort of stool that seemed to have legs made of bronze. It was fine and beautiful but I was afraid it wouldn't hold his weight. I was wrong.

I'd never seen anything quite like either the sofa or the chair. Celtic furniture, and the kind I'd had as a girl, was made for sturdy use, not decoration. Of course, the Romans had the luxury to build a world of elegance and beauty. It only infuriated me further.

But I sat quite still, kept my expression passive and my hands clasped demurely in my lap. Even sitting, he loomed above me, his height and breadth too large to minimize in any position.

"Why were you living with the Celts?"

"Because the Romans invaded my village and killed my entire clan."

His gaze intensified, not expecting that answer apparently. "Your sisters?"

Swallowing the grief that always swelled when I thought of them, I said simply, "Gone."

Pausing for a moment as if turning over this new information, he then asked, "What witchcraft did you use to help the Celts defeat my predecessor thrice before?"

I ground my teeth together, not wanting to tell him. When his indifferent expression hardened, his brow arching with superiority, it nudged me to be smart. To tell him and be done with it.

It wasn't as if it had been kept a secret that the Celts had been using a *witch*, as they called me, to help them defend against the Roman attacks. The warriors had spread the word themselves to encourage others to stand up and fight, not cower back into the lowlands and the deep woods.

"I have a gift." I paused, licking my suddenly dry lips. His gaze caught everything. "I can control the emotions of others."

Those dragon eyes narrowed. "And what did you do to the soldiers?"

Shrugging, I admitted, "I made them feel helpless, defeated, lonely for home."

He swore under his breath. "That's why there were so many desertions in the middle of the night."

Aodhan and two of his friends had taken me close to the encampment at night, where I'd sent out dark threads of fear and heartsickness to them.

I couldn't tether to too many at once, but I could connect to a great number through the nighttime hours, the weak-minded ones. It was enough. The plan had worked. Those who didn't abandon their post in the middle of the night fought with the belief that they would be defeated. It was self-fulfilling.

He stared at me with unnerving directness, but I didn't squirm or budge under his gaze. I remained still and obedient, my chin lifted.

"Most do not understand that fear is a weapon against one's enemy in battle. But you do. A Dacian dancer from the Carpathian Mountains. How is that so?"

Clenching my teeth while I tried unsuccessfully to hold my tongue,

I finally snapped back, "Simply because I'm not a trained warrior with all the benefits of a *Roman* education doesn't mean I can't understand the basics of warfare."

His mouth ticked up on one side, and it seemed to have a direct correlation to my heartbeat, sending it speeding faster. He remained still and quiet for a moment, simply drinking me in.

"Enlighten me," he finally said in that superior, dark voice.

"The deathriders always come first. That is a fear tactic, to weaken the resolve of the Roman enemy."

"The deathriders create a perimeter with fire, to keep the enemy corralled in one place so that they cannot escape."

I scoffed. "You're telling me it isn't the Roman intention to paralyze the enemy with the roar of dragons and the threat of a fiery death by using deathriders first?"

He didn't answer, simply stared at me with that irritating half smile.

Having little thought to my survival by speaking so directly to my superior, I continued. "Regardless of whether you admit it, I'm well aware what fear can do to assist one opponent and defeat another in battle."

Still, he said nothing, his golden eyes glowing in the semidarkness of his bedchamber. I became suddenly aware of the large bed looming in the near distance, wondering if I'd have a chance to escape if he tried to drag me to it. I wondered if I could press my magic into him, perhaps put him to sleep.

"Don't try to use your magic on me," he warned, his voice rumbling deep.

I started at how easily he'd predicted my thoughts. It wasn't my place or my right to ask questions, but I couldn't control myself.

Licking my lips again, I asked, "Why did you kill your own soldier who was attacking me?" A flash of sharp jaws and blood spray flitted across my mind. "Why did you bring me here?"

"Silvanus disobeyed a direct order."

"What order was that?"

"The prisoners of war were to be left unspoiled."

"Why?"

"Because slaves are a profitable commodity. And damaged ones don't fetch much coin."

His response gutted me. I felt it like a slap to the face. He wasn't concerned about my welfare or the fact that his soldier had planned to violate me, likely to the point of death. He was concerned with money. Gain and profit. Of course. He was a Roman.

Swallowing the ire that stirred acid in my stomach, I asked, "What will become of me now?"

"That was exactly what I was trying to determine," he said. "You need a role in my house."

"I can cook," I told him.

"I already have a cook."

"I can wash clothes and linens," I offered next, my skin prickling with awareness at the way he was intensely staring again.

"My cook, Kara, is my laundress as well."

"Then what?"

Golden eyes coasted down my frame, a phantom caress I could practically feel where it traced. "You will be my body slave."

"Your . . . what?"

A body slave attended to a Roman's physical needs—dressing and grooming—but they also often followed the dominus. Serving him in whatever needs he had, whenever and wherever he went.

"I have need of a body slave. You will serve as mine." The tenor of his voice dipped lower, deeper.

"Wouldn't you prefer a male like Ruskus to serve your . . . personal needs?"

"Ruskus manages my house and business affairs." He leaned forward, his elbows on his knees, his hands clasped casually between them. His voice was a husky rasp between us, his eyes golden bright. "I prefer you."

I sat very still, soaking in his words and unwavering attention. I should've been terrified at the prospect of attending a Roman general so intimately, but I was afraid that wasn't why my heart raced wildly with the idea of it. I wasn't afraid at all. That telltale thrill of adrenaline running through my veins was excitement.

"You will report to me every morning at dawn and every evening. You will assist with my dressing, my bath, and my meals. And though Kara tends to most of the household laundering, you will now take care of mine. You will keep my room and bed linens clean."

My gaze shot to the monstrosity of a bed behind him, pulse thrumming swiftly in my throat.

"Unless Kara needs your specific help in the kitchen, this will be your domain." He gestured with one hand to the room.

He paused and examined me with that unsettling, all-knowing gaze, as if he expected me to protest. At the moment, I had nothing to say. He wasn't selling me off or beating me for being the witch who helped the Celts, but keeping me here. Very close to him.

After what felt like an eternal breathless moment, he stood. I jumped to my feet as well, readying to defend myself. His mouth quirked in that amused manner again.

"Go. Get some rest. I start early in the mornings."

I was probably supposed to bow or curtsy or something, but all I wanted to do was get away.

"Goodnight . . . dominus," I muttered, then hurried for the door.

"I'll show you back to your room," he said behind me.

"*No,*" I practically shouted, needing to get away from him. "I'm fine. I can find my way back."

Then I was gone, rushing down the dimly lit corridor, wishing he hadn't dismissed Ruskus so the old man could direct me. I took a left, remembering Ruskus had taken a right at this turn. Or was it the last one? I came to the end of the corridor and had the option to go left or right, but I couldn't remember, panting now in the quiet hallway.

"It's right," rumbled Julian directly behind me.

I gasped and jerked my head over my shoulder, mesmerized by his eyes glowing like a predator's in the dark.

"Follow me, Malina."

He stepped around and in front of me, seeming to ensure he didn't touch me. I blew out a breath, fixating on the sound of his deep voice saying my name. I shouldn't like it. I shouldn't want to hear it again. Something was wrong with me.

I followed him through the maze that was his palatial home, taking in his expansive size and knowing I'd have to escape this place by stealth and with a good head start when I did. After winding back around the atrium and trickling fountain and down yet another corridor, we finally ended up at a familiar doorway.

An oil lamp now burned inside my bedchamber. I sighed with relief, thinking the gruff Ruskus wasn't so bad.

Julian turned to me at the door. Ducking my head to avoid his piercing gaze, I swept past him. But he caught me by the arm and firmly but gently turned me to face him.

I flinched when his hand came up toward my face. He slowed his movement, but rather than touch me, he tugged the leather thong around my neck. The backs of his fingers grazed my collarbone as he pulled the coin from beneath my tunic and then held it.

"The aureus," he whispered, seemingly to himself.

I couldn't look at him, my breaths coming quicker at what he was seeing, what he now knew. That long ago, a foolish girl was fascinated with a centurion who gave her a coin for good luck.

"Lady Fortuna smiles on you, Malina."

Instant rage burned inside my chest as I met his gaze. "How can you possibly *say* that?" I swallowed the lump forming in my throat, blinking back the stinging of tears. I often cried when I was angry, and I was currently fuming. "My family is dead by the hands of *your* people. My adopted clansmen are dead or enslaved, and now I'm to be the body slave to a general of the Roman army. Lady Fortuna *hates* me," I seethed.

I didn't even care if he decided to punish me for my insolence. I might've even welcomed a good beating after all that I'd lost today. How could my life possibly get any worse?

But he didn't react with anger or a hard hand. He stared at the coin he held carefully in his long fingers, then finally let it go, setting it on the outside of my tunic. He met my gaze, completely unfazed by my fury.

"You would have died tonight," he stated indifferently, "had I not intervened. And now you are safe here in my home."

Huffing out a breath, I asked, "Am I safe?"

Golden eyes trailed over my face—cheeks, brow, lips—then he stared down with unwavering confidence. Dominance. "Good night, Malina."

He turned and disappeared down the darkened hall. I shut the door—there was no lock to bolt it—then blew out the oil lamp and climbed into bed. Surprised at the comfortable pillow and the soft blanket, I tried to calm my whirling thoughts and erratically beating heart.

My hand found the aureus, clutching it tight as I had so many nights before, hoping and wishing. Somehow, my sad little heart never stopped doing both of those things, no matter how much trouble entered my life. I sniffed, slipping into a dream.

No, a memory . . .

"What if you're wrong about my gift, and it never comes?"

"Patience, little Mina. I have seen it. You are an empath. Time will tell the truth of it."

She brushed my hair as I sat cross-legged on the floor of her hut in front of the fire.

"It doesn't matter. What good is knowing people's emotions? I can tell you that without any gift. Papo is grouchy every minute of the day. There, see? I'm an empath."

Bunica chuckled in that low, husky way of hers, still brushing my hair with infinite patience.

"Your grandfather isn't grouchy all the time."

"Pfft. When is he not?"

"When he's in bed with me."

"Ew, gross, Bunica! Don't say things like that." I shivered at the thought of my grandparents rolling around in bed together.

She laughed again. When silence settled between us, her soothing strokes with the brush lulling me into a sleepy state, she spoke gently but firmly.

"Emotions are powerful, Mina. Listen to me. One day you will not only be able to read them, but you will be able to control them. Change them. That will be your true power. You can bring hope to the hopeless, joy to those in sorrow, and calm to those in peril."

She stopped brushing and urged me to turn around. I twisted to face her, still sitting, and looked up into the warm brown eyes of my grandmother, knowing she liked to see me eye to eye when she had something important to say, something that was touched with her gift of sight.

"One day, your gift will turn the tide of war. It will help vanquish the enemy. It will strike fear into the hearts of fierce, dangerous men." She touched her wrinkled fingers under my chin, holding my gaze. "You, my darling Mina, will hold the world in your thrall." She cupped my cheek, her eyes glassy in the firelight, distant with premonition. "You, and your sisters, will save us all."

But Bunica was wrong. I couldn't save anyone. Not even myself.

MALINA

I awoke to the smell of baking bread and the prickling sensation of being watched. When I bolted upright and looked at the door, a curly-haired boy quickly ducked outside, leaving the door wide open.

"She's awake, Kara!" a boy's voice echoed, obviously the one who'd been spying on me.

"Stop being a pest and get me that goat's milk or you'll have no breakfast at all," a woman snapped back at him.

"But I want to meet her," whined the boy.

The morning light in the window told me the sun was well up. I'd slept hard, which was strange in itself, considering where I was.

Quickly, I got out of bed and straightened it, then looked for my shoes that I'd left behind the changing screen. They were gone, as were my torn and soiled clothes I'd come in.

The washbasin was empty, but there was a pitcher filled with clean water and a bowl on the side table along with a frayed stick and tooth powder for cleaning my teeth. There were also small ties set beside the comb I'd used last night. For tying back my hair, I presumed.

Strange. This wasn't what I expected to wake to.

I combed my hair and braided it into a long rope down my back, then used the abrasive, gritty powder and frayed stick to brush my teeth before rinsing thoroughly.

"Are you ever going to come out of your room?" came that same boy's voice.

I stepped from behind the screen to find a tall, gangly boy probably around ten. He grinned wide when he saw me, revealing dimples. "I'm Stefanos."

He was a handsome child wearing a brown tunic and dark pants. He frowned down at my feet. "You need shoes."

"The ones I came in are gone," I told him.

He walked to the foot of my bed and opened my trunk. "Try these." He set a well-made pair of sandals on the stone floor. "Or maybe these." He set out another pair that covered more of the foot.

The second pair actually fit fairly well. I sat on the bed to strap them on. "You keep random pairs of shoes in the house?"

"Here, let me help you." He quickly knelt at my feet and took over looping the straps around my ankle. "Yes. Dominus never knows when a new member might join our household."

Member. I tried not to laugh at his kind tone, mentioning *members* joining the house like it was a choice. Like we'd *want* to join this household.

"My name is Malina."

"You're very pretty," he said sweetly, flashing me that wide smile again.

I peered down at him with warmth, having nearly forgotten the openness of children, saying what they thought without a care. Still, he seemed rather old to speak so freely.

"Thank you, Stefanos."

My gut clenched when I realized what he was wearing around his neck. A rudimentary metal chain, and chiseled into a steel plate at the middle was the name JULIANUS IGNIS DAKKIA. It was his slave collar. Then my stomach flipped with nausea again at what the collar mostly hid—a deep scar running the length of his thin throat. This boy had once nearly been killed by someone's blade.

"Thank you for helping me with my shoes," I told him kindly, hiding the anxiety I felt for him.

Another sweet smile then he finished the last strap.

"Come with me," he said excitedly. "You must meet Kara."

We went down the hallway only a few feet before we stepped into a long kitchen with a row of windows open to a stable yard. A large pen of chickens clucked outside. But my attention was on the short, stout woman with dark hair rolling dough onto her work table.

"Stefanos," she snapped. "Get the milk or there'll be no breakfast for you."

He rolled his eyes but then hurried out the door leading to the stable yard, disappearing somewhere to the left beyond the windows. When I turned to the woman, she was still kneading the dough but her hard gaze was on me.

"You're not Celtic." Her voice sounded accusing.

I shook my head. "Dacian."

"Dominus brought you from the Celtic battlefields, Ruskus said."

"That's correct." I straightened under her scrutiny, realizing this was an interrogation. "My people were killed. The Celts took me in."

She continued to knead, glancing my way with sharp, dark looks. "I'm Kara. I run the kitchen."

I remained quiet under her accusing look, then nodded. If she thought I was after her job, she was mistaken. I was hoping to go as unnoticed as possible. It would make it easier for me to escape.

She slapped the dough down and dusted her hands on her apron. "I understand you're to attend the master. But when you're not, you can help me. There's always work to be done."

And yet, last night, Julian had told me he had plenty of slaves to do all of his household chores.

"How many are there serving this house?"

"There are four of us. Five now." She gestured toward the window. "Ivo keeps to the stables and yard most of the time. His room is in the stables." She arched a brow at me. "Though he doesn't speak, he can hear well enough. So don't think to sneak off that way. It would do you no good. You'd never get far."

I don't know how Kara could tell I was already planning my escape. I forced my features into blankness. "I had no intentions."

She humphed while I peered through the window at the gargantuan man feeding the chickens. He had short dark hair and clucked to the chickens while they paraded around him.

So five of us. That seemed like a small staff of servants for a house this size.

At that moment, Ruskus entered the kitchen. He shared a look with Kara, then walked toward me, his limp not as prominent this morning. He reminded me of a man back home in Dacia who had a similar lame foot. His limp always worsened as the day went on.

"You need to put this on, girl." He lifted a chain similar to what I'd just seen on Stefanos.

I quickly noticed they both wore their own collars as well.

Ruskus stopped, seeming uncomfortable and frowning as he turned to Kara. "You'd better help her."

I remained still, staring at them while Kara went and took the chain from him. "Well, come here. Stop gawping."

It wasn't as if I had a choice. My fate was sealed, and yet that reckless part of me wanted to scream in defiance. I didn't, of course. I gritted my teeth and clamped my mouth shut tight as I walked over to Kara.

"You'll have to take whatever that other thing is off."

That was when I found my voice. "No."

Kara frowned at me. "It'll chafe your neck, the two rubbing against each other."

"This one is leather. It'll be fine."

I didn't pull the necklace from inside my tunic. I always kept it hidden. It was a miracle it hadn't been snatched from my neck after having it so long.

Lady Fortuna smiles upon you, Malina.

I shivered as the memory of Julian standing with me in the darkness last night came back. How could he say such a thing? She had abandoned me. I wondered if my own gods of Dacia were punishing me for putting my faith in a foreign goddess.

Yet still, I couldn't remove the coin. It was a talisman I couldn't give up, even when I knew it was likely causing my own misfortune.

Kara finished linking the chain beneath my braid. "Stop your scowling," she snapped. "This necklace will keep you safe."

I snorted a laugh. "Safe? My master's collar?"

"The master's name," she corrected, wearing a deep frown. "No one will dare harm you with his name around your neck. You should be thankful."

A sharp pang of grief struck me then. What would become of Enid now?

"Enough. The master is up," snapped Ruskus gruffly.

Kara nodded to Ruskus and rounded back to her table and her dough. "You can eat breakfast later."

I wasn't hungry, so it was no difference to me. I followed Ruskus along the path I'd taken last night, but in the light of day I was able to see how opulent and beautiful Julian's home truly was.

Tall columns painted in red and gold adorned every entryway. There were intricate mural mosaics on every wall—floral and pastoral scenes. There was a giant one in the floor near the atrium in what looked like a gathering hall for guests. The mosaic was of Diana the huntress in half-skin drawing her bow, her wings flared, her tail curling behind her, and her gaze intent as she aimed for some unseen prey.

The hall with the Diana mosaic was filled with low chaise sofas, velvet cushions on the floor, and a large plush rug beneath—a lounging room for feasts and entertaining.

I wondered how often Julian held celebrations here. I hoped never. The idea of a room full of Romans drinking and feasting while I was forced to serve them made me nauseous. Besides, rumors of how Romans used their slaves for entertainment at bacchanal gatherings filled me with a new dread. I refused to become a toy to be used and abused by these creatures. I had to make a plan of escape before that happened.

Ruskus wound us back down the long corridor to Julian's bedchamber. He stopped at the open doorway, waited for me to go in, then left. He didn't wait to be dismissed like last night.

The room was unchanged from the night before. I glanced at the chair and sofa where he'd interrogated me. His large bed sat facing the open terrace doors. It was sized to accommodate him, of course, with thick wooden posts and a canopy holding sheer curtains. The bed linens were rumpled where he'd slept. I frowned at the intimate scene and at the fact it would be my job to tidy it for him.

My gaze caught on a shelf to my right filled with both papyrus scrolls and bound books. Unable to help myself, I wandered to it, dragging my finger along the worn spines. Not bothering with the papyrus rolls, I plucked a bound book from the shelf. I expected something on military warfare, frowning down at the title of a Greek tragedy.

Setting it back, I pulled out another and opened to the middle. This one was written in Latin. The author droned on about the key to happiness and finding inner peace. I huffed a laugh.

"Something funny?"

I snapped the book shut at his deep voice. Julian stood just beyond a dressing screen, watching me. He wore a short red tunic that revealed far too much of his thick thighs, and he was wrapping the extra fabric of the robe across one shoulder.

Hurrying to put the book back in place, I turned and waited for him to yell at me for touching his things.

"You're late," was all he said. His expression was calm as he stood with the robe only partially draped over one shoulder.

"I apologize," I stammered quickly. "I am not yet used to . . ." I shook my head, trying to find the words.

"Your new home?" He raised his brows in question.

I merely nodded.

"Come here." He watched me carefully, as if waiting for me to defy him.

I walked closer.

For a brief moment, he simply stared, but I couldn't hold that gaze any longer. It made me feel confused and uncertain. I didn't like feeling that way. The one thing in my life I'd always been able to control was my emotions—and those of others when I needed to.

"Tuck this fold in the back." He turned.

It finally dawned on me that he'd simply wanted me to do my job, to assist in dressing him. After taking some instruction on how to properly drape and tuck it, I stepped away.

"Kara is always up with the sun," he said as he turned to face me. "I'll instruct her to be sure you're up as well."

Though his tone held no anger, it was obvious he was displeased with my tardiness.

"And do you always wake with the sun?" I asked, wincing at my own sharp tone.

I instantly dropped my gaze toward the ground, but I didn't miss his stiffening posture as he crossed his arms.

"Look at me, Malina."

Inwardly cursing myself, I lifted my gaze to his. There was now certainly a look of displeasure creasing his brow.

"Now look behind me. Do you see the number of archways facing east? I wake with the sun."

"You could add drapes if you wish it."

He scowled deeper, then scoffed. "So that I could lounge in bed all day," he said with disgust, more as a statement than a question. "I am a busy man. There is much work to do. I expect you to adhere to my schedule and to do your own work while I am away from my home."

His tone was clearly chastising, declaring his irritation. I blew out a shallow breath, realizing, as Lela had always told me, that I was reckless. My mouth often got me into trouble.

He remained still, watching me with those unnatural eyes, jaw clenching.

"I'll be gone most of the day. After you see to my room, you are to help Kara with whatever she needs."

"Where are you going?"

He huffed a sigh of irritation. "It is none of your business where I am going. It is not your place to ask."

"I apologize. Again." I wrung my hands together in front of me. "I often ask too many questions."

A tension-filled pause stretched between us as he continued to examine me with those golden eyes. I was the one to break the stare and lower my gaze demurely, trying and failing to be the submissive slave he expected.

"You may ask me anything you like . . . in private," he said softly but then added with cold command, "Outside of this house, you will be submissive, obedient, and silent."

Again, I was confused. Why would he allow me any leniency at all? But I knew when I was being granted a boon. I nodded.

When he walked around me toward the hallway, he cleared his throat and seemed to add begrudgingly, "If it satisfies your inappropriate curiosity, I'm going to the forum today. I have business to attend."

"Is the slave market in the forum?"

"Yes." He rounded, his scowl still in place. "What of it?"

"Would you—" I licked my lips, suddenly nervous, knowing desperation shook my voice. I'd already angered him but I simply had to ask, "Could you please take me with you to see if there is one person from the Celtic tribes? Would you please buy her?"

"Why would I do that?"

"She is an excellent seamstress."

"I don't need a seamstress." He turned to walk away.

I fell onto my knees and gripped the hem of his toga. *"Please."*

Slowly, he turned back to me and stared, his eyes burning brighter. "What are you doing?" he growled.

"It's obvious. I'm begging you to save a woman. She is a hard worker." My heart raced faster as I clung to his robe, realizing how vulnerable I was on my knees before him.

"I don't need another slave," he growled. "I didn't even need *you*," he added gruffly, frustration obvious in his voice.

"Please," I pleaded, voice shaking. "She took me in. When no one else would. I owe her my life."

Holding my gaze, he reached down. I didn't flinch or move away when the pads of his fingers coasted from the base of my throat up the column, two fingers lingering where my pulse beat hardest.

"You're afraid," he stated, brushing the pads of his fingers along the hollow of my throat and back up to my chin.

"For her, yes. For Enid."

His fingers lightly held my chin, his voice rumbling in a low, silken voice. "And what will you give me if I do this for you?"

I swallowed hard, terrified at his quiet question and all of the favors he might require for this trade. My chest rising and falling faster, I whispered, "Whatever you want."

He arched a dark brow, pinching my chin softly between two fingers. "Is that so?"

I didn't move a muscle, but held his gaze. Or rather, he held mine. I was his complete captive in that moment, unable to look away, unable to move.

"You know they think you're a witch, don't you?" His voice was soft, melodious, even as his grip on my chin hardened.

"Yes."

"I want to know more of your craft, little witch."

"I've already told you."

He huffed a laugh, though there was little merriment in it. "You've told me very little. Just enough to get the Roman general to stop asking you questions. But I want to know more of what you can do."

"So that you can use it against others in battle?" I snapped, even while I was on my knees at his feet.

He smiled. "Does it matter what I do with the information? You are mine, Malina, to do with as I will."

I scowled, and there was no doubt he could misread the anger burning in my eyes. It only made him smile wider.

"There's the firebird." He loosened his hold, brushing his thumb beneath my bottom lip, lingering in a way that made me shiver before he withdrew his hand. "Do we have a bargain? Every night when you serve me dinner, you will answer any question I ask about your mystical gift. Honestly. In return, I will save your Enid. If she is still alive."

I flinched at that last part but then I nodded.

"Say 'yes, dominus' so that I have your unwavering agreement."

"Yes, dominus," I said on a quivering breath.

He dipped his chin and straightened to his full height. "Stand up."

I did. But then I gasped when he gripped me around the upper arms, drawing me close. His features hardened, but his timbre was even harder when he said, "Do you know the significance of what I'm wearing?"

I shook my head.

"It is the color of my house. Do you know the lineage of dragons?"

Swallowing hard, I whispered, "Yes. My grandmother taught me."

He grunted. "Smart woman. You can pick out the Roman citizens in the crowds. The patricians will be wearing a toga, stola, sash, or even a pendant with the jewels of their house color." His penetrating glare kept me silent. "Do you know all of the houses?"

I nodded, unable to speak.

"Good." His eyes narrowed. "Your gaze is too direct. Don't look a dragon in the eyes. *Ever.* Do you understand? Remember who you are."

"I know who I am," I snapped back, pride burning the words out of my mouth.

For some reason, that softened his expression. "No, Malina." He drew me closer, the anger gone, some other emotion dancing in his golden eyes. Even as an empath, I couldn't place it. "In Rome, you are no longer one of the beautiful Bihari sisters dancing for crowds under the shadow of your beloved Carpathian Mountains."

My breath hitched that he'd known my full name. That he spoke to me with such tender intimacy, all while he was obviously putting me in my place.

"You are no longer the witch who aided the Celts against the Roman legions," he said softly.

"Who am I, then?" I asked on a trembling voice.

"In Rome, you are no one. A slave. One of many."

My entire body shook with both fear and fury, a commingling of emotions that kept me speechless. For what could I say? He was right. I'd lost everything. And everyone. I was alone and nothing more than what my Roman master allowed me to be.

Finally, he let me go. "Follow me."

JULIAN

This was not good. Or smart. And yet, here I was, strolling down the hill toward the forum with Malina a few steps behind me.

It chafed to force her to make the long walk, but taking her on horseback would only draw more attention. She'd draw plenty on her own without a patrician of my status trotting around the city with his new slave on the back of his horse with him.

When we entered the outskirts of the city, I slowed, wanting her close. Needing her close. Thankfully, the forum wasn't that far. I'd bought my home specifically because it was closer to the business end where I could discover news of the battles and the senators quickly and where I could meet friends discreetly.

Though I trusted my servants absolutely, the emperor had spies everywhere. I didn't trust that my neighbors within sight of my home might not be watching who was coming and going.

The forum was the best place for covert meetings. Ones that wouldn't seem planned or suspicious in any way. That was my hope this morning. To meet a certain friend and exchange some information without incident.

But now, I had Malina with me. And the quest to find and buy her caregiver from the Celtic clan. Her friend may not have even survived the journey in the slavers' nets. They weren't always gentle when carrying their cargo in their talons. If she was an older human, she would have to be tough as bones to have survived.

We took the long path through a row of apartments. This part of Rome wasn't as filthy as others, but I reached back and grabbed Malina's forearm, keeping her close anyway. When I glanced over my shoulder, she was staring wide-eyed at the people bustling here and there, then her gaze caught the graffiti along one long wall.

I followed her gaze. The graffiti was always of one mind. Vulgar, with many large, exaggerated phalluses. There was a depiction of the emperor in half-skin, standing on top of the Colosseum breathing fire to the sky, his erect penis larger and longer than his tail. There were others of various Roman senators and generals doing foul things.

My attention caught on one scene. It was a caricature of me, wearing my military uniform with the red tunic, my sandaled foot on a dead man, a Celt by the blue woad on his face. Beyond him was a line of dead Celts that went all the way until the wall was broken by a doorway to another apartment. My gut clenched.

This was recent, for I'd only returned home last night. Of course, the news may have carried to Rome sooner. The praeco liked to send one of his lackeys to the battlefields to get his news out quickly.

Malina stared at the depiction of me. I steeled myself and faced forward, tugging her closer and focusing on the boisterous crowd growing louder as we approached the forum.

The forum was an assault to the senses, as always. The vendors crying out their wares, customers haggling, a bull bellowing, the clopping of hooves on stone, and sheep bleating. Then there were the smells—a mingling of musky bodies, both man and beast, the sweeter scent of fruit and baked bread, and the definite whiff of decay on the wind. But it may be the sights most of all that had Malina's green eyes so wide and round.

A push of people wound through the makeshift paths of food carts, animal pens, slave pens, and past the Curia—the centered building where the senators met and decided the fate of all Romans. Acid burned in my belly.

But it was the sight lining both sides of the Curia that held Malina's attention.

She leaned close to me, her scent locking me in place. "What is that?"

I stared at the heads in various stages of rot—some mere skeletons barely hanging on to the pikes they'd been thrust upon.

"To the left is the Wall of Victory. Emperor Igniculus likes the kings of his enemies posted there." I noted the most recent on the end, blue woad covering his face, his reddish-brown hair floating in the wind, tongue hanging from his gaping mouth.

"You're running out of room," she murmured quietly.

It was true. The wall's residents extended to the corner of the forum and kept going. There was little space left where the wall ended at another building, the granary.

"The emperor will simply build another one for his heads," I told her without emotion. "He won't give those up."

"And the other side?"

To the right of the Curia was a longer row of victims' heads. Many were dragon heads, some skulls in half-skin, their horns shorn white to the bone by the wind and elements slowly peeling away the flesh. Traitors had been executed in various stages of shifting.

"That is the Wall of Traitors. Romans who have betrayed the emperor."

"How long has he been collecting traitors?"

"Since he took the throne, seven years ago."

Had it been so long? My pulse quickened at the reality that we'd been living this way for nearly a decade.

She paused in the middle of the square and stared at the giant bronze statue, a tribute to our forefathers, which stood above the crowds. Romulus and Remus suckled from the she-dragon who raised them, who gave them her milk and her blood, and a power as great as the gods. She curled around them as they fed, her wings folded. Romulus was the first red dragon, Remus the first black—the oldest and most powerful houses of Roman nobility.

"Come," I snapped, weaving a path through the people toward the slaver's pens.

Everyone jumped out of my way as I expected. If they didn't recognize who I was, they noted the color of my robe and that was enough.

The red house, the Ignis line, and the black house, the Media Nocte, were the oldest and most prestigious lines of dragon families. By birth, we were naturally most dominant, the most powerful, and the most deadly. It wasn't a mistake that every emperor was either from the Ignis or the Media Nocte houses.

The slaver Menteo, a weasel of a man with only half his teeth, wore his usual long gray toga—signifying him of the house of Griseo. He shouted from his short pedestal where he could direct his workers to bring out the next human to the auction block. There were many in the pens in the garb of the Celts I'd conquered only yesterday—most of them young, healthy women and children old enough to work.

I gritted my teeth, wondering if they'd killed the old and too young from the Celtic encampment, defying my orders again. Usually, I oversaw the transition from battlefield to Rome, but last night, I. . . .

I, what? Had lost my mind in the moment. No, it hadn't been me. It was my dragon. He saw her in danger and there was nothing I could've done.

Behind Menteo, the auction block was busy and bustling. A young woman, stripped naked, was standing and trembling while the auctioneer was pointing out her assets to the Roman men and women at the foot of the stage who shouted out bids for her.

"Menteo," I bellowed from outside the gates. He worked from inside the pen, directing his wishes close to the property for sale.

Those beady eyes found me, then he smiled that toothless grin. "Legatus! Legatus!" he cackled. "What a healthy crop of treasure you've brought me. There will be plenty of profits for your coffers, I promise. Do you need coin now?"

That slithering sensation crawled down my spine, but I pushed it away.

"No, Menteo. I'm looking for a woman to take off your hands."

He chuckled again. "Ah, yes. A pretty one to match her." He pointed at Malina. "A nice pair would do you good. A healthy legatus needs good sport to release his aggression, does he not?"

Malina stiffened next to me, her pulse jumping in her veins beneath my fingertips. Fucking Menteo.

"Not for sport," I declared in an easy tone. "An older woman."

Menteo frowned, but then Malina tugged on my tunic. I followed where she pointed. The woman wasn't as old as I'd thought, her copper-red hair barely graying at the temples. Her dark, watchful eyes were on Malina but she didn't make any attempt to show that she knew her.

"That one." I pointed to the woman Malina had shown me. Enid. She was a fair-skinned woman and small-framed. She was also filthy with blood and dirt, like most all of them. She hunched her shoulders forward, bracing her middle with both arms, leaning her weight on one leg.

"Sir?" Menteo stared at the woman I wanted.

I didn't have to explain myself but I wanted to get the fuck out of this wretched place before my nausea rose even more.

"She's the mother of the Celtic king," I lied, pointing to the Wall of Victory. "She has information on other clans I need to find. Get her," I commanded, deepening my voice.

Menteo's expression shifted to fear and he instantly snapped orders at one of his men, pointing to the woman Malina was anxiously staring at. They shuffled her through the throng, unshackling her ankles but keeping the ones on her wrists, then pushed her through the iron gate. She hobbled forward.

Instantly, she and Malina clasped hands but made no other sign of affection. I tossed a gold coin over the wall to Menteo, who snatched it out of the air. That was far more than an elderly slave cost, but it was a bribe as well. Menteo knew that I liked my privacy and no hassles. He wouldn't go blabbing to any other Romans that I'd gotten myself a slave with important information about one of our enemies.

All generals were competitive, and information was the most important treasure of all. To most.

"Thank you, Legatus!" he shouted, winking, and went back to bellowing at his men to get the next one up on the auction block.

"This way," I called over my shoulder, having released Malina's arm.

She helped Enid, who was smaller than her, walk and they followed closely. By the time we made it halfway across the square, the praeco—a thick, jowled man—had stepped onto his dais and began shouting his news to the forum.

"The honorable Legatus Julianus Ignis Dakkia has defeated the Celtic hordes and has returned their king's head for our Wall of Victory. We now await to discover where Caesar will send his brave and strategic nephew next. All hail Legatus Julianus, the Conqueror!"

My blood ran cold. As the cheers of the crowd went up, I refused to look back at Malina. And I thanked the gods the praeco hadn't seen me.

"Even more good news for Rome," he continued to bellow out over the throng. "With the courage of a great Roman, Prefect Ciprian crept into the Thracian camp and beheaded their general. The Thracians are defeated. Our victory owed entirely to the valiant Prefect Ciprian of the Media Nocte. Hail to Prefect Ciprian!"

A louder roar erupted in the crowd, my gut souring with every word. That snake Ciprian had most likely disobeyed his legatus and managed to come out the conquering hero over the Thracians on the southern border, for that was where they were moving next according to my uncle's last intelligence.

Now I'd have to suffer more of that sycophant's ego, for fuck's sake.

I caught sight of a tall Roman with dark wavy hair. Trajan needed a haircut. He was beginning to look disheveled.

He leaned against a fruit cart, smiling to the woman who owned it, his sapphire-blue toga haphazardly draping over his shoulder.

When I drew closer, he straightened and nodded. I nudged Malina on the arm.

"Go over to that fountain." A small drinking fountain off to the side should keep them out of the way and out of trouble a few minutes. "You can get her some water. Stay there till I come get you."

Those green eyes darted at me, but she did as I told her, which was the only thing going well so far this morning.

Trajan took the pear from the fruit vendor's cart and followed me to an alcove where we usually met. From here, I could still see Malina. Enid sat on the edge of the stone fountain while Malina washed the dirt and blood from her arms.

"You left with one and now you have two?" Trajan bit into his pear, looking nothing at all like the warrior he did last night when I left him in Gaul. He grinned, knowing he was sparking my anger.

"You need to get your man to cut your *pretty* hair."

"The ladies like my pretty hair."

"The emperor likes us to look militant."

He heaved a sigh. "I'll cut it before the victory feast." He waved his half-eaten pear toward Malina and took another bite. "Aren't you going to tell me what that's all about?"

"No."

His carefree smile vanished. "Are you withholding something from me?"

"Nothing you need to know." Not yet anyway. "What did your grandfather say about the senate while we've been gone?"

He chuckled darkly. "Quite a lot has been brewing."

"Tell me."

"For one, Valerius put forth the vote to outlaw slaves from marrying free humans or other slaves. They cannot marry at all now. The vote was won, of course, though Otho offered some dispute that I'm sure Caesar didn't like."

I contemplated that a moment. Malina was on her knees, washing the older woman's bare feet. The woman had lost whatever shoes she'd had between last night and this morning.

"Makes sense," I finally said, turning back to Trajan.

"Why's that?"

"If the slaves cannot marry, they have no true ties to anyone but their master. That bond even between two slaves can give them courage."

"Courage for what exactly? To start a family?"

"Rebellion, Trajan. Revolution."

"There's no way the slaves of Rome would have the gall to start a revolution."

"I don't know." My gaze swung back to Malina, her dark hair shining with a reddish tint in the sunlight, her braid hitting her hip as she washed Enid's ankles. "You'd be surprised what's in their hearts."

"You would know," added Trajan, tossing the core of his pear into the bushes. "Your house is different."

I darted a warning at him. "Don't say anything like that aloud ever again."

"There's no one here, Julian," he assured me, calm even while my voice had dropped dangerously, the dragon always riding me too hard.

"Besides"—I turned back to our conversation—"I'm sure the edict said nothing at all about them starting families. Igniculus has made it clear he's fine with them reproducing. That means more property." I rubbed at a pang in my sternum.

"True," agreed Trajan. "As long as those children aren't begotten by a Roman patrician."

It was my turn to heave a sigh. "Of course not. He's made that law clear enough." I rubbed my chin, realizing I needed a shave.

"Caesar forgets," added Trajan. "There are some Romans who have familial ties to slaves."

My mother's face flashed to mind, her kind smile, her kinder eyes.

"No. He doesn't forget. He's simply missing that part of himself that would remind him of that."

"What part do you mean?" he asked.

"A heart." I clenched my jaw, tension riding me hard. "He's a demon, Trajan. Never forget that."

He stared back at me grimly. "What I wonder is—" He broke off, a sharp female voice interrupting our conversation.

"Get off me!"

I didn't even think. One glance at the man touching Malina and I was across the small square with my hands around his throat.

"Have you lost your mind?" I asked the man I'd lifted off the ground.

His face reddened as he fought to remove my hands and gasped for

71

air. He was a soldier by his uniform, a human. Not one of mine. But the fear on his face told me he recognized who I was.

"Sorry . . . Legatus," he managed to whisper hoarsely, his face almost purple now.

"Did you not see her collar?"

His eyes darted to Malina, which only enraged me more. My muscles bunched and swelled, my dragon urging me to shift into half-skin so he could take the head off this fucking fool.

The soldier only managed to shake his head since he was now gasping for air. He couldn't speak if he tried.

"Or perhaps you don't believe the laws of ownership and property apply to you."

He shook his head again, his eyes rolling.

"Julian," said Trajan, right behind me now, speaking in that ever calm voice. "Let him go."

Always the voice of reason. If I killed this bastard, I'd have to explain why. It would draw attention to my overreaction and my obsession with my new slave. It would also force Trajan to speak on my behalf and would alert the emperor that we were meeting in the forum, far from any battlefield.

I dropped the offender at my feet and waited while he sucked in gulps of air, until he'd mostly recovered. I wanted to be sure there was oxygen getting to his brain before I gave him my last word on this subject.

"Know this, soldier," I said, noting the dark rumble of the dragon in my voice. "If she isn't yours, don't touch her." I squatted down and spoke low, "And if you ever touch mine again, I'll rip your spine from your body where you stand."

He panted and stared, wide-eyed and terrified. As he should be. "Yes, Legatus," he rasped, dropping his gaze in submission.

Dragons were a violently territorial and possessive species. The laws on property were strictly enforced and almost always followed. Otherwise, the city would fall into complete chaos. This soldier was lucky my beast hadn't leaped from my body and killed him.

Even now, I felt the burn deep in my gut, my beast wanting to taste the soldier's blood for his offense.

When I finally stood and turned, it was to find Malina staring at me with a touch of fear shining in her eyes. She had her arms wrapped around the obviously unwell Enid, who drooped against her.

Trajan had crept back into the shadowy alley, giving me a quick nod before he disappeared.

Not wanting to linger any longer, I scooped the sickly Enid into my arms. "Come." Then I led us back toward home.

Thankfully, Malina didn't comment on my overzealous behavior. I wasn't simply angry or defensive that another man had been near her, harassing her. I'd been so overcome with rage that I'd nearly murdered the man.

Not that I had to explain anything to Malina. The burning in my belly reminded me that eventually I would. There was no escaping that dreadful fact.

Of all the people to enter my life at this moment in time, when my focus must be razor-sharp, when any distraction might stray me from my cause and would definitely endanger my life, the firebird appeared. I'd thought to never see her again, even knowing what she was to me then, all those years ago, as we stood in the woods beneath the moon and the shadow of the Carpathian Mountains. I'd walked away, knowing it was the only safe path to take. For the both of us.

She had not merely entertained me with a whirling dance, she'd captured me entirely. The dragon too. And though I'd had a fleeting thought of a life where a Dacian girl fit into mine, I dismissed it at once. My uncle had already taken power then and his ruthlessness had been stamped across Rome. I'd seen it as a centurion far from the city. Now, I knew it was far worse than I ever feared.

So I'd dismissed any fantasies of returning to the Carpathian

Mountains and finding the girl who haunted my dreams these past years. Now, here she was, thrust into my life through violence and blood. I feared that was the only future the two of us could possibly have. For my destiny, my sole purpose, could only end in violence and blood.

She shouldn't be here. I shouldn't want her to be, and yet, I homed in on her light footfalls two paces behind me, on her every breath, on her scent of lavender oil mingled with sweat.

It didn't matter what I wanted. The gods have their own designs, and Lady Fortuna will not be ignored.

MALINA

I wiped Enid's brow where she lay in the bed in an empty room next to the kitchen. She hadn't said a word since we'd taken her from the slave auction.

After we'd gotten home, I'd helped Enid change, only to find a gash near her ribs. The wound reopened and began bleeding. Kara summoned a healer who tended to slaves and plebeians. He was a stern-looking but efficient man of the healing arts, it seemed.

He stitched Enid's wound while I continued to wipe her brow. He spoke softly to her after he examined her, finding she had several broken ribs and a fractured leg as well.

"Most likely happened in the net being carried back to Rome," he told me and Enid, who seemed to be drifting in and out of consciousness. "She's lucky. Most of the elderly and weak don't survive the netting."

Kara entered quickly with a steaming cup. "I have a sleeping draught that should help her rest."

"Good," said the healer. He then instructed us to bind her ribs and keep her in bed so the bones could mend. "I'll check on her next week." Then he left.

I remembered how Julian had carried me carefully in his claws back to Rome. That was horrifying enough. I couldn't imagine how it must've been for Enid being crushed into a net like an animal and carried away without a care in the world.

I helped Enid sip the draught. "Just a little more," I told her.

Finally, she gave me a weak smile and drifted off. Even though Enid was a tiny woman among the Celts, she'd always been full of life and vigor. Not now. It sickened me to think what she went through.

"What can she do?" asked Kara, gathering the soiled rags and dirty bowl of water. "If she survives."

"She can sew. Very well, actually. Not just practical clothes either. She has a gift for decorative embroidery. She can do laundry too." I smiled, tears pricking my eyes. "Not much of a cook though."

When we'd lived together in her hut with the Celts, I'd done most of the cooking. She'd either undercook our meal or burn it to a crisp.

"Don't get your hopes up, girl. She looks like she's got one foot in the underworld already."

I turned away from Enid to find Kara's usual frown. But this one seemed to be of concern rather than the ornery scowl she'd worn for me since I'd met her.

"She's not your relation," said Kara.

I shook my head. "She's one of the Celtic clan. The one who took me in when my family was killed."

With a sniff, she lifted the bowl and soiled rags. "I'll make a broth for when she wakes up."

"Thank you, Kara."

Kara paused without looking at me, but then nodded and left.

I tucked the blanket around Enid and left, quietly closing the door to her small room. I left the oil lamp burning in case Stefanos's voice in the yard behind the kitchen drew my attention. I followed sounds of something thwacking together.

Outside, I found Stefanos play fighting with Ivo, both of them using sticks like swords.

"Aha!" Stefanos shouted, spinning deftly and play stabbing Ivo in the side of the gut.

Ivo made a dramatic show of dying and falling to the ground. Stefanos laughed, then Ivo sat up, laughing too, before he stopped suddenly when he caught me watching.

"Sorry. I didn't mean to interrupt."

Stefanos's grin was a league wide. "Did you see me defeat Ivo?"

"I did."

Ivo stood, revealing he was almost as tall as Julian, easily the size of other pure-blood Romans, though obviously he wasn't one if he was a slave.

"Hi, Ivo." I stepped forward. "My name is Malina."

He seemed to be somewhere in his thirties, but he blushed profusely and ducked his head, dropping his dark gaze to the ground when I moved closer.

"Oh, sorry." I looked at Stefanos. "Does he not like meeting new people?"

"He's just shy." Stefanos grinned wider and patted Ivo's shoulder. "Especially around pretty girls."

Ivo shoved Stefanos, which almost toppled him to the ground, but the playful boy simply laughed and bounced right back.

"He cannot hear?" I asked Stefanos.

"He can, but he doesn't speak."

I nodded, then asked brightly, "So you like to sword fight?"

Stefanos shrugged. "Well, pretend anyway. I could never truly sword fight."

Tension tightened the silence after he admitted that.

"It doesn't hurt to train though, does it? You might have to defend the master's home one day," I offered since he truly seemed upset by the idea he would never fight in the Roman legions.

Stefanos's blue eyes lit with excitement. "Yes! That is what dominus told me as well. That I might even fight in an army one day too."

Ivo knocked him on the chest with the back of his hand and gave a quick shake of his head.

Surprised, I asked, "Why would dominus say that to you?"

Common-born Romans—humans—could be soldiers, but not slaves. Not even freed ones.

"Did you know Ivo can juggle?" He laughed and picked up his sword, swinging it around, but with less spirit than before.

Ivo kicked a rock on the ground with his large sandaled foot, avoiding looking at me.

"I didn't."

"Stefanos! Ivo!" called Ruskus, both hands on his hips in the kitchen doorway. "You've got a lot of work to do in the stalls to be playing in the yard."

The both of them instantly marched for the stables, heads down.

"The master's dinner is ready." Ruskus eyed me carefully. "It's your job to serve him now."

"Of course." I stepped toward him where he still remained in the doorway. "Where is Ivo from?" I asked.

"Macedonia."

"He's been here long?"

"Three years."

"Dominus bought him from the auction?" I stopped in front of him. Ruskus arched a brow. "You ask a lot of questions."

"Am I not supposed to?"

"It depends why you're asking. What are you after?"

He stared at me with a touch of accusation, and it finally hit me. His wariness of me, as well as Kara's, wasn't because they simply didn't like me or that they were annoyed with another mouth to feed in their home. They were protecting their master.

"Because this is my home now," I answered. "I'd like to know about those who live in it."

He continued to stare; the scar that bisected his top lip grew tight as he pressed his lips together. When I remained still under his scrutiny, he finally answered.

"Ivo was the slave of another Roman, one of the consuls."

"The consul of the Roman senate?"

A stiff nod. "Valerius is his name." He paused, narrowing his eyes before continuing. "Ivo stepped between his master and another slave. A woman. He was trying to . . . protect her from Valerius."

I swallowed hard. No need to explain what horror of a scene that must have been.

"What happened then?"

"Valerius had Ivo beaten near to death for interfering. But servants talk." He shrugged a shoulder, seeming uncomfortable. "Word came to our house what had happened. Dominus stepped in and paid a handsome sum. He needed a big stableman anyway, to handle his horses, he'd told Valerius."

I stared, wide-eyed, trying to absorb what he'd just told me: essentially that Julian had saved a condemned slave from death.

"Enough talk. Get to your work. Dominus is waiting on his supper."

I walked swiftly past him into the kitchen where Kara was already setting food onto a tray. There was a large portion of everything—cuts of spiced pork, fresh bread, slices of fig and pear drizzled with honey, and a half round of sliced cheese. There was also a decanter of red wine set on the tray.

"He prefers to eat on his bedroom terrace. Take it quick before it gets cold."

I didn't hesitate since I'd already been scolded that morning for being late. Making my way through the center atrium and beside the fountain, I found my way back to his bedchamber with little difficulty this time.

He stood on his terrace, his hands clasped behind him as he gazed out at the city of Rome, torches and oil lamps beginning to burn bright in the homes as the sun set in a flourish of pink and gold.

"Your dinner, dominus," I stated evenly, wanting to choke on the title I was forced to use with him.

He turned and walked toward the low chaise and pillows strewn on a carpet beneath an awning that jutted out on his terrace. I noted that it was on a dais so that he could still see the view of the city from a lounging position. Somehow, he gracefully lowered his large frame onto the chaise, half reclining and facing out.

I set the tray on the low table at the center of the cushions. A goblet half-full of wine already sat there. As I stood to leave, he said, "Sit."

When I didn't obey right away, he arched a brow with superiority. "Have you forgotten your bargain so soon?"

"My mind was preoccupied for most of the day," I managed to reply evenly and without the irritation I felt.

I lowered myself and sat sideways on a pillow close to the low table opposite him. He'd already taken a slice of bread and folded it around a piece of pork, eating with unhurried but large bites.

"How is she?" he asked casually.

"Not well," was my curt reply.

He showed no emotion whatsoever, and I had no interest in tethering to him with my gift to find out what he felt. Or to discover that he had no feelings at all.

"Have you eaten?" he asked as he reached for more meat.

"No." I had little stomach for anything since I'd arrived.

"Eat." He gestured toward the platter. "Kara always prepares too much for me."

I didn't want to eat his food. "Wouldn't that be inappropriate? For me to eat with you."

He held my gaze for an uncomfortable moment, then he spoke in a conversational way, rather than dictatorial.

"A philosopher once said that while we cannot always control our circumstances, we can control how we react to them. It is better to take advantage of the smallest of gifts in these hard times. Take what you can, cherish what will give you peace and strength for the difficult roads that lie ahead."

It was baffling. He was my enslaver and yet he was offering me such odd and somewhat wise advice. Starving myself or denying myself good food was foolish.

"And you've traveled hard roads, dominus?" I tried but couldn't quite hide my bitterness.

"Eat, Malina." His commanding voice was back. "Besides, this is my house, and I make the rules. I want you to give me what you promised in exchange for your friend's life, and I don't want to listen to your stomach making those noises the entire time I enjoy my meal."

I scowled, ready to protest when a low gurgle of hunger rumbled in my belly. I hadn't eaten all day, I was so sick with worry over Enid.

"Eat," he commanded with more roughness.

I picked up a piece of fig and took a bite, savoring the honeyed fruit on my tongue. He watched as if waiting for me to eat more, so I did. I ate a chunk of cheese on bread, then another fig, and then picked up a slice of spiced pork, humming with pleasure at the savory deliciousness.

"Kara is a good cook, I see," I finally broke the silence, licking one of my fingers.

"She is." He'd stilled, gazing at me with unwavering intensity.

That stalled my feeding frenzy. I settled back from the table, feeling self-conscious and not a little bit uneasy.

He filled his cup of wine from the decanter Kara had set on the tray. Belatedly, I realized I was supposed to serve him, but he didn't seem to care about the formalities.

"Tell me about the first time you knew you had this mystical gift." He took a sip and waited while I let my mind drift back.

"The first time I never told anyone. I was very young, only six years old." I looked out at the city, pinpoints of light from windows below. "My mother's father died and she'd been crying uncontrollably the entire day it had happened. My father had tried to comfort her, but eventually took my sisters out of the house to give her privacy."

"But you stayed behind," he said quietly as if he'd known that's what I'd do.

I turned to face him, finding his fixed attention thrilling when I should not.

"Yes, I did," I confirmed. "She'd been sitting at the hearth, staring into the fire while she wept. I curled up beside her and laid my head on her lap. I can't explain how I did it. I only knew that I was desperate to help my mother. To make her pain go away. When I wished for that to happen, I reached out with my first bond."

"A bond?" he asked.

"It's the line I create to connect with someone. I did it for the first time without really knowing what I was doing. But when I felt my mother's pain feeding through the line, I just wanted to help her. To stop it."

I'd poured my love through that connection. For some reason, that part felt too personal to tell.

"It worked. My mother stopped weeping a few moments later.

And by the time my father and sisters returned, she was cooking dinner. She was still sad, of course, but not overwhelmed with the grief."

I could still remember exactly how she'd stroked her palm over my head and hair before she pressed a kiss to my temple and whispered, "Thank you, sweet Mina." I didn't want to share that part either. Or how next time I saw Bunica, she patted my cheek and stared into my eyes and said, "It's finally arrived. And now you know."

I remained quiet while he seemed to be contemplating my story.

"And does anyone else in your family have this gift?"

"No," I answered honestly. They did not have *my* gift.

He drank his wine, his gaze flicking over the lights below, the sky growing darker.

"About today," he said.

My entire body locked into place remembering that scene in the forum. Actually, we were in a very secluded alcove off of the forum. I'd wondered about the man he met there and what they'd talked about. But all of that had fled my mind when Julian nearly burst into half-skin after the soldier passing by harassed me.

The sight of Julian was terrifying. He was beyond menacing, his eyes glowing fiery gold, his muscles bunching, expanding, as he fought to control his beast and nearly murdered the soldier. I hadn't known any Romans personally. Julian was the only one I'd ever spoken to. My other interactions had only ever been violent and brief—from a far distance when I helped the Celts and that one other time when I lost my entire family.

So I wasn't sure if his reaction was normal. Did all dragons nearly lose their minds when someone touched their property? Everyone knew they were innately possessive beings, but Julian had looked . . . maniacal, monstrous, horrifying.

"About today," he repeated after setting his goblet down on the low table. "We must ensure that doesn't happen again."

I blinked at him, saying nothing. I certainly didn't want to witness a scene like that again.

"You won't leave the house except in my company or with Ivo." When I said nothing still, he added, "Do you understand?"

"Yes." A burning stirred at the center of my chest. He didn't trust me, and that was understandable, but now I was to be essentially imprisoned at his house. "Does Kara require an escort around the city?"

He clenched his jaw before answering. "No. But Kara isn't you."

"Surely, there are other young slaves who go about the city doing business for their masters. Why am I—"

"Because you don't behave in a subservient way," he snapped. The sinking sun cast half his face in shadow. "I told you this before we left."

"My direct gaze?" I huffed in anger. "So you're saying I invite the attention of other men?"

"Yes."

I flinched at the insult.

He sat up from the lounge and faced me. "You may not mean to, Malina, but that fire burning in your eyes is a challenge to any man. But to a Roman and especially to a dragon, it's like a summoning, a siren's call. Not to mention the rest of you."

I straightened my spine, my ire stoked, and unfortunately, my ego as well. My bravado took over beneath his intense stare.

"What about the rest of me?" I immediately wished I hadn't asked that question.

His gaze flickered over my face and trailed down my throat, so tangible I could feel its caress, a tingling, delicious burn. I shouldn't have done it, but I reached out with my empathic gift, finding his aura was already waiting for me, the tether faint but still there.

I gasped. A wave of heady lust, hot desire, and powerful need hit me so hard, I braced a hand on the table. It prickled through me, filling my veins with heat and igniting my own arousal. Or was that simply his feeding through the tether?

The strangest part of all was that altogether, his myriad of emotions weren't repulsive. They staggered me in their intensity, and yet, I wasn't running from the room as I should've. Rather, the witch inside me basked in his emotions, bathing in their brilliance and power. She liked the strength she held over the dragon.

Stupid witch.

My pulse beat fiercely in my throat, my body beginning to tremble.

Finally, he leaned forward, his eyes glowing with supernatural luster. "Your defiant spirit," he whispered, almost like he was sharing a secret, his timbre rough, "coupled with your beauty." He shook his head. "It is dangerous. So very dangerous."

"For me?" I asked, wondering why I could never keep my mouth shut, because then I kept going and asked, "Or is it dangerous for you?"

His wide mouth ticked up into a smile so devilish it stole my breath. Rather than frighten me, I wanted to capture that smile in my palms and hide it away for only me to ever see.

"Both, sweet firebird." His voice was a velvety, dark caress. "We might both burn for what's to come."

MALINA

My pulse thrummed in my throat as I walked through the corridors toward his domain of the house, carrying his morning meal on a tray. It wasn't fear that beat wildly in my chest—as it should be—but a twisted sort of excitement combined with anger.

Enid was awake this morning when I entered her room before dawn. I assured her she was safe and that I would take care of her. But she barely seemed to hear me, her face contorted in pain.

She simply closed her eyes and turned her head away when I reassured her again. I wanted to stay longer, but I could couldn't as Kara called me to the kitchen moments later with the master's meal.

As I drew closer to his bedchamber, the same heaviness of the air that surrounded the master of this house began to press against my chest before it slipped over my skin and enveloped me entirely. It should've sparked terror, an innate instinct to claw out of his hold— the deadly predator's strong embrace. It did not. It only increased the anticipation of seeing him again.

It was the same sensation I felt beneath the moonlight so many years ago, a sort of wonder and awe and interest that my inner witch would *not* let me walk or run away from. And now, the feeling was stronger, the pull was greater, and it only made me angrier—at fate and him and myself—as I finally stepped through the doorway into his vast bedchamber.

He stood beneath one of the arches leading to his terrace facing the city, hands clasped at his back, the same posture I found him in last evening.

Still, his figure was arresting. Even wearing a simple white tunic without his formal red robes or his general's armor, he exuded electric power. He was an intimidating force. I tilted my chin up and stepped forward with all the confidence I could muster.

I made no noise, and yet, he knew I was there. There was a subtle stiffening of his shoulders, and he curled one hand at his back into a fist.

I remained still and quiet, waiting to serve him as was my duty. A mixture of anger and, yes, excitement again, flared in my breast. It was obscene to have such feelings. There should be absolutely nothing living inside me but disgust and hatred for this man. This Roman.

"Where would you like your morning meal, dominus?"

He turned with only a flickering glance my way and gestured toward a side table, not out to the terrace. I set the tray down.

Without looking at me, he quickly ate a piece of bread and cheese, then washed it down with the cup of milk, leaving the rest untouched.

His manners were abrupt and hurried, unlike his usual cool demeanor. He then strode toward a screened area. "Follow me."

I followed, slowing when I rounded the screen to find this was his bathing chamber. There was a large bath set into the floor, surrounded by decorative tiles. Bathing oils shimmered along the surface. There was a small window to one side where he'd have a view down Palatine Hill.

Rather than disrobe and horrify me further, he sat at a table in front of the window in a chair with a high back that was thickly cushioned. He patted the stool next to him. "Sit." He watched me.

Confused, I moved at his command, perching stiffly on the stool.

"I need a shave." He gestured to the bowl of steaming water. "Kara just brought this and it won't stay hot long. Do you know how to shave a man?"

I shook my head. Where would I possibly have occasion to learn such a thing?

"It's easy. Apply the olive oil to my chin and neck area, then use the novacila to scrape the bristles off." He gestured to an instrument lying on a bit of toweling.

I picked up the shaving tool. The top was a bronze, flattened dragon in flight with three finger holes beneath it, the dragon's claws clasped around the sharp copper blade extending at the bottom. I slipped my three middle fingers through the holes and pressed it into my palm.

"That's correct. Scrape upward along the bristles. That's the most efficient way as Ruskus does it."

Still clutching the blade in my hand, I asked, "Why don't you have Ruskus do this since he knows how to do it properly?"

"It's your job now as my body slave. The light from the window will help you see."

He seemed almost amiable as he tilted his head backward and rested it on the top of the cushioned high-back. I realized the chair must've been made for this exact purpose.

"Don't forget to put the oil on first." Then he closed his eyes and waited.

For a moment, I did nothing. Slowly, I set the shaving tool back on the toweling atop the table. Standing, I then poured the scented olive oil into my palms before I gently rubbed it along his abrasive chin and jaw, the roughness sending prickles over my skin. He let out a small grunt of pleasure, not opening his eyes while I used my fingertips to smooth the oil up to his ears and down his neck where the dark bristles grew.

My pulse raced as I wiped my hands clean on the rag, then slipped the instrument back on my fingers, using my free hand to tip his chin up. His eyes were closed, his body relaxed, his throat exposed. He was completely vulnerable and unaware of the sudden thought beating its way to the forefront of my mind. This was a sharp blade. I could escape right now.

I stared at the strong column of his throat, the cords of lean muscle, and the vulnerable dip at the base. Then I raised the razor toward his neck, my hand trembling and frozen mid-air.

"What will you do after?" His deep, silken voice made me flinch.

"After what?" I whispered.

"After you slit my throat."

His eyes remained closed, his neck curved as if daring me to do it. I was frozen in place, my breaths coming quicker.

"You can't escape over my terrace. The cliff is too steep on the other side of the wall. You have no money, though I suppose you could rob me of what I have in my private coffer beside my bed. Then you'd have to get past Ruskus and Ivo, who keep watch of the back gate. They'd turn you in to the emperor's praetorians for killing their master, the emperor's nephew."

The emperor's nephew? My stomach rolled with nausea, while my hand trembled, with the blade still aloft. He opened his eyes and turned his head on the cushion, so calm and cool.

"Then there's your friend. She'd be killed for her association with you. And you wouldn't make it far, even with my coin. The emperor's soldiers march the streets at night. The moment my death was reported, deathriders would be sent out in search of you. And they wouldn't be kind in their capture of a murderess."

My heart beat so hard, I was sure it would hammer right out of my rib cage. He gently gripped my wrist and steadied my quivering hand.

"It's a foolish thought, Malina. Killing me won't help you escape. It'll only end in your torturous death."

I stared, completely bewildered. "Did you know I would try?"

Not that I actually had tried. I wasn't sure that I could do it, but I was certainly considering it with the sharp blade in my hand and his bare throat mere inches away.

"I know you're thinking of ways to escape," he said in that even, steady way of his, his thumb brushing along the pulse point in my wrist, which somehow calmed my trembling. "I would be if I were you."

A strangled laugh came out of my throat. "But you'd never be in my position."

"You never know," he added so easily, with a pensive expression creasing his brow. It was strange for him to say something like that. A powerful dragon and Roman such as himself would never find himself held captive as I was.

"I want you to see that there is no way free of here that doesn't end in death," he added. "This isn't some woodland clan you can slip away from into the night. You're at the heart of Rome, surrounded by your enemy." His grip firmed and his voice deepened. "You must trust that I will keep you safer than any other."

"Trust you?" I huffed another laugh. "My slave master?"

"Yes." He softened his tone, his thumb sliding sweetly over the thin skin of my wrist before he let me go. "Now that your hand is steadier, let's try again."

He leaned his head back and closed his eyes as if he hadn't nearly caught me about to murder him in his own bedchamber. The level of trust he had that I wouldn't cut his throat anyway was astonishing. I refused to believe that he knew me so well, because the fact was that he was right. And though I might be reckless, I wasn't a fool.

Inhaling a deep breath, I blew it out slowly, then pressed the blade to his skin and scraped the bristles up the side of his neck to his jaw, wiping the excess on the rag. Then I repeated the movement over and over until I'd shaved his throat and jaw clean, having only nicked him slightly at one sharp curve. After dabbing his face with the rag, he sat up and felt his face.

With a grunt, he stood. "You won't have to serve my dinner tonight, but I'll expect you in the morning as usual."

A pang of disappointment had me frowning, but I kept my gaze averted as I cleaned up the vanity table holding the shaving instruments. "Where will you be tonight?"

He seemed to pause behind me before he moved again, the shush of fabric brushing fabric. I wiped the table clean of spilled oil and turned to face him.

He'd draped a simple sash of red across his tunic, the fabric hanging in loose folds at his hip.

"I have a feast to attend at the emperor's palace."

"To celebrate your recent victory over the Celts?"

He scoffed as he refolded the red sash at his waist, though it already looked perfect. I was surprised he hadn't made me dress him as well, but he seemed in a hurry. He likely didn't want to teach me yet another duty that might make him late for whatever work he had to attend to in the city.

"Yes, Malina." He seemed perturbed. "The emperor likes his victory parties."

"Emperor Igniculus. Your *uncle*." I couldn't hide my distaste.

He lifted his gaze to mine and stared a moment. I thought he might say something more but he simply clenched his jaw and walked past me, then out of the bedchamber into the corridor, his heavy footsteps fading away.

"Reckless," I whispered to myself, knowing my sister Lela would chastise me for it if she were here.

I never could hold my tongue when I ought to. What was he supposed to say, that he might be the emperor's uncle but he wasn't a cruel dictator like his kin? That would be a foolish hope. He might not have abused me, but he was still a part of this frightful, monstrous machine of Rome, the one that kept burning and killing and taking more lives for their own pleasure.

It was appalling.

"I should've cut him when I had the chance," I muttered as I set about to make his bed.

Even if I died for it, at least there would be one less tyrant in this world.

JULIAN

I dismounted from my black stallion, Volkan, closer to the stable entrance, noting that many of the patricians were exiting their extravagant litters at the palace doorstep. Torchlight spilled onto the steps leading into Caesar's home, illuminating the senators, generals, and their wives in elegant dress as they ascended.

"I'll take care of him, Legatus." The young stableman who I tipped to handle Volkan for me on my visits to the palace held his reins.

"Thank you, Jovan."

I slid a small silver piece into his palm, then removed my formal red toga from the satchel on the saddle. Jovan stepped up to help me arrange it properly over my short white tunic, the thick folds draping over one shoulder, the hem nearly brushing the cobblestone. I held the silky fabric up to keep it from dragging in the dirt and walked toward the palace steps, my gut tightening as it always did when I entered my uncle's home.

The dragon's lair, indeed. But I was costumed perfectly to please my uncle. There was nothing that gave him more pride than his nephew, the Coldhearted Conqueror, wearing the red of our house.

I followed behind Senator Otho, frowning to see a young woman with long, silky brown hair on his arm. He wasn't married. Or he hadn't been when I left on my campaign to Gaul.

The servants at the entrance holding platters of goblets bowed as we entered. I took a chalice of wine right as Otho took one from the same tray.

"Salve, Julianus. How wonderful to see you." He smiled genially, gesturing to the young woman at his side. "May I introduce to you my new bride. This is Sabina Amethystus Candida. Darling, this is the famous Legatus Julianus Ignis Dakkia."

"Such a pleasure to meet you, Legatus." She leaned forward, batting her kohl-lined eyes, her plump breasts spilling out of her low-cut purple stola. "Is it true you are called the Coldhearted Conqueror because you've single-handedly killed more barbarians than any general in history? And that you drink the blood of your enemies?"

Gods, the rumors of this city.

"*Sabina,*" Otho chastised her with a laugh. "Don't be rude."

"Oh, I'm so sorry, Legatus." She placed her jeweled hand on my wrist as I poised to take a drink of my goblet. "I meant no insult."

I glanced at her hand, then switched my goblet to my other hand, releasing her hold. "I'm afraid those tales are exaggerated."

Otho wasn't usually invited to the palace. In fact, I could only remember him being here once, many years ago, before he began opposing

Caesar in the senate house. His ignorance of his precarious situation was only exacerbated by the fact that he hadn't heard or listened to the tales of the emperor's infamous parties.

We followed the other line of guests down the marble hallway to the grand hall where my uncle held his large feasts. My gut tightened the closer I grew to my uncle's inner sanctum.

"Well, the other rumors aren't exaggerated," she said when Otho stopped to greet another senator. Her gaze roamed my body with obvious interest. "You're the finest general in all of Rome."

"Sabina!" a woman yelled from inside the throng of guests.

She hurried over to the other woman dressed in a green stola, one of the Chrysocolla line. They'd socialize in the same circles, of course.

There were few of the middle-ranked dragons present—the Amethystus, Chrysocolla, and Sapphirus houses. And none of the Griseo. Uncle would never allow the lowest caste to attend his feast. There were mostly black and red robes milling about the room, dotted with blue, purple, and green.

"She's a beauty, is she not?" Otho stood next to me.

"You shouldn't have brought her," I told him honestly, wishing this man, one of the few dragons who still voted his conscience in the senate house, was smarter than I'd thought. "You should take her and leave. *Now.*"

"What do you mean?" He frowned, finding his young wife giggling with the girl in green.

"I know you haven't been to the palace much, but you are aware of my uncle's tendencies at his feasts, are you not?"

Otho turned his frown toward me. "My voice holds power in the senate," he said haughtily. "Caesar knows this. He would not disparage me in such a way."

"You are a fool if you believe that," I told him with pity.

"Caesar invited me," he protested, becoming more agitated. "I couldn't reject his invitation. It would be tantamount to treason."

"You're right, but you could've left her at home."

"The invitation was for both of us," he added nervously, then looked over at his wife. "Besides, my bride loves parties. I couldn't disappoint her. It didn't seem fair to keep her at home."

"Not even to protect her."

Otho scowled at me. "You can't be implying what I think you are."

I opened my mouth to answer but then that deep, familiar voice that always skittered across my skin, nearly raising my scales to the surface, interrupted me.

"Julianus!"

Ice bled through my veins as I turned to Caesar as he ascended the entry steps to his famous feasting hall. Or rather, infamous, depending who you were and how you viewed the debauched and violent events that had happened here. That sickening swell I had to keep down in my stomach and the revulsion I had to keep off my face whenever I came to his palace began to claw at me. All while I pretended I belonged here.

My uncle opened his arms, his red toga perfectly fitting his large frame. His short black hair and clean-shaven face cut his jaw, chin, and brow into too-sharp angles. It was as if he could never completely shift back into the man he was supposed to be. Though he wasn't in half-skin, his beast always seemed to be lurking on the surface, waiting to burst free.

"Caesar," I said, bowing as he approached and then enveloped me in an embrace.

He pressed a kiss of greeting on my cheek and held my shoulders hard, his dark gaze full of pride. "I knew you could do it," he said, low, for only me to hear. "You slayed that rabble in Gaul and brought me the head of the king in a fortnight after that fucking bastard failed me time and time again."

"Thank you, uncle." I filled my voice with admiration I didn't feel, forcing the nausea down. "All for you, Caesar. Always for you."

He squeezed my shoulders, his grin spreading wide, his eyes already growing glassy from drink. "Come. Take your seat at my side."

My stomach lurched, but I nodded and walked beside him, the crowd opening as we walked through the throng. My gaze caught on Trajan—hair shaved nearly to his scalp, his face clean-shaven. I caught his smirk before I looked away. At least he took my advice to heart.

We passed the fountain at the center where the statue of a naked male dragon in half-skin stood. Two nude female dragons in half-skin knelt at his feet. His hands gripped one of each of their horns, forcing them to gaze up at him adoringly. This statue was the first change I'd noticed in the palace when my uncle took over.

The palace was filled with similar signs of his dominance, of his demand that all bow beneath his strength. The truth was, my uncle was an incredibly strong dragon. In half-skin and in his dragon form, he had never been bested, not even in bouts of strength between warriors. My father had told me that even when my uncle was an adolescent, he'd defeated another dragon twice his size.

So while I detested the way he flouted his dominance, I couldn't dismiss it as arrogance. History had proven that anyone who went against him would likely not survive the encounter. Yet again a reminder that our plan must be solid to be successful.

"You know Prefect Ciprian," said Caesar, gesturing toward the man in a black toga sitting opposite me. My uncle lowered onto the highest seat between us—a kind of short throne with a high, gilded back and gilded arms—sitting among a cascade of cushions and plush carpets of red and gold.

"Yes." I nodded at Ciprian, clenching my jaw to keep from saying something nasty.

Ciprian annoyed me for many reasons. Besides being a malicious deviant and reprobate, he received favor from my uncle, and I didn't understand why.

When I was a centurion, I'd once had the unfortunate experience of having Ciprian assigned to my infantry. He didn't like my more methodical way of leading and would often rouse some of my men to his side and make rash, foolhardy decisions in the midst of battle that went against my orders.

When he explicitly went against my command in a campaign in Thrace, causing the death of three men who charged ahead with him, I had planned to formally punish him for undermining my authority. A public lashing for getting his brothers-in-arms killed wasn't equal but it would've gone on his record.

By the time the battle had ended and we'd tended to our injured, I summoned him to my tent only to be told that he'd been suddenly called back to Rome. I'd assumed the emperor had found him guilty of some other crime worse than getting his brethren killed. But the next thing I knew, he had been promoted to centurion of another unit.

Knowing it was unwise to challenge my uncle's decisions, I never asked. But it never sat well that this arrogant, selfish bastard had only risen over the bodies of others. Now he was fucking prefect.

"I hear congratulations are in order," I told the man through gritted teeth. I took my seat, facing out toward the mingling guests, some now taking seats along the many low feasting tables on pillowed carpets.

"They are indeed," drawled Ciprian, already deep in his cups. "I'll be taking my Rite of Skulls soon."

Another wonderful tradition instituted by my uncle. Acid roiled in my belly.

"That's right, Ciprian," said the emperor. "The first king's head you've brought me. I daresay it won't be the last."

"You can count on it, Caesar," replied Ciprian, raising his goblet to him before drinking.

"Of course," added my uncle in that superior tone of voice that always prefaced him saying something provoking, "you'll need to kill quite a few more kings before you catch up to my nephew."

Ciprian's black gaze cut to me, his nostrils flaring in fury as he drank from his goblet. "Too true, Caesar. But I will."

"You think so?" I challenged.

My uncle laughed gleefully. He loved conflict, probably the only thing beyond power and violence that put a smile on his face.

Ciprian held my stare. "You've had a good head start on me, Julian. But I'll beat you. I always achieve my goals."

And now his goal was to beat me?

I huffed in derision, not even bothering to reply, surveying the room as half-naked dancers began twirling along the paths between feasting tables. They all wore the golden slave collars stamped with IGNICULUS, their breasts bared, their skirts mere gossamer. Red-painted serpents wound around their bellies, backs, and between their breasts. They twirled to the soft tunes of the musicians playing the flute and tympanum in the corner.

"I heard a rumor about you, Julian," said Ciprian, using my shortened name, which only close friends were allowed to do.

His face was objectively handsome, carved into sharper lines than most, like all aristocrats of the black and red dragon houses. But all I could see was the ugliness hiding within. Ciprian was a foul creature. No wonder my uncle liked him so much.

A woman in a green toga, the one Otho's wife had greeted when she entered, plopped down next to Ciprian with a rumbling purr in her throat, a female dragon's way of flirting. He wrapped an arm around her waist and pulled her close, his fingers teasing the side of her breast. She was obviously here with him, though he didn't even bother to introduce her.

"What rumor is that?" I asked cavalierly, holding my goblet up for one of the servers to refill.

A pretty slave filled my cup, made a quick curtsy, and disappeared. *Smart girl.* It wouldn't take long before things would get vulgar in here.

"I heard," said Ciprian in a singsong sort of way that made his woman giggle, "that you shifted into your dragon on the battlefield and killed a man over a Celtic wench, then carried her away into the sky."

I'd wondered who would bring this up first. It didn't shock me that it was Ciprian. And she wasn't Celtic, but I wasn't going to correct him.

"What's this? You shifted on the battlefield?" Igniculus asked me in disbelief. "Over a woman?"

Roman generals didn't shift on the battlefield, not into half-skin or their dragon. It was considered a sign of weakness if they were forced to leave their human form during battle. They weren't even supposed to get their blade bloody since that was the job of their soldiers.

"Yes, Caesar." Ciprian laughed again. "That's what I heard anyway."

I remained unruffled as I'd been expecting this to come up at some point. "Your source is obviously addled in the head. And if I meet them, I'll remove it for him."

"What is the truth of the incident?" Caesar asked in a way that was a command, not a question.

I held his gaze steadily. "The truth is that one of my men disobeyed a direct order. And for that, I severed him in half." I shrugged. "I could've done the same without shifting, but my dragon wanted his blood. And I wanted every man present to understand clearly the consequences of disobeying my orders and that my dragon would stand for nothing less than complete *obedience*." My gaze shifted to Ciprian, who wasn't laughing anymore. "That fucking rabble that Bastius left me is wholly undisciplined." I swiveled my gaze back to my uncle, letting my dragon deepen my voice with promise. "They'll obey me. Or they'll die."

Just as I suspected, my uncle grinned wide, that insane look of both bloodlust and pride mingling in his gaze as he leaned over and placed a hand on my shoulder, giving it a squeeze.

"That's correct, nephew. You did the right thing. Use brutal force to teach them the way." Then he chuckled darkly. "By Dis, my blood certainly runs through your veins."

We clinked goblets. Ciprian fumed since I'd stolen his moment. He'd thought to show me weak in front of my uncle. That wasn't going to happen. Yet he still continued to try.

"So, you didn't carry that witch off? The one who supposedly helped the Celts evade Bastius?"

"Oh, no. I took her. She's quite the beauty," I confirmed, having to give some reason for why I took her. "It's the general's prerogative to take the choicest spoils of war. But you wouldn't know that, *Prefect*. You aren't a general."

His eyes filled full black with his dragon. He was itching to shift and claw me, which only made me smile and lift my goblet to him. It was improper etiquette to shift at the emperor's palace. Only the emperor himself could do so.

Caesar tilted his head back and laughed uproariously. When he settled, he said, "Don't worry, Ciprian. I believe you'll be seeing a promotion soon enough."

"Thank you, Caesar," said Ciprian, now openly fondling the breast of his companion.

She didn't seem to mind, drinking down her wine and watching the guests below us.

"That must be one sweet piece of Celtic cunt," said Ciprian venomously.

Fury swirled like a snake in my belly. But I kept my face cold and impassive.

"Speaking of cunts." Caesar glared at Otho sitting at the table directly across from us, the dancers swirling between us.

Why had that fool even come to this feast? After openly arguing against a law the emperor had wanted passed. And especially with his young wife.

"Otho!" called Caesar over the music. "What lovely creature have you brought as a guest?"

Otho stood with a smile, helping the brazen girl in purple to her feet. "Caesar, this is my new bride, Sabina Candida of the Amethystus."

Caesar flicked a hand to summon her. "Come closer, Sabina."

She looked down at Otho, unsure. He nodded while his expression revealed the wariness he should be feeling. If my predictions were right, he should be feeling much more than that right about now.

I girded myself for what was about to come, keeping my expression indifferent as I sipped my wine.

Sabina wove her way up to the carpeted dais and pillows, around other generals and their wives to stand before Caesar.

"Candida?" Caesar wore his charming smile for her. "Was your father not a deathrider?"

"He was, Caesar," she answered brightly. "He was very sad to retire from service."

"Very loyal to Rome, if I recall correctly."

"Indeed, Caesar."

He flicked his hand for her to come closer. She glanced nervously at me, then at Ciprian, who watched her with feral lust, still groping his companion with his free hand.

Sabina stepped forward. Caesar leaned against his high-backed chair and spread his legs. "Closer, sweet."

She returned his smile, one similar to how she'd looked at me in the corridor. He coasted his hand along her thigh, pressing the silk of her stola to her skin.

"So how do you like married life to a senator?" he crooned while caressing her.

"I . . . I like it very much, Caesar."

"Does your husband satisfy all of your needs?"

She gulped hard, then giggled nervously. "I don't know what to say," she finally answered, a hitch in her voice.

Caesar slid his hand up the side of her waist, stroking the back of his knuckles over one breast. Then he grinned at the taut nipple teasing through the silk of her purple stola.

"Caesar!" Otho stood. "Please, do not—"

Two praetorian guards shoved Otho back down into his seat and stood over him. Sabina snapped her head to look at her husband, seeming confused, worried. Then my uncle guided her chin back so that she looked at him. I couldn't even look at Otho, especially when I'd warned him. He thought himself so important, like so many others, that the emperor wouldn't dare target them for humiliation and their women for crude sport and public shame. He was wrong.

No one seemed to recognize the depths of the evil in my uncle but me.

"Don't worry about him," Igniculus told her. "I am the emperor. It is my right to touch beautiful things." He opened his palm and mounded it over her breast. "You are a beautiful creature, Sabina. Your husband won't mind."

"Because you're the emperor," she whispered, her breathing quickening, her pulse speeding in her throat.

I could hear it flutter even faster when Caesar pushed the strap of her stola off her shoulder, revealing the breast he'd been fondling.

"That's right." He slid his hand beneath her stola and gripped her thigh, tugging her closer. "I'm the emperor. I can have whatever I want. Open your thighs."

She slid her feet wider, eyes dilating with desire.

"I want you, Sabina." He moved his hand between her legs. "And according to your dripping cunny, you feel the same."

She giggled, like this was a game. Of course, it was. And the emperor always won. He stroked between her legs and she moaned.

I coolly surveyed the feasting hall. This foul game my uncle liked to play was showing not just Otho, but all of Rome, who held the most power. And what he could do with it, who he could steal and hurt with it.

Some of the generals and their wives pretended not to see what was happening on the dais. Legatus Titus, the general I served under for my entire military career until my recent promotion, quietly assisted his wife to her feet and slipped out the side entrance. That was always the interesting part. My uncle demanded everyone's presence when he sent invitations to his so-called celebrations, but he didn't appear to mind when some crept away once his target had been established.

Through his cruel behavior toward Otho and his wife, Caesar was now announcing to the entire lot of senators present that they'd better vote only in his favor or suffer similar consequences.

Others had taken it as the sign that the orgy could commence and were now groping and fucking at or around their feast tables. But my gaze skimmed to Otho. I wished I hadn't looked. The shame and fear and fury mottled his face red as the praetorians held him in place. He simply watched, and it wasn't nearly over yet.

"Why don't you come sit on my lap, sweet Sabina," growled my uncle, his eyes sparking gold with his dragon.

"Yes, Caesar," she cooed.

When she went to drape her leg across his lap, he twisted her quickly to face away, her back to him. He hiked up her stola and then pulled her onto his lap. She gasped as he maneuvered the flap of his toga aside and sank inside her with a hard thrust.

"Ah!" she cried out in pleasure, dropping her head back to his shoulder.

My uncle, however, had his eyes on Otho as he fucked the senator's wife, baring her breasts completely and licking her neck with his forked tongue. Always, his dragon rose when he was being cruel. He wouldn't shift into half-skin unless he wanted to kill the girl. But that wasn't her purpose. She was a tool to show Otho he'd better not vote against the emperor's wishes in the future.

There was a reason beyond my number of kills that they called me the Coldhearted Conqueror. I'd become a master at remaining completely emotionless no matter what was happening around me. Whether my men were taking the head of a king, slaughtering an entire army, or my uncle was fucking another man's wife in front of all the patricians of Rome.

For a split second, I contemplated killing my uncle now. I could obviously take him by surprise. But then his praetorians and the others loyal to him would certainly kill me right here and now. And like a hydra, another of his ilk would sprout his head and take the throne. Nothing would change.

And then there was Malina.

My stomach churned with acid even thinking of her while Otho's bride writhed on Caesar's cock, crying out in pleasure. All while the dancers and musicians continued on, the guests laughed and drank and fucked, like one of their own wasn't dying inside at the center of the feast hall. Otho's head was now bowed in humiliation.

Ciprian had joined in the fray, pushing the head of his woman down beneath his toga. Her head bobbed furiously as he growled with lust, watching the emperor with fiendish glee.

A few of the honorable couples slipped away quietly, leaving the feast hall before the depravity intensified. I remained fixed in place, summoning the servant with the wine to fill my cup.

Finally, Otho's bride screamed with her climax. Caesar pitched her forward onto all fours and finished with a few hard thrusts, fisting her hair and forcing her face up so that Otho could see what he'd done to her. That he'd fucked and pleasured his wife and there was nothing the senator could do about it.

Caesar slapped a palm to Sabina's bare ass and pushed her aside as he heaved back into his throne, his breathing labored. "Otho! I give you and your bride my blessing."

Ciprian laughed cruelly, his hand still on the nape of the woman sucking his cock. "You might even get an extra blessing from the emperor in nine months!"

Caesar tilted his head back and laughed, then reached for his goblet, his gaze falling to me, ever cold and watchful.

"Julian. You need to take the edge off. Take Sabina. She's a good, tight fuck." He gestured toward the woman, who was still crumpled in the cushions, her face flushed both from exertion and the new shame that kept her from looking over at her husband.

Otho's head was still bowed, his fists clenched. The praetorians no longer held him in place, though they kept watch at his back, just in case he tried to avenge his honor. He wouldn't though. No one ever did.

"No, thank you, Caesar," I said evenly. "I'm fine with just the wine."

"That's right," said Ciprian. "He's got that Celtic cunny at home." Then he grit his teeth and orgasmed. The woman between his legs gagged and coughed, but he held her down a second longer before letting her up. "Well done," he told her, handing her a goblet of wine.

It was a miracle I could sit through these events and not vomit. It was a miracle I wasn't insane from it all. The excessive debauchery in this den of hedonism had grown over the years. My emperor's insatiable appetite for power was fueled by his malice, his lust for flesh and his lust for blood in equal measure. The madness was rising, and we needed to set our plan in motion soon.

When it was an adequate time for me to take my leave, I did so quietly. Ciprian was preoccupied with another woman wearing a sapphire-blue stola, the one in green he'd used moments earlier sulking at his side. Caesar was engaged with some of his generals, who'd gathered around to regale him with their recent victories.

No one took note as I wove quietly through the party and toward the exit. Speeding down the corridor, I left the sounds of sex and laughter and a corrupt, rotting kingdom behind me.

Once out of the palace, I strode at a quick clip, nearly at a run, eager to get the fuck away from there.

A shadow moved before I reached the stables.

I reached for the blade hidden beneath my toga before I realized it was Trajan. Relaxing, I joined him in the shade of a line of Persian cypress trees.

"Otho should've known better," he said quietly. "He won't be opposing any more laws in the senate."

"The senate is useless."

"Don't tell my grandfather that."

"We need to move soon," I spat, bile still trying to rise up my throat after my uncle's display. "I can't take this much longer."

"You've witnessed that before. We both have. Even worse than that. At least Otho's bride was willing."

Another wave of nausea rose as I remembered some of my uncle's past public demonstrations with wives who weren't at all keen on the emperor's attentions.

"We all need to meet to devise the final plan," Trajan was saying, his blue eyes glinting with a flare of his dragon. "There can be no confusion on what each person's role will be. Just let me know when to arrange the meeting."

I gave a stiff nod. "Soon."

Then I strode away. Jovan brought Volkan out quickly. I swung up and galloped away, needing the wind on my face, needing to scrape that foul place from my soul. It wasn't enough. It never was.

As I trotted into the courtyard, a candle burned through Ivo's window in his little room where he preferred to stay near the horses. He stepped out as I dismounted and took Volkan from me.

"Thank you, Ivo."

Normally, I'd take care of him myself after a late-night party, but I needed a bath. Now. Even a cold one.

Even so, I couldn't help myself, diverting my path through the house toward the servants' quarters. Slowly, I inched her door open.

The moon shone through her open window, bathing her beautiful face, shining on the black tresses of her hair. The crescent shape of her dark lashes, her full mouth relaxed, the slightly upward slope of her nose—everything about her was both like a balm to my soul and an ache on my heart.

I couldn't imagine how those jade-green eyes would look at me if she'd been there tonight, if she'd watched me sit idly by.

Quietly, I walked to the window and closed the shutters, locking them. I had an insane need to haul her to my bedchamber. To have her near me so I could protect her.

What I should do is shed my human skin and carry her away to the farthest point from Rome. Somewhere she might have a chance at being safe, in a life far from me.

An instant burn erupted in my core. The beast raised his head, a feral growl rumbling in my chest. Then I heard him.

Never.

The single word vibrated through my bones and echoed through my soul.

Pulling her door shut, I exhaled a breath I'd been holding and marched toward my bedchamber.

He was right, of course. I could no more part with her than I could shove my blade through my own heart. Not when the gods had given her to me, not when she was designed to be mine.

A distant whisper floated to the surface, reminding me why I could never part with her:

Treasure.

I walked to my terrace and stared toward the palace, where torchlight shined bright, where Romans wallowed in licentiousness, where my uncle, the emperor, luxuriated in his corrupt power.

There was nothing to be done, then, except to move forward with our plan and to somehow not die in the process. I didn't mind dying for the cause before, but now there was *her*.

My loyalties had shifted the second I saw her on the Celtic

battlefield—bloody and terrified, defending herself against that filth in half-skin. My cold heart was engulfed in flame, and there was nothing I could do to stop the wheels Lady Fortuna spun for me.

For us.

That night in Dacia four years ago, I was newly appointed centurion by my uncle, who I'd known was not a good man. I'd left our camp with three of my trusted men that night only to get away from this oppressive feeling that I was on a path of my uncle's choosing and there was nothing I could do to escape from him or his appalling plans for Rome. There was a constant pall of gloom pressing down on me.

Then, unexpectedly, I'd watched this young, beautiful woman dance with fire in her heart and defiance in her eyes as she looked upon me, an enemy. For our brief encounter, she'd given me hope.

As I watched her, an inner voice, not my dragon's, had nudged me to give her the gold coin. Whether it was the gods guiding me or my own intuition, I believed that I owed her for what she'd given me that night. It wasn't simply a dance, but an unexpected courage to walk my new path. If she could look upon a dragon with such fearlessness, knowing I had the power to kill her and her entire clan, then I could summon the same to face my own future beneath my uncle's power.

That was why I'd paid her with such a precious coin that had been so dear, never knowing it would one day guide her right back to me.

I bowed my head and prayed to the gods who would listen that we weren't both now doomed together.

MALINA

"Why can't she just use the mill in town?" I asked as I turned the quernstone around and around, grinding the grain.

"Because their flour is shit!" shouted Kara from the kitchen window.

I made a wide-eyed face at Stefanos, which made him burst into laughter. He was always smiling or laughing, this child. I laughed with him, even while my arms were burning from the exertion of grinding the grain into the fine powder Kara required.

"Here. My turn." Stefanos shooed me off the handle attached to the quern, sitting on a low stool opposite me in the yard.

For such a gangly boy, he was strong, grinding twice as fast, and seemed not to wear out like me.

At this time of day, I'd normally be cleaning the master's bedchamber or washing his linens. I had laundered all of his togas and robes yesterday afternoon since he was at the emperor's feast.

This morning, I'd arrived to his bedchamber with his food on a tray only to find him already gone. I'd tidied what little there was to do, checked on Enid—no change—then found Stefanos grinding grain for bread flour.

"Do you know where the master was off to so early?" I asked casually.

"No." He kept grinding in a circle at his swift, even pace. "But he's an important man. Loads of people want to meet with him. He's the emperor's nephew, you know."

My stomach shriveled inward. "Yes. I discovered that."

"He'll be next in line." He shook his head. "Though Caesar won't be going anywhere anytime soon, I daresay."

A darkness smothered my spirit at the thought of Julian ascending the throne and taking the cruel wheel of this city. I don't know why it bothered me so much. I knew him to be the conqueror everyone proclaimed him to be. Gods, even the graffiti declared him to be the cold monster whose sole ambition was to kill more, enslave more.

Skrr, skrr. The wheel went round.

And yet, there were signs that he wasn't a cruel man, that there was compassion in him. He'd rescued Ivo and brought him to his household when he likely would've been killed by his former master. He'd taken Ruskus in, a man with a decided limp, and a boy who—my gaze flitted to his throat where the vicious scar raised beneath his collar—must've had a violent past. My intuition told me he'd rescued Ruskus and Stefanos from some horrible fate as well.

"Stefanos, did dominus save you from something . . . or someone?"

I'd been considering it all week, noting that Julian kept few slaves and the ones he did all seemed to have one thing in common—a fault of some kind, a reason most nobles would not want them.

He gulped, then picked up speed again. *Skrr, skrr.*

"He did. He's still saving me."

"How do you mean?" I asked curiously.

"I—I can't say. Kara says not to tell."

It was the first time I'd seen Stefanos seem nervous or scared. "It's all right," I assured him, deciding to switch the subject. "How did Kara come to the household?" I asked quietly.

"She was his mother's slave. When his parents were killed, he inherited her."

My heart tripped faster. "His parents were killed? Who killed them? Why?"

"Some plebians looking to rob them. His uncle's men found and executed them. That was his brother they'd killed after all." His eyes widened as he whispered, "Kara said it was ghastly. Slaughtered in their beds. Killed the slaves of the house too. Kara was midwifing for a neighbor. She found them the next day."

"Where was Julian?"

"Away at military training. Somewhere in Dacia. He was a centurion then."

My entire soul shrank inward. "It happened around four years ago?"

He shrugged. "Unsure. I'm never good with time."

But I believed I knew. It was about the time we met. Perhaps even the same night, his parents were being murdered half a world away. All I knew was that when I met him that night, he seemed more carefree, not as angry as he appeared now. Not as cold. Something had hardened him, and I knew as well as any that the deaths of one's parents could certainly change a person.

So strange these ties we seemed to have. I wondered where he was when my family was attacked and slaughtered by Romans. That was three years ago, and he certainly wasn't among the men that night. I'd have known. Just as I did on that Celtic battlefield. I'd felt him there.

That night, there had been an awareness building inside me, my magic tap-tap-tapping on my tether. I thought I was simply in sensory overload after the slaying of my adopted clan and the near-assault by that monster Silvanus.

But when Julian stepped into view, when I heard his voice, my tether locked on him. I refused to open the empathic link but it didn't keep my magic from grasping tight. I didn't understand.

Bunica had always said my sisters and I were given our gifts to defeat our enemies. While my sisters were dead, I still had my gift. So why would it drive me toward this Roman dragon? Not to control or defeat him, but to keep him close. The witch inside me longed for the dragon, Julianus. I didn't understand.

A steady clip-clop of hooves drew our attention to the entrance into the stable yard. Julian entered astride his black stallion, and my entire being warmed at the sight of him. Not because he appeared strong and powerful and majestic—though he did—but because he was simply there before me.

He pulled on his reins, his impassive expression locked onto me. We remained like that, holding each other captive until Ivo stepped out and took the reins.

Julian dismounted and strode toward us, Stefanos still grinding, then he stopped in front of me.

"I'll take dinner in an hour. Don't be late."

Then he strode away.

I cringed at the amount of pleasure that suffused my entire body. I was ashamed of my attraction, that I was completely captivated by a Roman—a sworn enemy, one of the kind who killed my entire clan and family.

Stefanos stopped turning the handle of the quernstone, his brow raised so high it disappeared behind his draping bangs. "You dine with him?"

I managed a shrug like he'd done earlier. "I'm his body slave. I serve his meals."

Stefanos grinned. "He doesn't want you to serve him. He wants you to join him."

And then I saw it, right before he lowered his gaze to the quern—a flicker of golden fire flaring bright in his eyes. The otherworldly spark of a dragon.

I gasped and stood quickly. Stefanos continued on, not noticing my reaction. So that was why Julian was "still saving him." All dragon bastards must be killed, but here he was. Living and breathing.

In complete and utter shock, I hurried away to prepare for dinner, trying to understand why the Coldhearted Conqueror of Rome would be hiding a dragon bastard in his home.

MALINA

Kara had provided roasted pheasant, fresh bread served with a soft cheese, stewed leeks with garlic cloves, and a bowl of olives. And while the meal smelled heavenly, my stomach rolled with nervousness as I set the tray down on the table inside his bedchamber. I could hear water dripping where he must be taking his bath.

"Malina," he called softly, "come here."

Blowing out a shaky breath, I steeled myself and marched behind the screen to find him waist-deep in his luxurious bath, steam rising off the surface. Avoiding his naked body, I kept my gaze on the floor, realizing I could feel heat seeping from the tiles and through the thin hide slippers I was wearing.

"There's a chamber beneath the floor. Ivo feeds the fire to heat the water when I need the bath."

I frowned, not liking that he seemed to know what I was thinking so often. Then my thoughts scattered as he walked up the steps, water sluicing down his muscular frame in rivulets.

Mouth agape, I couldn't stop my gaze from roving up his thick frame and sculpted body to where he held out a hand. When I finally met his gaze, no doubt wide-eyed with shock, he arched a brow.

"The towel, Malina."

I jumped at once and turned to find the drying cloth hanging across the stool I'd sat upon to shave him. I snatched it up and held it open with both hands. He walked forward, pressing his wet body against the open towel and taking the ends from me. A drop of water dripped onto my forearm, making me flinch. I chanced a glance at his stoic face; the only part of him showing any emotion at all was his eyes—burning embers of gold.

I turned while he finished drying his body, thankful he didn't ask me to do that for him as well. I didn't dare reach through my magical line to discover what he was feeling in that moment, with that look in his eyes. It was better I didn't know.

"Fetch me a clean tunic." His voice was cool and steady as always.

Glad to gain some space, I moved away from the bathing area and to the shelves where his clothes were stored. I pulled out one of the plain, loose tunics I'd folded and put away yesterday then carried it to him.

He finished toweling off his hair and wiped his chest once more before tossing it aside, leaving him completely naked before me. I'd seen him nude before, the night he'd carried me here in dragon form. But then it had been dark and I'd been half-mad with the trauma I'd endured.

This was different. While he seemed perfectly at ease, waiting for me to help him dress, my pulse beat wildly in my veins. I'd helped him dress before, but not for bed. This was disturbingly intimate.

"Are you going to assist me, Malina, or stand and stare all night?"

His tone wasn't teasing or reprimanding. Somehow, that made it easier to get past my anxiety. I opened the tunic to help him slip his arms through, then he slid it on and walked toward the terrace without another word.

Relieved, but also knowing the image of him stepping out of that bath would haunt me later, I hurried back to the tray and carried it out to him. He was already seated, sitting up this time with his back to the outer wall of the terrace, his gaze out at the setting sun.

I sat in my usual place on a cushion opposite the low table and waited. He was tensely silent, something obviously worrying his mind. But I wasn't his friend or his comforter, I reminded myself.

Finally, he looked at me, expression heavy, and asked, "Why didn't you use your gift when your village was attacked?"

Surprised by the question, I straightened and decided to answer honestly. "I couldn't."

"Why not?"

Clearing my throat, I pushed away the remorse and regret that always laced those memories. "I didn't know my magic well enough then. And I—"

Should I be this honest?

He stared at me with such intensity, I found myself being more truthful than was wise. "I've always had trouble focusing my gift when I'm afraid."

He nodded, seeming to understand.

"When was the first time you used it in defense?"

He wasn't simply curious. This was an earnest interrogation.

"Aren't you hungry, dominus?" I gestured toward the food.

He gave a sharp shake of his head but poured two goblets of wine and passed one to me. Without commenting on the master serving his slave, I took it and drank deeply, remembering.

"After my family was attacked, I'd found a small town in the south of Gaul, serving in a tavern. The owner let me sleep in his storage room, and he was a kind old man. But I was a woman alone."

When I paused and met his gaze, I noted the sudden hardness taking over his expression.

"Did someone hurt you?" he asked, a darkness seeping into his voice.

"Not exactly. A man in the tavern had offered me coin for sex. When I told him I wasn't a prostitute, I could tell I was going to have trouble with him. He and his friends were a loud, drunken bunch. Their minds were easily pliable, and I needed to protect myself."

I took a sip of my wine. Julian kept silent and waited.

"Using my gift, I filled them with fear and announced to his table that deathriders had been seen coming our way." I huffed a small laugh, recalling their terrified faces. "They fled the tavern at once, screaming in panic. When a few others in the tavern stepped outside to check the skies and returned confused to find me laughing, the tavern owner asked what I'd done to those men. I didn't answer and cleaned their table. But that was how a rumor had started that I was a witch. It helped keep unsavory men away. It also led a particular Celtic clan to come looking for me not long after."

He reached forward and tore a piece of bread from the loaf and dipped it in the soft cheese. He seemed to be mulling this over as I set my cup on the tray.

"Is that all, dominus? I will leave you to your meal."

"No," he said quickly when I moved to stand. "Stay and eat with me. I have more questions."

I was eager to check on Enid. And while I understood my role well in his home, it still sparked an angry flame when I wasn't *permitted* to leave.

"The bargain, dominus, was for one question each night. You've already asked two."

He continued to eat, then asked as if he hadn't heard me, "You claimed that they were drunk and their minds were easily molded to your will. Do you have trouble using your gift on stronger minds?"

"I will answer the rest of your questions, dominus, if you answer some of mine after."

"Agreed," he snapped easily.

Clasping my hands in my lap, I said, "Yes, I can have difficulty tethering with some minds."

"You have difficulty, but can you connect with the strong-willed?"

I thought about how easily I'd connected with him. "I can, yes."

His expression showed a glint of excitement. "Could you tether to someone powerful like the emperor?"

I couldn't suppress my surprise. "Are you asking me to?"

He said nothing, firming his lips together, his jaw clenching.

"Why would you want me to use my gift on the emperor?"

He stared, a taut silence stretching heavily between us. This seemed to be one question he wasn't going to answer.

"What kind of work keeps you away every day?" I asked, curious where he went and what he was doing.

"I've had to meet with my military tribunes. Among others."

"For your next war campaign?" I asked, not disguising my disgust.

"I'm a legatus in the emperor's armies. That is my job."

I snorted indignantly. "And when will Rome have enough?"

He clamped his jaw again, not answering. Somehow, that made me braver.

"Will Rome never stop until the entire world bows at her feet? Enslaved and groveling before the mighty dragons?"

His eyes flared with golden fire, his dragon watching me. That reminded me of Stefanos. Was he hiding a dragon bastard because the boy was his? My stomach curdled at the thought. If Stefanos was his son, where was the mother? What did he do with her? And why did he let the boy live?

That law enacted by Caesar when he took power rang around the world, all the way to Gaul and beyond. The law that demanded any dragon born of a lowborn must be executed at birth. That the Romans could be so callous wasn't a surprise. It was Caesar's way of keeping control, not allowing slaves or lowborn freed men or women to have the strength of the dragon. It kept him in power.

Not only that, but it was said that all lowborn dragons begotten before this law was enacted were sentenced to fight in the gladiator pits, a punishment for their birth. Apparently, the emperor had been smart enough to know that the people wouldn't applaud and clap their hands in watching the deaths of some of their own, of women and children, but they would applaud them becoming warriors in the pit.

"I thought all surviving dragons were to be put to death or were sent to the gladiator pits in the far provinces. Even children." Julian was defying his own uncle's law. "Why are you hiding Stefanos in your household?"

He angled his head, arching a superior brow, seeming unsurprised that I'd figured out Stefanos was dragon-born. "Because he will be killed otherwise."

"You could be executed for hiding a bastard dragon, couldn't you?"

"I could," he acknowledged coolly, sipping his wine as if he hadn't just discovered that one of his slaves now knew his deadly secret.

A smart woman would've kept her mouth shut or made promises that I'd never tell for survival and self-preservation. But as I was always told by my grandmother, my mother, and my sisters, I was reckless. I'd rather walk into the fire than have it chase and burn me as I ran away. I blamed the witch who lived inside me.

"Why risk so much for Stefanos? Why him?" I asked.

He observed me for a moment, that cold, unreadable expression hiding his emotions. I could tap into the tether, but right now I liked wondering as he watched me in that calculating way. Was he considering how to dispose of me once this conversation was over? And why wasn't I afraid?

"Because it is not his fault he was born a bastard," he finally answered evenly.

Such a simple, honest answer. One that contradicted the almighty ambition of the true Roman.

"When I held that small boy in my hands," he continued, holding out his hand, palm upward, staring down as if he saw the newborn babe in his own arms, "he was so innocent. So pure." He dropped his hand, meeting my gaze again. "I realize you see me as a monster, Malina. But I am not." He glanced away, raising his goblet. "Not entirely anyway."

Rather than want to run away, I wanted to hear more. I wanted him to keep talking and to listen to his low, rich baritone telling me words he should never utter if he were a true, loyal patrician to Emperor Igniculus.

I still couldn't ask him whether Stefanos was his, because I was afraid of his answer. Of how it would make me feel if he only saved Stefanos because he was his own blood or if he actually had enough of a heart to save him regardless.

A trembling had taken root deep inside my core. I wasn't sure what caused it. Whether it was his honesty about Stefanos, that he wasn't a Roman who followed the orders of his emperor, or that this thread of humanity strengthened the tether between us.

"That man in the forum." I changed the subject. "He is one of your tribunes?"

"He is."

"Then why meet in secret?"

"It wasn't secret. It was in the middle of the day in the forum."

"It was on the outer edges in a deserted alcove off the forum center where no one could see. You whispered in the shadows of an alley," I challenged. "It was a clandestine meeting."

He arched that brow at me again. "You're sure of this?"

"Positive." Yet again, I wished I could hold my tongue, but there was nothing for it. In Julian's presence, I could be no one but myself.

He smiled but it vanished quickly. "It wasn't entirely deserted."

He meant the man who had grabbed hold of me, the man he nearly killed for committing such an offense.

"Your reaction that day," I began, plucking at a piece of bread, "it was rather extreme." When he said nothing, continuing to watch me, I asked, "Why did you nearly kill that man? He hadn't harmed me."

For the first time since I'd sat down, his expression shifted from cool indifference to a harsh scowl. He stared for a breathless moment.

"He'd taken liberties where he shouldn't," he rumbled in that darker voice of his dragon. Then he snapped, "Next question."

"Why am I eating meals with you?" I sat back, though I'd barely eaten a bite tonight, my stomach in knots. "It isn't my place . . . as your slave."

He abandoned the food as well, wiping his hands on a cloth. "Would you rather dine with Kara and the others? You can if you wish."

"That's not what I asked."

His gaze was sharp and searching, the shimmer of gold burning brightly. "You don't know?"

His question was accusatory, and it sent my pulse racing. I shook my head.

He smiled again, but this time, it wasn't sardonic or cynical. It was seductive, whether he intended it or not. The harsh lines of his face softened to an expression of welcome and promise. He was so beautiful, it hurt. I couldn't drag my gaze away if I'd tried. The witch inside me luxuriated under his sultry gaze.

"Do you remember our first meeting?" he asked gently.

"Of course I do. You gave me the gold piece. The aureus. Your mother's."

A pang of sorrow hit me at learning of his parents' death. His expression didn't change, still calm and intent on mine, still alluring with that crooked smile.

He glanced at my throat. Though the aureus was hidden beneath the high neck of my tunic, he knew it was there.

"You wore it all these years," he declared. "You could've used it for any number of things. Food, shelter, weapons for your Celts. But you didn't. Why?"

Then I couldn't help it. My fingers went to the coin. Even beneath the fabric, I could feel it cool against my skin. "I couldn't."

"Why not?" He leaned forward off the wall. "It was given to you by a Roman centurion. A stranger you'd never see again." His smile widened. "Or so you'd thought."

Swallowing hard, I answered honestly. "I couldn't part with it."

"Because of its value in gold?"

"No."

"Because of its connection to Fortuna, then. You thought the goddess would protect you if you kept it."

"Partly." My voice was shaking now.

"And what of the other part?"

"I . . ."

His attention was fierce and intense. I couldn't hold his gaze, nor could I answer him. Standing, I pulled the aureus from beneath my tunic and held it as I walked to the terrace banister overlooking Rome. The light was fading, dots of yellow torches and oil lamps lighting up the homes and taverns below.

I felt him standing behind me. "Tell me of the other part." His voice was silky dark, sweeping over my skin in an intimate caress.

When I didn't speak, he gently turned me to face him, one hand on my shoulder. I held the aureus tight in my fist, a pulse beating there. For a moment, I wondered if it originated from the coin or if it was simply my own heart beating wildly in my palm. He lifted my chin with a finger.

I inhaled at the tether drawing tight, the connection my magic strengthened at his touch.

"Tell me," he urged.

I shook my head. "I can't."

I couldn't admit that I was wholly attracted to the Roman who'd enslaved me, who spent his life killing and enslaving others to grow an empire of malevolence and malice. The very thought made bile rise up my throat, and yet, I couldn't resist the powerful need to be near him, to draw him nearer.

I suppose that's why I didn't move, barely breathed, when his large hand cupped my jaw, the pads of his fingers sliding into my hair.

"Shall I tell you?"

I kept silent, a war of morals churning in my breast.

He swept his thumb across my cheek. "I'll tell you since you're too coward to admit it." His hand on my shoulder slid to the side of my neck, and it felt heavenly. "You kept this coin, because it tied you to me. The gods had bound us together. Your gods, mine, it doesn't matter." His thumb continued to sweep, stroking sweetly. "I never thought to see you again either. But I'd never forgotten you. Do you know there were so many nights I lay alone in my tent in some foreign part of the world, feeling disconnected from everyone and everything in my life? When I felt the absolute loneliest, you would visit me."

He chuckled at my shocked expression, continuing to hold and stroke my face softly.

"I'd see my firebird dancing across that stage. I should've known that night that you held magic inside of you. You bewitched me with that first glance. I'd wonder where you were in the world. Who you were dancing for. Who had the privilege to watch you."

"My dancing days ended long ago," I told him. When the Romans had invaded my village and killed everyone I loved.

"I hope that's not true." His thumb brushed close to the corner of my mouth. His gaze dropped there, his expression soft and yearning. "I hope you'll dance once more. For me."

Then the pad of his thumb swept over my bottom lip. He wanted to kiss me. I could *feel* it. If I allowed that, it would be a betrayal to everything I was. It would be a betrayal to my family, long buried in their cold graves. His burning gaze swept over my face, then he let me go and stepped back suddenly.

While I caught my breath, Ruskus entered the terrace carrying a scroll of parchment. Julian must've heard him coming. Dragon senses, of course.

"Excuse me, dominus." Ruskus limped closer, his wobbly gait much more pronounced in the afternoon. "This just came for you."

Julian stepped aside and unrolled the parchment. He read it quickly. There was a pinch between his brow when he turned. "That will be all, Ruskus."

He nodded a bow, then left, never even glancing in my direction. I wondered what he and Kara thought of me, eating with the master. Probably that I was sleeping with him as well. A stab of guilt darkened my mood when Julian turned to me.

"What news?" I couldn't help but ask. He'd given me permission to ask my questions and now I couldn't seem to stop.

"War."

My stomach twisted. "Where?"

"Barbarians are attacking Roman provinces in Moesia."

"That's not far from Dacia . . ." I heard my voice trail off, remembering how I'd fled west toward Gaul rather than south toward Moesia when I'd escaped the Roman attack on our village.

"It's in the southern region close to the Thracian border." He stood closer.

I snapped my head back to him, my thoughts having wandered quickly. "When do you leave?"

"Three days." He crumbled the scroll in one hand. "I have a mind to take you with me."

"Why would I go?"

"You're my body slave. It's common for generals and officers to bring them." He paused, then added, "Many slaves travel with the campaign."

"How else would Romans eat or dress themselves?" came my tart reply.

I winced at my sharp accusation. He edged closer and corralled me against the stone banister.

My back hit the railing while I kept my chin up to face him.

He placed his hands on the banister, caging me in but not touching me. I kept forgetting how large he was. I couldn't even imagine what he'd look like in half-skin. And why the thought of seeing him that way didn't repulse me was another mystery.

"True enough, firebird." He dipped his head lower, studying my eyes carefully.

"Why do you call me that?" I asked, angry that my voice trembled.

"You don't know the tale?"

"No."

His smile turned fiendish, then he stood straight and stepped back, removing his heat and intoxicating presence. "Good night, Malina. Be ready to leave in three days." Then he walked away down the terrace steps and around the corner toward the stables.

* * *

I found Enid awake when I ducked into her small room. Her hair was pulled back in a neat bun away from her face, the way Kara wore hers. I realized the older woman must've helped her with it.

"You're awake," I whispered happily as I rushed to her side.

The single oil lamp burning on her bedside shadowed her thin face. She'd lost weight.

She smiled when she saw me and reached up a hand from the bed. "Malina."

Her voice was raspy from disuse. I sat on the edge of her bed, hugging her gently. She smelled of the lavender oil Kara set out for me to use in bathing. Kara had been taking good care of her.

It made me smile to think of the rough Kara tending so kindly to Enid.

"How are you feeling?" I asked, easing her back to the pillow.

Rather than answer, she asked a question of her own. "How did you manage it? To get the general to save me?"

I'd begged.

The tether wound tighter.

I shrugged. "You're here now. That's all that matters. You'll be well enough soon."

"I don't know if I will." She fell into a coughing fit.

I helped her sit up more and grabbed the cup of water on the small table to help her drink. She gulped it down, then settled again. A wet wheeze squeezed out of her lungs every time she breathed.

"Why would you say that? Kara said the wound is healing."

I held the cup in my lap in case she needed more water.

"There's something wrong on my inside." She grimaced as she tried to move to get more comfortable. "Don't think any healer can help me now."

"Don't say that, Enid."

Dread gripped me hard that she might be right. Her face was paler than before, her lips dull and gray. Shadows danced across her eyes as she got a faraway look.

"Do you remember Brigid?"

Setting the cup aside, I gripped her pale bony hand in both of mine, swallowing the lump swelling up my throat at the thought of the frail, white-haired woman Brigid, who was a little addled in the brain.

"She begged for her life," whispered Enid hoarsely, "when they were loading us into the nets. They killed her with one swipe of a claw." She sniffed. "Now I wish they'd done the same to me."

"Please don't say that," I begged her, squeezing her cold hand in mine.

"I thank you for getting your master to bring me here. Better to die in this bed looking at your pretty face than in that cold pen or all alone somewhere else."

"Please don't give up, Enid."

"Don't worry about me." She gave my fingers a weak squeeze. "You're in a safe place here. There's no shame in doing whatever you have to in order to survive, my sweet girl."

Whether she thought I was using my body to placate the general, I wasn't sure. It didn't matter. All I wanted was for her to find some peace.

I sought her core with my magic, connecting easily with her since our souls were so familiar, then pushed a wave of solace through the line.

She stared up at the ceiling, the candlelight casting strange shadows over her face. She winced again in pain.

"Sleep, Enid," I said softly, pouring tranquility through our tether, giving her spirit the balming peace she needed. "Rest."

I curled up and laid my head next to hers as we used to do on cold winter nights. Though now I made sure not to jostle her, feeling the excruciating pain bouncing back through our connection. I closed my eyes and wept silently, listening to Enid's ragged breaths in the dark, pushing my soothing magic into her aching body.

My mind drifted back to my conversation with Julian tonight and his dogged questions. He wanted me to use my power on the emperor? The thought of tethering with that dragon sent a terrifying chill through my blood. But Julian didn't ask me that randomly. He had a purpose, though he refused to confide in me what it was.

Bunica had taught me to have faith in my magic, to rely on it, and now, that inner knowing reached desperately for Julian. Not as a target to vanquish, not as the enemy, but as an ally.

I reached out to that witch who lived inside me, thinking of Julian and all that had passed between us. I clutched the coin around my neck, and a familiar rightness settled deep in my bones. I determined then and there that I must know why he asked me such a question about Caesar.

Dare I hope, was it possible, that my enemy could become my ally?

JULIAN

I awoke well before dawn. My senses prickled again. Something had pulled me from a deep sleep. Pushing my bed curtains aside, I stood and looked around, listening.

A soft whimper on the other side of the house. *Malina.* I rushed through the dark corridors toward the slave quarters, knowing she was in distress.

Passing her room on the way to the end of the corridor, I pushed open the door that was ajar. She knelt beside the bed, her friend Enid's hand clutched in her own. I could already smell the first whiff of decay.

By the oil lamp burning, I could see the tears streaking her face when she looked up.

"She's dead."

I held myself rigid and witnessed her agony. It wasn't proper nor was it my place to comfort her. By all means, I was the one who'd killed her friend. It was my army who'd killed her entire clan.

She sniffed and stared at the dead woman. "She told me she was going to die. I just didn't want to believe it." Her chin quivered as another tear slid down her cheek. "She was the last person alive who loved me in this world. Now, I have no one."

I shouldn't, and yet there was no stopping me. I couldn't stand there doing nothing and watch my fiery girl consumed with pain and grief.

Moving slowly, I closed the space between us and scooped her into my arms like a child.

"No, I can't leave her." She struggled.

"Shh." I settled in the chair beside the bed, likely where Kara had sat tending to the sick woman.

Malina settled, her gaze turned toward the bed, her chest heaving with each sob. I pressed my chin to the crown of her head, holding her close in my lap, my entire soul engulfed with the small pleasure of it.

"Pluto will take care of her now," I assured her.

"She doesn't believe in your Roman gods," she hissed tightly, body trembling. "Pluto does not wait for her."

Even in grief, my firebird let her voice be heard.

"There are some who believe that it doesn't matter whose gods you worship. There is an order to the world we cannot comprehend. To life and death. Pluto will grant passage into the underworld for those who deserve it, where her soul will find peace whether she believes or not." I looked on the woman in the bed, who seemed peacefully asleep rather than dead. "For your kind friend, he'd take her in."

Malina pushed out of my arms and to her feet. "One of your philosopher's beliefs?" She swiped the back of her hand roughly over her cheek. "It's all nonsense."

"Would it comfort you to believe she was granted passage to Pluto's realm of peace?"

"Of course it would."

I shrugged. "Then what could it hurt to believe?"

She turned to look at Enid. "It doesn't matter anyway. I heard Ruskus say she'd be dumped in a mass pit outside the city where all the dead of the poor and enslaved must go." She turned her head back to me. "She can't go to any afterworld without the proper rites."

"We could burn her in a pyre here if you like," I offered calmly. "With whatever prayers and to whatever gods you'd like to send her on her way."

"Why would you do that?" she asked, disbelief coloring her words.

"Do you want to? Because if you do, we'd need to do it now and quietly before the world awakens and wonders why there's a plume of smoke coming from my back terrace."

"Yes," she rushed eagerly, "of course I do. But I need more time with her," she begged.

"I can't give you that. But I can give your friend a funeral pyre. We must do it before first light."

She nodded, my brave girl. Then we both hastily wrapped Enid in the blanket on the bed together. When she grabbed an oil lamp to guide us into the corridor, I shook my head.

"We don't need it. Just follow me."

I could see clearly in the dark, and I didn't want to wake anyone. Ruskus and Kara would ask, no doubt, when they saw the woman gone, but I wanted Malina to have time alone to say goodbye.

"We'll need the lamp to set the pyre," she protested.

"No, we won't. Leave it."

Frowning, she did as I said, then followed me. We walked briskly past the atrium and to the larger back terrace that I used to entertain politicians and soldiers whenever I had to and the platform I used to come and go in dragon form. Malina followed me in silence, the half-moon shining softly on the expanse of white marble.

"I have no dais to raise her up. The ashes will simply blow away," I told her as I set Enid's wrapped body near the balcony railing, which was made of slim columns of stone.

"It doesn't matter. The Celts often buried their ashes from the pyre in their native land. But Enid wouldn't want to be buried here."

"Stand back," I told her, gesturing with my hand for her to move to the side.

I waited until she was a safe distance, then I summoned the fire and let the dragon overtake me. I gritted my teeth as the sound of my cracking bones splintering and lengthening filled the air. Rather than giving the dragon full reign, I halted the transformation, allowing my wings, horns, and tail to sprout, my body bulking into the beast in half-skin. The mutation took only a moment, but the power electrifying my veins made me feel like another man entirely. I was, actually, though I was still sound of mind.

It always made me wonder why I was able to hold on to my humanity in this form when so many others could not. There were many who couldn't even speak in half-skin, so overwhelmed by the creature they shared minds and bodies with. But I always could. Even as a gangly boy when I first shifted into this half-formed beast, I kept my reason.

Lashing my tail, I pulled away my ripped tunic that still dangled at my waist and threw it aside. Finally, I chanced a glance at Malina.

She'd remained in place rather than cowering farther away, and her expression wasn't one of fear. It was more of wonder and curiosity. She actually took a step toward me, seeming to want a closer look.

I faced her, knowing my red scales shone beneath the pale moonlight and that my body in this form was impressive. Her eyes roved hungrily, which only made me stand straighter and spread my wings wider.

"Can you speak?" she asked.

"Of course," I answered, noting that though my timbre rolled deeper, my pronunciation was clear.

"Why did you transform?"

"So that I could send Enid on her way." When she only seemed more confused, I explained, "I can make fire in this form. And my fire will burn far hotter than the one from an oil lamp. We need to send her on quickly."

She nodded, her gaze still devouring my appearance. I couldn't help but notice that her expression was one of admiration.

"Step farther back, Malina."

She did.

"Go on and start your prayers."

She stared toward her friend's wrapped corpse and began to mutter in Dacian, words I didn't understand.

I stepped closer to the small bundle, then I inhaled a deep breath and poured out a stream of fire. The impact flicked a flap of the blanket open but I didn't stop, blowing a continuous flame until she was entirely engulfed. As I knew would happen, the flames licked high, greedily consuming the dead woman.

The flames had barely been lit when the blanket, her clothes, and her flesh had all been burned away, her small skeleton charred and smoldering. I blew a softer flame down the length of her. Then I waited while Malina and I watched her bones, glowing with fire, finally dissolve into ash, orange embers carrying pieces of her away into the night.

Malina continued to whisper her prayers, her cheeks dry now while she seemed to pray with all her heart, holding her palms in front of her, facing up toward the heavens. When there was nothing but a long pile of smoking ash upon the terrace, I inhaled another deep breath but only blew out air to send what was left of Enid over the balcony.

Some ashes fell to the earth while the rest drifted away and upward on a draft. When I'd blown all of the evidence away, leaving behind only a smudge, I turned to her and commanded, "Go to sleep, Malina. I'll be taking my morning meal in the city. You won't need to tend to my needs."

I hadn't planned on leaving until noon to make my appointment in the forum, but she needed rest. And I couldn't have her dragging into my room, carrying a tray, with circles under her eyes and grief plain on her face.

She let her hands fall to her sides, still staring past the balcony.

"Malina," I said with a deeper rumble.

Her head snapped to me.

"Go to bed. Rest."

She gulped, her expression still full of heartbreak, then she finally nodded. As she walked away, I heard her faint whisper, "Thank you."

Her gratitude only slid the dagger deeper. I was the cause of her friend's death. And so many, many more innocent lives. I didn't deserve gratitude.

My mother's lovely face flashed to mind. Then my father's. I couldn't bear to think how they'd look at me now if they'd seen all the destruction and death I had caused. A son they'd tried to teach better than following the ways of Rome.

I stared out at the city, where only a few lights glowed in windows, the city still asleep.

"It must end," I hissed into the night. "It *will* end," I swore. "Soon."

XII

JULIAN

"Valerius is as much a tyrant as Caesar," said Gaius, Trajan's grandfather.

It was early afternoon and most vendors were beginning to close their shops. There was no auction block today and the praeco had already made his pronouncements earlier. I liked coming to the forum this time of day. Most patricians were readying for an evening meal at home, or somewhere else. No one of importance was usually here, no one to wonder if I chatted overlong with a senator like Gaius.

I looked over at him. He was the head of the Tiberius household and also the oldest dragon of the Sapphirus line still living. It was said his ancestors could be traced back to the first blue dragon, born of a coupling between Romulus's daughter and the god Neptune. The son begotten on the Roman maiden was named Tiber, giving them their distinguished and well-respected surname.

Their family's lineage was also why his and Trajan's alliance in the plot was so important. Together, the three of us lent legitimacy to our planned coup. Our assassinations of Igniculus and his followers would not only free the people of Rome from tyranny but our political positions would also lend credibility and support to us while we formed a new Rome. Or that was what we hoped. For the road in front of us, even after we'd severed the serpent's head, would be a long and hard one.

"Now that Caesar has silenced Otho," Gaius added, "there will be no resistance left."

"Except for you, Grandfather." Trajan stood to his side eating a date he'd picked off a cart nearby.

"Any public resistance in the senate would be unwise," I said to Gaius. "We all know Caesar's tactics to control are cruel at the very least."

"My grandmother is no longer living," Trajan said bitterly, "so he couldn't do to Grandfather what he did to Otho."

"No," Gaius agreed, looking regal in his midnight-blue linen robe, his still-black hair cut short, the noble lines of his face setting him apart as a pureblood no matter what he wore. "But I do have two granddaughters. Your sisters."

Trajan froze, his dark eyes instantly sparking bright blue with his dragon, the air sizzling with the energy before a shift. "I'd kill him if he touched my sisters."

"Trajan," I said in the cool timbre I would use on the battlefield.

His gaze snapped to mine. Immediately, he came back to himself, closing his eyes and blowing out a breath.

Gaius put a hand on his grandson's shoulder. "Need to control that temper, my boy. We must all be very careful. The emperor may act the monster, but he is cunning and perceptive." He patted him. "No wayward looks or flares of temper. And certainly never allow your anger to bring out your beast."

One of the many laws enacted since my uncle's reign was that shifting into half-skin or dragon in Rome was illegal. Only military personnel had the legal right to shift into dragon form in order to leave the city to join their campaign.

"Perhaps Junia and Marilla should leave the city for a while," said Trajan.

"They're visiting their great-aunt in Ravenna at the moment," added Gaius.

"That's not far enough." Trajan's mood had soured quickly.

"It wouldn't matter," I said, surveying the crowds in the forum. "If Caesar finds offense, he'll do everything necessary to make that person pay. So we simply won't offend him."

"Until we take off his head," murmured Trajan.

"The senate is powerless," Gaius stated flatly, a sense of somber finality in his tone. "I'm glad my own father isn't alive to see what it's become."

He heaved out a sigh, his gaze sweeping across the forum to the Wall of Traitors.

"When I was a young boy, in my grandfather's time," he continued, "we were a proud state, content within our boundaries. We didn't murder indiscriminately. Even slaves had the right to earn their freedom and find a better life. But now"—he shook his head—"Rome is no better than the rotting heads mounted above our city."

He waved a hand to the corpse in half-skin that had been staked to a wall near the hall of justice. His purple scales were so dark they were almost black, a noble of the Amethystus house.

"We'd never find a criminal punished in such a shameful, morbid way. If a man was sentenced to death, he was at least allowed his dignity or to fight for his life in the gladiator pits. Now, all Igniculus wants is blood and rot. The city reeks of it."

There was no telling what the Roman had done to be staked through the hands and feet and chest, exposed to the elements and jeers of on-lookers. No one looked at him now, his tongue swollen and hanging grotesquely from his gaping mouth, a pool of blood nearly black in the cobblestones at his feet. A man leading a steer past him didn't even turn his way.

"True, Gaius," I agreed, holding Gaius's hard gaze. "And that is why our plan is so important. You say the senate is powerless, but this is only for *now*. It will not be forever. We need those of you who stand against the emperor to remain in office."

He sniffed. "Even if we have to vote against our own conscience to protect our loved ones from the emperor's wrath."

"Even so," I agreed. "Trust me. I've been leading campaigns for too long, murdering clans who weren't even our enemies but only trying to make a life in their own lands. I've given countless slaves to Rome to appease my uncle when it *galls* me," I spat, my gut tightening at the truth of it. "When the tide turns—and it will—we will need loyalists to give their honest votes on new laws to come. Righteous laws for a new Rome."

Trajan crossed his arms, huffing out a breath. "The picture you create seems impossible, Julian. He isn't just well guarded. He's sur-rounded by sycophants and powerful men who agree with his laws. Who agree with wielding power by the sword and claw."

"They may not all agree with him," I offered. "They may be pre-tending, just like I am, just like you are."

Gauis grunted assent. "We won't know who is truly on our side until we strike."

I was well aware that killing Caesar alone would be much like cut-ting the head off a hydra. There were plenty more to take his place in a heartbeat. We had to take many more down with him, once we could determine who truly supported Igniculus and his tyrannical Rome.

"The timing must be right," I said calmly. "The plan must be solid before we strike. I don't want any of Caesar's followers fleeing to other provinces and gathering their armies."

"Perhaps Caesar should be our final target, rather than our first," said Gaius thoughtfully.

I stared at him, taking in this strategy. "That's an idea. Weaken him by removing his allies first."

"Caesar has no allies." Trajan watched the dwindling crowds. "He has only lapdogs seeking his favor and brutal men who relish the playground of blood and sex he provides."

"True enough," I agreed. "His new pet Ciprian grates me to no end."

"Ciprian Seneca?" Gaius asked.

"Yes. Do you know his family well?"

"Not well." He shook his head. "He's from a branch of the black dragons most don't associate with. They're not of the quality of most patricians of their dragon lineage."

I remembered the foul way Ciprian treated the women at the emperor's feast, the way he spoke of Malina. Slave or not, most patricians didn't speak of others with such vulgarity, especially in public. Except my uncle.

"That doesn't surprise me," I added.

"So who do we take out first?" asked Trajan, having turned his back to our small circle. He was anxious for action.

"Don't be in such a hurry." Gaius scratched his chin. "Let's think on it."

"I'm tired of planning. It's time to act," grated Trajan, his frustration apparent.

"I understand how you're feeling," I said, the need to act building inside me.

I'd been wanting to kill my uncle for years, ever since the day I found out he'd dragged his sister, my aunt Camilla, from the Temple of Vesta. All my aunt had ever wanted, my father once told me, was to devote her life to Vesta. Aunt Camilla was born a white dragon, a Vicus, after all, and from a high noble house. Only white dragons could serve as priestesses in the temples. She'd been a priestess at the Temple of Vesta ever since her fifteenth birthday.

But within the same month my uncle took the throne, he hauled his sister from the temple and back to his palace. I didn't want to know what he did to her there, but I could imagine well enough. Whatever it had been, it was awful enough to make her transform into her dragon and never shift back.

All I knew was when I returned from the campaign I'd been on with Legatus Titus, I was told my aunt Camilla now resided in a dragon pit with a chain around her neck to keep her from escaping. Caesar had built the pit near his palace, where he kept her prisoner to this day, to keep her from escaping.

That was so many years ago, and yet she remained in dragon form. My only solace was that my own father had died before that had happened. It would've broken his heart to see his sister that way. He would've fought my uncle, and he would've lost and died trying to free her.

"But your grandfather is right." I returned to the conversation. "I believe switching tactics to go for his supporters first is smart. However, if my uncle catches even a whiff of insurrection, he'll go to ground to plan a counterattack. And he'll have plenty of forces to gather around him."

"Agreed." Gaius shifted his toga higher up his shoulder. "We'll meet again when you both return from your campaign. I hope it's a short one." He gripped Trajan affectionately by the back of the neck like one would a child, even though Trajan stood a foot taller than his grandfather. "Be safe on the battlefield, my boy. Come back whole."

"Yes, Grandfather."

Then Gaius nodded farewell to me and melted into the shadows along the edge of the forum. Trajan and I stood in silence for several minutes, watching the vendors pack up for the day and a few women getting water from the public fountain. A young girl dipped her pitcher in the fountain and tried to balance it on her head like her mother, following in her wake.

"Otho has taken a leave of absence from the senate," I told him. "He's taken his new bride on a trip to the southern shores."

"Smart man." Trajan snorted. "I imagine he might set his young wife up in a villa far from Rome for quite some time."

"I tried to warn him that night. The hubris of senators. Have they learned nothing?"

"Unlike you, they don't read nearly as many philosophy books."

Growing weary of the topic and thinking of Otho's idiocy, I heaved a sigh. "I'll see you tomorrow in Moesia. Be sure to lead your legion out at dawn. I've already spoken to the other tribunes and given them orders."

Trajan was frowning while watching something over my shoulder.

"Did you hear me?"

"Isn't that your witch over there?"

I snapped my head in the direction he was looking, instantly spotting her dark hair, braided into the long rope she was accustomed to wearing. She was on the far side near the circle of temples. Ivo loped along behind her as she disappeared into one of the white marble buildings.

"See you tomorrow, Trajan." Then I was gone, snaking through the forum to discover what Malina was doing.

MALINA

"Wait for me here," I told Ivo.

He nodded and leaned against the outer wall at the entrance of the Temple of the Dead. I'd passed other temples, the one for Vesta where the vestal virgins kept the goddess's eternal flame burning, the most prominent in the forum. But if I was betraying my own gods to pray to a Roman one, I didn't want any of the others. This was where I longed to be.

Bunica was likely screaming at me from the afterworld for entering a Roman temple. But I'd prayed to our gods Zamolxis and Bendis for years in the wilderness. Look where that had led me. I needed more powerful help.

It was the witch inside me who pushed me now, so I obeyed. I wrapped a scarf over my head as I walked inside. Down a short corridor, I passed a line of columns into a grander domed space, the interior of the temple, which was cool and silent. Shocked, because I was expecting the god of the underworld, Pluto, I froze at the sight of the figure looming large above me.

At the temple's center stood a magnificent white marble statue of Proserpina, a beacon of light shining on her from an oculus above. She took my breath away.

In half-skin, she spread her arms and wings wide as if in welcome. She was bare-breasted with a sash tied loosely around her hips, one clawed foot and slender leg extending from the drapery. Her tail curled in a way that indicated she was in movement. She was heading somewhere with a fierce, determined expression on her lovely face, coils of hair falling over one shoulder.

Heavens, she was lovely. If the real Proserpina was half as beautiful as this artist had rendered, she would be almost too magnificent to behold.

To the right, a white marble statue of Pluto loomed in an alcove, lit with oil lamps. I gave him a cursory glance. He was also beautiful, horns and spikes sprouting from his head in half-skin as some dragons bore them. But he didn't occupy this space and dominate the temple as his wife did.

A priestess in white, her head and face veiled by gossamer fabric, walked to the front of the temple, knelt, and whispered a quick prayer. I watched her, wondering about the white dragons, the females who were born being an anomaly to their kind, forced to become priestesses at Roman temples simply by expectation of their birth.

Of course, what choices did any of us truly have? By birth, we were forced into some circumstance and place in this world that wasn't of our choosing. But of the gods'.

I stared up into the fierce expression of Proserpina. She'd been stolen from her home above and forced to marry Pluto and live in his world below. But fear or grief or remorse wasn't what I saw on her expression now. She'd taken control of her fate. She'd become a queen in her own right. And she was stepping forward to greet and welcome the souls entering her husband's kingdom.

The priestess rose from her kneeling position. She glanced at me and was about to walk right past when I asked her, "Why do you worship Proserpina and not Pluto?"

The priestess moved in her fluid way to stand and face the statue with me. "Because she rules the underworld." Her voice was soft and pleasant.

"No, she doesn't." That wasn't what I'd always been taught about the Roman gods.

"Trust me," said the slim priestess, standing nearly a foot taller than me, as most patricians did. "She does."

"How does she do this?"

The priestess faced me. I could barely see pale pink eyes behind the veil. "Because she rules her king's heart. He will do anything for her. Therefore, supreme power is always in her hands. Not his."

Then she slid away and disappeared down another corridor leading to the back of the temple while I remained pleasantly dumbfounded.

Without waiting another moment, I stepped forward and knelt before Proserpina, removing the cloth bag I carried with me. I'd borrowed the one that Stefanos used when gathering eggs for that was all I could find.

I pulled out four red geraniums. Kara had tended the pot of flowers that decorated the atrium of Julian's home, and I didn't think anyone would miss a few buds.

Two petals had fallen off but otherwise they were just as perfect as they were in Julian's atrium. They reminded me of my baby sister, Kizzy. She loved flowers, always plucking them from meadows and adorning her hair, skipping along and smiling.

I say she was the baby, though she was only a few minutes younger than her twin, Kostanya. But Kizzy always seemed younger, so innocent and sweet. Kostanya was serious and watchful, the leader of the two.

My hands trembled as I placed the first flower before the altar of Proserpina where other offerings had been laid—food, flowers, even silver denarii, and promises to the gods scrawled on parchment.

"For Enid," I whispered. "I pray you've found peace, my dear friend."

Then I placed the second red bud on the floor.

"For you, Kizzy." I pressed my forehead to the cold stone and whispered a prayer that Proserpina would look after her in the underworld as well.

Sitting straight, I said, "For you, Kostanya." I thought of my solemn sister, who'd always watched out for us, mothering us when Mama wasn't with us as we traveled. Then I placed the flower next to the first and pressed my forehead to the stone again, whispering another prayer.

I set the final flower as a tear slipped free. I was closest to Lela since the twins had each other. That night we were attacked, she'd looked so beautiful in the gown Bunica had made for her, love shining in her eyes as she gazed up at Jardani.

When the Romans in half-skin had charged into the wedding at the center of our village, I'd frozen. I'd seen the one who swiped a claw across Jardani's throat, spraying blood on Lela's dress while she screamed. Papa had jerked me aside and shoved me toward the woods.

Run! His voice echoed in my mind now. I'd instantly obeyed him, noting the flash of relief on his face, and through the tether I'd attached to him the second he'd grabbed me. I ran as fast as my legs would take me deeper into the woods, panting and sweating, then I sensed a sharp pain through the tether, and instantly after, I felt nothing. The connection severed even while I reached and grasped for it with my magic, the ghostly frays slipping away into the ether.

That was when the tears had begun to fall. My papa was dead. And the rest of my family with him.

Later, I asked every traveler from Dacia if they'd heard any news of my village. One man had scowled when I mentioned it, saying he'd heard of the attacks, having lived a few villages away. He'd said that part of a Roman legion was drunk on bloodlust and had used not only my village but also several others to gorge themselves. Something about dragon madness had overtaken them.

When I'd asked the stranger about survivors, he'd shaken his head and said, "No one survived."

Sniffing at the memory of Lela's lovely face, I pressed my forehead to the stone and let my tears fall on the altar of Proserpina.

"Please, mother of the underworld, queen of the afterlife, watch over my sweet sister Lela."

Then I gathered my bag, wiped my face, and headed toward the exit of the temple.

Right as I walked through the columns, a wintry wind passed through me, kissing my flesh and bones, the scent of wildflowers swirling around me.

Pausing, I turned and looked. "Kizzy?"

For some reason, the ethereal touch felt and smelled like her. Peace was left in the wake of her scent. "Sleep well, my darling."

Then I wiped my eyes and left the temple. The sounds of a cart rattling and people shuffling about and talking loudly brought me back to reality. Ivo stood straight and smiled as I approached.

"Let's get home," I told him, knowing I'd be leaving tomorrow morning for Moesia. Not that I had anything to prepare for. Still, I wanted to wash and pack a few tunics, what little I had.

We walked side by side at a leisurely pace out of the forum and past some other shops toward the road that wound up to Julian's home.

A sound coming from a tavern pricked my attention. The familiar instruments called to me like a siren song. The soft clink of metal zills, keeping in tempo with a lute and a tympanum beating a slow rhythm. My body jerked at the memory of Rukeli and Yoska. I could still see their grizzled, smiling faces as we took the stage.

Instantly, I hurried to one of the three doors of the tavern open to the street. Ivo followed and stood at my back as I leaned in the doorway.

Disappointment washed through me when I saw the faces of the musicians. I didn't recognize them as anyone I knew in Dacia, not in our village or the ones close by. And yet, they felt familiar, especially when they played that music. The sound of home.

Then the woman, a dark-haired Dacian dressed in a plain tunic, not the colorful wardrobe of our homeland, her slave collar fixed around her neck, stepped up toward the front of the makeshift stage. She clicked the zills and danced slowly in a circle, a memory of Lela dancing the same way twisting my broken heart.

Then the Dacian woman sang, and my heart shattered a little more. She sang in our tongue, not in the common Latin. I covered my mouth to hide my sob. I hadn't heard my own language in so many years. I'd forgotten how beautiful the lyrical sound was, a sweetness I'd been without for far too long.

A Roman soldier walking by stepped up to the open door ahead of me to listen, but I'd heard enough of the song to know he shouldn't be hearing it, even if he didn't know Dacian.

Unraveling my tether, I latched onto him instantly, recognizing the authoritative presence at once. Without even thinking, I poured an unwarranted fear into him, whispering through the magic that something must be wrong at home, urging him there.

The Roman soldier instantly stepped away from the door and

marched up the hill in a hurry. Relaxing, I turned my attention back to the singer. Instantly, her words hit my heart.

"What does she sing?"

I spun at the sound of Julian's voice, and looking over my shoulder, I was surprised to see it wasn't Ivo hovering at my back.

Julian's steady, golden gaze held mine, a touch of sympathy in those depths.

"What words does she sing?" he clarified, since I'd done nothing but stare.

Turning back to the tavern, I noticed the audience was a mixture of slaves from different countries and a few plebeians, free Roman men and women. No soldiers, like the one I'd sent away. I focused on the singer, who could've been my mother. She bore the same regal face—a woman who'd lived hard, and loved hard as well.

She clinked the zills and twirled once, then began singing the chorus again in that slow, sonorous tempo.

"We live in the moment, for a stolen heart and a pretty face . . ."

"Malina," he interrupted. "You're speaking in Dacian. I don't understand."

Another tear rolled that I'd lapsed so easily into my native tongue, my heart yearning for home like never before. But some part of me wanted him to know the singer's words, the hurt they caused as she sang them so beautifully. So I began again in Latin.

"We live in the moment, for a stolen heart and a pretty face . . . we stare into an abyss, with a brave soul and the gods' grace."

I swallowed hard as she paused. When she began singing again, I continued to translate for Julian, who'd eased closer, his chest pressing against my shoulder blade. My body automatically leaned back, needing his strength, needing someone to lean on and help me with this heartbreaking burden of loss.

"We must not imagine a future that cannot be . . . we must bow to the demons and cherish what they cannot see."

I stopped translating on the next line. My pulse quickened as he remained fixed behind me, his hand wrapping around my waist as he lowered his head to whisper.

"Keep going, Malina." His words vibrated against my skin. "Tell me what the demons cannot see."

The demons were Romans. The demons were him.

I listened to the Dacian singer until she'd repeated the lines again. I leaned back, pressing more fully to his chest. He stiffened and kept still as I continued on.

"For we have hearts greater than they know, that fire cannot burn, that spilled blood cannot show." The Dacian's voice rose with heavy emotion, and I translated the last. *"No chains or pain will ever hold us here. If we ever hold the sword, it is us they will fear."*

The crowd erupted into a roar of applause, even the freeborn. That should've been a warning to him, that not all Romans felt truly free under his emperor's reign. But Julian didn't rage or seem angry. The tether between us remained calm and still. He simply squeezed my waist, then nudged me away from the tavern.

"Come on."

I didn't resist, walking at his side along the more deserted road to his home. Ivo was waiting not far ahead. He loped toward us, then followed behind.

The cheers grew more distant but her words were stamped on my very soul, burrowing into my bones like a charm. Then I suddenly worried for them.

"You aren't going to punish them, are you? Turn them in?"

I felt his sharp gaze on me as we walked. "For singing? No."

"For singing about rebellion." She likely sang in Dacian knowing very few Romans would even understand her words.

"Malina, if they didn't sing about a day when they'd be free, they'd be nothing but lifeless shells."

"Wouldn't your emperor be upset if he knew slaves were openly singing about such things? Threatening violence to your kind?"

He paused and drew me to a stop, both his hands wrapping around my shoulders. There was no one on the road but us and Ivo, who suddenly stepped to my side as if to protect me.

Julian sighed and looked at him. "It's all right, Ivo. We are only talking."

Ivo stepped away and pretended to be enamored with a bush on the shoulder of the road.

I gritted my teeth, preparing for a lecture. But that wasn't at all what he'd intended.

"The emperor won't ever know," he said gently, sliding his palms to my throat, one thumb brushing softly at the base where my pulse beat. "Do you know why? Because they sing in a foreign tongue he doesn't know nor does he care to learn. And no one in that tavern would tell any of his men. No one there cares about coin or allegiance to their masters."

There was a stinging behind my eyes. "I did," I admitted, shame engulfing me. "I told my master." The tears slipped free now. "I told you without any hesitation."

"Oh, Malina." He cupped my face now, wiping the wet trail from my face. "I won't ever betray them." His thumb stroked the crest of my cheek. "Or you."

I wanted to laugh, because his declaration was so absurd. "You *own* me. That in itself is a betrayal. We are not *equal*. Not in the eyes of Rome." I stepped back and pushed his hands away, the heat of anger and shame climbing into my cheeks, because I longed for his hands on me. I wanted them back the second I shoved them away. "I thank you for not betraying them"—I pointed down the road where we'd come—"but there is no bond or trust between you and me that can be broken."

Trembling with anger—at myself more than him—I stormed toward home. No, not my home. His home. My prison. I had to keep that in mind and stop imagining some connection between us. Even if there was, what did that mean? That I would live a quiet life at his heels, at his beck and call, and be happy with that?

The words of the tavern singer wafted around me as I marched up the hill. It was nonsense. A dream she conjured so they didn't wallow in the despair of their circumstances.

Julian was right, which only incensed me more. If they had no hope at all, they'd simply wither and die like a flower.

Flowers. Kizzy.

A sob wracked my entire body, a tangible grief for all I'd lost hitting me hard. My clan, my parents, my sisters, Enid. I stumbled and fell onto my hands and knees, relishing the pain in one palm where I hit a rock too hard.

Strong arms were around me, lifting me. I struggled, knowing that familiar drugging scent, yearning for it. For him.

"No!" I kicked uselessly. "Don't. Not *you*." I cried harder.

"Ivo," he snapped, then he was handing me over.

I stopped struggling as I was cradled in Ivo's arms, burying my face and my grief-addled shame into his chest.

"Be sure Kara sees to her," he ordered.

Ivo grunted and strode on. Then I felt the air crackle, and the distinct sound of bones cracking pulled me out of my stupor. I knew that sound.

"*Stop,* Ivo," I hissed. "Turn around."

Ivo turned just in time for me to see a giant red dragon lift off into the air, beating his black-tipped wings, his regal horned head tilted toward the afternoon sky. His powerful frame knocked the breath out of me, even as he flew farther away.

"Gods," I whispered, staring as he rose higher and higher, my entire soul going with him.

Ivo turned and continued on toward home, but my gaze was fixed over his shoulder on the dragon growing smaller in the sky. I suddenly felt bereft, the realization that perhaps he was going on his campaign without me. That I'd pushed him away.

Maybe it's for the better, I told myself, wishing I believed it.

MALINA

I awoke in the dark to a hand on my shoulder shaking me gently. When I opened my eyes, I expected Kara or Stefanos, not Julian. But there he was, shirtless and squatting next to my bed, his expression back to cool passivity.

"You didn't leave me?" I blurted, my sluggish brain from sleep not yet allowing me to think clearly and keep my feelings hidden.

His expression softened, a line pinching between his brow. But all he said was, "No." Then he stood, revealing he wore only a cloth wrapped around his waist. "It's time to go."

I pushed out of bed, dressed only in a thin, short tunic for sleeping. He turned toward the window, moonlight still peeking through the shutters, silhouetting his large, lovely frame.

Quickly, I jerked the thicker tunic hanging on the screen to me and slipped it on, shapeless as all the others, and tied a rope-like belt around my waist. Then I slid into my sandals and secured my hair back with a strip of cloth.

I grabbed the small bag I'd packed yesterday. I didn't think over-long why I was so eager to join a war campaign.

"Ready," I whispered.

He turned, his form barely visible in the dim light. Even so, I could *feel* him, his presence large and imposing and dominant. The tether shivered between us, but I ignored it and dutifully followed him through the darkened house.

He didn't head toward his bedchamber as I expected. Rather, he walked straight out to the larger terrace, the one where he'd first landed when he took me from Gaul and the one where we'd said goodbye to Enid.

"Why are we leaving in the middle of the night?" I asked.

"It's morning, actually. A few hours from dawn." He stopped in the middle of the terrace and faced me. "But there is a reason I wanted to leave under the cover of night."

"And that is?" I could hardly force the words from my mouth, my gaze flicking over his broad chest and the stack of tight muscles down his abdomen.

"Because," he said in that deep rumbly voice, "I don't want to carry you the way I did before." His scowl deepened. "That hurt you, and I can't"—he cleared his throat—"I don't want to injure you."

I blinked up at him, my heart fluttering at his admission. I shouldn't be so pleased to know he was concerned about my welfare, but I couldn't help the overwhelming sensation of pleasure. Then I realized what he intended.

"Wait. You want me to ride on top of your dragon?"

He erased the small space between us, those golden eyes glittering in the semidarkness. "Yes, Malina. I want you to ride my dragon."

We stood intimately close, my chin tilted up, staring into those hyp-notizing eyes, trying not to hear his voice in my head telling me to *ride his dragon*. But it was hopeless. That simple sentence conjured a sudden, jarring image in my mind that I couldn't wipe away quickly enough.

I bit my lip and closed my eyes, squeezing my thighs together as well. Heat already pooled low in my belly.

Julian dipped his head low, still not touching me, but I felt his body heat and his warm breath at my ear. He inhaled deep, a growl vibrating in his chest.

"You'll let me know when you're ready. Won't you, firebird?"

I snapped open my eyes. He held my startled gaze, for he knew what I'd been thinking. Of course he did. Dragons had heightened senses. He could smell my arousal.

Still, no shame bloomed in my chest. Quite the opposite. He'd given me the power to decide when I allowed him to touch my body. For a Roman, that was almost unheard-of. They took what they wanted whenever they wanted it.

He glanced toward the sky and stepped back, breaking the spell. "We need to go."

"I've never heard of someone riding on a dragon's back."

"That's because it's illegal now. One of the many laws enacted by my uncle's senate since he took the throne. It was rare even before that."

"But you're willing to break his law?"

He looked back down at me, his chiseled face kissed by shadows and moonlight, two slivers of gold holding me captive. He appeared to be calculating his response before he answered rather smoothly, "For you. Yes, I'll break his laws."

The tether tightened yet again, the shabby wall I'd erected between us crumbling that much more.

"I've ensured our tent is set up and ready."

"Wait, you flew there and back this night?"

"I'm a fast flier," he assured me with confidence and a touch of arrogance, which I found made him even more attractive. Damn him. "Most of the legions will be arriving later today. If we arrive by night, no one will notice."

"And if someone did," I countered. "If someone saw and threatened to report you to your emperor."

He angled his head, a hardness returning to his features. "Then I suppose they'll die, won't they?"

I gulped hard, knowing he meant it. Whether it was in defense of my safety or his own that he'd do such a thing, I wasn't sure. But it was another reminder that Julian wasn't like other Romans. He had an agenda not in line with his uncle, with Caesar.

"Stand next to the banister," he ordered, snapping me from my thoughts.

I instantly obeyed, already sensing the spark of magic in the air. He was readying to transform. The first time I'd seen him shift, it was a blinding distortion of limbs, his beast leaping from the man's body with sudden, powerful violence. The second, he only mutated into half-skin, but again it was a swift and surprising transformation.

This time was different. He walked a few steps away and untied the cloth at his waist. I held my breath, chastising myself while I ogled the strong contours of his back, his round, muscular backside, his thick legs.

He bowed his head between his shoulders, the sound of breaking bones making my heart trip faster. He morphed into half-skin first, his spiked tail lashing as red, black-tipped wings sprouted from his back. Horns curled out of his skull, spikes down his spine, but he kept me at his back.

Then he chuffed a chestful of air and the dragon was set free. Within seconds, his body elongated and fell to all fours, his giant, red-scaled body towering above me, eating up the space on the wide terrace. He curled his long neck toward me, those familiar yellow eyes watching with interest. He seemed to be asking a question.

"No," I snapped haughtily, "I'm not scared."

I was, of course, but I wouldn't admit it. The dragon rumbled a sort of purring sound as he lowered himself until his belly rested on the stone, then stared expectantly.

"All right, then," I told myself, stepping cautiously forward as I looped my bag over my head and across my back.

Julian's dragon extended a claw, obviously for me to climb up toward his back. I thought his scales would be rough and hard, but they were rather smooth and soft. I had trouble near the shoulder but Julian shifted just enough for me to climb onto his spine.

There was a trail of small spikes along the top of his neck, with coarse hair jutting along the back of his head down from his horns, but the spikes stopped at the perfect juncture where I decided I should ride astride. Once settled, I took the loose ends of my belt and tied them in a double knot around one of the spikes, where I also held on.

Julian made that rumbly purr again, curling his neck around to look at me.

"I'm ready," I assured him.

He stepped gently over the terrace where it dipped down a hill toward the city, then he leaped off. I squealed, but he beat his wings and lifted higher at a gentle slope toward the sky.

After a breath-stealing moment, he leveled off and soared north. Finding my courage, while still holding the horny spike tightly, I leaned forward enough to see between his shoulder and wing.

Rome fell away, dots of torchlight slowly fading as we passed over the wilderness beyond. A forest of trees blurred together, a silver river winding through it. By the gods, the world was beautiful from up here. Like an ethereal mirage that couldn't touch me or hurt me. It was a strange and wonderful gift to glide through the night sky upon a dragon.

I laughed, unable to control the unfettered joy I felt flying above the world. Not as a captive. Here, sitting atop Julian's dragon, I felt free. The tether between us didn't unravel when he shifted into the beast. Rather, it wound tighter, not a constricting kind of bond, but a firm, unbreakable one.

That was the moment I knew the gods meant for me to be bound to Julianus Dakkia. And no matter the evidence to the contrary, that he was the Coldhearted Conqueror, I knew otherwise. I'd witnessed his true nature in countless ways.

He'd saved Ivo, and I'd bet Ruskus as well, with his lame leg—two unwanted, doomed souls. There was also Stefanos, who he had apparently saved from a horrible fate. And Enid, who he didn't need to rescue from the auction, or pay a healer or even offer a proper funeral rite for. And then there was how he treated me, not with the cruelty I'd expected but with a marked kindness.

But this, breaking his emperor's laws to see to my comfort, to see that I was unharmed on this journey, spoke volumes, much more than I believe Julian realized. Because it wasn't only my comfort he saw to. He gave me something more.

I marveled at the moonlight glittering on a lake far below, shimmering like glass and beautiful to behold. We soared higher through the clouds, closer to the heavens, the earth so far away now. The stars above were so bright I was sure I could touch them. The gods felt closer too, their power and beauty as sure as the wind in my hair.

He showed me the unparalleled beauty of the world as the gods saw it, as he saw it.

We traveled across the heavens as equals.

"Oh, Lady Fortuna," I breathed on a whisper. "What have you done to me?"

JULIAN

When we landed, the first light of dawn lined the mountains in the distance. The encampment was just stirring, so I lowered onto the meadow on the far side of the trees that encircled our camp. I didn't want to take the chance of anyone seeing that Malina rode on my back and not in my claws.

I was honest when I told her I'd kill anyone who threatened to report me if they discovered it, but I didn't want to bring any attention to myself now.

Caesar trusted me wholly and completely. I didn't need to give his paranoid mind any reason to doubt me. I'd managed to turn the incident with Silvanus to my advantage, proving to my uncle that it was simply my brutal nature to punish the disobedient with death that had caused me to shift into dragon form and kill my own soldier. He understood that. Thankfully, he had accepted my story and not the rumor Ciprian had relayed that I was bewitched by a slave girl.

However, if Caesar heard a second rumor that she was riding on my back—a sign that he believed meant a dragon was being submissive to a human, which can never be done—he wouldn't believe another excuse so easily. I had to tread carefully.

Malina walked quietly beside me as I led us through the copse of trees toward the waking camp. I noticed how she purposefully avoided looking at me.

Fortunately, the chilly air during the flight had helped me manage to get my body under control. Even so, I couldn't help but be amused how her gaze would flick to me, then quickly away. She was trying so hard not to look at my naked form.

"You can look at me if you like."

"*What?* I don't want to look at you," she spluttered quickly.

"You've been trying so hard to *not* look at me, you've probably got a stiff neck."

"I do not!" She stopped and turned to face me. "*See.* I'm looking at you."

I stopped as well, knowing the sun was coming up behind her, giving her a good view of my body. Stubbornly, she stared only at my face, her jaw clenched tight. At first.

Straightening my shoulders, I held very still. "Look all you want, firebird."

Then she did. She finally gave in, taking a leisurely stroll down my chest, abdomen, lower. I regretted my boldness, because her slow perusal stirred my cock to life again.

While her cheeks flamed pink, it was my shoulder that caught her interest and held it. The tattoo there in black ink. "SDCR?"

"Senatus Dracones Romanus," I told her, turning back toward the camp. I wanted to get her inside soon, before the legions began to arrive.

"The senate and dragons of Rome," she mused, walking at my side. "Do all Romans wear this *uniting* mark?"

She couldn't filter out her disdain, and I didn't blame her. "All military, actually."

"I suppose it adds to your superiority."

"It is a rite of a Roman soldier, a badge of pride, yes."

"Pride. That's one way to look at it."

I nudged her toward the largest tent we were approaching from behind. The door had been constructed to face the interior of the camp.

"Romans weren't always what we are now."

"As long as I've drawn breath and at least in my parents' time, your kind have always been the same."

That was not a compliment. Not that I expected one.

I moved ahead of her to enter the tent first, as I heard and smelled a familiar scent inside. It was Koska, a stout Macedonian who usually tended to my tent and needs on campaigns.

He immediately stood at attention near the war table, where he'd been spreading out maps of the territory as I'd requested.

"Legatus." He lowered his gaze. "I have made all of the accommodations you commanded."

There was one in particular that had given Koska a moment's pause, but only a short one, then he'd gone about to do as I asked. I'd left him late last night in order to make the journey back to Rome, knowing I'd be making the trek a third time.

I'd never arrived early to tend to my tent arrangements. It had never been important to me. But this time was different. And though

Koska certainly recognized my behavior as odd, he never said a word or looked anything but conciliatory and professional.

Remembering what Malina had said, that dragons had always been the same, cut me deeper than she might know. I wanted a different Rome, a different legacy for my kind. But could I trust to tell her?

"That will be all, Koska."

He kept his head bowed, his gaze on the ground, and hurried past without even looking at Malina. She let out a low whistle.

"Is that how I'm supposed to behave?"

"Koska is accustomed to working around temperamental military men. He is efficient and brief."

She snorted and wandered around the room like she owned it, reminding me of the first time I caught her snooping through my books in my bedchamber. Then, she'd been afraid of me. Watching her curious nature take hold, without fear of me now, opened a bloom of warmth in my chest.

"You can put some clothes on, Legatus," she said, staring down at a map on the table. "Am I supposed to assist you?" She swallowed hard, still observing the map, or simply avoiding looking at me.

"That won't be necessary. Today."

Smiling, I ducked behind the curtain that would serve as our bedchamber. Koska had done well, constructing two low beds within the chamber. Between them there was a small space with a low table and a rug beneath. The rug wasn't of a fine weave like I had back in Rome. But I didn't expect it. I only wanted a private space where I could keep watch over Malina at night, where we might share time together over dinner when the war talks were over. Where I might listen to her voice telling me stories of her past.

Opening my trunk, I pulled out my uniform and began to dress, needing to costume myself in all the trappings of the conqueror. Especially since I'd brought a female on a war campaign, and I'd never done that before.

I'd contemplated the risks of bringing Malina, but the thought of leaving her behind in Rome where anything could happen to her was beyond my forbearance. I needed her near me, no matter what others might think of my behavior. It wasn't as if women weren't often brought on campaigns to satisfy men's urges. But it was highly uncommon for a Roman legatus, specifically me, to bring a female to war.

And still, I didn't fucking care. Malina was mine to protect and keep safe. The only problem was how this changed my other plans with Gaius and Trajan and the others. It put a shrinking timeline on how long I could keep my new attachment a secret from my uncle. For once he caught on—and he would—he'd begin to doubt me and he'd use Malina as leverage against me. The thought sent a cold chill through my blood. Not to mention that my advantage in our plans would vanish like vapor.

"The doors are over tall and wide," she called, having wandered a circuit of the tent twice. I was constantly attuned to her movements. "Does that mean that soldiers wander around in half-skin often in the camp?"

There was a nervous trill to her voice that I didn't like. I fastened my paludamentum, my red cloak signifying my rank as general, to the clasps on both shoulders, then I stepped from behind the curtain.

She turned from where she stood near the opening of the tent, her eyes widening at my appearance. A Roman in military uniform should instill fear, or at the very least disgust, in her. However, there was the hint of admiration in her gaze.

"Did you hear what I asked?" She was using bravado to hide her concern. And perhaps her surprised attraction.

"No. The men do not walk about in half-skin. But the officers will return from battle in that form, of course."

"Why just the officers?"

"Because only Roman patricians can be officers. Only dragons. And they'll be hot-blooded when they return from battle. You're to always stay in this tent unless I'm accompanying you."

She nodded. "So what happens now?"

"I need to walk the encampment and see my soldiers. They'll all be arriving within the hour."

"Is that normal for a Roman general? Seems rather tedious."

"It's necessary since I inherited my army from an undisciplined general who had no control over his men. And since the last time most of them saw me, I'd ripped one of their own in half following a victory." I stepped closer, forcing myself to stop within a foot of her, curling my hands into loose fists to keep from touching her. "That is not normal behavior for a general."

"Then why did you do it?"

"I couldn't stop my dragon from what he wanted," I answered too easily.

Her feline green eyes never wavered from me, letting my words sink in just as she pretended to ignore them. "So you're saying that your soldiers are undisciplined and the dregs of the Roman military?"

"I've culled most of the waste. The men following and assisting Silvanus at the Celtic camp have been demoted and transferred to the farthest and most remote army from Rome."

Her mouth parted in wonder. "Truly?"

"And others who did nothing but stand by and watch or who abused the prisoners after we'd won the field in Gaul have also been replaced."

"Won't that bring unnecessary attention to that . . . incident?"

"It will remind them that I am the Coldhearted Conqueror and that my commands will be obeyed or they'll suffer the consequences. I require discipline and order. That is something they understand."

Her breath quickened, pupils dilating as she seemed to be considering me and my actions. What she thought of them, she didn't say. She glanced away when I would not.

"What do I do while you're wandering the camp?"

"Whatever you like. As long as you don't leave this tent."

I gestured to the low shelf behind the war table. I always had Koska supply me with a small library on campaign. The nights could be long and lonely. She seemed curious about my books back home.

"There's plenty to read if you're interested." I angled my head lower, entranced by the ring of palest green around her pupils. "Can you read Latin as well as speak it?"

"Of course I can," she snapped back, her brow furrowing. "My grandmother taught me well." She looked over at the library of books and scrolls. "Though I'm not the devotee to philosophy that you are."

Dipping my chin, I added, "There are plays and books of poetry as well. Koska will bring meals twice a day. We eat more sparingly on campaign."

She shrugged. "Two Roman meals is a feast compared to what I was used to."

My gut clenched, reminding me that she'd lived a hard life with the Celts on the run from the Romans.

"Besides," she added, "someone recently told me to cherish what may make me stronger in difficult times."

Her expression wasn't mocking, almost as if she believed it. I hoped she did.

"I'll be back before the afternoon." I turned for the exit but stopped. "Don't leave this tent, Malina."

"I'm not a fool, Julian," she said before turning to the shelves.

I pushed open the tent flap, the air chilly, and even so a hot rush flooded my veins. I couldn't pinpoint what had caused the jarring sensation until it dawned on me how easily, how casually she'd used my name. Like we were familiar, like we were intimates.

Perhaps, that's because we were. I knew she felt attraction for me as well as disdain. If I wanted her to understand, I'd have to be the braver one.

That meant risking my life. And I would. For her, it was a risk worth taking.

MALINA

He was not back by the afternoon. I'd read an entire book by a Roman philosopher who thought very highly of himself, yet still made some valid points on the ethics, morality, and responsibility of dragons. It must've been written an *extremely* long time ago, for I'd seen little to no ethics or morality in the current dragons ruling Rome.

Koska had come in once with some bread, figs, and cheese. I'd devoured the meal alone, then spent the remainder of the day sitting at the entrance and peeking stealthily out of the tent flap.

I was mostly surprised at what I witnessed. Soldiers working together alongside slaves to build tents and fire pits. They'd even laughed together over a meal around a fire. One of the younger soldiers passed his water flask to the slave he'd been working with the whole day.

To my relief, Julian had told me the truth, that no one marched around in half-skin. They appeared so . . . normal. And yet, in my mind, the Romans had always been monsters. I never imagined them working amiably and laughing together.

Koska came again, setting a tray of roast hog and vegetables with more bread on the table in the private quarter of the tent, behind the curtain. He also brought a pitcher of clean water and a bowl to wash with.

He didn't speak a word to me, and I didn't ask if I was permitted to use the water. But I did use some of it to wash up. I was about to blow out the oil lamps and change into my night dress when I heard voices approaching. Remaining behind the curtain, I watched as Julian entered the tent with another man.

"Malina," he called, summoning me.

I walked out to realize that the man with him was the one he met with in the forum when we brought Enid home, one of his tribunes. He was the one who talked Julian down from shifting into half-skin when that soldier manhandled me.

He was near the same height as Julian, but that was no surprise. All dragons were built much larger than humans. His skin was a deep bronze, his eyes a clear blue, and they glinted with mischief. He was extremely handsome and seemed to know it.

"Malina, this is Trajan."

"Salve, Malina." He nodded a greeting, smiling to himself at some joke I didn't get.

"Hello."

"If you ever need anything, and I'm not here, you can go to him. His tent is directly to our left."

I stepped closer, frowning at his amused expression. "What are you smiling about?"

Seeming surprised, he laughed. "I apologize. I'm not laughing at you."

Julian grunted disapprovingly. "Now you've met her, you can go."

"I'm laughing at him." He gestured toward Julian, ignoring his suggestion to leave. "He was very put out when I suggested we meet in case you ever need something when Julian isn't here."

When I made no reply at his rather familiar teasing, he went on.

"These campaigns can actually be rather long and boring. As it is, we don't even know where our enemy is."

"Really?" I moved closer to them. "And who is your enemy this time?" That was something Julian hadn't bothered to tell me yet.

Trajan glanced at Julian, seemingly for permission. After Julian nodded he said, "We don't know. They've sacked several provinces, burning one to the ground, and yet none of the survivors can even tell us who they were."

That was unusual. Most clans would leave something behind or would proudly leave a mark so everyone would know who had destroyed a Roman province.

"What language did they speak?"

"They didn't," answered Julian. "No one heard them speak at all."

"That's strange."

"Exactly," said Trajan. "Quite the mystery, these marauders. But we'll dig them out soon enough." He turned for the door. "Good night, Legatus. Malina."

Then he was gone, and I was alone with Julian.

"What are you thinking?" he asked with that pensive look he often wore when he regarded me.

"I was feeling sorry for the marauders that you'll be killing soon."

"Do you not feel sorry for the families, the women and children they murdered for no reason at all? They weren't all dragons living in these provinces. There were free men and slaves alike who were killed."

"Of course I don't want any innocent person—dragon or human—to die. But they weren't killed for *no reason*. It's a rebellion against the Roman state."

He smiled that crooked smile and walked past me toward the living quarters, disappearing behind the curtain.

"But you know that already," I called.

The sound of him removing his uniform kept me from confronting him face-to-face.

"Yes," he finally answered. "I know that."

"And so"—my voice vibrated with anger—"yet again, you will root them out and kill them all and put their king's head on a pike on your Wall of Victory as a sign that the Romans are the almighty rulers of all." I paced beside the war table, breathless and furious. "Always the same thing," I muttered to myself.

"Malina." He stood in a plain tunic, holding the curtain aside. "Join me for dinner."

"I've already eaten," I snapped. "What's left is yours."

"Join me anyway. Let us talk."

"I don't feel like talking."

He paused, then used his heavier, more dominant voice. "Then come assist me. I require a bath."

There was a heavy promise in his words and in his eyes. He seemed tired. Not physically exhausted, but weary emotionally. It tugged on the tether between us, killing the ire that had inflamed me only a moment before.

He turned but I could see him clearly enough, pulling his tunic over his head. Even though I was in fact his body slave and was required to assist him in such things, he hadn't demanded that of me yet. There was nowhere for me to go, and even if I could, I didn't want to go anywhere else. Or be anywhere else. I couldn't refuse him.

Moving the curtain aside, I found him seated on a stool that Koska had set over the small tub, nude but for a piece of linen draping his lap. I also noted the small table next to him with a bottle of oil and the strigil, the concave instrument made of bronze to scrape the oil and dirt from the body. I'd seen it used before, though I never had used it myself. I preferred a wet cloth or a stream, like the Celts did.

He watched me, almost daring me to do my duty. If he thought to scare me off by having me cleanse him with oil and strigil, he would be disappointed. I marched across the small chamber, the room lit by a single oil lamp, and stood behind him.

Pouring an ample amount of oil in my palms, I rubbed them together, then spread them across the expanse of his back. He stiffened, then shivered beneath my touch. I couldn't help smiling at how intensely quiet and still he was, his hands on his knees.

Once his entire back was covered with the oil, I took the strigil and curved it across his shoulders first, admiring the taut lines of muscle. I scraped the oil in silence, shaking the excess off into the tub beneath him. I set to my work with ease and comfort while my pulse beat wildly from seeing and admiring the lovely lines of his body so closely. It was almost meditative.

By the time I circled around to his chest, he couldn't hide his heavy breathing. He was as affected as I was. I refused to meet his gaze, concentrating on being thorough as I applied the oil to his chest and began methodically scraping with the strigil along the firm lines of his pectorals. He kept still while I did my work, his body heat radiating to me, both of us breathing the same air.

It was when I pulled the strigil down one side of his abdomen, all the way to where the linen in his lap stopped my progression, that he finally moved. Like a viper, he caught my wrist. I flinched and finally met his gaze—all fire and embers glowing burnished gold.

Breath caught in my throat; he held me still but I hadn't even tried to move.

"Enough," he grated, his nostrils flaring as he let me go and stood to move around me, avoiding my touch.

Now I was panting, glancing over my shoulder to get a full view of his naked body, unable to pry my eyes from his hard cock. I turned quickly, biting my lip so I wouldn't make a sound.

I busied myself setting the strigil and oil to a side table. After a moment of shuffling and the sound of cloth moving on skin, he heaved a sigh and said, "You can turn around."

He took a seat on his bed beside the low table where the tray of food had been waiting for him. He ate quietly, picking at the meat rather than devouring it like he usually did. I sat across from him on the carpet.

There was a tremor of unease surrounding him, my empathic senses quickly picking up on whatever was circling in his mind. I assumed he was anxious or frustratingly aroused or both, like I was. But when he finally looked up at me, abandoning his meal altogether, he seemed apprehensive, nervous. Scared, even. That wasn't what I expected. That wasn't what I was feeling.

Then he broke the silence. "I don't want to kill them."

At first, I didn't follow, my mind reeling and my pulse racing from the sensual experience of scraping oil from his body. Then I remembered what we were discussing before, what had gotten me annoyed and made him use his *master* voice to get me to obey.

"The marauders?" I asked.

"Not any of them. Not the Celts or the Macedonians, the Greeks, the Persians, the Carthaginians. Not the Dacians." He held my gaze and said, almost in a whisper, "None of them."

"But you're the Conqueror. That's what you do."

"Yes. I must. To stay in my uncle's favor. Because that is the only way I can stay close to him. To maintain access to him."

My heart tripped faster, trying to reconcile what he was telling me. What I believed he was confessing to me.

"And why is that important?" I asked softly.

He was sitting with his weight leaning back on one arm, one leg stretched out on the carpet, the other slightly bent. He leaned closer across the table and spoke low.

"If I tell you this, it could jeopardize something very important." The gold flared even brighter in his eyes, his dragon waking to the danger of the moment.

"Then why do it?" I asked.

"Because I need to earn your trust. So I must give you something valuable."

"What's that?"

"My life," he answered easily, as if it were nothing.

I stared, breathing heavily, and not for the reason I was moments before. He was serious. He was willingly giving me power over his life—or death—in whatever he was about to confess.

Holding his gaze, I commanded confidently, "Then tell me."

I could feel it in the thread still weaving us together, that what he was about to say would indeed change the balance between us.

"There are a number of Romans, including myself, who are not happy with the regime my uncle and his predecessors have created."

"And," I asked, near breathless, "what do you plan to do about it?"

The small flame from the oil lamp on the table glittered in his eyes, his expression softer than usual, more vulnerable. Even so, his dragon watched me carefully. Always watching.

"We plan to kill him."

I gasped and held very still, unable to move or even blink. He went on.

"But we also know that killing Caesar will not be enough. Every emperor for the past hundred years has been worse than the one before. My uncle is the most insane and vicious of them all by far. Rome has created its own society of degenerate and corrupt leaders. We mean to eliminate all of them and create a new world order. A new Rome."

I stared without breathing for what felt like forever. When I finally let out a sharp exhale, I nearly fell forward reaching for the cup of water on the table.

"Here." Julian managed to stretch an arm across and brace me by the shoulder, then he handed me the water. "Drink."

I took several gulps, my head spinning while I slowly recovered. He eased back to his side.

"Are you all right?"

I chuckled as I held the cup in both hands in my lap. "That was rather . . . shocking."

"I imagine it was." His expression and voice were both grave and somber.

"You're serious."

"I am."

"Trajan is one of your allies."

He paused, then said, "I won't give you the names of my allies. If I'm to risk any life, it will be only mine."

"Do you mean you think I will report you?" I laughed. "To the emperor?"

He remained quite sober. "You could. If you wanted revenge on me."

"For what exactly?"

"For killing your adopted clan, the Celts. Enid. For stealing you away to be a slave in my home. Or to avenge your family, whose deaths you could surely lay on my head. It was my people who killed them, and I don't blame you for hating me for it."

He was serious. He believed that what he told me might be his doom, that I might turn against him and get him executed. A flash of his sightless eyes staring out from the top of the Wall of Traitors made my blood run cold.

"Julian," I said quietly, kindly, "I will never turn you in to the emperor or anyone else. I couldn't."

"Wouldn't? Or couldn't?"

There was a distinct difference. It was like he knew about the tether, about my magic sinking her claws into him, winding deeper, curling around his bones, seeking the essence of his soul. My magic never wanted to let him go.

"Your secret is safe with me," I assured him, unable to confess how far I'd fallen already. "But . . . why tell me?"

"Because while I'm forced to maintain my role as legatus, I would do anything to relinquish it. I don't want to kill those rebelling against us. I understand them and why they fight so fiercely. Battling them is like battling myself."

He combed a hand over his short hair, mussing the longer strands toward the front. I suddenly had the urge to comb my hands through it, to see if it was soft or coarse.

"But I must." Then he looked at me again with a plea in those amber depths. "It's all a means to an end, you understand. I must play my part until we are ready to strike."

I shuffled closer on my knees and reached across to place my hand on his where it rested on his knee. "I will help you."

He turned his hand and opened his palm, closing his large hand around mine. "All I need is for you to be near me. And safe."

I swallowed hard at the implication he was making. I couldn't protest, for I couldn't deny what the gods had already told me. Their magic was my gift and it pronounced loud and clear that this Roman, this dragon, was bound to me. And I to him.

He gave my hand a squeeze and rose to walk toward the pitcher and bowl. "It's late. And I've got to get an early start tomorrow. Let's go to sleep."

His weariness was evident, but there was a lightness between us that had never been there before. I rose quietly and tucked myself in the bed that was constructed a foot off the ground. His was a bit longer and wider, on the other side of the carpet.

I didn't watch to see if he was naked when he blew out the oil lamp and climbed into his bed, the creaking of the wood proclaiming it had been used many nights on many campaigns. Strangely, I felt calmer and more peaceful than any night since I'd been captured by him.

I thought he'd fallen asleep but then he spoke in that deep, low timbre.

"My mother rode my father as a dragon."

I turned to look at him but, sadly, could not make out even the slightest curve of his face in the dark.

Surprised, I asked, "Your mother was human?"

"Yes. She was a slave in a Roman province in Thrace when my father met her."

I could barely breathe. His mother had been a slave? It hardly seemed possible.

"She worked in the household of a noble family, one of his comrades from his legion. My father—" He broke off with a chuckle. "He told me, 'one look at her and my heart was gone.' He begged his friend's mother to sell her to him. She protested but my father had always been rather charismatic and persuasive."

"He was a charmer, your father?" I asked lightly, even while I was breathless with this new revelation.

"Believe it or not, yes. I've always been more stoic like my mother."

He shifted in his bed and when he spoke again, it seemed like he was facing my direction.

"My father said he took her back to Rome and straight to the public office of records and signed the papers to free her."

"Right away?"

"Instantly. He knew he couldn't marry a slave. Under Emperor Adolphus's rule, it was also illegal to marry a slave, but you could marry any freed person from any country."

Yet again, my poor heart galloped faster, knowing these intimate confessions tied us even tighter to one another.

"My uncle never accepted the marriage. Of course, he and my father were never close. My father was content to retire early from his military career as prefect, while my uncle continued to rise in the ranks."

"What did your father do when he retired?" I asked.

"He started a family." There was a bittersweet tenor to his voice. "They could only ever have one child."

"I'll bet you were spoiled," I teased, wanting to ease the pain I knew he was feeling since his parents were gone.

"Ridiculously spoiled."

I laughed, and he paused a moment. "I love that sound. When you laugh."

"I don't believe I've ever laughed in your presence," I said with a teasing lilt again.

He said nothing in response, so I asked, "You are favored by your uncle?"

"Yes. He has claimed I will be his heir."

"But your mother wasn't noble-born. I'm surprised he holds you so highly because of it. No offense to you."

"None taken." He chuckled. "I was surprised myself. But growing up, he'd often come visit my parents' home and take me in the yard to teach me some training tactics. He always said my Dakkian blood ran thick. I suppose on top of all his sins, my uncle was also a hypocrite because he easily overlooks my *muddied* bloodline."

"Not muddied, Julian."

"I know. But I'm not any different than Stefanos. It just so happened that my parents were married and my father was born of a higher class. When the decree that bastard children of mixed breeds must be sent to the gladiator pits was declared, I was simply fortunate that my father loved my mother enough to marry her, making it all nice and legal that I remained alive and well and climbed the ranks as the emperor's nephew."

A somber silence stretched between us. Then he added, "It's also why I must prove my brutality as the Conqueror. If I show any signs of weakness, some upstart will claim it's my mixed blood and try to challenge me." He paused, then added, "I haven't had as hard a road as yours, Malina, but lately . . . the path has become more difficult."

I had never thought to feel sorry for Julian's plight. But to be a man in his position with the legacy of his father behind him but also the expectations of his cruel uncle in front—an uncle he obviously hated—I couldn't imagine that kind of pressure and strain.

No wonder he was so grave and stoic, wearing the mask of a statue for the world to see. So that they could never *truly* see him. But I was beginning to, and the sight of the man beneath the mask curled tenderly around my heart.

"I've heard you laugh many times," he said softly, changing the subject. I didn't mind at all.

"When have you?"

"In the yard with Stefanos."

The reminder that Stefanos could be his child, his own family, cut into the sweet sensation I'd been feeling. I'd told myself to leave it alone, that it didn't matter. But now, after tonight, after his confession and the undeniable truth that I couldn't sever myself from him now if I tried, I had to know.

"Julian, may I ask you something personal?"

"Anything."

Inhaling and exhaling a deep breath, I asked, "Is Stefanos your child?"

There was a brief pause where my heart nearly leaped out of my chest. Then, "No. He isn't mine."

It wouldn't have made a difference, not really. I loved Stefanos. But I could finally admit to myself that I was jealous he might have had a child with another woman, a woman he loved.

"Kara was a midwife for a while. She delivered the child to a freed woman, the daughter of a shopkeeper. She'd been seduced by a Roman soldier. The girl died during the birth, and the father took Stefanos out back to do what he was ordered by law to do."

"To kill him." I shuddered. "That's why he has that scar."

"After Kara cleaned up the mother as best she could and left, she heard the baby squalling in the trash. When she found him, he was in dragon form. That's what saved him. His scales kept the wound from gaping too wide, from losing too much blood. So she brought him home and when I looked at him, I saw myself."

There was a thickening silence, and I thought he might not continue.

"How do you mean?" I asked, wanting to hear more of this compassionate side of him.

"Had I been born when he was, my father wouldn't have been allowed to marry my mother. I'd have been a bastard child, likely forcefully taken from my parents and killed in a back alley as well. Saving Stefanos was like saving myself. I could do nothing else but keep him." He huffed a sigh. "It was about that time my plan against my uncle first took root."

Suddenly, I sat up. "Wait, how old is Stefanos? He looks to be about ten or eleven, but I didn't think Kara had been in your household that long."

"She hasn't." He laughed. "Stefanos is only six. Dragons grow and mature faster. That's another reason he knows he's to stay at home as much as possible. I don't want the neighbors catching on."

"There aren't many neighbors close to your palace on the hill."

He chuckled again, the sound warm and lovely, melting sweetly at my center. "Would you be willing to live in a real palace, Malina?"

"What do you mean?"

Then he went silent for a moment.

"Nothing. Let's get some sleep."

I heard him turn over, the bed creaking some more, his body rubbing against the coarse sheets. I rolled to my side as well, trying to make him out in the dark, but I didn't have the heightened senses of a dragon.

His question kept me awake for some time, the one he didn't want to clarify. Because I believe it meant he intended to be the new Caesar, and he wanted me there with him.

The loveliness of the night dampened under the thought of him ruling Rome. I believed him when he admitted that he intended to overthrow the current Caesar and all the corrupt men beneath him. But one thing history had taught us about the Roman throne: it corrupts absolutely. I wasn't sure that would be a path I could take, to join him there. Not if I had the choice. The idea was hard to imagine in my current status.

There was no guarantee he would even survive the coup he was planning with his allies. That thought cut me the deepest.

He couldn't die. I wouldn't allow it. I'd do whatever I had to do to keep Julian on his path to overthrow Caesar. I simply wasn't sure I would be able to walk with him the entire way.

XVII

JULIAN

We'd been encamped near Singidium, the Roman town that had been burned to the ground, for two weeks. During the day, I joined my men in learning our surroundings and trying to track down the marauders. At night, I told stories of my childhood to Malina. I told her of how I'd broken my arm the first time my father put me on a horse and how my mother would scold me for stealing sweet-cakes from the kitchen. And with every story, she seemed to soften further toward me.

I'd managed to keep my hands to myself, though that was a feat all its own. She'd pushed me away once when I'd tried to calm her in the street that day when we heard the Dacian singer, and the rejection had cut deeply. I wouldn't risk that again. So I spent the days with my men, and my quiet nights closed in my tent with Malina. It had been peaceful and perfect, until the last week when my attention became focused on these barbarians we couldn't seem to capture.

They were a strange enemy. The first week, we'd thought they'd fled the territory altogether. They'd done their damage and left the moment Romans were sighted in the area. That had been wrong. My men had discovered signs of them camping in glens and woods nearby.

Frustrated, I joined Trajan and some of my men in half-skin to seek their whereabouts. While it was almost unheard-of for me to scout with them, my men didn't argue, knowing my frustration at our lack of progress was mounting.

We flew over a nearby gorge, and I smelled them, a foreign scent of human sweat where there was no village or town. We flew down into the ravine, finding nothing more than an abandoned fire, still smoldering, near a cave entrance. There was no sign of them in the cave either, which we spent a full day searching.

Two mornings ago, we spotted three of them running below us near a misty riverbed that ran down from the hills. We swooped down only to have them vanish in the foggy foothills of the mountain. Even my own heightened senses as the strongest dragon among them couldn't find and capture these damned barbarians. Their constant evasion was maddening.

Whatever means they were using to elude us was extraordinary. And then, last night, a party of warriors whooped and bellowed in the dead of night, waking the entire camp. I led a troop of us into the woods toward the sounds. We found only recently warm fire pits in the ground and no barbarian warriors at all.

We'd had enemies that fled when Roman soldiers moved in to attack before. But this was different. There were signs of large parties camping in the vicinity. Never in the same place twice and never maneuvering farther away. Rather, they seemed to be simply circling our perimeter, but refused to face us. To compound it all, they escaped us like ghosts.

We were accustomed to victory. Easy victory, for the most part. Or at least an enemy we could see and fight. The longer these barbarians eluded us, the more desperate we all began to feel. It was like they were toying with us.

But then, early this afternoon, the barbarians had finally shown themselves and *not* fled. One of my deathriders flying above had spotted a horde of them in the woodlands north of the burned town, Singidium. Our encampment was only a few leagues south.

I hadn't ordered the deathriders to do their usual job of corralling them with fire because we couldn't even see the entirety of our enemy. I didn't want to divide them. I wanted to be sure we had all of them surrounded so that we could be done with them all at once. There weren't that many of them. A thousand, maybe two. We could easily surround them all and end this little rebellion quickly enough.

"This is unusual." Trajan stopped beside me in half-skin, lashing his tail and staring down into the dense woodlands where part of a legion had gone in to circle around our enemy.

They hadn't fled. We could hear them moving around and see shadows flitting just out of reach. But our heightened senses told us they were still there, at the center of the woods. We simply had to completely surround them, then attack.

I'd marched down the hill, needing a closer look when my men entered the woods without any resistance at all. Not even an arrow shot from the cover of shadows. Yet, we knew they were in there.

The other half of the legion had divided and were moving in flank formations from the sides of the woodland. The slate-gray sky promised a storm, darkening the landscape. But that was no matter for my soldiers in half-skin.

"What kind of enemy runs from their opponent?" Trajan's speech was thick and deep, but easily understood. "Cowards."

"Their boldness in attacking the villages doesn't speak of cowardice." I walked down the small incline that led into the woods, Trajan alongside me. "And yet, why are they hiding?"

"Perhaps they were only bold when there were no Roman soldiers to defend the towns."

"Perhaps." I stopped at the mouth of the woodland, listening to my men move stealthily through the trees, no sounds of swords clashing or the snarling battle cries. "Something is off here."

"What are they doing?" Trajan's frustration was evident.

"Either they're cowards like you say, on the run."

"Or?"

"Or this is part of their plan. They're luring us into the woods."

Trajan looked in all directions, then behind us. "You should return to the top of the hill, Legatus."

I glanced back at the soldier in half-skin holding the standard of the golden dragon where I'd left him. From here, the entirety of the woods would know the Roman soldiers were descending upon them.

That was always our way, announcing boldly that we were setting upon our enemy. The enemy was here, and yet they weren't. Something was wrong.

"Order the men to retreat," I told Trajan.

"General?" His deep scowl on his half-dragon face pulled his snout into a snarl. "Retreat?"

"We'll use deathriders and burn them out." Even though I wasn't sure our enemy was wholly nestled in these woods, my instincts told me it would be better to keep to the higher ground. Something was definitely off.

Trajan didn't hesitate. He marched into the tree line, calling the orders to retreat.

Suddenly, the entire woods erupted in screams and fire. Streams of

flame launched across the pine boughs, igniting the trees into a conflagration. Confusion halted my men. I could see several dozen below
the line of fire, staring up and around them for the enemy while nets
flew through the air and trapped them.

"Prefect!" I called to Salvo, one of my officers not far into the woods,
his green wings spread wide, illuminated by flames licking around him
and the men. "Retreat!"

"Back, Legatus!" Trajan shouted before he flared his giant midnight-
blue wings and flew into the melee.

I couldn't, running forward to help Salvo, who had heard my call
for retreat but not before inhaling too much smoke. He coughed and
stumbled to the ground, crawling from the din of cries and crackling
fire.

"Hold on to me!" I reached him, hefted him up with one arm
around my shoulder, his wings a dragging weight as I half carried him
quickly into the grass where he could breathe the open air.

I looked back to see a purple-winged soldier still in half-skin taking
flight to escape the inferno, though it blazed through the treetops and
forced him back to ground. A massive wave of fire billowed across the
tops, creating an impenetrable roof of flame, while I could see nets still
falling from the trees. Thick black smoke billowed and clouded the
interior until I could see no one at all.

"Fucking hell!"

My soldiers couldn't fly out of the blaze without injury, even
those who weren't trapped by the nets, and most of my men were in
the center of the woodlands now surrounded entirely by a wall of
flame. Their half-skin scales wouldn't protect them in that intense
of a blaze.

Suddenly, dragons—dozens, then hundreds—burst through the
burning branches toward the open sky, their wings smoking, leaving
trails of embers and ash. The men had shifted completely into dragon
form, the only way to break through the fire wall. And still, some of

their wings and tails were on fire as they fled from certain death. But I had human soldiers trapped in there as well.

The entire woodland had been engulfed in seconds. Many of my men were already at the center, still seeking our enemy. They wouldn't have been able to get out fast enough. As I had predicted—too late—it had been a trap. I'd given the order to seek them out, giving up the higher ground to root them out. My impatience had killed my own men.

"Legatus!" a strange voice called from behind me.

I turned to see the standard bearer up the hill, holding the staff of the golden dragon that was now in flames. A giant of a man stood behind him, a sword thrust through the back of the standard bearer, the blade sticking out of his belly. It was the gigantic stranger who'd called me and then spoke again.

"This is the future of Rome," he spoke in accented Latin. Germanic. He held the burning standard high in his left hand, the symbol of our might and dominance, and shoved the bearer to the ground with his right, sending him rolling away.

The barbarian was naked but for a leather skirt and boots, his entire face and body coated in black war paint. His dark hair blew wildly around his shoulders, but it was his eyes that held me still—bright and feral and mocking.

Without hesitance, I charged up the hill, my bones stretching against my skin, bursting through my uniform as I broke into half-skin. The throbbing pain of horns, tail, and wings sprouting free from my body was only a split second before I launched myself at the barbarian.

He laughed when I tumbled him to the ground, then snarled when I slashed him with my claws, barely missing his face, catching his upper chest when he twisted away.

We were both on our feet, facing each other and circling.

"You aren't ghosts, then," I growled. "You bleed well enough."

"Yes," said the barbarian, his size impressive for a human. As tall and wide as me in human form. "We have bled quite enough for the likes of you, *General*."

Animosity dripped from his tongue.

"Who are you?"

He stopped circling and planted his feet wide, completely fearless even while I stood several feet taller than him in half-skin.

"You will know soon enough." He tilted his head, his grip tightening on the bloody blade in his hand. The one he'd used to kill my standard bearer. "All the world will know who we are when we are ready."

Faster than was humanly possible, he streaked toward me. I swiped at his throat this time, but he ducked unnaturally fast and dragged the serrated edge of his blade across my abdomen and side. Roaring at the sharp pain, I twisted to defend against his next attack.

But he was already at the woods' edge along the outer ring of fire, staring back at me, thick plumes of smoke billowing behind him. In that single moment, it wasn't the pain in my abdomen or the cries of my men or the roaring inferno screaming toward the sky that catapulted my pulse and sent a chill down my spine. It was the otherworldly flicker of gold flaring bright in his eyes before he vanished into the smoke.

"General!" Salvo was flying up the hill in half-skin, eyes wide, having recovered from the smoke.

That's when I finally noticed the trail of warm blood gushing from between my clawed hand where I'd pressed it to my abdomen. Looking down, I saw that the giant's knife had cut me deep, opening a wide gash nearly to the side of my hip. Blood streamed down one leg, pouring into the ground at my feet. Searing pain pulsed from the wound, more than it should.

"*General.*" Salvo caught me as I fell to one knee, the quick blood loss pulling me into darkness.

XVIII

MALINA

"Julian," I breathed out on a gasp as I rushed toward Trajan and another soldier, both in half-skin, carrying him into the tent.

Julian was in human form but naked, barely conscious. He must've shifted on the battlefield. Dark red blood dripped from his waist down his body.

"Gods! What happened?"

"Move, woman," said the emerald-scaled soldier I didn't know, shoving me to the side.

Julian erupted into a savage snarl and launched toward the man, hands reaching for his throat. The soldier fell back on a cry, knocking the war table over, maps scattering.

"Julian!" Trajan hauled him back and lifted him bodily, carrying him toward the sleeping quarters.

I leaped into action, drawing the curtain back so that Trajan could carry him through, his wings scraping the top of the tent. Once Julian was laid upon the bed and Trajan moved out of the small sleeping space, I set to work, finding the rags used for washing and what little water was left in the pitcher.

"Send for Koska," I snapped, sitting on the edge of his bed with the wet rag, beginning to wash the wound.

"He attacked me," the soldier said to Trajan, both standing near the entrance to the bedchamber.

"He's delirious," said Trajan. "Likely imagined you were his attacker for a moment. Go fetch Koska."

The soldier instantly obeyed and headed toward the tent exit, leaving me alone with Trajan. His half-skin form was unsettling. Especially since he was so big and broad, his dark blue scales covering most of his body, his eyes gleaming bright blue. I would've been terrified had I not known him first in human form.

"What happened?"

Trajan shook his head. "One of the barbarians. He cut Julian, then Salvo saw them fighting but the enemy fled into the smoky woods."

"Cut him," I muttered, my attention back on washing the wound, wincing at how deep it went. "It's more than a cut."

Koska hurried into the tent and remained on the other side of the bedchamber curtain, his figure visible through the sheer fabric.

"Koska, I need fresh water, thread, and a needle. And salve for the wound. Hurry," I snapped.

"Yes. At once." He fled the tent.

"You know how to suture wounds?" asked Trajan, his guttural speech eerie.

"It's no different than stitching fabric." I dipped the rag in the bowl, the water cloudy red, then wrung it out.

"It's different, but I believe you'll manage it well enough."

"Why do you say that?" I tried to wipe more of the blood, hands trembling because it didn't seem to be stopping.

"Because the gods wouldn't have given Julian a weak female."

My hands paused but then more blood gushed, and I couldn't think about what Trajan was admitting while Julian was losing so much blood.

"The blood should be clotting but it isn't."

I heard Trajan step closer behind. "He'd already lost a lot before I got to him and Salvo."

Julian rocked his head to the side, his eyes—pure, bright gold—slit open, his brow beading with sweat. He murmured something I couldn't hear.

"What?" I leaned forward, holding his feverish gaze. "Repeat that, Julian," I urged him.

"Poison," he muttered. "On the blade."

I gasped, glancing up at Trajan, his scowl so deep he looked like the savage beast he was. "Do your healers have something to draw the poison out?"

"I'll find out." Trajan stormed through the curtain and out of the tent.

Quickly, I reached for a clean, dry tunic folded on top of the chest in the corner where I'd left it. I pressed the thick fabric to his wound, trying to stop the excessive bleeding.

Rough fingertips caressed my jaw. Startled, I jerked my gaze to his half-lidded one.

"Thank you," he whispered.

"I don't know if I can even stop this bleeding," I admitted, panic gripping me hard. "I believe the poison at the wound is preventing the blood from clotting."

He shook his head to the side once. "Thank you for being here."

"I had to be," I snapped, keeping pressure on the wound. "You dragged me here, remember?"

His mouth quirked on one side, even while sweat rolled down across his forehead and into his hairline.

"Not here. In this tent." His eyes slipped closed. "For being in this world. In my life." He chuckled, more blood seeping out of the bottom of the fabric. "The gods love to play their games with me."

"Stop talking. And by Pluto, stop moving and laughing. You're only making it worse."

My hands shook as I noticed the beige tunic was nearly soaked completely dark red.

"Where the devil is Koska?" I muttered.

As if summoned, he rushed into the tent and the sleeping quarters and knelt on the opposite side of Julian's bed, setting a tray down. A woman followed behind him, older and confident looking as she sat on the bed with a bowl in her hand.

"Remove the cloth," she commanded.

She didn't wear a slave collar, but her dress was plain. She was a free Roman, a healer they kept during campaigns.

I did as she ordered, then she began to wipe and press a ground-up, dark green herb onto the wound. Julian hissed but his eyes remained closed.

"Apologies, Legatus," she whispered, then her gaze snapped to me. "This will draw out the poison. Watch how I do it."

I did, observing how she packed the entire wound with the earthy, pungent-smelling herb.

"Leave this on till he begins to bleed through. Clean it off, then add a second layer. Do that until the wound stops bleeding. Then clean it thoroughly and stitch the wound, covering it with the balm Koska has there."

She finished stuffing the wound, then thrust the bowl out to me. I took it.

"Don't you want to do it yourself? To be sure it's done well."

She eyed me from head to toe, seeming to take my measure. "There are many dying soldiers and officers who need tending." She stood and shrugged a shoulder. "Besides, it is known the general has a body slave with him. Something he has never had before. He will prefer you doing the mending of his body."

Then she left. I stared after her, open-mouthed. For a brief moment, I wondered what others were saying about me, about the slave Julian had brought on campaign. Likely, they assumed I was his sex slave. That seemed the only reason a general would bring a female body slave on a war campaign.

The thought of their gossip stung for only a second until I realized the truth. I wasn't an object to Julian. A slave to be used. Since we'd arrived, he hadn't even touched me, except for a few moments ago when he was delirious with the fever burning through him.

He'd been careful not to touch me. It had been frustrating, since I now longed to feel his calloused hands on my face, my throat, my body.

"Malina?" Koska gestured toward the wound where blood began seeping through the barrier of medicinal herb.

"Yes. Sorry." I snapped back into action, wiping away the layer of soiled herb dressing. "Go empty the bowl please, Koska."

He took the water bowl, dark red with Julian's blood, and left the tent.

After completely cleaning the wound, I settled to pressing the mash of herb along the wound again, relieved to see the blood release was slowing. It was working.

"You're beautiful." Julian's voice startled me again.

Blushing and smiling at the ridiculousness of his compliment at a time like this, I said, "Hush. You need your strength."

"You are my strength." His voice was deep and raspy, his breathing labored from the fever.

I finished pressing the second layer of herb all the way to the side of his hip, then wiped my hands and poured some of the clean water onto a fresh rag from the tray Koska had brought. I leaned closer to wipe his sweaty brow.

"You're talking nonsense, Julian."

"I haven't been saying the right words." His eyes slid shut as I pressed the cool cloth to his brow. "Been wasting time telling stories."

"I enjoy your stories." It was true. I loved hearing about his family, his childhood. His parents had been lovely people. We never spoke of their deaths.

"I have to tell you what you are to me," he mumbled, leaning into my hand as I wiped the cloth along his cheek.

My pulse catapulted faster.

"Shh," he soothed, his voice sleepy. "Don't be frightened by it."

"I'm not frightened," I said tartly.

His mouth quirked again, even while his eyes remained closed. "You are. But there is no need." Those golden slits opened and held me captive. "You are my treasure, Malina."

I huffed out a bitter laugh. "Like a coin."

"No," he answered quickly. "We are touched by the gods, you see. With the beast that lives inside us."

I knew that. Everyone knew that. It was why so many easily bowed to them. They had a power given to them by the gods.

He continued. "We have a sight into the gods' will like no other creature on earth."

I wouldn't refute that but I was sure I had my own connection with the gods' will. At least whichever one had given me my magic.

"Every dragon waits for his god-given treasure his whole life." His hand groped on the bed, finding my wrist and wrapping his long fingers around it. "And I have found mine."

I wanted to brush off his words as fever-addled nonsense. I wanted to reject his declaration and scream at him, *the gods would not choose me for you.*

But the tether between us tightened, and the witch in my soul whispered, *yes.* And a comfort like I'd never known wrapped me in warmth and rightness and utter contentment at the realization he was right.

"Shh," I whispered to him, like he'd done a second before to soothe me. "Get some rest, Julian."

He seemed to listen to me, falling deep into a slumber. Koska returned shortly after, and I settled to wiping off the second layer of herb, then added a third, though there was little blood at all oozing from the wound now.

Still, I wanted to be sure. I needed my dragon to heal and be well. I wasn't sure what was in store for him, for us, but we'd both need to be strong for the fight ahead. For there was *one* thing that was certain and clear to me now. If he planned to kill Caesar, I was going to help him in any way I could.

MALINA

Trajan stood looking over the war table at maps. I was folding some of the clothes I'd laundered on the rug in the open area of the tent while Trajan stared at one, making some notes with a stylus.

"What happened to the barbarians?" I asked.

"Vanished," he said, still bending over the table, shaking his head.

"That is unusual in your experience?"

"It's unheard-of. Especially considering their attack on us had been successful."

"They defeated you?" I hadn't thought to inquire about the battle, my sole obsession being in getting Julian better.

For the past three days, Julian had slept, waking in brief moments as the fever flared up. The healer, whose name was Polla, came to check daily, assuring me that I'd done well with the sutures and that the general was on the mend.

"Nearly four hundred dead," said Trajan.

"How many of them were killed?"

He looked up at me from the table. "None. We found not one of their dead once we were able to scour the forest when the fire was put out. And we captured none of their wounded for interrogation." His brow furrowed. "This is certainly a defeat."

Koska had told me there was a raging fire that had burned the entire forest to the north of us. I'd paid it no attention at the time, my sole concern being Julian.

"That was the other thing," added Trajan. "Fire."

"What do you mean? Romans always use fire in their attacks." An image of burning trees in my village flashed to mind.

"True," he said flatly. "But we *didn't* use fire. They did."

Shocked, I stood with the folded linens in my hands. "Has that ever happened before?"

"Never," came the rusty voice of Julian from the private quarters.

Instantly, I rushed to him behind the curtain, Trajan following quickly behind me. I placed the linens on the rug and poured a glass of water.

"Here. Lift your head." He allowed me to help him and drank the entire glass.

It was good to see him without a trace of fever, even though he appeared pale and weak. Not the powerful man I knew. But his fever breaking for good was a start.

He tried to push up into a sitting position but struggled. Trajan and I helped him to sit up. He panted with the effort, seeming completely drained.

"How are you feeling?" asked Trajan.

"Like I've been gutted and sewn back together."

"Well, that's accurate, then." Trajan smiled. "You look less like Pluto's meat today."

"Good to know." Julian sighed, his gaze skating to me, softening for a moment.

"They knew how to use fire to their advantage." Trajan switched quickly to business. "They used nets to entrap us. They were all pre-set with mechanisms that were triggered by our men walking on the forest floor. Somehow, they evaded the nets and the fire altogether. Now, they've disappeared for good. No sign of them anywhere."

Julian remained quiet, but his expression was dark and pensive. Finally, he said, "I believe I spoke to their leader."

"The one you fought with?" asked Trajan.

Julian nodded. "This wasn't an attack."

"Julian," Trajan scoffed, "they killed almost four hundred of our men. It was an attack."

"It was a warning," he replied. "Actually, it wasn't even that. It was a prelude to what's to come."

Trajan crossed his arms, still standing at the foot of the bed while I remained seated on the edge next to Julian.

"What did their leader say to you?" Trajan demanded.

"Only that we would meet again."

"But that isn't what has you so pensive," I remarked, knowing it with my empathic sense. "What is it?"

He turned his head toward me, a smile tugging on his mouth. "So perceptive, firebird."

I took his hand in both of mine and squeezed, so relieved he was awake and talking. Then he went on.

"I saw something before the leader disappeared. I thought I was imagining things, but now, seeing their use of fire, I know I'm right."

"What did you see?" asked Trajan.

"The flicker of a dragon living inside him."

Trajan balked. Then he laughed. "Are you sure?"

Julian didn't laugh, but held his tribune's gaze. "The man who moved with inhuman speed and cut me with a poisonous blade was a dragon, Trajan. I know it."

Trajan glanced away and bit his lip, soaking this in. Then he added, "Not just the leader. All of his men as well."

A chill prickled along my skin, raising goosebumps on my flesh. "Yes," I said, knowing yet again with my magic that this was true. "That's how they were able to use fire against you."

"Because they could breathe it," said Julian. "And they must've soaked the boughs with oil so they would ignite instantly, the nets trapping my men so they smothered beneath the dome of smoke and flame."

Nodding, Trajan heaved out a sigh. "That would make sense, but Julian"—he shook his head—"there were hundreds of them. Were they all dragons? How did they escape?"

"There were hundreds flying through the tops of the trees," he said. "I thought they were our men, but now . . ."

"They were the enemy," finished Trajan. "The barbarian horde flying to safety, disguising themselves as our own men."

"It was chaos," continued Julian. "And the air was covered in the scent of smoke and burning flesh. How could anyone scent that they didn't belong to us amidst that mayhem?"

"Smart." Trajan shook his head. "Very smart."

"Indeed."

"What was the leader like?" I asked.

"Formidable," answered Julian. "He sounded of Germanic origin. He spoke Latin clearly but he had an accent."

"Fascinating. How on earth could he have gotten that many Romans to defect and join him? I can't imagine that many would do such a thing."

"Perhaps disgruntled in their foreign province with their governor. Or bitter from some slight under my uncle's rule." Julian shrugged.

"That's easy to imagine, actually," Trajan corrected himself, "but to go up against a Roman legion. One of hundreds. There can't be that many of them."

"I don't know. But we need to find out." Julian winced as he shifted in the bed. "This stays between us. No one is to know who or what these barbarians are."

Trajan smiled. "Because if we can contact them without them burning us alive"—he dropped his voice to a whisper—"they could be our allies."

Julian smiled. "We are of the same mind."

"We always are. I'll leave you to rest." He slipped out of the bedchamber curtain. "Get him strong, Malina. We need to return to Rome."

I stood and went to the water bowl, dipping a fresh cloth and wringing it before I returned to his bedside. Julian's gaze rested on mine, a soft smile curling one side of his mouth as I wiped his brow.

"Aren't you tired of waiting on me?"

"No," I answered softly and wiped his neck and upper chest.

The clean linen covered his naked body. It had taken Koska and I nearly an hour to wrestle the soiled sheets from underneath his body and replace them with new ones after I'd sutured his wound.

"Let me put on some more salve."

I lowered the sheet just enough to see the long scar from beneath his naval to his left hip bone. The flesh wasn't puckered and red as it was the first day. It seemed to be healing well.

"It will leave a nasty scar," I said while gently adding the salve.

He flinched beneath my touch, then settled. "Will that bother you? If I have an ugly scar?"

Shocked, I snapped, "Why would I care?"

"I don't know. But"—he cleared his throat nervously—"I wouldn't want to appear . . . ugly to you."

I sat back and stared at him, then laughed. "Oh, my. The great Legatus Julianus is a vain creature."

He tried to keep from smiling as a flush of red crept into his cheeks. "I am not vain."

"You are."

"Only when it comes to you. Your thoughts of my appearance are all that matters," he added with levity.

He hadn't tried to touch me. I wished he'd reach for my wrist or hand as he'd done in his fever.

"Well," I added soothingly, "I think a man with a battle scar is rather attractive."

He pushed himself up a little. "Do you?"

"Yes," I added, not knowing why I was inflating his ego. He didn't need it. "Scars show strength. That you can survive pain and injury. That your body is strong and can take on more."

"I can take on anything. Except an injury you might give me."

Walking to the washbowl, I cleaned my hands of the salve. "I have no reason to injure you."

"You might do it all the same."

Smiling, I turned to tease him, but his expression was so hard and harsh that I couldn't say another word. He wasn't speaking of physical injuries and I couldn't mock him for it, showing me his vulnerability. It was too serious a conversation that we hadn't had clearly enough.

"Come," he beckoned. "Tell me a story of something happy in your life."

He sensed the too-tight tension as well.

"More stories of my gift?"

"No," he said solemnly. "Any story of your life that was a happy one."

Nodding, I walked to his side and thought back to find some good memory to share. It didn't take long. I settled on a low stool next to his bed.

"It was a trial for my mother to raise four daughters who were all so active and opinionated. She would send us once a week to a neighboring village, Aldava, to trade at market."

Julian settled farther down, lowering his head to the pillow, watching me and smiling. I could become addicted to the adoring expression on his handsome face.

"There was a small creek we always had to cross. The bridge into Aldava was farther down, but we could reach the market faster by crossing a fallen log we'd found. Well, one day, I decided to make our trip more adventurous."

"Of course you did," he rumbled.

I refolded the scrap of cloth in my lap to busy my hands, unable to hide the grin from spreading across my face.

"I dared my sisters to dance across the log. Whoever did successfully, I'd buy them a honey roll from the baker at the market. But"—I raised a pointer finger and arched a brow—"they had to mimic a dance I created on the spot."

"Show me."

I paused. "What?"

"Show me the dance," he dared me, like I'd dared my sisters that day.

With a haughty lift of my chin, I set my linen rag on the stool and stood at the foot of his bed. I laughed, clutching a handful of my tunic and lifting it slightly so that I had more movement around my legs.

"Let me remember." I looked at the tent ceiling, unable to meet his gaze at the moment.

I swayed my hips in a sinuous line from one side to the other, then I shimmied two steps to the right, twirled once, then kicked my right leg before spinning to face away, where I repeated the soft circling of my hips, twirled, and kicked with my left, then took a giant leap on a resounding clap.

"That was as close as I can remember," I said, laughing, finally looking at Julian.

His amused expression was part joy and part hunger, his golden gaze flicking down my body, then back up.

"Lovely," was all he said in that dark, velvety voice.

"It was a simple dance," I added lightly, ignoring the allure of his voice and his gaze. "But it was more difficult on the log."

"So who was successful in getting their honey roll?" he asked.

"Lela refused to do it, of course. She was always too mature. She scolded all of us for being so foolish. But Kostanya was competitive, so she did the dance. Kizzy—" I stopped and laughed again. "She wasn't so successful. She fell into the creek on the second twirl."

Julian chuckled and the soft, rumbly sound warmed me from the inside out. "Was she upset?"

"Kizzy? Never." I remembered the way Kostanya and I ran to her aid while Lela scolded us and said, *I told you so.* "She laughed it off, even while her stockings were wet the rest of the day. It was summer and warm enough. But I bought her a honey roll anyway. I could never refuse Kizzy anything she wanted." A fleeting pang of loss gripped me.

"Of course you did." His eyes drifted partly closed. "You were a good sister."

I tucked the covers higher beneath his chin. "Yes." A lump swelled in my throat. "I was." I blew out the oil lamp on the side table. "Now get some rest."

I left the tent, my memories having stirred me to full wakefulness. It was dark so no one saw me slide between the tents to the back where I could get a breath of fresh air and peer up at the moon.

I wondered if my prayers to Proserpina helped my sisters at all. I liked to think of them all together in the afterlife with Papa and Mama. And Bunica. I hoped that Lela's and Jardani's spirits found each other too, and that they walked in peace together.

The memory I shared stirred both joy and deep sorrow in my breast.

I hadn't thought of the good times in so long. Of the many sisterly arguments and petty grievances that turned into hugs and tears more times than I could count.

A tear slid down my cheek as I gazed up at the moonlit sky, the stars a canvas of glittering shards as far as I could see.

Bunica had said that my sisters and I would turn the tide, that we would defeat our enemy, and change the fate of our people. She'd never said the Romans, but we both knew that's who she meant. Bunica had the sight, and she was so sure of her premonition of us.

Now, my sisters were gone.

"But I'm still here, Bunica."

I swiped the tears from my cheeks with the back of my hand.

I was still here, and I'd risk my life to make her prophecy come true. I'd do it all by myself if I had to. Yet, I knew I wouldn't have to. I wasn't alone anymore. I had Julian, and the allies he trusted. For the first time in so many years, hope stirred like a fluttering bird trying to finally take flight.

"I promise, Bunica," I swore up to the sky and to any gods who might be listening.

MALINA

Those Roman soldiers who'd been injured by the smoke and fire—and had not died trapped beneath nets—were mostly recovered, according to Trajan. Julian had been the only Roman physically attacked by one of the barbarians face-to-face besides the standard bearer, who hadn't survived his injuries.

Trajan informed me that their scouts had found no trace at all of any of them camping nearby. They'd truly vanished this time. And while the remaining soldiers had begun to pack, they still awaited their general's recovery. None would leave without him.

Julian had slept most of the day, the color returning to his face. It was near sunset, and yet he slept on. But there'd been no more fever and last I changed his bandages, the wound seemed to be healing well. Trajan said that was due to his dragon blood and my good nursing skills.

I lit a second oil lamp as the tent darkened with the setting sun outside and sat beside Julian on his bed. He was no longer feverish, but I liked wiping his brow with a cool cloth.

Over the past week, I'd had many opportunities to observe him closely. As he lay quietly, his eyes closed and not bewitching me, I could look all I liked.

Right now, for example, I observed that his harsh features—his blade-like jaw, his sharp cheekbones, his long slash of a nose—appeared more beguiling on close observation. And his mouth. Soft lips that made me wonder and imagine, that made me reach out and touch them.

I trailed my fingertip along his lower lip, then leaned in closer, easing my weight onto my other elbow and stretching my legs down the bed. Settled closer, I went back to my inspection, drawing a line with my fingertip along that sharp jaw and over his brow.

He wasn't scary at all. Not to me. He was utterly beautiful. I was in the process of grazing my fingertip along his cheek when those golden eyes slid open.

I froze, holding his gaze as I continued my tactile exploration, reaching his mouth yet again. His lips parted when I went back to tracing his lips, his breath hot on my fingertips, my gaze fixated on his mouth.

He said not a word, nor did I, both of us afraid to break the spell we were under.

I wish I could say I hated him from the start, from that moment he snatched me off the battlefield from my Celtic clan. I should've loathed him. But I never had.

The Romans, his dragonkind, yes. I'd always hated them. But Julian, he'd been set apart. Ever since that night he wandered into our

216

traveling troupe as a centurion, since he watched me dance and gave me a coin for good fortune.

I grazed my fingertips along his jaw to his throat, where his pulse beat furiously.

"I'm your treasure, the gods have said?" I whispered, wondering, if I spoke it too loudly, if the gods might hear and refute my declaration. But I wasn't listening to the gods now.

I trailed my fingers lightly across his prominent brow and back along his jaw.

"I care not what they say, for what I feel is all my own. Not forced or given to me by the fates or anyone else. It comes from my own soul."

The witch inside me may have luxuriated in the maddening desire Julian sparked, but this feeling went deeper than my magic. It was my own will guiding me now, speaking a truth I could no longer hold inside myself.

"I can finally confess to you," I murmured, stilling my hand where it cupped his jaw, my thumb settling at the corner of his wide mouth, "that you are my treasure too."

Julian lay perfectly still, not speaking a word, watching me with that otherworldly gaze burning bright hot like the summer sun.

Gripping his shoulder, I shifted my weight up, leaning across his chest, then lowered my head carefully. He waited, still as stone. Until I brushed my lips against his.

His giant hand cupped the back of my skull as he groaned and swept his tongue into my mouth. This kiss morphed quickly from slow and tentative to hot need. He nipped and licked and ate my mouth hungrily. When I made a soft sound of pleasure, he rolled me beneath him and pressed my body into the mattress.

It was divine. He made sure not to crush me but wedged his glorious weight between my open legs. His free hand slid underneath my tunic, bending my leg and gripping my thigh to make room for his body to settle more deliciously.

"Malina," he groaned, nipping along my jaw and down my throat.

I speared my hands into his short hair, scraping my blunt nails along his scalp, arching my neck so he could lick and kiss me to his heart's content.

Desire sizzled through my blood. I rocked my hips up, feeling his hard cock press sweetly at my core. Only a tangled sheet and my thin tunic separated us.

His mouth was back on mine, delving, sucking, biting, bruising my lips as I moaned, "More."

A steady, low, rumbling purr vibrated from his chest to mine, his dragon making himself known. I had a fleeting thought that I should be disgusted, but I banished it at once. I would no longer rebuke myself for what I felt for Julian. I trusted myself, and everything inside me yearned for him. I ground harder against him, my sex soaking the linen sheet between us.

Through the tether binding us—the one I could not and would not ever break—I felt his desperate longing, which spun me higher, increasing my arousal.

"Gods," I shuddered as I rocked up and rubbed my quim against his hard length.

He gripped the inner neckline of my tunic and ripped it open, one breast popping free. Instantly, he lowered his head and sucked the tight peak into his mouth, that low purr stimulating me further.

I was a writhing mess when his hand on my thigh moved between my legs and stroked my slick slit.

"Mmmm," he moaned against my nipple before he slid a finger inside me. "Malina," he groaned, his raspy voice beckoning me toward climax.

I cried out and arched my neck, already coming when he thrust a second finger inside me, pumping deep and fast, his teeth grazing my breast.

Then he was hovering over me, still stroking his fingers, his thumb pressing against my clitoris, his gaze ever watchful, burning me with want.

Still holding his gaze, my mouth dropped open as I came, a keening moan pouring from my throat. The pleasure was so great, I couldn't quiet myself if I'd tried.

"Mmm," he hummed again, holding his fingers deep as I pulsed around them. He lowered his mouth as I panted, brushing a soft kiss against my swollen lips. "You come so sweetly, my wild firebird." Another sweep of his mouth. "I had no idea you'd be so soft and perfect."

He pulled his fingers from my body, causing me to gasp and squeeze my thighs together. Shifting his body up, his weight on one arm, he watched me as he sucked his fingers clean, letting out another purring groan.

It was frightfully shocking to discover that made me squirm with desire yet again. He grinned, his canines sharper than they should be for a human, but not what they would be in half-skin.

"Did you let your dragon slip his leash?" I asked while a blush flushed my cheeks.

"I can't deny him what he wants." He stared at me with soft adoration.

I gaped at Julian, trying to reconcile myself with the boundary we'd just crossed and how I still wanted more when he winced. I pushed him off me, and he let me roll him onto his back, where I saw dark blood had seeped through the sheet and onto my tunic.

"Gods! You're bleeding."

"I believe a suture or two popped while we were . . . engaged."

"Julian! Why didn't you stop?"

He frowned. "Not on my life. I couldn't stop even if I wanted to."

I pulled the linen down gently, trying not to hurt him further. "Only a man would rather bleed to death than end his pleasure."

"It was your pleasure I wasn't willing to end."

I glanced up at him while I pulled the cleaning rag I kept folded over the bowl beside his bed.

"You should've stopped anyway," I snapped, dabbing the blood clean. Only one stitch had popped, but two more were stretched wider.

"By Jupiter," he rumbled, cupping my chin to make me look at him, "I'd have bled to death just to see that look of sweet ecstasy on your face. Knowing I'd put it there."

"Stop it, Julian." I shoved his hand away and leaned across the small side table where I'd been keeping the medicinal supplies, including the needle and thread. "You're embarrassing me," I said low as I bent to restitch the one that had come loose.

His laugh was soft and deep, his hand finding my knee and giving me a squeeze. I kept my eyes on my work.

"Malina," he rasped when I ignored him too long. "Thank you."

Finally, I looked at him. "For what?"

"For being exactly who you are and nothing else. For not pretending this"—he gestured between us—"doesn't exist." A frown pinched his brow. "I was afraid you might deny me. Deny us. I was afraid you wouldn't allow even this."

"Will there be more than *this*?"

"So much more, Malina. There will be forever."

I laughed, finishing the suture without him even wincing. "You jest."

"Not at all."

I swallowed hard against his certainty. I'd only recently given in to this madness between us. The idea of forever felt a little terrifying.

I set the needle and thread aside and wrapped a clean bandage around his wound. When finished, I tidied his table and replaced his bed linen with another. I'd have to wash tomorrow. I blew out the oil lamp on his table and walked to my side, where my smaller bed was waiting for me.

"Malina," he called to me.

I stood above the second oil lamp burning on the table where we usually ate meals, about to blow it out. Julian outstretched his arm.

"Come sleep with me."

"Absolutely not. I just redressed your wound."

"Just sleep," he teased, his mouth quirking in that insanely attractive half smile.

"I could still jostle you."

"Please, Malina." He sighed. "I just want to lie beside you."

I glanced through the sheer curtain toward the tent opening, wondering if that was wise. What if someone caught us? Then again, what if they did? They all thought I was his pleasure slave anyway, so who cared?

Julian wanted me beside him for comfort, and I couldn't deny him. Not anymore.

I blew out the lamp and climbed in beside him. Instantly, he pulled my body close, my head lying in the crook of his shoulder and chest, his arm wrapped down my back. He exhaled a heavy sigh, then a grunt of satisfaction when I tucked my hands between our bodies against his side.

"There," he whispered. "That's perfect."

There were a dozen sharp protests on the tip of my tongue, about how this was stupid considering we'd just reopened his wound. But I didn't say anything at all. I snuggled closer.

"Good night, Malina," he murmured against the crown of my head.

"Good night."

I'd known that our tether had never broken, but I'd often kept the connection closed, fearful what I would feel if I opened it wide. Tapping into the line, our bodies warm and entwined, I opened our connection.

Stunned but not surprised, I exhaled deep relief at the overwhelming affection pouring into me from Julian. I let his potent emotions soothe me into a warm cocoon of sleep. I relaxed further into his embrace, grateful that for tonight I could let my worries go, that I was wrapped in the strong arms of Julian, my dragon. Nothing had ever felt more right.

JULIAN

I thought I was dreaming. Her slight weight was molded against my chest and my side, her drugging scent filling my nostrils. The strangest thought came to me as I stirred awake: this was how I wanted to die. With her in my arms, many years distant from now after a full life together.

Immediately afterward, reality and true fear set in. How was I going to keep her safe in Rome? There had been an ominous cloud hovering over me ever since I'd taken her from that battlefield in Gaul. The danger of losing her had become a constant obsessive thought.

That was why my dragon had been so wakeful as of late. He didn't want to slumber beneath the man's machinations. He wanted to strike and kill anyone who threatened her or us. Seeing as I needed to continue my charade as the compliant Conqueror for my uncle, that suddenly became a problem. The dragon didn't want to pretend anymore. He wanted to drag her far away, where she'd be safe, and fuck the rest of the world. Let them fend for themselves.

As if divining my worries, Trajan stepped into the tent. I could see his scowl through the sheer curtain between the living quarters and the rest of the tent. He stopped right on the other side.

"Julian."

"Enter."

He stepped through the curtain holding a scroll, not even bothering to make a face about the woman sleeping in my arms. Since we'd known each other, I'd never had a woman sleep in my bed.

"From Rome." He held up the scroll. "From Caesar."

Malina instantly sat up. I had wanted to linger awhile together, but it seemed Rome would not wait. I pushed myself into a sitting position, noting my uncle's seal, then broke it and unrolled the scroll.

My gut tightened as I read the brief missive and rolled it back up.

"What does he say?" asked Trajan, while Malina watched me with concern.

"To return to Rome at once and report on our enemy here."

"He's heard news from our camp." Trajan scowled deeper.

"Of course he has. We know he has spies everywhere."

"But you're still injured," objected Malina. "You shouldn't move just yet."

My annoyance instantly vanished. That she cared was enough to quell the anxiety about my uncle. For the moment.

"Nevertheless, we must break camp and return. Caesar wants me to return *with* my army."

"What of the burn victims still too wounded?" asked Trajan.

"Have others carry them."

Trajan clenched his jaw. Returning to Rome wounded by our enemy was a sign of defeat. Though we weren't defeated here, we'd lost our one battle with the marauders. We'd been hit harder than expected. And by an enemy who simply vanished into thin air.

"We leave this afternoon, Trajan."

He nodded and left to put my orders into motion, though there was also a look of concern on his face when he glanced at Malina. He didn't have to voice it. I knew his worries already. They lived inside my flesh, my bones.

"You shouldn't fly yet," she protested. "What if you rip all of the sutures when you shift?"

"It's mostly sealed. Except for that one tender place."

She shook her head, scowling at me prettily. "That one tender place."

She pushed out of bed and hurried to her small table, where her few tunics and linens were folded neatly. Then she started shoving the garments into the small bag she'd carried them here in.

I sat up and swiveled my legs around to plant my feet on the floor. My side stung but I didn't feel the sutures pull. She was right though. While my wound would only be a mere scratch in dragon form, I'd break the sutures and it would need healing yet again once I transformed back.

"So strange." I watched her busy herself, my elbows on my knees, hands clasped.

"What is?" she snapped, walking to my other bedside to pack away the medicinal salve and supplies.

"That the woman I . . . treasure so much can pack herself into a bag so small."

She snorted and glared at me, then continued shoving things into the sack.

She didn't understand the depth of my affection, how long I'd dreamed of having her. And though last night was only a kiss—a little more—it was enough to buoy hope in my heart.

"You don't regret what you said before."

She settled on her knees to fold the blankets that had made up her bed while we'd been here. "Before what?"

I smiled at the thought those linens had gone unused last night, my own body and bed keeping her warm instead.

"Before you kissed and ravaged me in my sickbed."

She stopped her hurried movements and gaped at me. "I believe you were the one doing the ravaging."

"You kissed me first," I teased.

She shook her head as she went back to folding, her loose hair brushing along her back, refusing to answer my question.

I stood, my muscles stretching for the first time in days. A flight in dragon form would do me good. But right now, I had to set Malina straight. "Come here."

She frowned up at me. "What? I'm packing."

"I see what you're doing. Stand up so I'm not talking to the back of your head. Though it is a lovely view."

She huffed in frustration and stood before me, chin lifted, jaw clamped. I was aware that I was smiling, which only made her frown deepen.

"Do you know how often I've thought of you since that night I first saw you dance?"

She shrugged a shoulder. "I haven't thought of you at all. What of it?"

I reached toward her throat and tugged the chain holding the coin I'd given her, the one my father minted to celebrate their wedding. Gripping the coin in my fist gently, I murmured, "Not at all, firebird? Not once?"

She tried to tug back but I had her fixed in place with her necklace. Those captivating eyes softened, even while I could see she wanted to deny me.

"No, I do not regret what I said or what we did," she admitted softly.

226

"Then why are you so angry?"

"I'm not angry, I'm concerned."

"About?"

"Oh, I don't know," she snapped sarcastically, "trying to kill Caesar, being killed by Caesar."

"We will win," I stated emphatically, willing it to be true.

"And then what?" she asked. "There will be years, if not decades, where your new Rome is set to order. I can't—" She bit her lip and looked away.

"Can't what? Tell me, Malina."

She exhaled in frustration and turned back to me. "Julian"—she gusted a breath—"you *own* me. I am your slave. My heart cannot want *more* with you while I am."

A sickening sensation tightened low in my belly. "Then you are free. I'll take you wherever you want to go."

She laughed. "Right now?"

"Yes. We can find some faraway place in the wilderness. Far from any Roman province."

Her smile dimmed. "You'd leave your position as a Roman general, as next in line to the throne? You'd leave your allies floundering, your mission to—" She glanced to the side, though there was no one else in this tent, nor did I hear anyone nearby outside. "To do away with this regime. To create a new, freer Rome."

My spirit faltered at the thought of leaving the work unfinished, at leaving my uncle in power. Of leaving the people in pain and bondage.

"If that's what you want. I'll take you anywhere. But I can't leave you there alone and return here." I couldn't yet explain to her that it was my dragon who would forbid me abandoning her in some wilderness, leaving her without protection. I could never do that. Not now. Not even if I tried.

Her expression tightened with both frustration and anger. "No," she added roughly. "I could never ask that. I do not want that. It would mean that all of those beneath the clawed feet of your uncle and those like him would continue to suffer. I could never be that selfish."

I released the coin of her necklace and cupped her face, pressing my mouth to her forehead. "Then know that you are free. At any time that you would will it, I'll fly you anywhere in the world. Any place your heart desires."

Suddenly, she wrapped her arms firmly around my waist, pressing her cheek to my lower chest, and hugged me tightly. I wrapped her close. As a human woman, she felt so delicate and small in my arms, reminding me yet again how vulnerable she was among dragons. I clenched my jaw and held her tighter.

"Oh, Julian. I don't want to be anywhere else." She squeezed me around my waist. "This is where I'm meant to be."

Cradling the back of her head with one hand and banding her waist with the other, I rocked her in my arms and pressed my lips to the crown of her dark glossy hair.

"Then we are bound together, as you said before."

"I suppose we are," she admitted in a whisper, her mouth muffled against my chest.

After a moment of indulging in her affection, I pulled back, sliding my palm around her nape beneath her hair and tipping her chin up with my thumb.

"I am sorry, Malina. For the plight of your people, for the death of your family, for all those who suffer beneath the yoke of Rome." I coasted my thumb up the silken line of her jaw. "But know this. We are not all the same. There are many dragons who do not agree with my uncle and how he rules. How so many before him have ruled."

She wrapped her small fingers around my wrist. "Then they'd better come out of hiding and stand beside you."

"They will. They all will. When it's time to strike." I coasted my free hand up and down her back soothingly, keeping her body close to mine.

She smiled.

"What is it?" I asked.

"This soft Julian. I don't recognize him. Or see him often."

"It's dangerous for me to be anything but the Conqueror outside this tent. Outside my home. Only for you can I be this Julian," I whispered, bending and lowering my mouth to hers.

She tilted her mouth up, lifted onto her toes, and met me partway, our lips brushing in a soft exploration, different than our first kiss. I wanted her to know that I could be tender for her—soft. I touched my tongue lightly to hers, brushing with slow, exploring strokes. While my heart hammered in my chest, my desire yearning for more, I kept my hold gentle. I kissed her with the reverence and deep affection that I felt, wanting her to know she could trust me.

I wasn't the brute she thought all dragons were. There were many others like me. And she was right. There would be a time—soon—when we'd all need to come out of hiding.

For now, we simply had to return to Rome, and I had to face my uncle.

After a moment, I went back to simply holding her. She pressed her cheek to my sternum, panting softly.

"Before you came, all of this was easier," I admitted.

"What do you mean?"

"I never cared about losing my life."

"But now you do?"

"No." I hugged her close. "I care about losing yours."

JULIAN

Upon arriving home, I'd let Malina suture my wound yet again while she glared and muttered curses about stubborn men. Shifting had pulled all of them loose, of course. I knew that it would, but I wouldn't let anyone take her back but me. I'd waited until all but Trajan had left the encampment to be sure we weren't seen.

After she'd stitched me up, I bathed and changed into a regal toga in deepest red, then set off on Volkan to the imperial palace. It was dark when Volkan trotted up the winding path bordered by tall cypress trees.

I slowed Volkan to a walk near the stables, hardening every part of myself, locking my emotions for Malina into the chamber where my dragon slept. I wore the mask of the Coldhearted Conqueror by the time the stable boy Jovan stepped forward. This was the only version of me that my uncle could ever see.

My wound smarted as I dismounted and handed Jovan the reins, but I kept all of the discomfort off my face. There could be no sign of weakness.

Walking briskly up the marble steps, I marched past the praetorians at the door and stopped at another guard standing outside my uncle's parlor, where he usually met with his generals and politicians.

The guard saluted, then said, "He is not in his parlor, Legatus."

"Where is he?"

His expression remained stoic when he replied, "At the pit."

I dipped a nod and walked on, cursing to all the gods in my mind. Seeing my aunt in her current state tore a piece of my heart away every time.

Stalking through the open courtyard where Caesar held his last feast, I steeled myself for what lay not far beyond the outer gate. I'd contemplated attempting to set my aunt free somehow multiple times. But my uncle kept her so well-guarded, I wouldn't be able to do it without certain capture. It was one of the many wrongs I planned to set right whenever we'd implemented our plan, a plan I was becoming more and more desperate to accomplish.

Exiting through the garden's back gate, I took the rough trail through the long grass, well-worn by my uncle's visits to his sister. There, upon a platform he had constructed that jutted from the edge and hovered over the pit, stood my uncle, two praetorians, and Ciprian.

My steps faltered for a second but thankfully it seemed Ciprian was taking his leave. My uncle clapped his shoulder before Ciprian stepped away and onto the trail toward me.

His eyes widened slightly, not expecting me. Then his expression relaxed into its usual arrogant sneer.

"Legatus, I hear you had trouble in Moesia."

"Nothing serious, Ciprian. I didn't lose as many men as you did in Macedonia."

His smile vanished. "At least my men and I won the field."

"*Your* men. Those weren't yours. You've yet to lead a campaign of your own. You are merely prefect," I reminded him.

"Not for much longer." He stopped in front of me, blocking my path, and snapped the length of his black toga higher up his opposite shoulder. "Looking forward to your hospitality and getting a look at your slave girl soon."

My entire body locked, muscles stiffened. Willing myself not to strangle him where he stood, I replied steadily, "I have no intentions of entertaining soon. There are more important things to do, like wars to be fought." Just the thought of him ogling Malina made me sick with dread.

"That's what you think." He laughed and walked on by me. "Go talk to your uncle."

It took far more energy than I imagined to keep from snatching him back and demanding him to tell me what the fuck he was talking about. Expression passive, I walked on to meet my uncle standing at the edge of the platform railing, holding a golden goblet in one hand. I refused to look down just yet.

"Caesar," I greeted him.

I always reminded him of his powerful station when I could, using his formal title rather than being familiar first.

"Julian."

His mouth quirked into a smile as he turned sideways to greet me, his eyes glassy with drink and gone full dragon, with serpentine slits down the middle of the gold. He clasped my forearm and shook it hard.

"Report," he commanded as he always did directly following a campaign.

"The town of Singidium was completely destroyed by the enemy, as we were informed. No survivors could attest to who had attacked their province and the two surrounding ones. I sent scouts to seek them out in the woods and foothills nearby. They evaded, remaining hidden for more than two weeks when we finally corralled them in one central area, a dense forest north of Singidium."

I kept my voice even and confident and my gaze on his, despite his somewhat inebriated state. He was always dangerous, no matter what state he might be in.

"It seemed they were a small force as my legions closed in on them, when they started a quick-burning fire that ignited the entire forest above my soldiers' heads. They used nets to keep my officers from shifting and fleeing but most of them were able to free themselves regardless. We were forced to retreat. Four hundred eighty-three were lost in the blaze. Two hundred thirty-six were wounded and will make a full recovery. The barbarian horde fled and vanished from the vicinity."

"Did you discover their origins? What tribe they must be from?"

"No, Emperor."

I had an idea, but I wasn't sharing it with him.

"You didn't recover any of their injured?"

"I'm afraid not. They had planned this well and apparently had an escape route that we never discovered. We couldn't have pursued them once the blaze was ignited. It was a conflagration."

My uncle's brow furrowed. "Fire. Curious that they would use our own key weapon against us."

"I believe it was a statement, Caesar, declaring exactly that. That they could use Roman weapons as well. They had no intentions to fight us man-to-man. They simply wanted to taunt us and run."

He huffed and turned his attention back to the pit, where I could hear my aunt feeding on something. Someone. A grotesque wet, crunching sound made my stomach curdle.

"Cowards, then," he said. "Rabble. No need to pursue it unless they strike again."

And they would. Though I had a feeling the next target would be a bigger one.

Igniculus stared down. I finally turned and forced myself to look into the pit. My aunt in her white dragon form chomped on the remains of a human man. There was only the bottom torso and one leg left.

"Is he tasty, Camilla?" Igniculus called down to her.

She turned her head up to us, the chain around her throat keeping her staked to the ground. Blood dripped from her fanged muzzle. Her jaws gaped and she released a guttural growl, her red eyes narrowed on my uncle. Then she caught sight of me.

I was never sure if she recognized me. But she let out a piercing sort of cry, a sad, birdlike wail, then she returned to her ghastly meal.

"Eat well, sweetheart," laughed my uncle, raising his goblet to her before drinking. "She loves the fat ones."

I didn't bother to ask who had the luxury of being my aunt's meal tonight. He usually used one of many he believed were against his regime, or a recent prisoner of war before they were sold off at auction.

Aunt Camilla's permanent state of dragon form was a mystery. My uncle had had numerous physicians to study her and delve into the archives for cases of this kind, to find a cure. The only conclusion they offered was that she had succumbed to dragon madness and could no longer shift back into her female human form.

Uncle Igniculus had gutted the first physician who'd given him that diagnosis. But he'd spared the second and third, realizing perhaps they were right.

I'd done some studying of my own, finding a case in my own father's books of the early dragon families. Dragons were protectors, and there had been a case of a young boy who'd been separated from his family while traveling. He shifted into his dragon form and remained that way even after distant family members found him living in a cave years later. They tried to coax him back to their village, but he blew fire to keep them distant and lived his entire life as a dragon.

The theory was that his dragon knew he was best protected in dragon form and he feared being vulnerable as a man.

Whatever my uncle had done to his sister, Camilla, it had terrified her so much that she preferred living as a dragon in chains in his pit over returning to her womanly form. I hoped that one day I might finally free her from this miserable life in chains.

She'd finished her meal and glanced up. She made that shrieking chirp again, then curled into a ball, jangling her chains, giving us her back as she went to sleep.

"All you have to do is come back to me," my uncle slurred down to her in a sickeningly sultry voice, "then I'll remove the chains, my sweet."

She didn't make a sound or move, her back heaving in deep breaths as if she were already in slumber.

Igniculus grunted, turning to me. "Come have a drink."

Fuck. The last thing I wanted to do.

"Of course, uncle. It would be a pleasure."

His praetorians followed us back, but I was mindful of the ones stationed in permanent watchtowers on two sides of my aunt's pit, my uncle's watchdogs.

We crossed through the back gate and door leading into his feasting hall, then into the central part of the palace, then his parlor.

"Jana!" he bellowed as he lowered onto a chaise.

A pretty female wearing his slave collar entered the room quickly. "Yes, dominus."

I recognized her as one of the wine-bearers at the feast.

"Get me more wine and one for my nephew."

"Right away, dominus."

While Jana fetched us wine, I stretched out, pretending to be comfortable in my uncle's home when in reality, my entire being revolted at being here. The palace reeked of rot and corruption and sin.

"Do not let this loss weigh you down, nephew. They are inconsequential."

"Thank you for saying so, but I'll be there if they raise their heads from the sand again."

"Indeed, you will be. You're a Dakkian. My blood." He thumped his chest.

Jana delivered the wine and speedily left.

My uncle's gaze was bleary from drink, and his mood was sentimental. This was rare.

"You know, Julianus. Augustus never knew the proper way of the dragon."

I didn't flinch at the sound of my father's name. No one spoke of him anymore, too afraid to resurrect old ghosts or to offend the Conqueror.

"He was different," my uncle went on with a sigh. "You are more like me than my brother."

"I've always thought so," I lied.

He chuckled after gulping more wine. "If I'd ever had your mother, I'd swear you were my trueborn son and not my brother's."

I grunted with a smile and swallowed the wine, which tasted like bile. It would be so easy for me to kill him now. Yet again, that was only one part of the plan. Many heads needed to come off at the same time if we were to be successful in our coup. So I held my tongue and smiled through the pain of him jesting at defiling my own mother.

Though I could imagine his assassination happening on an evening like this, my uncle half-drunk and espousing obscenities like they were truths. Me listening to him like I cared, like I agreed.

"I have always been grateful for your guidance," I told him, injecting emotion and sincerity into my voice.

He smiled, his eyes—still slit like his dragon's—softened toward me. "And you shall be rewarded for your great leadership, my son. And your loyalty." He pointed at me with a wink. "That is why I've chosen your house as the venue to hold Ciprian's Rite of Skulls."

Motherfucking gods of hell.

"My house, uncle?"

"It is always the senior general of the Roman legions who hosts the rite." He pointed at me again. "And that is you, Julian. You are my most senior general, the bloodiest conqueror this world has ever seen. With the exception of me." He laughed at the last.

"I appreciate such an honor."

"But you do not like the idea. I can see it on your face."

So much for keeping myself unreadable.

"I don't like Ciprian," I told him. "He's arrogant and thinks too much of himself."

My uncle tipped his head back and laughed, leaning farther back onto his chaise lounge. "You're two of a kind. Yes, he's arrogant. He's ambitious. He is not your equal yet, but he's trying to be. You could be his mentor."

I snorted. "I doubt he'd accept me as his mentor."

"He sees you as a rival." Uncle set his goblet on the low table beside him. "He wants to be first in my affections."

I dared to let my emotions show for once, my disgust for Ciprian. "He is greedy and undisciplined."

"Do not worry, Julian. You speak from fear that he will replace you. That will never happen." He picked up his goblet again. "You are the son I never had. My blood runs through your veins. You will continue my work as a true dragon when I am gone."

Frowning, I sipped my wine, stewing in the thought of Ciprian taking the throne after my uncle. I'd never allow it. If we failed and never removed my uncle, I'd come back from the grave and slit Ciprian's throat. But my uncle was right. Ciprian wanted my place, and he'd do anything to supplant me, including turn my uncle against me if he could. That made him even more dangerous.

"You will host the rite, Julian," he declared in his authoritative tone.

"Of course, uncle. As you wish."

"I do wish it. I want everyone to know you are my favored general. And not simply because you're my nephew but because you deserve it."

"How many should I plan for?" I asked casually, wanting to vomit at the thought of Ciprian's closest friends in my home.

"I've told Ciprian his invitation list must be kept at a maximum of fifty. The Rite of Skulls is an exclusive ceremony. And though I'm sure Ciprian would like the whole world to see him receiving the rite, he will bend to tradition."

"I agree." I was glad to know there would be a small number of guests in my home at least. "When will we hold the ceremony and celebration?"

"Four days' time. The skull master is preparing the king's skull for the ceremony. The purification process will be complete in three."

I nodded as if all of this was acceptable to me while I wanted to hunt Ciprian down now and murder him for achieving this rite. My dragon sniffed the air, well aware there was danger on the horizon, that untrustworthy men would be near our treasure.

It took everything in me to keep from growling my displeasure. I downed the rest of my wine and stood. "It seems I have preparations to take care of, uncle."

"Indeed you do. Until then." He began loosening the belt of his tunic. "Send Jana in on your way out."

Cringing, I gave his parting order to one of the praetorians at the parlor door. I in no way wanted to see the expression on Jana's face when she was summoned to my uncle.

Yet again, I left the palace with haste, needing to cleanse myself of all that I still endured. I wasn't sure how much longer I could pretend, how much longer I could keep from killing him. But I had to be sure I could survive his assassination. I had someone to protect now.

Malina. My bright firebird.

As I hefted myself into Volkan's saddle and trotted down the drive, the realization sank in that my uncle, Ciprian, and more of their ilk would be filling my home soon, where Malina was. If I hid her away, Ciprian would make a show to point out my affections for my slave to my uncle. Only a dragon who cared too much would hide a treasure from others. My uncle knew that. So she'd have to be present, serving them.

"Son of Dis, save me," I muttered, hurrying home.

I needed her sweet company, her soothing voice to quiet my soul, to wash away the horror of this place. And all that was yet to come.

XXIII

MALINA

Since the night Julian returned from Caesar's palace and the news that he'd be hosting a feast under his uncle's orders, he'd been tense and the house had been thrown into chaos. Kara had sent me, Ivo, and Stefanos to the market and the butcher multiple times a day, to fetch the freshest peaches, berries, and figs or the choicest bits of pork or the plumpest pheasants. We'd return with what she requested only for her to continue barking orders, sending us back out for fresh herbs and honey and cheese.

Under Julian's orders, Kara had also hired two free women from a local taberna in the plebeian neighborhood, the Aventine, to help with the cooking preparations. They'd arrived every day the last three days shortly after dawn and stayed all day, busily washing and chopping vegetables and salting meat and marinating everything in between. They'd begun cooking the meats and vegetables early this morning, the day of the feast.

When I wasn't running an errand for Kara with Ivo and Stefanos, I was cleaning the great hall, where the atrium and fountain stood. Julian had only been home once during the day the past several days. He'd stopped when he saw me cleaning the tiles around the atrium, frowning and seemingly displeased. When he stepped forward to tell me something, one of the newly hired had walked into the room and he continued on to his bedchamber without saying a word.

He was nervous. I could feel it through the tether, tapping anxiously like a frightened heartbeat. The only time I could soothe him was at night, when the free women had gone and the house was quiet and still.

Julian was always distant and anxious. Especially after his visit with the emperor. Each night, he demanded that I sleep beside him in his bed. I'd ask what bothered him. He'd lie and say, "Nothing," then he would hold me close until we were both asleep.

He hadn't tried to be intimate with me, nor had I tried to kiss him. I didn't want to reopen his wound yet again. It was finally healing properly, even while he was gone from the house all day, every day.

When I mentioned that the others in the house would know that I hadn't slept in my bed and was sleeping in his, he'd merely said, "They should know."

I suppose it didn't matter. I knew what was in my heart, the fire of a red dragon's love. I felt it kindling, burning sweetly every night that I climbed into his bed and laid my head upon his chest. He may not have said the words, but I could feel it all the same.

Last night, something remarkable happened. While Julian was asleep, he made a familiar low, purring growl deep in his chest. I knew that sound came from his dragon.

Bunica had once told me that I could use my magic for defense and for revenge, but I could also use it for love. I understood that in the way I could calm an upset sister or help my mama sleep when she was anxious, but lately, as the binding between Julian and me became tighter, more intimate, I thought maybe Bunica meant something more.

So as Julian slept on, I snuggled closer and shut my eyes, then sought the beast that lived inside him. I wound the tether that tied me to Julian around the slumbering dragon as well. His essence was immensely powerful and terribly magnificent, my magic flinching for a moment before coiling tenderly around him. Then I poured my affection and loyalty through the line.

Julian's growl deepened, a steady thrum of pleasure. I felt a definite nuzzle along the line, and my entire body melted at the sensation. Then suddenly, the line between us rippled in a way that made me gasp. I felt a jolt, then electric power vibrating back into me.

I clenched my arm, which I had wrapped around Julian's waist, breathing deep gulps of air as the sensation hummed through my body, speeding my pulse, until finally the sensation leveled and I could breathe evenly again. Julian never awoke, but the dragon purred like before, reveling in our connection, burning his powerful force directly through the tether into me.

No one had ever reverberated their essence back through my tether. I didn't think anyone else could, unless I let them. But what Julian and I had was special, beyond a simple connection. It was a deeper bond.

When I fell asleep, I felt as if I were in both Julian's arms and his dragon's protective claws, and I didn't want to be anywhere else.

We hadn't spoken of anything that mattered since we'd returned—not the strange barbarian he'd encountered, not his confession that he and others were plotting to assassinate the emperor, and not our new and fragile relationship.

Nor had I even spoken of the incident when I connected with his dragon while he was sleeping. We'd never had time, and he seemed so tense readying for this feast that would host the emperor along with many other unsavory people he didn't want in his house.

"The three of you hurry to the butcher. I want the biggest ducks he's got," Kara shouted to us.

The other women were chopping endives and parsnips as I asked Kara, "How many do you need?"

"Five," she told me. "Six, if he has them. And fill at least one of those baskets to the brim with pomegranates. Fill the others with whatever is ripest."

Then Ivo, Stefanos, and I left for yet another trek to the butcher. The butcher she used actually had a shop in a neighborhood outside the forum. It would be quicker to get the fruit first, then stop at the butcher's on the way back.

The streets were busy today, people bustling everywhere. The forum was uncomfortably packed, especially for me and Stefanos carrying the empty baskets for the fruit. Kara didn't want it packed in sacks because it would bruise too easily. She was planning a monumental feast for tonight and wanted everything perfect for the aristocratic guests.

"Over there, Malina." Stefanos pointed to a cart with a canvas top to the left.

I nodded and we wove through the crowd together, Stefanos in front, me in the middle, and Ivo at my back.

The town crier shouted news again from his dais toward the center of the forum. His droning voice blended with the other noises of the forum until the mention of Julian's name caught my attention.

"Julianus Ignis Dakkia will host the honorable Rite of Skulls for the newly appointed general, Ciprian Media Nocte Seneca. This is a great honor for the house of Seneca. The emperor and exclusive guests will attend to witness Pluto's blessing upon our new general and the might of Rome will grow greater in the light of the gods."

He passed a scroll to his assistant beside him and took another in hand and began his loud oration again on a new topic of the senate. But I didn't hear any of it. Julian had told me there would be a ceremony at his home and there would be guests, including the emperor, and I was aware he wasn't happy about it. But he'd never mentioned this Rite of Skulls.

We reached the fruit vendor and made quick work of haggling, filling one basket with pears, figs, and dates, and the second with pomegranates as Kara had instructed. Then Ivo led us through the thick of the crowd and down an emptier lane to the butcher's shop.

"What is the Rite of Skulls?" I asked Stefanos when we were mostly alone along the narrow street.

Stefanos frowned, which he rarely did, and said, "It is one of the ceremonies Emperor Igniculus started. That's what Ruskus told me."

"What is it for?"

"It's to celebrate a Roman who takes the life of a leader or king of our enemy."

"What happens at this ceremony?" The name of it sounded rather ominous.

He shrugged. "I don't know. Never seen one myself."

Suddenly, someone grabbed my arm and jerked me down an alley, my shoulder nearly popping out of socket as the basket of pomegranates tumbled to the stone pavement. Stefanos yelled while Ivo launched himself at the one trying to drag me farther down the alley.

He was a big, brawny man in commoner clothes, his face bearded and eyes cold. "Get him!" he yelled at a third man who wasn't nearly a match for Ivo.

"Stop!" I cried out. "I belong to Julianus Dakkia!"

The man with an iron grip around my forearm chuckled darkly. "We know who you are."

That was when I had the presence of mind to see he was wearing a slave collar. I couldn't make out the full name but I saw enough. It was the name I'd just heard shouted in the forum by the crier.

Ivo tussled with one of the men while my captor continued to drag me farther away. Then a chill ran down my spine as Stefanos erupted with a bellowing, inhuman roar. It froze everyone in the alley, all heads swiveling to the boy.

The man facing off against Stefanos backed away, his palms up. "I don't believe it."

Stefanos's nails extended, curling into black claws, his body swelling bigger. I managed to pull free from my dazed captor and ran to him, pressing my palms to his face and making him look at me. His eyes glowed red, his pupils split like a serpent's.

"No, Stefanos," I murmured, pushing a wave of calm into him. "Don't do it, love. Calm down."

He trembled, fuming, his eyes closing, as he accepted my balm of peace, the force of my magic soothing his inner beast.

"That slave boy's a fucking dragon," spat the bearded one who'd attacked me.

At once, I turned to face them and snapped my tether out like a three-headed viper. They jolted as I grasped hold of their souls with frightening speed.

"Hear me now," I commanded, my voice resonating with fury.

Ivo slid away to my side, an arm around the shoulders of the shaken boy.

"If any of you speak of what you think you saw here, you will be *cursed* forever by the gods." My voice trembled with power. "You and your families will be plagued by illness and death. But you yourselves will die in pain and agony. You must *never* say a word to anyone or you will suffer dire punishment."

I pushed terror through the line, injecting them with a taste of the agony they'd suffer if they disobeyed my command.

The bearded one jerked backward, his eyes round in horror, then he turned and fled, with the others right behind him.

We watched them disappear around a corner, then I turned to Stefanos. His eyes were back to normal, his claws retracted, but he heaved with fear and blinked away tears.

"No, no," I told him, pulling him into my arms. "Don't cry." I rubbed his back.

"I'll get dominus in trouble," he muffled into my shoulder.

"No, you won't. Those men will never say a word. They won't tell. I promise."

"What did you do to them?" he asked, pulling back and wiping his tears with the sleeve of his tunic.

Ivo watched me with a curious expression, seeming to want to know the answer too.

"You must keep it secret," I told them, "but I have a mystical gift." "You do?"

I nodded. "So don't you worry, Stefanos. I won't let them do you or dominus any harm."

Romans feared curses more than anything, and these men felt the power I held, the pain I could cause them should they disobey me. I was certain we were safe. At least from them telling about Stefanos. As far as myself being nearly abducted, that didn't make me feel safe at all.

Stefanos and Ivo stared at me in wonder, while I was already picking up the dropped basket and the pomegranates that had rolled away.

"Come on, now. Let's pick this up and finish our last errand, then get home, or Kara will have our heads."

After we'd gone to the butcher's and were nearly home, I'd made them swear not to tell anyone about what had happened. I didn't want Julian to have another concern weighing on him before tonight. And while I would tell him eventually, I couldn't explain how I knew my magic would keep those men quiet.

But all my plans of keeping quiet and calm were thrown to the wind the second we arrived into the stable yard and Stefanos said to me, "Thank you again for saving us."

"Saving who from what?" came the deep voice behind us.

I spun to find Julian standing there, Volkan's reins in his hands. His expression was cold and hard, much like he often looked when I first came here. He was wearing a casual tunic with red capping on the sleeves and a red belt. It was still early and he was already home. But of course, he would be. He had a feast to host.

"Stefanos"—I handed him my basket—"get those to Kara. Ivo, bring her the meat."

Ivo and Stefanos slunk off quickly toward the kitchen entrance through the yard.

"Tell me what he was talking about, Malina."

"You don't have to worry."

He reached out and wrapped his fingers around my forearm. When I winced, he instantly dropped Volkan's reins and lifted my arm gently in his fingers, bending his head closer. Purplish bruises already marked the underside of my arm.

"Who?" His voice was rough and dark.

"Some men, slaves, on orders from their master, no doubt. They attacked us in the street. One tried to take me."

"*Whose* men were they?"

"I saw his name on one of the men's collars." I tapped mine hanging outside the neck of my tunic. "I also heard the same name in the forum today. Ciprian." When his golden gaze met mine, I added, "Isn't he the one to be honored at your house tonight?

"I'm going to kill that fucking bastard." His voice vibrated with rage while remaining low and eerily steady.

"Who is he?"

"A dead man soon enough."

"No, Julian." I grabbed his arm when he tried to turn away. "Who is he?"

He clamped his jaws tight, staring back at the house. "A rival."

"A rival being honored at your house tonight? Why would he try to anger you by . . . attacking us?"

"He wants a war between us. That can be the only reason."

"But why?" I wondered.

"Because I'm next in line for the emperor's throne, and he wants that position." He combed a hand through his hair. "Ciprian knows that taking you away from me would enrage me into acting out against him."

"How could that help him in the eyes of Caesar?"

"Because it would be illegal for one Roman officer to attack another over—" He swallowed hard, his expression showing his distaste as he continued. "Over property. Disputes must be overheard and judged by the emperor himself. And Ciprian knows that my uncle would not like me displaying irrational emotion over a woman."

"And a slave," I added. "Caesar would see such behavior as weak."

He gave me one stiff nod. We remained quiet a moment as the sun dipped lower behind his house. Volkan had lowered his head and nibbled on some hay strewn over the stable floor.

"Ciprian wants you angry tonight, so you must focus on *not* letting him get his way."

He huffed out a disgusted breath and pulled me gently into his arms. "Having him here in my house makes me want to—" He squeezed me a little hard and gritted his teeth, a dark rumble vibrating in his chest.

Wrapping my arms around his waist, I pressed my body to his and instinctually pushed a wave of calm into him. Though I was fatigued from using my gift within the last hour, I would always have enough for Julian.

He grunted and lowered his mouth to the crown of my head. "I told you not to use your gift on me, didn't I?"

"I don't care. You'll take it whether you want it or not."

He chuckled and squeezed me tight. "Are you all right? Did they hurt you?"

"I'm fine."

"Why did Stefanos thank you for saving them?"

"Because I used my gift against them."

He pulled back to meet my gaze, his brow pinched. "How?"

"I made them feel terror and made them believe the gods would kill them and all those they love."

"You can do that?"

"Emotions are powerful."

"Indeed." He grinned. "There it is."

"There what is?"

"My feisty firebird. Proof that you are meant to be mine. My dragon would only choose a powerful female for his mate."

My pulse pounded in my ears, and my throat went dry, remembering Trajan had said the very same thing. His smile slid away as he cupped my face gently, brushing his thumb along one cheek.

"Oh, Malina. You know this to be true. Why do you look so surprised?"

"I'm not. But when you say it aloud, it feels . . ."

"Real?"

I nodded, my chest squeezing tight, my legs wobbly with a rush of energy. He lowered his head and pressed a soft kiss to my lips, then murmured against them.

"You are mine and you are his, and we'll both die protecting you." He pressed his forehead to mine. "If we ever see the man who bruised your arm, the dragon will rip from my body and eat him alive."

"I'd think you were exaggerating but I've seen him do it before."

"That's right," he murmured. "No one hurts my woman."

A sharp foreboding pierced my chest. "Be careful, Julian."

"I always am."

"I'm serious. This Ciprian is trying to provoke you."

"I'm aware of it."

"Then don't fall into his trap. Don't allow it. It's like you said, he's trying to cause trouble between you and your uncle."

He straightened to his full height, one hand still cradling my nape. "I won't."

"Your mission is important," I said with emphasis. "We'll be all right if we keep our heads."

He tightened his hold on my nape. "Don't worry. I've got it under control."

But as we both walked back into the house, the sun dipping lower, an ominous tendril wove into my spirit. A whisper of warning bade me be alert and ready. For what, I wasn't sure, but it weighed heavily like a coming storm. The eerie part was, when I looked up, there wasn't a cloud in the sky.

JULIAN

The lilting of flutes drifted across the grand hall beside the atrium, where the musicians played from a corner. Guests mingled and laughed, drinking wine and picking at the platters of food now being set out for them. The night had barely begun and I was ready for it to end.

I had hired extra servants for the night from a neighbor who kept more slaves than he needed. I watched them working the room, Malina with them now, setting out one of many of Kara's impressive platters—a tiered display of honey-drizzled figs, pears, and pomegranates. Malina kept her head down and returned to the kitchen. I blew out a breath of relief and turned to survey the room.

I'd managed to acquire the musicians from that tavern where I'd followed Malina to. But I'd requested they play lighter, celebratory music rather than the melancholy tune they'd played in the tavern. So far, they were doing their job well.

I'd also hired dancers from one of the brothels in town, promising the madame extra denarii if any of my guests wanted more than to watch them dance. This was my job. Procuring prostitutes for my uncle and Ciprian's guests.

There were a few ladies of noble houses here as well. That should've alleviated my fears of my own party turning into an orgy, but I knew Ciprian. And I knew my uncle. I dreaded the moment this feast descended into debauchery. Not only because their hedonistic practices disgusted me, but because Malina might witness it.

"Nice guest list." Trajan had sidled up next to me, wine in hand.

"Isn't it?" I remarked dryly.

"There's that fucking Valerius. Snake in the grass if I ever saw one."

I loved the way Trajan had a talent for saying heinous things with a jovial smile on his face. Valerius, one of the consuls—the one most devoted to Caesar—stood next to Igniculus, chattering on about something that made my uncle smile. He was lithe and lean-muscled for an older dragon. Though his hair was more gray than black and he didn't spend his days on the battlefield, he wouldn't be easy in a physical fight.

Only six months ago, Valerius had been attacked in the street late at night by a group of thugs trying to rob him of his purse. Likely because it was dark and he was unescorted, they thought him a human, not dragonkind. He managed to break one robber's arm and stab the other in the eye with the knife he was trying to use against Valerius. Then he shifted into half-skin and killed the other three.

"We'll have to plan well to take out that one," I said under my breath.

"No worries. Grandfather and I have our plan almost perfect."

"Let's meet on it tomorrow." Trajan looked at me in surprise, but I kept my gaze on the guests. "We need to act soon."

"What's happened?"

"Nothing yet. But Ciprian is going to be a problem. He seems to have targeted me as his chief rival and wants to stir trouble between myself and my uncle. We need to put the plan into motion before Ciprian's machinations get in the way."

"Tomorrow, then." He stepped away and greeted Fausta of the Media Nocte line, a recent widow who may be looking for a new husband. Her glass-blue gaze caught mine over his shoulder, then she gave me her scintillating smile and angled her neck in a submissive pose.

It was a sign to other dragons that she was yielding, flirting. Her stola in black silk was draped in flattering folds over her slim body, pinned at one shoulder with a dragon-head brooch, the eyes glittering rubies. She bared one shoulder, the fabric of her silky gown a perfect complement to her fair skin. Her honey-brown hair was coifed in intricate braids on top of her head, with loose curls falling to her shoulder. She was the epitome of Roman beauty.

I nodded in greeting but didn't take her bait to walk over and talk. My uncle had undoubtedly invited her. He'd made mention more than once that she would make a good wife. Instead of engaging with Fausta, I remained fixed on the outer edge of the party, using my role as host as a reason to stand apart and make sure all was satisfactory for my guests.

As if on cue, Ruskus appeared at my side. "Dominus, the skull bearer and his attendants have arrived."

Gut tightening that I'd have one of these foul rituals take place in my house, I said, "Have them set up on the terrace. I'll let the emperor know."

My gaze found Malina circulating through the room and filling wine glasses. I'd had all of the servants wear formal attire—white tunics with red sashes—to represent my house. But it only accentuated

Malina's beauty more. Her sun-bronzed skin and glossy black locks contrasted against the clean white of the more fitted tunic. Her figure was on fine display as well, which had me even edgier.

If I could've gotten away with it, I'd have put her in a dowdy sack. But Uncle Igniculus would be insulted. Like all dragons, he desired to be surrounded by pretty, shiny things. And me trying to hide her would've only emphasized how important she was to me.

"Julianus!" my uncle called across the room and waved me over. My gut clenched.

Ciprian was now standing beside him, looking as smug as ever. I strode slowly across the room, stopping to greet a guest here and there. Most of them were from the Media Nocte dragon line, as expected. Ciprian would've ensured more of his own kin was present to witness his rite.

"Salve, Ciprian. I didn't see you come in."

"Salve," he replied. "Thank you for hosting my Rite of Skulls, Julian."

The way he casually used my name grated along my spine. "Of course. I am happy to host the newest legatus on this prestigious occasion."

"That's what I like to hear," said Igniculus, grasping me by the shoulder affectionately. "The two rising stars of Rome coming together."

I didn't miss the menacing glance from Ciprian before he widened his smile agreeably. "Indeed, Caesar."

"The skull bearer has arrived," I added quickly. "If you'd like to get started."

I wanted it done and over with as soon as possible.

"Yes. Let us begin," proclaimed my uncle.

I waved a hand to the musicians. They all stopped immediately. The musician with the large drum between his knees, the hide pulled tight on a wide brim, stood and carried his instrument quietly toward the terrace. He would serve as the only player during the ritual.

"Friends and guests," I called to the room, "please make your way to the terrace. We will begin the sacred Rite of Skulls momentarily."

A buzz of excitement rippled through the room. There were no priests or priestesses. This rite wasn't held in a temple or in the forum, but in the house of a general of the emperor's choosing. That's because this rite wasn't sacred. It was created by Igniculus to celebrate his might and that of his elite generals of the greatest power on earth—Rome. And anyone who witnessed it was considered the most privileged of dragonkind.

Igniculus grinned and grasped Ciprian's shoulder. "Ready to join the highest ranks?"

"I am, Caesar."

"Who will be your *sanguis auctor*?" he asked.

The role of blood giver was considered an honored position and was always chosen by the one receiving the rite.

"I think she will do." Ciprian nodded toward Trajan where Malina was refilling his goblet.

"No," I automatically snapped, fire licking through my veins and locking my muscles tight.

Ciprian chuckled. "It's my choice, is it not?"

"But she's a slave," I argued, trying to ignore my uncle's keen observation. "You didn't bring a highborn female to serve as your *sanguis auctor*? I assumed that's why Fausta was here." They were cousins, after all.

"Fausta would rather gut me than serve me her blood. Our families have never gotten along." He turned to my uncle. "Correct me if I'm wrong, but the *sanguis auctor* doesn't need to be a dragon, do they? I was told that General Antonios chose his own favored slave in his Rite of Skulls."

"That is true," agreed Igniculus, staring at Malina with new interest, sending a prickle of unease along my skin. "But why her?"

"That's the slave girl, the witch they say helped the Celts overcome

Bastius and his men somehow. The one Julian snatched from the battlefield."

If I could've killed him right then for bringing her to the emperor's attention, I would have. But I remained stone-still, even while I scowled at the bastard.

"Ah, I see," said Igniculus. "Your pretty new plaything, Julian."

"I think it would be appropriate for a conquered slave who once served our enemy to serve me her own blood." Ciprian's smile skated chills over my flesh. He turned his attention to Malina winding her way toward the kitchen with the wine decanter. "Besides, look at her. She's a feast for the eyes, is she not?"

"You have no problem with that, do you, Julian?" My uncle's question was not a question.

Through gritted teeth, I replied, "Of course not."

"Good." Ciprian clapped me on the back like we were friends. "I'll see you on the terrace. I must prepare."

My other guests were filing outside onto my wide terrace, which opened down toward the city. But I couldn't remove my gaze from Malina and what I was about to ask her to do.

"I can understand, my son," my uncle said in that familiar, intimate way when he had advice for me. "I had an obsession over one of my own slaves once, a long time ago. Best cunt I ever fucked."

His crassness grated while I pretended it didn't.

"What happened to her?" I asked, watching Malina disappear down the corridor.

"I had to kill her, of course." He sighed like it had been a reluctant duty that pained him only a little. "She disobeyed me." Then he turned to face me, his expression sharp and grave. "They can lead you astray with that cunny of theirs. It would be best you get rid of her soon." He leaned closer and told me in that authoritative tone, "Ride her hard for another week, then sell her. Don't keep that one."

It was a command.

Swallowing the bile that tried to rise up my throat, I simply nodded. "Of course, uncle. Good advice."

"Trust me. You can't keep a crafty whore in your house."

"You're right," I agreed yet again, forcing my expression to remain passive while I was dying inside. "I'll go instruct her for what she must do."

I parted from him and marched toward the kitchen, while dread twisted a knife in my belly. I now had a week to implement our plan. Because my uncle wasn't making suggestions. He now thought me bewitched by a slave girl, and he wouldn't have that. Not his prized nephew.

Of course, I *was* bewitched—body and soul. Happily, blissfully entranced by my mate.

I found her refilling the decanter beside Kara, who was plating more food for the feast to follow.

"Malina," I called to her.

Nausea swelled as she came to me.

"What's wrong?" she immediately asked.

"There's something I need you to do."

Tugging her to a corner away from the servants bustling through the kitchen, I explained the ceremony that was about to take place in my home and that Ciprian had requested she be his *sanguis auctor*, which was his right.

I waited for her to refuse, or at the very least, to show her disgust. But she did neither. She placed her hand on my arm, her touch a gentle warmth, then said, "Of course, Julian. Whatever needs to be done, I'll do it."

Then I felt that tiny hum of serenity pouring into me, an intoxicating tranquility. She was using her gift to keep me calm. She'd done it more and more of late.

"Thank you," I told her, glancing around to be sure the hired servants didn't hear me.

They'd certainly spread rumors if Julianus was thanking his slaves, something the emperor and most Romans disapproved of.

She leaned closer and whispered, "Whatever it takes to get through this night."

Her green eyes glittered by the lamplight. She didn't say more, but I knew exactly what she was thinking. We had to keep the farce going long enough to get through the night, to make sure everyone—most importantly my uncle—believed I was one of *them*.

I was not. I was woven from another cloth. The ghosts of my mother and father haunted me in my dreams. More than once, I'd woken drenched in sweat, the soft cries of my mother echoing from a nightmare, her shame of what had become of her son a constant, stabbing grief in my heart.

Malina straightened, wearing that fearless expression I knew so well. "Lead the way."

MALINA

It was quite fascinating that Emperor Igniculus had labeled all non-Romans barbarians, and yet, he was the true savage. The Rite of Skulls was nothing more than a barbarous ceremony to highlight the cruelty and brutality of the dragon's reign. Of *this* emperor's reign. And I was to be a part of it.

Standing exactly where Julian had told me to, next to the skull bearer, I waited. The skull bearer was dressed in a plain black toga, depicting his lineage. His head was shaved clean and his face was painted to mimic a skeleton's head.

The guests stood on the far side of the terrace behind a line of torches, near the long banister. They faced inward, the lights of the city glowing below Palatine Hill. They were all of dragonkind. Standing in a long line to witness this rite in hushed silence, their towering figures and regal attire, serpentine eyes glittering in the dark, made an ominous spectacle. A chill skittered over my skin.

A long, crimson carpet had been placed across the terrace for this ceremony. Along both sides of the carpet stood ten of the twelve generals of Rome, staggered down the line, Julian the farthest away. Near him, at the far end, Emperor Igniculus sat upon an ornate throne made of brass, the arms shaped like dragon's claws, spikes cresting the chairback. It had been set upon a dais so that he could oversee the ceremony from on high. Or, he simply liked to look down upon his subordinates, to remind them of his status. Perhaps, it was both.

The throne must've come with the skull bearer and his attendants—also wearing painted faces like death heads—who all stood in the shadows behind me.

Directly at the end of the carpet stood Ciprian. He was bare chested now, except for his leather sheath with his gladius strapped across it, a black linen wrapped loosely around his waist.

Julian had explained the procedure of the ceremony, so I was aware what would happen. But knowing something and experiencing it were two entirely different things.

A drum began to beat in a slow tempo, the signal to begin. If it weren't for the steady buzz of dragon power wafting in the air, the otherworldly glow of their eyes in the semidarkness would tell me I was standing among the most dangerous predators in all the world.

I turned to face the skull bearer, who held the gold-plated skull on a pillow—what was left of the king Ciprian had killed. I lifted the ghastly thing, shining under the moonlight, and upturned it where the empty hollow of the dead man's skull became a bowl. The back rim had been smoothed into a perfect dip for someone's mouth to drink from.

The skull bearer poured wine into the empty skull until it was half-full. Then I turned and began my long march up the red-carpeted aisle.

Stopping at the first general, a behemoth of a man with a square, flat face and a horrifying scar across one eye, I held up the bowl. He unsheathed his gladius, pulled the blade across his palm and let it drip into the skull. After a few seconds, he lifted his hand away and resheathed his blade.

I walked diagonally across the carpet as Julian had instructed, the cool wind pushing on my tunic. But it wasn't the chill in the air that had the hairs on the back of my neck rising. It was the low, deep rumble of dragons growling while the beat of the drum continued.

It wasn't simply the generals in the ceremony, it was all of the guests too, like a choral song of beasts, harmonizing for this obscene display. I kept my eyes down except when I had to present to the next general.

On and on, I went down the line, head bowed and skull bowl up while they poured their blood into the ghastly goblet. When I finally made it to Julian, I still kept my eyes down. I didn't want anyone to notice the way I looked at him, or to shake his resolve in seeing one ounce of fear in my eyes. Because there was fear inside me, so much of it.

My gift from the gods could be wonderful, but right now, I wish I could turn off the scraping of bloodlust beating against my flesh, trying to rip into my psyche. The beasts on this terrace smelled fresh blood, and they all wanted a taste. Except, perhaps, *my* dragon.

I dared not look into his eyes as he cut his palm and let his blood drip into the bowl. Afterward, I slowly walked and stood before Ciprian. Until now, I'd held the skull goblet with two hands.

I had no idea what would happen if I spilled the contents in this skull, but I knew the punishment would be severe. And Julian would either have to stand back and watch, or worse, he'd intervene. And that would be a death sentence for both of us.

Gripping the skull tight with one hand, my thumb hooked tightly around the dead king's gold-plated mandible, I presented my left palm to Ciprian.

A dragon can't taste blood and not transform. He will shift into half-skin.

Julian's words repeated in my mind, the ones he'd whispered quickly to me in the kitchen, preparing me for the inevitable. Still, I couldn't keep from trembling.

Ciprian gripped my wrist and unsheathed his blade. His chest began to swell, his shoulders widening, his entire body stretching taller, yet he remained mostly in human form.

"Look at me, witch," he commanded.

I ignored the deeper growl rising from Julian to his left. I recognized the sound and presence of his dragon above all others, yet I couldn't let anyone know.

So I obeyed the order of Ciprian, lifting my gaze to his red eyes, slit like a serpent's. He grinned, revealing a row of sharpened teeth, two canines lengthening as I stared in a stupor.

He reached out with his gladius and slit a shallow cut on the fleshy part of my palm. I didn't even flinch, then my blood was dripping into the bowl.

"Mmm," Ciprian hummed and sniffed the air, still more human than dragon, "such a sweet sacrifice."

It was a mockery to the gods to call this a sacrifice. There were no priests. No priestesses. This rite was presided over by the self-appointed god, Igniculus. An unholy horror of a creature.

Ciprian gripped my wrist harder and dipped his head down. His long, black forked tongue licked out and across my palm. I made a small sound of distress that caused movement where Julian stood, but then he froze. I dared not even look.

Ciprian's red eyes bored into mine. I felt true evil looking back at me. Then he grinned and let me go. Instantly, I gripped the skull with both hands and knelt at his feet, presenting the bowl high above my head as Julian had instructed.

Almost over, almost over, I repeated in my head.

Staring at Ciprian's bare feet, I heard the cracking of bones and his guttural moan as his wings and horns emerged, his body growing even taller. All I could see were his feet, which elongated and formed sharp, black claws that curled from his toes.

Then I felt his heavy hand on my head. I flinched again, terrified he was going to rip it off. But his crooning growl was one of pleasure, his voice low when he said in garbled speech, "I like."

Whether he meant me or the fact that I was kneeling submissively before him, I had no idea. He patted my head like I was his dog, only briefly, then his hand was gone and the bowl was lifted from my hands.

But it wasn't Ciprian who'd lifted the bowl. I hadn't even noticed that the emperor had slid from his throne and now stood beside him. The emperor's rough, booming voice jolted me where I still knelt, my gaze on the ground.

"Romans! Children of the gods! Hear me now." The growling hum and the drums stopped at once. "I lift this golden chalice, made by our might and our power, which yet again proves our right to rule this world."

A chorus of applause and a few cheers of approval lifted from the audience as if they were merely at the theater. Then they fell silent. The wind ghosted across the terrace, a few stray leaves scraping on the marble. My heart remained in my throat, the oppressive energy in the air threatening to strangle me where I trembled on my knees. I wrapped my hand around my other where the cut still dripped to the white stone, squeezing to stop the bleeding, but also because it kept me sane in this horrifying, surreal moment.

"We gather tonight to celebrate Ciprian Media Nocte Seneca. He has earned his first king's skull and his right to stand among the generals of Rome. We salute him."

Another round of applause mingled with growling dragons this time. I glanced up to see Igniculus holding the golden skull above his head, a gruesome trophy with my own blood mixed in the swill.

"We welcome him. Legatus Ciprian Seneca."

Ciprian walked past me toward the emperor, brushing his tail along my thighs, the tip curling slightly in a possessive motion before he was out of reach. The audience erupted in more applause as the drum began to beat again. I glanced up to see Ciprian draining the mixture of blood and wine from the golden skull, but then my gaze found Julian.

Bona dea.

He was the only one not applauding or cheering or smiling or even watching Ciprian. His golden gaze was hot and furious and on me. I finally reached out through our tether, flinching at the rage filling his entire being. Swallowing hard against the fury threatening to engulf him, I poured my affection as well as serenity through the thread.

At first, it had no impact at all. Julian remained rigid and fuming while the rest of the nobles stepped forward to congratulate Ciprian. He slowly shrank back into human form, clutching the linen at his waist, which had come loose.

The whole ceremony was an odd juxtaposition of monstrous and civil. The patricians applauded him like he was receiving a garland around his head at a triumph. In reality, he stood there half-naked, holding a man's skull that had been dipped in gold, his new prized goblet.

Trajan sidled past Julian, whispering something before maneuvering closer to me, still applauding and keeping his gaze on Ciprian, pretending to celebrate. When Trajan was close enough for me to hear, he whispered, "You may rise and go back to the kitchen. Best you stay out of sight for the night."

Without wasting a second, I was on my feet and hurrying past the drummer and the skull bearer and away from this nightmare as fast as my legs would take me.

XXVI

JULIAN

Ciprian had never been on our list of those to execute for our coup. Now, he was at the top of mine. Most of those on our list were present right now. Too bad Legatus Drussus was leading his campaign in Bthynia. He was practically my uncle's twin in cruelty and brutality. Trajan's grandfather insisted he must be in Rome before we put our plan into action.

As I watched Ciprian, holding his golden trophy and laughing with my uncle, I realized I wouldn't be able to wait much longer. I needed Ciprian's head severed from his body. Especially now that my uncle had given me a week to get rid of Malina. I couldn't send her away without going with her. Perhaps Trajan could hide her in his home or somewhere else for me. He and his family had homes in provinces near and far.

Ciprian tipped his head back and laughed at something my uncle said. I was also well aware that his performance with Malina—licking her hand and caressing her with his tail—was specifically done to draw my anger out. In that, he had been entirely successful. The only reason I hadn't shifted into half-skin and gone for his throat was because of her.

Yet again, she'd opened her gift to me, to keep me from going mad with rage. And it had worked. I was no longer wrestling my beast back into his cave. I was now calm enough to lead our guests back into my home, where there would be a grand feast and dancers for entertainment.

"Caesar and guests," I called loudly from the arched entrance where light spilled onto the terrace, "come and feast in celebration."

I ignored Ciprian's smug glare and led the others back inside.

Kara and the servants had created a beautiful bounty of roasted pheasant, boar, and venison, along with decorative platters of seasoned fish with whole roasted cloves of garlic. Platters of garlic-seasoned endives, asparagus, leeks, and legumes were stacked in silver bowls around the feasting area. There were even more dishes of cheese, olives, and marinated artichokes, as well as baskets of honey cakes, berry tarts, and fresh-baked bread set out with decanters of oil and honey.

Some of the guests audibly gasped at the sight of the bounty spread out among the low tables and pillows, the many oil lamps lighting the room in a welcoming glow. While the musicians played a lively tune, I saw no dancers.

The guests made their way to the lounging area and reclined among the pillows and chaises to serve themselves. All I wanted to do was sneak off to the kitchen to see how Malina was feeling.

Taking a goblet of wine from one of the hired servants, I ambled past the atrium near the musicians. Ruskus appeared from near the foyer entrance of my home, his expression concerned. I met him so that he didn't have to mingle among the guests.

"What is it?" I asked.

"The girls from the brothel. They aren't coming."

"Why not?" I demanded.

"There was an altercation at the brothel house. Some foreigners fighting over a girl, which turned into mayhem and started a fire. Some of the women were injured. Madame sends her apologies and returned your denarii."

"Son of Dis," I cursed.

Entertainment was always required of a host at these events. And music was not traditionally enough. Romans liked to be entertained, more specifically by beautiful women. I'd also hired prostitutes for favors they might give when the rowdy ones had drunk and laughed enough and wanted to fuck.

"Don't worry. We are improvising."

"What do you mean?"

Igniculus stepped to my side. Ruskus disappeared back toward the kitchen.

"Come, Julian. Have you met Fausta?" He guided me to the female dragon of the Media Nocte house I'd met on more than one occasion.

"Yes, we've met." I gave her a nod. "Welcome to my home, Fausta."

"I am pleased to be among your noble guests tonight, Julianus. Won't you sit with me?"

My uncle's grin was nothing less than telling. He wanted me to tie myself to a noble house and beget a pure-blood heir. He had only ever begotten bastards, who were killed at birth, if the rumors were true. I'd asked him once if he planned to marry. His nauseating reply was that the only woman he would ever make his wife lived in the dragon pit behind his palace. I believe my aunt Camilla knew this, and that was why she remained in dragon form.

"Such a succulent meal you've provided us," Fausta was saying as she draped herself on her side among the pillows, her gown slipping enough to reveal the elegant curve of her shoulder without being too immodest.

"I am pleased to provide it." I stretched out on a nearby chaise, propped on my side as well, doing my best to look at ease.

"Your home is quite lovely." She stared at the mosaic on the opposite side of the atrium, the one of Diana hunting with her bow, her wings flared and tail curling, her hair billowing in the unseen wind. "You have an affection for the huntress goddess? Or just beautiful women?" she teased.

"You would think me a fool if I didn't enjoy the beauty of graceful women, would you not?"

She tipped her head, baring her throat in that submissive pose again, her curls sliding over the silken skin of her shoulder.

Ciprian, now back in human form, lowered himself and sprawled beside us, dressed in his toga once again, completing our circle. "Julian enjoys beautiful women. Don't you?" He plucked an olive from the tray between us and popped it into his mouth. "Where's that pretty slave girl of yours?"

"Ciprian, you are a guest in my home. Though I accord all guests what comforts and pleasures I can provide, my servants are not on the menu."

"Keeping her all to yourself, are you?" He popped another olive and chewed obnoxiously. "Too bad. I enjoyed the taste of her blood."

Fausta's expression pinched in annoyance or disgust or both. What I knew of her was that she came from a more noble family than her distant cousin Ciprian, and apparently she didn't seem to relish his vulgarity. She turned her head toward the musicians, pretending not to hear his obscenities.

Ciprian leaned toward me and whispered loud enough for her to hear, "Have you tasted her?" He chuckled darkly. "What am I saying? Of course you have. That's why you don't want to share." He then raised his voice. "Fausta."

She turned to look at him with undisguised annoyance.

"If you catch Julian here for a husband, be sure and sell his slaves first. I'll take at least one off your hands." He laughed when both of us didn't.

"I'll die first," I growled, unable to hold my tongue.

That had Ciprian grinning with glee. "That good, eh? Seems I need to try her magic cunny."

I was across the carpet on my knees, lifting him by the front of his toga. "I know what you tried to do today."

"Almost had her too," he admitted freely, unruffled. "I bet she sucks good cock with that full mouth of hers."

"Keep talking, and I'll kill you right here."

"Julianus!"

I froze and turned to see my uncle, standing close with the scarred General Sabinus beside him. The murmur of guests talking died, all eyes on us.

"Let him go, Julian." The emperor scowled, his disapproval apparent in the tone of his voice.

Dropping Ciprian, I stood. "My apologies, Caesar."

His frown remained tight, but his voice relaxed as he said, "It seems you two need to draw a little blood before this rivalry will settle. I can understand that."

It had nothing to do with our rivalry. It was the fact that he continued to insult and threaten my mate. But no one knew that, except Trajan. No one could know or I'd instantly be charged a traitor to Rome. A dragon fated and mated to a common-born citizen was considered a curse by the gods. To be mated to a foreign enemy would be considered worse. My uncle wouldn't stand for that shame. I'd be publicly executed alongside Malina.

"No need," I said, fisting my hands at my sides.

"I wouldn't mind drawing a little of his blood," added Ciprian, now plucking a roasted wing from a pheasant off the platter beside him.

Igniculus chuckled. "It is necessary. When dragons target one another, there will be no peace until they've battled it out. Therefore, you two will meet tomorrow in half-skin. In the Colosseum."

A murmur of excitement drifted over the guests. A public fight always pleased the people of Rome, especially when it was between two dragons. But rarely did they meet on the Colosseum floor.

"I accept," said Ciprian frankly, chewing his pheasant and smiling up to where I towered over him.

I simply nodded in agreement.

"Good," said Igniculus, clapping his hands and rubbing his palms together. "So where is our entertainment, Julian?"

I was about to reply with my apologies—my mind still reeling with the fact that I'd be fighting Ciprian in the arena tomorrow—when the music stopped, only the tympanum drumming a steady beat.

"My, my," crooned Ciprian. "You decided to bring her out of hiding after all."

Snapping my head toward the atrium where everyone else was staring, I nearly groaned in pain.

Malina was stepping dramatically, gracefully to the beat of the drum from around the fountain. She was no longer dressed in her slave tunic. She wore very little at all. A bandeau top of red silk bound her breasts and tied behind her neck. Her stomach was entirely bare down to her hips, where a gossamer material of white draped to her knees, slits open at the sides for ease of movement. Because she obviously was preparing to dance.

I moved away from Ciprian and off to the side of the guests to lean against a column.

She clapped her hands over her head and swayed her hips to the easy tempo of the drum, her gaze to the side and down, her waves of hair hiding her face and draped to her hips. Then the flute players joined in, playing a tune that seemed familiar. My pulse tripped when memory reminded me where and when I'd heard a similar song—beneath the Carpathian Mountains by moonlight.

Malina snapped her head up and began to shine like the jewel that she was. Her eyes were smeared with black kohl, giving her a mysterious visage, making her green eyes glitter brighter by the lamplight. She spun and leaped, the panels of her skirt flaring wide, revealing her bronzed, toned legs. And there I was, entranced yet again, just like the first time I'd seen her on that stage.

Only now, she was a full-grown woman, her body so beautiful and graceful as she spun in circles across the atrium, silhouetted against the white fountain behind her. Some of the guests gasped in awe as she arched her back until her hair draped the floor, then braced her hands on the marble and flipped her legs entirely over, spinning away again.

"Oh, how lovely!" one of the wives gushed and clapped somewhere to my right.

Several others did as well, all enamored with my dancer for the night, the entertainment I hadn't procured at all.

"Not bad," grunted Consul Valerius. "I've got a prettier one at home."

But I barely heard his insult or the applause, my gut tightening that she would come out in full display for them.

What is she thinking?

That's when I realized that Ciprian wasn't heckling her or yelling obscenities as I'd expected, nor was he fondling himself while he watched her. Rather, he was nearly asleep. His eyes were half-lidded, his head resting on his shoulder as he leaned on his side.

I glanced toward the kitchen, wanting to catch Ruskus to see if perhaps they'd put something in his wine. They wouldn't poison him as he was an honored guest in my home. I'd be blamed for sure if he was poisoned.

Then I noticed that Igniculus had taken a seat on a chaise as well, his own eyes blinking heavily. When I searched the faces of the other guests, there were no signs of drowsiness. I didn't understand.

Malina danced on, spinning and swaying and hypnotizing the crowd with her bewitching dance, her sinuous movements. The song went on and on, and Malina never stopped, a bead of sweat trickling down her temple and dropping onto the white marble.

I was about to step in and stop the dance—etiquette be damned—when the music came to a crescendo. Malina spun faster and faster until she struck a final pose, reminding me of the girl on the stage in Dacia.

Everyone applauded while Igniculus barely roused and Ciprian was dead asleep on my carpet. My uncle pushed to stand groggily and ambled toward me, seeming more than a bit drunk when I knew he hadn't imbibed nearly enough to be intoxicated.

"Thank you for hosting, nephew. I'd best be going." He yawned and clapped his hand on my shoulder. "The day's been long."

"Yes, uncle. Happy to be of service."

As he walked toward the foyer, his praetorian guards melting out of the shadows to flank him, he called back, "The Colosseum tomorrow. At noon."

My gut clenched, but a sense of relief washed over me. The emperor leaving meant it was time for everyone to leave. The guests began to thank me for a lovely evening while I summoned Ruskus with a finger.

When he was at my side, I leaned down to say, "Fetch Ciprian's litter bearers to come and get him off my carpet."

"Yes, dominus."

Fausta stopped and bowed before me. "Thank you, Julian, for having me in your home."

She didn't simper or flirt or make any of the overtures she did earlier. I wondered if she had that feminine intuition and understood that Malina meant more to me than a slave should. She cut me with disapproving eyes as I expected, but she held her chin high, her gaze cold, full of the poise of a woman of the dragon aristocracy.

"Good night, Fausta. Thank you for coming."

"Good night." She followed the others filing through my foyer toward the front, where their litter bearers and litters had been waiting all night to carry them home.

Trajan stopped before me. As always, he'd kept his distance from me. Though he was my military tribune, we'd tried to keep a show of only casual acquaintance off the battlefield.

"So," he murmured, his expression dark, "I suppose we won't be meeting with my grandfather tomorrow."

"Fuck." My temper had thrown everything off course. "I am sorry, Trajan."

"Don't apologize. To be fair, you handled him with more calm than I imagined you would."

"I wouldn't have been able to for much longer."

"Then Malina came to the rescue. Her dance seemed to distract everyone." He watched as four of Ciprian's large male slaves carried him, dead asleep, toward the exit. "Seems Ciprian drank too much. Can the blood do that to him?"

"No." I searched the atrium, finding no sign of Malina. "It wasn't the blood that put him unconscious."

Trajan seemed about to ask another question, but then nodded. "I'll be in touch." Then he called to General Sabinus, complimenting him on the spoils of war he brought back from Macedonia on his last campaign.

Trajan always knew how to work the crowd, how to make them like him. I never had that in me. Tonight, I'd been as amiable and cordial as I could possibly manage. But right now, I wanted everyone gone. I wanted no one's company but hers.

Storming back toward where she struck her final pose, I inhaled deeply and followed her scent straight down the corridor toward my bedchamber.

MALINA

I stood at the entrance to Julian's private terrace in his bedchamber. From here, I could see a corner of the street where his guests were being carried in their litters down Palatine Hill to their own homes. I remained in the shadow of a column so no one could see me.

When all of the litters seemed to be gone, hearing no more of the sandaled bearers clomping along the stone street, I finally exhaled a sigh of relief.

But then I felt him near me. When I spun, my breath caught. He stood only a few feet away, having moved with predatory silence. His eyes burned so bright, like sparks of glowing embers.

"I know you're angry." I was aware he wouldn't want me to dance, to be in the line of sight of Ciprian. "But I knew that I could solve two problems at once. You had no entertainment, and I, of course, am a dancer. But also"—I gulped hard as he stepped slowly toward me—"I knew that I could tether Ciprian and the emperor. I could make them sleepy and want to go home."

It was strange, that knowing, when the idea had come to me in the kitchens while Ruskus argued with Kara over what to do since the dancers weren't coming.

I felt it—a hard, strong pulse of power light me from within. It was the same sensation I had when Julian's dragon responded to my tether, when he gave me some of his own strength. I knew then and there that I could tether a powerful, dangerous man like Caesar. So I didn't hesitate. I knew what I must do to end this awful night.

"You put Ciprian into a coma." He walked closer slowly.

"Good," I whispered from the shadows. "Then you won't be able to fight him tomorrow."

"How did you do it?" He stopped only inches from me, his voice gruff as he began to remove his toga. "Sleep isn't an emotion."

I stared as he unwound the fine red material, his eyes lit from within. "Isn't it? Anyone can feel sleepy."

"It's more than that." He dropped his toga to the floor and then lifted his fine white tunic beneath over his head, revealing his entire nude body, his muscles locked tight. His wound was reddened but completely sealed and mending. "Sleep is a physicality," he stated calmly, while I couldn't seem to catch my breath.

His body was so beautiful, so strong and powerful. His cock hung half-hard as he reached down and stroked it. I was no virgin, having explored sex a few times with Hanzi the year before our village was attacked. But Hanzi had been more of a boy, not a man, and certainly not a dragon of Julian's proportions.

"E-every emotion is a physicality," I whispered breathlessly.

"Indeed they are, Malina." His voice was velvet dark as he stepped even closer. "And my emotions have run riot through my blood all night."

He reached his hands beneath my hair to the knot where I'd tied the strip of red cloth and slowly unwrapped the bandeau from around my breasts until I was bare. I remained perfectly still.

"The emotions you stir in me have become all-invasive. A painful physicality I can no longer endure."

"Julian, I—" I'd lifted my hands to his chest, but he quickly wrapped my wrists in one hand and pressed them over my head, against the column at my back.

He lowered his head until we were eye to eye. Heavens, his gaze was feral.

"I may burn in Tartarus for all the evils I've done." His large hand mounded one of my breasts, squeezing till I whimpered with pleasure. "But by the gods, I'll fuck my mate before I'm sent there."

His mouth was on mine, a deep growl vibrating up his throat as he stroked his tongue inside. I could do nothing but accept him as he pressed his hard body against mine, pinning me to the column, his thick cock against my bare stomach as I lifted onto my toes to reach him better. Heat pooled between my thighs, soaking the fabric I'd tied beneath the skirt to hide my sex while I danced.

He broke the kiss on a grunt and fell to his knees. He went for the fabric of my skirt, his claws out as he slashed through the material and ripped it off, making sure not to cut my skin.

"Julian." I sank my fingers into his hair right before he roughly pushed my thigh over one of his shoulders and opened his hot mouth on my sex.

"Juno save me," I murmured, my head falling to the pillar behind me.

Julian ate me with ravenous intensity, and I could do nothing but whimper and rock my sex against his mouth.

"More, Julian. *Gods.*"

He'd retracted his claws and slid one hand between my thighs, then pumped two fingers inside me. His glittering gaze was on me as he licked out with his forked tongue over my clitoris.

I gasped, then I was coming too soon. He pumped his fingers faster and sucked my throbbing nub into his mouth as I climaxed on a deep moan, thighs trembling, fists clenching.

Before I'd even come down, he lifted me in his arms and carried me deeper into his bedchamber, into his private lair, sliding me between the canopy curtains and onto the center of his bed. I bent my legs and opened my thighs as he settled between them, but he sat back onto his heels. Then he grabbed my hips and propped my bottom on his lower thighs. Gripping his cock, he wet the head along my folds.

"I need you, Malina," he growled, a desperate yearning creasing his face.

I moaned as he sank slowly inside me, then gasped when he grabbed my hips and thrust to the hilt. A full body shiver went through him, then he ground his hips in a sensuous circle, allowing my body to stretch and accommodate him. Exquisite pleasure filled me at the tight sensation.

His eyes slid closed, his brow furrowing like he was in pain as he murmured, "Gods help me. So good, sweetheart."

He made that low purring sound deep inside his chest when he began to thrust, nice long glides that made me whimper as I fisted my hands in the sheets. His golden gaze made a slow trek from where he impaled me all the way up my torso to my breasts and then to my face.

"Sweeter than I could've imagined," he said in that cool, unaffected way. But I caught the roughness in his tone, the passionate longing in his eyes.

My desire met his, an innate need to *feel* him everywhere. I raised my arms, unable to reach him.

"I need to touch you."

Slowly, he leaned forward and braced his hands on either side of my head, widening my thighs as he lowered his body to mine. We both groaned as I skated my heels up the backs of his thighs.

He lowered to his forearms, his face inches from mine. But he didn't kiss me. He scooped one of his hands behind my head, cradling me tenderly while he stared with searing heat in his dragon-slit eyes.

"So beautiful," he whispered.

I coasted my palms to his muscular back. Then he withdrew and impaled me deep. I whimpered at the intensity and clawed my blunt nails down his back.

"Yes, my firebird," he murmured, pulling out to the tip and thrusting back in. "Mark me all over."

"More," I begged.

His dark growl vibrated from his chest, sensitizing my nipples as he began to thrust faster, deeper.

"Unh . . . yes, Julian. Need more of you."

He angled his mouth over mine, kissing me hard as he drove into me, over and over, his cock swelling bigger when I scraped my nails hard down his back again. He nipped my lip but didn't break the skin, even while his canine teeth had sharpened. He hadn't gone half-skin but parts of his dragon were pushing through, needing to be known. To be seen.

Panting, I plunged my fingers into his hair and pulled his head closer so I could whisper in his ear. "Is your dragon fucking me too?" I shivered, knowing full well the dominance drenching my skin and pressing into my soul was that of the beast that lived inside him. "Is he claiming me too?"

He ripped away and out of me so fast I gasped. He flipped my body, my cheek pressed to the mattress, my bottom in the air. Then he drove his cock deep and scooped one hand over my sex; the other gripped the front of my throat as he blanketed his large body over me, pressing against my back.

I was perfectly pinned by his cock and his body. I couldn't move. And it was glorious.

A guttural rumble rolled from his chest, his mouth at my ear.

"That's right, Malina." He stroked inside me slow and deep now, with precision, his forefinger rubbing my clitoris in a circle, his other hand cradling my throat gently. "You're mine." His voice was so deep, I hardly recognized it. "This sweet cunny, this beautiful body, your bright soul." He pounded harder. "It's all *mine*." He squeezed my throat tenderly. "Tell me."

"Yes," I whispered as he nuzzled his mouth below my ear, licking and nipping my neck. "I'm yours."

That deep rumbling growl returned as he stroked and rubbed and squeezed and sucked me. "You're burning me up, firebird." He started to thrust faster. "I knew you always would."

His overpowering body held me in an iron grip while he impaled himself deeper and deeper inside me. Beyond my sex and right into my soul, my dragon breathed fire, blazing his way, leaving a fiery trail I knew would scar. He was leaving his mark as well.

I screamed my climax, knowing I'd never be the same. That no man would ever replace Julian. He was indeed the one the gods intended for me. Our tether vibrated with emotion—a myriad of need and want and desperate, overwhelming, obsessive affection. Love.

He grunted on every thrust, finally driving himself inside me one last time, his grip on my sex and my throat spasming and squeezing as he emptied his seed inside me. His groan was more animalistic, gruff and grating, as he held himself deep, his cock throbbing with release.

He panted and nuzzled my neck. "Malina." His voice broke with emotion and softly pressed his lips to the skin of my throat. "What have you done to me?"

"No more than you've done to me," I breathed.

Gently, he pulled from inside me and rolled me beneath him.

His gaze captured me, wholly and completely. The fire had dimmed from within his eyes, but they still glowed with a preternatural luster. The beast lingered close by. But it was the deep affection I saw there that gripped me so tenderly.

We said nothing as I traced the sharp lines of his face with the tip of my forefinger and he simply stared, both of us breathing hard from our coupling.

"I don't want you to fight Ciprian tomorrow," I finally said.

He searched my face, still gazing in wonder. "I have to."

"When will you and Trajan implement your plan?"

There was only one plan, but even in the quiet of his bedroom I feared to say revolution or rebellion. Or more clearly, assassination. I was afraid that if I said those kinds of words aloud that somehow the emperor would know.

Igniculus. He was a terrifying beast of a dragon. Even in his human form, he was horrifying. The way he watched the room, seeming to be always calculating.

"Soon," Julian replied, sighing as he rolled to his back, hauling me with him onto his chest.

I wrapped my arm around his waist and snuggled close while he pulled a blanket over us.

"Your uncle," I said softly, "is terrifying."

Julian stroked a hand down my back over the covers, soothing me. "He's a madman."

"How did he turn out so differently than your father? Your father seemed a good man." From what little I knew of him, he sounded like the polar opposite of his brother.

"Did you know my uncle was born in half-skin?"

I sat up, wanting to see Julian's face. "Is that unusual?"

He nodded. "Most Romans are born either in human form or dragon."

I winced. "How could a woman survive the birth of a dragon?"

"If they're in dragon form or half-skin, there is a soft membrane that coats them. And they have no horns at birth."

"Oh." I exhaled a breath, and his mouth quirked into a smile at my ignorance. "I didn't know."

"How could you?" He stroked a hand over my hip. "Depending what form we are born, the gods tell us which will rule them most. The man or the beast."

"Or the woman. There are female dragons." I tried to tamp down the instant flare of jealousy at seeing that noble lady flirting with Julian tonight.

"Yes. When a dragon, man or woman, is born in half-skin, it is believed by some that the dragon will be forever twisted."

"How so? A dragon in half-skin is simply another form of their animal."

"No," he said, staring at me while twirling a lock of my hair. "It is not. When in half-skin, we are neither man nor beast. We are an unnatural creature, both fighting for dominance. We're taught at an early age how to control our bloodlust while in half-skin. It's like the beast is fighting for domination when we are in between. It is never good to remain in half-skin for too long."

I laid my cheek back to his chest. "You do on the battlefield."

"And there, our primary goal is to kill the enemy. So there is no need for control. We can let our primal urges take hold. That is why after the battle is over, the general demands the men return to human form back at camp. That is also why it is illegal for a Roman to shift into half-skin in the city unless he's attacked and needs to defend him or herself."

"I'd think your uncle wouldn't care."

"He doesn't want random killing. He needs an empire to rule over, after all. Allowing dragon madness to take over would be disastrous to the citizens, particularly the plebs."

"Why does he even care about the plebs? Seems he only cares about the needs of the patricians."

"Because though the plebs don't have the power of the dragon, they do hold the power of the people. If there is civil unrest among the plebs, he will be blamed and hated. And that sort of hatred bleeds into both classes when we all live and work in the same city."

"There must've been civil unrest when he began taking dragon bastard children from homes and throwing them into the gladiator pits."

He paused, his hand still ghosting softly up and down my spine in a soothing sweep. "Yes and no. There were some protests, of course, but my uncle took care of them quickly and quietly and by the cover of night."

"He killed the plebs who protested?"

"Of course. Then he had the praeco give a long series of lectures to the public in the forum about the sanctity of marriage and that only children born in wedlock were true Romans."

"That's ridiculous. He can't actually care about the sanctity of marriage? From what I've heard, he's a whoremonger himself."

"You don't know the half of it. He's beyond a hypocrite, but he does know how to manipulate. And he knows the tradition of Romans holding sacred marriage and family."

"So he played upon their guilt and shame, the mothers who had children out of wedlock?"

"Yes. And he lied and told them that the gods would punish them by bringing dragon madness upon them, that the bastard children were an aberration and would go mad and kill them in their sleep."

"What a horrible lie." I thought of sweet Stefanos and how I knew in my soul he could never hurt anyone, least of all any of us, his family.

"It was," he agreed on a sigh. "As a final insult, he gave all of the plebs twenty-five denarii and threw a festival where he furnished the bread and meat in the forum, showing what a gracious emperor he was."

Igniculus truly was a monster.

A sharp memory invaded my mind. One of the man who'd told me about my village so long ago.

"I was told that it was dragon madness that caused the attack on my village."

Julian's hand stopped stroking, spreading warmly on my back. "The Romans attacked in half-skin?" he asked gently.

"They did." I remembered the carnivorous gleam in their eyes. "We hadn't done anything against the emperor. Our village was so small and far away from other Roman provinces. It never made sense to me why they'd come in and simply murdered everyone."

He wrapped both of his arms around me and hugged me close, pressing his mouth to the crown of my head. "I'm sorry, Malina. It sounds as if they were taken over by the bloodlust." He squeezed me again, whispering almost to himself, "Thank the gods you escaped."

"I used to curse the gods for letting me escape."

He rolled us both onto our sides, facing each other. Propping himself on one elbow, he cupped my face with the other. "Why would you do so?"

I scoffed. "Really, Julian? To be the only one of my village, of my family, to survive that nightmare? I thought perhaps the gods had spared me for a reason. And when I was able to help the Celts in battle, I believed perhaps the gods had set me there for that purpose." After all, my bunica had always told me as much. That I could save the people. "But then the Celts were defeated."

"By me," he added sourly.

"By you. And I was taken into captivity."

"By me."

"Yes." I scowled.

"So you believed your purpose was for naught. That the gods had abandoned you."

I didn't answer, because that's exactly how I felt.

He trailed his fingers down my throat and lifted the coin I still wore around my neck. I'd removed my slave collar for the night but I never removed the coin he'd given me.

"You *were* spared by the gods for a purpose."

"What?" I huffed. "To be your lover?"

"To be my wife." He pressed his forehead to mine. "To be my partner in this infernal world. To be my helpmate as we crush the Roman Empire and build a new one."

My heart catapulted faster, blood humming wildly through my veins. "You truly want all of that."

"To build a new Rome? I've told you so."

I pulled away so I could see his eyes better, then shook my head shyly. "Not that."

His widening smile made my belly turn over. "For you to be my wife?"

"I saw a rather beautiful Roman lady at your party. She seemed rather fond of the position."

His chuckle made me angry. "You're jealous."

Shoving him away, I turned over and threw off the covers. Before I could extricate myself from his bed, he had me around the waist and hauled me back to him, laughing fully now.

"Stop it," I demanded. "Let me go."

"No. Never," he murmured into my ear as I half-heartedly struggled to get free. He pinned my arms and squeezed me closer. "That woman is a dim, dying light compared to you. *Gods,* Malina. You were so fucking beautiful tonight, it hurt my heart to even look at you. And yet, I couldn't look away."

He sucked in a breath, nuzzling into my neck. I couldn't help but tip my head at an angle so he had more access. He growled.

"Do you know what that means among dragons?"

"What are you talking about?"

"When you bend your throat and bare your neck to me?"

"It means I want you to kiss it."

He chuckled and pressed a chaste kiss to my sensitive skin. I shivered.

"It means you're submitting to me. That you're offering yourself to me." He pressed his now hard cock against my bare backside. "Are you offering yourself to me, Malina?"

"You'll take me anyway," I snapped back, arching my back and rubbing my bottom against his hardness.

He hissed in a breath, his hand on my stomach rising to cup my breast. He rolled and pinched my nipple till I moaned.

"Tell me you're giving yourself to me," he demanded, pressing soft, light kisses up and down my throat.

"Always," I breathed out softly, sincerely. "Always, Julian."

On a groan, he sank inside me, my core sensitive and raw from our rough coupling before. He seemed to know, because this time he slid inside me with gentle, grinding pumps. He massaged my breast, pinching lightly, opening his mouth with feathery brushes along my neck. Then he began murmuring sweet, insane things that had my body clamoring for more of him.

"So beautiful, my firebird." Kisses to the base of my throat where he lapped at my pulse. "I want to take you to a dark cave. Far away." Gentle, deep strokes of his cock. "Where no one can find us. Where I can keep you forever. And fuck you over and over." He pinched my nipple till I cried out at the sting, then he coasted his hand to my stomach. "I'd fill you up till you became round with my child."

"*Our* child," I corrected on a gasping breath.

A grating rumble of satisfaction vibrated from his chest. He gripped my thigh and lifted my leg. I let it drape back until my ankle wrapped behind his thigh. He slid his fingers into the slick that was left over from our first coupling.

"I want to make a mess of you," he whispered, pinching my clitoris lightly.

I jumped and whimpered, reaching back to curl my fingers into his hip.

"I want you drenched with me so every dragon knows you're mine."

Arching my back, I angled so he could go deeper. "So drown me, Julian."

He did. He drowned me in his desire, his adoration, and his love. When the tether pulled tight at the end, an overwhelming wash of that unconditional emotion poured into my body and soul. It was as real as my heart thudding erratically in my chest. It was a living, breathing entity. I was immersed, engulfed in love. And it was the finest moment of my life.

I remember weeping when we were done and his soft murmuring, soothing me with "Shh, I'm here" until I finally fell asleep.

XXVIII

JULIAN

A thunderous roar echoed from the crowds above the subterranean chamber where I stood and waited beneath the arena floor. There were men below me in the basement corridor, their hands on a giant wheel, ready to crank it and open a hatch, then raise me into the Colosseum.

I closed my eyes, trying to calm the tremor of fear that gripped me. Not at battling Ciprian, but at the dread of something I couldn't see. That this fight was bending motions out of my control, that Ciprian was becoming a problem I couldn't remove without entirely removing *him*. But if I dared to strike him dead on the arena floor, Caesar wouldn't be happy. Worse, he'd suspect and distrust me. Then it would all fall apart.

Suddenly, the floor opened up, sunlight spilling into the chamber where gladiators rose out of pits beneath the floor, like gods themselves. As I climbed the stairs, the roar of the people vibrated the air. Directly across from me, Ciprian climbed to the sand floor from another chamber.

We entered the Colosseum at the closest positions to the canopied box where the emperor and his lackeys would watch the spectacle. I didn't even glance his way, my attention solely on Ciprian.

He grinned as if he knew exactly how badly I wanted to maim and mutilate him. We were both already in half-skin, dressed in leather skirts and nothing else, our gladii in hand. His black scales shimmered beneath the noonday sun directly above us. He was smaller than me, even in half-skin, which had my dragon chuffing, ready for violence and to stomp him down.

Attendants stood not far away, near the Colosseum wall where other weapons were available for us to use. My fist squeezed the handle of my gladius, my heart desiring to stab into his chest so profoundly.

He was a threat. Not simply to me. But to Malina. Ciprian had brought her to the attention of the emperor, and now my timeline grew short. We'd have to do it soon. I had only been able to get a hasty message off to Trajan before I had to report to the arena. I'd woken late and left Malina sleeping, hoping to be home before she roused. I'd kept her up far into the night, almost to morning.

Sweet nectar of life, my Malina. My mate.

"Until one is bested or yields!" boomed Igniculus, jarring me to the present. "Not to the death, Generals."

"Of course, Caesar!" Ciprian called up to the stands.

"Julianus."

I jerked my head sharply up to him. "Yes, Caesar."

"Then you may begin!" He clapped his hands once, signaling the start.

The noble Romans, commoners, freedmen and women, and slaves filling the stands roared their excitement, thirsty for blood and violence.

So was I.

I circled him, my tail lashing the air in anticipation, my beast uncoiling from the deep. He'd been with me all night, satiating his lust for flesh, for his mate. Now it was time to satisfy our appetite for blood.

Ciprian attacked first, lunging with a hard strike of his sword. I deflected, the blade skating along mine as I pushed him back a step. Then I took my own first strike, but he was fast. As I expected. I planned to wind him, beat him down before I could draw first blood.

He spun away and swept his tail across the sand, flinging it into my face, blinding me. Before he could slash across my chest, I beat my wings and flew backward just out of reach, rubbing the gritty sand from my eyes. The crowd screamed with excitement at the near miss.

My uncle's laugh carried across the open arena. With a thrust of my wings, I leaped into the air and drove downward, toppling Ciprian to the ground. His widened eyes of surprise thrilled the dragon in me as I beat him with the hilt of my sword across the jaw. Once, twice . . . on the third, he rolled and beat his wings to escape me into the air, then landed on the opposite side with a thud and scrape of his claws in the sand.

The small trickle of red at his lip had the beast growling inside me. Complete pleasure at the sight of it. But not enough.

I charged, dodging his initial swing and managed a swipe of my blade against the bone of his wing. A satisfying crack filled the air.

"Ahhh!" cried Ciprian, blood dripping from the wound.

"Oooooo!" shouted the crowd, loving the sight.

I chuckled as I circled again, whipping my gladius playfully through the air. "That shoulder's gonna need suturing when you shift back."

"On Juno's cunt." Ciprian spat a glob of red. "I'll have your blood on the sand before we're through."

"You'll be fucking dead before we're through," I promised.

He laughed, squaring off, his shoulders hunched as he readied to attack. "Now, now, Julian. Your uncle said no killing," he taunted.

"Who said I plan to do it here and now?"

Then he lunged again. I was ready, gripping the handle of my gladius with both hands, I swung just as his blade clanged against mine. With a deft twist, I launched his sword out of his hand.

Ciprian growled in frustration and walked toward the attendants. "The trident!" he bawled.

The young man ran forward and gave him the new weapon while I marched to my own.

I waved my attendant over to bring me the three-pronged trident as well. He carried the weapon toward me, then leaped back suddenly.

With a rush of beating wings, Ciprian launched himself at me on a harsh cry, nearly stabbing me in the throat. He barely missed when I dodged right and swiped the tip of my gladius blade across the back of his thigh.

Even with scales, the sharp blade cut through the skin. Ciprian's bellowing growl echoed to the skies.

"Bastard!" he yelled, his dark snout covered in blood, then he came at me again.

The clanging of trident against sword sounded through the stadium, the crowd completely enraptured, howling and screaming for more, for blood.

The sign of my opponent heaving deep breaths, weakening, seemed to rouse the beast within me. I launched forward at the same time I beat my wings hard and thrust both feet at his chest, sending him flailing and tumbling backward.

He pushed up onto his feet, stumbled and froze, winded and breathing heavily, seeming surprised by the hard blow. It was all I needed.

I spun my body sharply and swept him to the floor with my tail. His trident went flying out of reach.

Before he could scramble for it, I was on him, my foot on his throat, my gladius poised over his heart. Suddenly, almost at once, the crowd's cries transformed from nonsensical screams into one steady chant. A mantra.

"Conqueror! Conqueror! Conqueror!" they cried.

Someone in the lower balconies shouted, "Kill him, Conqueror!"

More cries for death and the spilling of this putrid excuse for a Roman's blood. The idea sank deep. I could see it, feel the power of it. Of taking his life and ridding the world of yet another would-be tyrant.

My gaze never left Ciprian, and his never left mine while the world howled for his head. We were frozen, locked in place, waiting. My grip on my sword tightened. Sweat dripped down my red-scaled arm, glistening in the sunlight. It would be so easy to end him, end the threat to Malina.

I was going to kill him.

The fact that Caesar might execute me for disobeying a direct command didn't seem to matter. The growling beast that lived inside me crawled up, filling me with the hard desire to be done with this pathetic rival once and for all.

The shouts grew louder. I lifted my head to look at the Roman people, and a bone-deep chill burrowed to my bones. I could rule these people. I could very well become the Roman emperor they'd always needed.

I gazed back down at Ciprian, his throat still under my foot, and bent over him. Ciprian struggled beneath my weight but couldn't get free. I grinned as I tightened my grip on my gladius, then—

No, Julian.

A tingling through my veins and her voice in my mind made me halt.

Don't do it.

Malina.

I jerked my head toward the crowds. She was here somewhere.

Suddenly, to my right there was movement. Emperor Igniculus

stood from his throne beneath the canopy and stepped to the edge of the box. He raised his hand high. As if he'd pulled a garrote tight around their throats, the crowd silenced at once.

"Well done, Julianus! A true son of the Ignis dragon!"

There was a clamor of applause and cheers that died quickly.

"Now you've tasted each other's blood. It is done!"

There was steel and violence in his voice. It did the job. I removed my foot from Ciprian's throat and stepped aside. Ciprian instantly stumbled to his feet, obviously wanting to come at me again.

"Come forward, Generals," called Igniculus.

Chests heaving, we both walked closer to the emperor's box and stood beneath it. The sun was high and hot.

"You have both done well. And though this is a draw—"

"I bested him," I bellowed.

"I didn't yield," snapped Ciprian.

"Because I was about to slit your throat!" I glared at him.

"Enough!" Igniculus's command echoed high into the rafters.

Nothing could be heard but a whoosh of wind through the arena, Caesar's ire clear and apparent.

"That is quite enough," he said in a calmer voice, still loud enough for those patricians in the lower boxes to hear. "To appease one another, you will each forfeit property of my choosing to end this feud once and for all."

He paused, and my entire soul screamed, for I feared what was coming.

"To Julian, Ciprian will give his prized Andalusian stallion." Ciprian hissed but said nothing. "To Ciprian, Julian will give his Celtic slave girl."

I flinched, willing myself not to react. My sword hand tightened on the hilt again. To anyone else, this wouldn't be a fair trade. A slave girl wasn't as prized as an Andalusian stallion. But they didn't understand that my *slave girl* was more precious to me than my own life.

Don't, I heard her voice again, begging me, reaching through our bond.

Any rebuttal or refusal now would mean my death. And Malina needed me.

Ciprian, smiling, called up to the emperor, "Yes, Emperor! As you wish."

I remained frozen, a statue in half-beast form, as I stared up at my uncle, who waited with a grave expression for my submission.

"Yes, Emperor," I finally said in a low, clear voice. "As you wish."

While the Romans laughed and filed out of the stadium, in good spirits from the day's entertainment, I bowed to my emperor and walked away, a sickening pall blotting out all the light in my soul.

XXIX

MALINA

"No!" Julian roared. "I won't *allow* it."

I'd arrived back home only moments after him to find Julian still sweaty and bloody and furious. He wouldn't let me look at the gash on his shoulder.

"I can control him," I said for the third time. "Just like I did at the feast last night."

Finally, he stopped pacing and strode directly for me, gripping my upper arms. "You listen to me, Malina." His eyes were wild, his behavior completely uncontrolled, so unlike him. "I know what he'll do to you. I can't let that fucking happen." He hauled me close and pressed his forehead to mine, his entire body trembling. *"Gods,* I'll go mad."

"Hush, Julian." I pressed my hands to his jaw. "Listen, listen, listen." I stroked a hand over his hair. "I can manipulate his emotions to my own will. He won't hurt me. I've done it before."

Julian lifted his head and stared at me with both fear and adoration.

"How do you think I've survived all this time?" I pointed out.

"Let us just leave now," he growled low. "We can go far away where they won't find us."

"And what about your mission with Trajan? What about the people of Rome?"

He didn't answer, his jaw clenching tight.

"She's right," came a voice behind us.

I spun to find Trajan standing in the corridor leading from the back stable yard.

He stepped out of the shadows beside the atrium, the quiet trickle of the fountain seeming more ominous than tranquil at the moment.

"You have to send her," said Trajan, "or all our plans are forfeit."

Julian gripped my shoulders and pressed his chest to my back, holding on for dear life. "So easy for you to give the orders when it isn't your female to give away."

Trajan shook his head, his dark eyes sad. "No, my friend. It isn't easy at all. But think about the chain of events if you refuse to let her go. The emperor knows you are attached to her. That's the only reason he's forcing you to give her up."

Julian huffed with disgust. "Because I'm in love with a slave girl, he can't allow it. He must take her from me."

I turned quickly in his arms, placing my hands on his chest, searching his maddened expression. "You love me?"

He tore his wretched gaze from Trajan and looked down, his expression softening as he murmured, "You know I do."

I smoothed my fingertips over the frown etched in his brow. Trajan was silent for a moment, seeming to recognize that we needed it.

But then he added quietly, "Yes, Julian. He's aware you're more than attached to her."

"Because of fucking Ciprian," Julian bit out, his gaze still on me, his hands on my shoulders, his thumbs brushing the bare skin of my neck.

"Yes. Because of him. And the emperor won't allow you to fall into what he believes is an ill-fated match, like your father did."

Julian cupped my cheek. "Too late for that."

I smiled, placing my palm on the back of his hand, pressing my cheek against him.

"Julian, we are *so* close, brother."

"How close?" He finally lifted his head to look over my shoulder.

I turned to face Trajan as well.

"They want a meeting tomorrow night. *All* of them."

"Where?"

"At my grandfather's house in Vulsinii. We can't take a chance in being caught altogether. We have to gather outside of Rome."

"Then we wait till then at least," I offered, turning to face him.

"Do you have any idea what you're asking of me? To willingly put you in the hands of a monster?"

"I can handle Ciprian." I put my hand on his chest above his heart, feeling the organ beneath drumming hard and fast. "And think of it, Julian. I might even be able to help."

"That's true," added Trajan. "If she's in his house, she can get us information on his comings and goings. How to best kill him."

I glanced back, not knowing Ciprian was on their list of death. But of course he was. I looked back at Julian.

"I can even do the deed," I offered.

He cupped my face, his lip quirking in a sad smile. "There goes my firebird again. Barreling toward danger without a fear."

I was riddled with fear, but I wouldn't admit that to him. It would only make this worse.

Ruskus shuffled into the atrium. "Dominus. Ciprian's men are here with the stallion," he said somberly, his gaze solemn on me. "For the trade."

Julian stiffened and clamped his jaw. "For the trade," he grated, fury lacing every word.

"It will be all right." I stepped away but he hauled me against him, crushing me into his embrace.

"If anything happens, you escape and come to me," he whispered, then he turned my face up toward him and kissed me.

Shocked, I froze, for we were in the full presence of Trajan and Ruskus. Then Julian coaxed my mouth open and I forgot everything but him. For a few brief seconds, it was only Julian and me, my deep, sweet love.

When he clutched me harder, closer, I realized I would have to be the one to sever this. There was no way he could. I pushed away, breaking the kiss.

"Don't worry."

He lifted a shaking hand and cupped my cheek and whispered in a heartbreaking rasp, "By the gods, he'd better not hurt you."

"I will keep him from it." I lifted his large hand and pressed a kiss into his palm. "I promise."

Then I turned and followed Ruskus out toward the front entrance to the street. Julian didn't follow and I was glad of it. I couldn't bear to have him watch me being taken away.

As I crossed the foyer, Kara was standing in an alcove, watching, solemn-faced.

I noticed Ivo standing behind her and Stefanos beside him, tears pouring silently down his face. Forcing a smile on my face, I told them all, "Julian will find a way. Don't worry."

"You just watch yourself, girl," said Kara, her usual scowl on her face but etched with concern.

"I will."

I hurried away and out the final corridor onto the street that wound along the finest houses of Palatine Hill. The men waiting for me were the ones I'd cursed, the ones who'd recognized Stefanos for what he was. A pang of fear gripped me hard, but Ciprian's men, including the big, bearded one who'd manhandled me, seemed almost scared as he handed the reins of the stallion to Ruskus.

"Ivo!" he yelled out.

Ivo hurried out and took the reins, giving me a parting sad smile before he took the horse around to the alley leading into the stable yard.

"This way, girl," said the bearded one, not touching me this time, and then turned downhill.

The other followed behind as I was escorted to my new home. I walked away with my head high and the sound of something shattering in the house and the sickening roar of an enraged dragon echoing to the skies.

MALINA

"You'll have to take that off," the blond-haired girl told me, pointing to my slave collar with Julian's name on it.

Her name was Rhea. She said she'd been sold at a very young age and didn't know where she came from originally, though she thought she looked like many Celts she'd met. She was extremely talkative.

I removed the collar but when Rhea reached out to take it from me, I jerked it back and pressed it to my chest. "I'll keep it."

She frowned, then shrugged. "If you want. But don't let dominus see it. He's very possessive of his slaves." Then she added sincerely, "He'll take it from you if he sees it."

I didn't bother telling her that I was not his slave, nor would I ever be any man's property again. I might be in this infernal house by force, but I had a mission of my own. To find the easiest way to kill Ciprian Seneca.

Staring down at Julian's name on the tin plate of my collar, I said, "I dare him to even try."

She giggled. "Feisty little firebird, aren't you?"

"What?"

"Oh, I meant no offense."

"No, why did you call me firebird?" I'd wondered for so long and Julian never bothered to tell me.

She shrugged. "It's just an expression. From that story about Aurelia. The gold dragon."

"I don't know the story."

"How do you not? It's a common one."

"I'm from Dacia, not Rome."

Rhea frowned. "Of course." She walked to the small chest at the foot of what was my new bed and opened it. "It's actually a wonderfully tragic romance."

"Will you tell it to me?"

Rhea smiled, making her pretty face even prettier. I noted the faint bruises on her wrists as she took out a black tunic from the trunk. It was the same kind she was wearing, which was tied with a length of leather as a belt. The material was thin and transparent, her body completely visible beneath it.

"Here, go change into this. Dominus likes us all wearing his color."

Grinding my teeth, I turned around and began to change, cringing that I would have to wear such a thing. There was no changing screen for privacy. The slave quarters were smaller, darker, and colder, without any windows, vastly different from those in Julian's house.

"Tell me the story," I urged her again.

"Aurelia was the last female golden dragon. She lived centuries ago. She was the only daughter, and only child, of the most prominent family in Rome. Because she was a gold dragon, the last childbearing female of her kind, the emperor wanted her as his wife."

"Which emperor?"

"Crusus the Red was his name. The problem was that Aurelia was a defiant child. She was well-known for being hotheaded and reckless. Her father had raised her with the independent will of a son. Furthermore, Aurelia was in love with another. A lesser nobleman's son. When her father told her she would marry the emperor, she refused."

"I suppose that didn't go over well with the emperor," I said, turning back to her while I folded my old tunic and placed it in the trunk on top of my collar necklace.

"Not at all." Rhea laughed. "She told her father she'd like to see them try to force her to marry the brute of an emperor. She said she'd die before she let him take her. When news of her refusal came to Crusus, he immediately gathered his praetorians and marched to her home, intent on dragging her back to the palace by force."

I sat on the stiff mattress and Rhea sat beside me, her eyes alight with excitement in telling the tale.

"So *then*," she said dramatically, "they stormed into her home and Aurelia fled into their outer courtyard, where she shifted into her golden dragon. She roared to the sky and took flight. Well, of course the praetorians and the emperor also shifted and chased after her."

"And they caught her?"

Rhea grinned. "No. They did not. She was so fast that she'd made it over the lands of Hispania before they finally began to catch up to her."

Rhea's expression turned somewhat sad.

"Aurelia knew she wouldn't be able to outfly them for long, and she refused to marry any other but her true love. She also knew the emperor would kill her lover the moment they dragged her back to Rome. So she allowed them to draw close. One of the praetorians blew fire to warn her to stop. That was what Aurelia had wanted. She sucked up his fire into her mouth and swallowed it."

"What?" I was confused. "But how?"

"She was a *golden* dragon."

"What does that mean?"

"Golden dragons had the ability to amplify fire. Suck it into themselves and expel ten times more. They could create an *explosion* of fire."

"So she was able to burn them and get away?"

Rhea shook her head. "Only the one. The emperor held back and waited. So she did the only thing she could. She slowed her flight and bared her neck for him, showing she was submitting. And when the emperor took her bait, latching onto her with his claws and clasping his jaws at her throat mid-air, she amplified all the fire burning inside her and burst her own body into flames."

I flinched, not prepared for that ending.

"She fell to her death, but she took the emperor with her, clutched in her claws. So that's where the term firebird comes from."

"Well, I don't have the ability to burn anyone to death. And I thank you for the compliment." My mind wandered to Julian for the hundredth time since I'd arrived at this new home, remembering the first time he called me firebird back in Dacia. I smiled at the thought of being compared to Aurelia, the golden dragon.

Rhea laughed. "You've got that same bold spirit though. Only"—she paused, her brow pinched, and placed a hand on my arm—"be careful around master."

I gestured toward the bruises on her wrists. "Does he hurt you often?"

"Oh, not really." She laughed while tenderly touching a bruise. "Just hold still when he's rutting on you. He usually only gets violent when you fight him."

"You fight him?"

"Me? Gods, never." She shook her head.

And yet she still had bruises from his rough handling. My heart sank into despair at this pit of hell I'd been dropped into. Ciprian truly was the epitome of cruelty and brutality, which made me even more determined to find a way to kill him.

"Rhea," said a large, burly man also wearing one of Ciprian's collars. "Dominus wants you and the new girl to serve him dinner tonight."

Rhea sobered instantly, her smile vanishing. "Yes, Adriano."

"Cook will have dinner ready in an hour."

My stomach rolled with dread. As much courage as I'd had coming here, it seemed to all fly away at that foreboding summons. But I'd sworn to Julian that I'd take care of myself, and so I must.

"Don't worry," Rhea assured me, taking my hand. "He won't beat you unless you are disobedient. So"—she shrugged—"just obey his orders and all will be well." She laughed but not nearly as heartily as before. "Don't be the firebird tonight, Malina."

I smiled back, knowing full well there was no way I could be anything but.

✳   ✳   ✳

"Stand over here and let me get a good look at you."

Ciprian's voice skated across my skin like a slithering snake, raising gooseflesh on my arms. I set the tray of roasted meat and vegetables on the low table in front of his chaise, then stood behind it, wanting the table between us.

I was beyond pleased to see his entire shoulder wrapped in a bandage and another around his middle. He was shirtless due to his many gauze wrappings on his upper body and wore only a black skirt ending above his knees. His left eye was swollen and purpling, and there was another cut that ran from his jaw to his neck. Julian must've barely skated his blade, Ciprian escaping a fatal blow there.

While I took in all of the damage my mate had done to him, he perused my face and body at length, knowing he could fully inspect my naked form through the sheer tunic I was forced to wear. It was indecent, and exactly what I'd expect from a man like him.

I held my chin high and stared directly at him, not letting him see that I was in any way uncomfortable in my new garb.

"Yes," he said at length, "I can see what Julianus is so bothered about. But tell me, witch."

He paused while Rhea poured his wine, then she stood against the back wall of his smallish parlor for dining. His house was not nearly the palatial splendor of Julian's—no marble floors or sculptures, nor the wide atrium filled with plants and a fountain. His home was at the foot of Palatine Hill, but still upon it, marking him a patrician. Yet it was obvious his family wasn't the level of aristocrat as Julian. Not nearly so.

It all made me wonder how he was in such good favor with the emperor, who seemed to only delight in the company of the wealthiest, oldest families of Rome. Ciprian's might be an old, aristocratic family, but they were certainly not the wealthiest.

"Tell me." Ciprian grinned and stared like the demonic fiend he was. "How did you help the Celts defeat Bastius three times before Julianus showed up and took care of business?"

"I don't know what you mean. How could a mere woman help warriors in battle?"

I kept my expression tightly blank, showing no emotion whatsoever.

He chuckled and sipped his wine. "A mere woman cannot. But a *witch* can."

"And what do you mean by a witch? Do you believe I enchanted the Romans my Celtic clansmen fought?"

"It was said you used some kind of witchcraft against them, made men abandon their legion and the battle itself. But strangely, no one who was there can remember anything at all."

"And how would I have such a gift to persuade warriors away from the field?"

"Only a witch could. One who's been touched by the goddess Minerva. Who's been given evil powers to use against men."

"I am not Roman, nor am I Celtic. I am Dacian, and we do not worship your gods." That was a lie since I'd already worshipped at Proserpina's altar, praying for the souls of my sisters, Enid, and family. "Why would Minerva give me such a gift? I'm not Roman."

"Minerva is a spiteful goddess," he said in a low, angry tone. "She thinks herself better than her father, Jupiter, and her uncles, Neptune and Pluto, who declare the rightful order."

"The rightful order of what, dominus?" I asked, playing the curious, submissive slave.

He smiled and shifted, placing his hand over his crotch and fondling himself. "Of your place. Minerva would give her powers to any she thought could use it against mankind. Like she did with Medusa."

A tremble of awareness sent a spray of chills down my back. I knew the story of Medusa. Bunica had told the tale to me and my sisters countless times. I never understood why she was so fascinated with a Roman story until I began to feel the power taking root inside my mind and soul. Until that first time I'd reached out with my gift and latched onto my mother when she mourned her father's death, and I had tethered to her for the first time to stop her pain. It was instinct. I didn't understand my gift, but I felt it living and breathing deep inside my flesh and bones.

And when Bunica retold the terrible story of Medusa and Minerva's gifts after that, I understood the intense look in my grandmother's brown eyes and the reason why she reminded us of the story over and over again. Minerva had bestowed these gifts on us. And now I was the only one left to use them.

"So answer me this, Malina." Ciprian's grating voice brought me back to the present. "Are you a witch?"

"Of course not, dominus," I answered easily. But I *was* a woman filled with a powerful mysticism, and I planned to use it on him with a vengeance.

He drank more wine, not touching his food, his eyes on me narrowing. "What does Julian say about me?"

"Pardon, dominus?"

"Don't play coy. I know he talks about me." He grinned as if proud of the fact. "And men like to talk after a good fuck. What's he said?"

I clamped my jaw tight, trying not to answer, but his insinuation that I was nothing more than a body to be used by Julian stoked my ire. We were so much more than he could ever imagine, this pale shadow of a man next to Julian.

"He says that you are arrogant. That you try to climb above your station to be close to the emperor and that you'll never replace him because his blood is from the Dakkia family." I paused while Rhea gasped. "And your blood isn't equal to his so you never will be good enough to sit upon the higher seats of Roman aristocracy."

He stared, seething, while his face mottled red with splotches from both drink and anger.

"Sharp little tongue you've got," he snapped. "I'm going to put it to better use."

He gulped down the rest of his wine and banged the goblet on the table, then he began unbuckling the belt at his waist and unwrapping the front flap of his skirt.

"Rhea!" he bellowed, though she was standing right behind me. "Come suck my cock. Let's show the new girl how I like it done. Then we'll give her a turn."

Fury shot through my frame. This disgusting piece of filth. He was going to put me in my place, but not before he degraded Rhea first right in front of me.

Rhea was already hurrying to kneel before him at the chaise. How many times had he made her do this, I wondered for a split second before I summoned my *witchcraft,* as Ciprian had called it.

With a violent snap, I latched onto his essence. Like last night, his spirit was cold and writhing and putrid beneath my tether, but I locked on hard all the same, coiling my power line around him. Tonight, I didn't want to put him to sleep. I wanted him in *pain*. Excruciating pain.

He had his hand on Rhea's head while she fumbled to open his skirt flap. He pushed her down toward his erection. "That's right. Let's show her how it's done."

Then he looked up at me, grinning.

I'd never done this before, but I instinctually sought the most roiling, nauseating, foul emotion I could muster, then I shot it like a poisoned dart through the bond.

One second, he was smiling, gloating at the power he had over a helpless girl like Rhea, then his face went ghostly pale and he shot upright, shoving Rhea away. He vomited a stream of red all over himself—the wine he'd been imbibing all night, it seemed. For there was quite a lot of it.

"Pluto's cock!" he gasped, choking, then he lurched forward onto his knees next to the chaise, heaving and vomiting onto the floor.

Rhea had screamed, jumped to her feet, and scrambled away. But I stood perfectly still and watched the master of the house expel his entire stomach until he had bile dripping disgustingly from his chin. Other slaves ran into the room.

"Dominus! Let me help you!" The big one who'd summoned us to dinner was there on the floor, helping him up and hauling him away, all while Ciprian dry heaved and moaned in agony, cursing in between.

When Ciprian's body slave had gotten him out of the room, and I presume into his bedchamber, we could still hear him crying out and moaning in torment.

"What happened?" yelled the cook, a thick woman, standing in the opposite doorway. "What food made him sick?" She wrung her hands, expression fearful.

"He didn't eat anything," I replied calmly. "He only drank the wine. Could be something the physician gave him?"

The cook frowned and nodded. "Could be. The physician gave me something to put in his willow bark tea for pain." Then she hurried back toward the kitchen, mumbling, "He'll need a sleeping draught."

I turned to Rhea, whose mouth gaped and eyes were wide with shock. "Do you think he was poisoned?" she whispered.

"No," I answered.

Rhea blinked. "I suppose we better clean this up."

We both stared down at the disgusting mess he'd left behind. "Much nicer job than sucking his cock," I said dryly.

Rhea burst into laughter, then covered her mouth. "Yes," she whispered, "I much prefer cleaning that than servicing him."

"Come on. Let's get started, then we can go to bed."

She stared down the hallway, eyes widening with distress. "Do you think he will come back after . . . ?"

Another loud moan echoed through the house.

"No. He's done for the night. And Cook is making him a sleeping draught." I held on to the tether, though it was loosening now that he'd left my presence. I'd never been able to hold on to someone for long outside of my sight. "Let's clean up and go to bed."

It was foul work, but I smiled the whole time. When we passed over the floors with soapy water a second time, my arms buckled and I nearly banged my head on the stone floor.

"Are you all right?" asked Rhea.

"Just tired." My body was weak from the energy I'd used on Ciprian. I hadn't been this exhausted from using my magic since I'd been with the Celts, tethering to the Roman soldiers in Legatus Bastius's legion.

Cook had given Ciprian the draught while we cleaned, but I'd held on to my tether to him, still worried he'd somehow recover and come after me and Rhea again. It had entirely drained me.

"Come," said Rhea, helping me to my feet. "It's time for bed."

I didn't argue as she dumped our rags in the bucket and carried it with us back to our quarters. We washed in her bedchamber, the one I was meant to share with her since there were no other available ones.

Wearied, I climbed into her small bed next to her, pulling the covers under my chin as I lay on my side, watching the open doorway. There were no doors on the servants' bedchambers. Apparently, Ciprian didn't think slaves needed privacy so he refused to give them doors. One more indignation.

Rhea faced the other way but her body heat warmed me. It was a small comfort in this desolate place.

"Does he ever seek you out in the daytime?" I asked, afraid he might come back in the morning.

"No," she answered sleepily, as if it was of no consequence. "He is busy with his new soldiers and officers all day now. He is preparing for his first campaign, whenever the emperor tells him where he is to go."

I exhaled a small sigh of relief, finally letting go of the tether I'd kept around Ciprian's dark soul. A well of release washed through me at being free of him. I fell instantly into a deep sleep.

That night, I fell into a vivid dream. A nightmare.

I flew through the night sky, my arms spread wide, a flowing white gown billowing at my ankles. Then a terrifying roar startled me, causing me to spin mid-air. It was Ciprian in dragon form, black scales shining beneath the moonlight. His red eyes glowed and he snapped his jaws as he barreled closer. I floated and waited for him.

When he opened his jaws to eat me, I wrapped my arms around his snout, and my tether—a tangible golden rope—burst from my chest and coiled around his legs and wings, binding him tight. I stared into one of his gleaming red eyes and whispered, "Fire."

Then we were diving down, the stars falling with us, streaming like burning souls toward the earth. Before we hit the ground, I burst into flames, and I heard Julian screaming my name.

JULIAN

Gaius's home in Vulsinii stood on a small cliff overlooking a vast lake, which now glistened under the moonlight. This home had been in his family for over a century.

Standing on the terrace with all of our allies, I barely listened as I stared at the marble statue of the first Roman dragons cradled beneath the wing of their adoptive mother, an ancient dragon. It was set in the inverted curve of a wall, a fountain cascading around them, turquoise tiles lining the rim.

History never tells us what happened to the dragons of old, the ones who were only beasts without the gift of transformation. They simply disappeared into obscurity when dragon skin-shifters began to populate and rule the world. I wondered if the first Romans killed them off, not wanting any competition for dominance over the land. It wouldn't surprise me.

"Yes, it's a risk we all take. If you did not think there was a possibility that this all might end with your deaths, then why are you even here?" Gaius snapped at Appius, an older, dignified senator of the Sapphirus line. He also happened to be Gaius's cousin.

"I am well aware of the risk of death," Appius stated in a deep-barreled voice, the kind I imagined he used on the senate house floor. "I merely want to debate if the risk is worth it. Will we all die for naught? Or do we have a plan put forth that is most likely to succeed?"

A round of bickering hummed through the dozen men gathered on the terrace. Trajan leaned against a gold-painted column with his arms crossed, scowling.

The men gathered were a mixed lot of senators and soldiers. Men we collected into our fold over careful scrutiny and time and who Gaius, Trajan, or myself had all personally witnessed their quiet but obvious disdain for the emperor and his regime. They were cautiously amassed. Some of their hatred for Caesar stemmed from his laws stifling their own climb to power and to better fortune. A few joined us out of fear of the violent world Caesar was creating and that it could get worse. And there were a few who also longed for a just, fair, and prosperous Rome without the brutality Caesar embodied.

I stepped forward and raised my hand, knowing all the motivations in the hearts of these men. Almost at once, there was silence. I lowered my hand and paused before I spoke.

"The gods gifted us with our power to transform into a creature who could reign over earth and sky. And what have we done with that gift?"

I stared at each of the very powerful men standing before me.

"We've burned and pillaged and conquered. We've enslaved and killed and gorged ourselves on the misery of others, of those too helpless to defend themselves against the strength of dragons."

The silence thickened with the weight of my words.

"With the might of our power, we have become more monster than man. We have glutted ourselves on greed and blood. And the time to change who we have become is *now*," I bellowed, the last word echoing into the night.

"You all may think my uncle cannot delve deeper into depravity or that he cannot sink Rome into a pit as dark as Tartarus itself, but you are mistaken," I practically whispered, emotion choking my voice. "Igniculus is no god. Nor is he gifted by them. He is *cursed*. A twisted, malformed creature who drags our people deeper into the hell he has created."

I felt my own dragon waking and shining behind my eyes.

"Have you not all heard, and some of you here seen with your own eyes, Caesar's most recent humiliation? That he took Otho's new bride in front of all the nobles of Rome? Have you not witnessed yourself in recent years, for those who were there, how he raped other Romans' wives and daughters?"

I held my fingers up one at a time as I named them.

"Clarissa Media Nocte Isthmus. Leta Chrysocolla Evander. Phaedra Amethystus Opius. Sylva Sapphirus Thetis."

I glanced toward Gaius on the last. She was the daughter of his cousin, now a ghost of the proud woman she was.

"And do not forget that Leta took her own life rather than live with the violation done to her. Now these women, *Roman* women, must hide themselves in shame and fear that he may choose them again for his sport or his manipulative games to control us."

I scoffed and looked from man to man, ensuring they were listening. They were.

"Trust me, gentlemen, he's not simply putting the men in place who have offended them with these tactics. He's making sure each and every one of you know that he can destroy you by destroying those you love if you do not do *exactly* what he wants."

I paused and held Horatius's hard gaze. He was the only Griseo in the senate, a tribune elected by the people because of his renown in the gladiator arenas. He would've heard of but not seen these atrocities. But he'd experienced others.

"And this is how he treats *nobles*. Let us not forget the barbarity with which he treats the plebeians and the slaves."

My heart lurched at the thought of Malina, but I kept my focus.

"I have a story to tell you. The other day when I met with Trajan and Gaius in the forum, I noticed a man in half-skin staked to a wall. Dead." I glanced at Trajan, who frowned, for I hadn't yet told him of my discovery. "I put my man Koska to work. You may know he helps me on war campaigns, but he's also a wealth of information and knows how to find it."

I'd let my voice even out and lower to a calm timbre. Gaius stepped forward, his face etched with concern.

"The man, a dragon of the Amethystus house, who'd been killed for his crime in half-skin, had apparently fallen for the butcher's daughter. She was a plebeian and not a noble. He decided to defy Caesar's law that nobles must not marry outside their class and secretly married her anyway. Not only that but he also got his young wife with child. This was reported to his legatus, General Sabinus."

I stepped closer to them, hands clasped at my back.

"His crimes of marrying the woman he loved from a lower class and getting her with child may have been forgiven if he'd promised to kill the child at birth or send it to the faraway gladiator pits on the other side of the empire and divorce his young bride quietly. But this man did something worse."

"He planned a coup," said Appius, his voice rusty with emotion.

I nodded to him. "He did. He confided in his brothers, the soldiers he was closest to in his regiment under General Sabinus. But one of them lost his courage and reported it to Sabinus, and he took no time to tell Caesar, who gave the order to stake the man. All of his soldier brothers were killed too and dumped in the Tiber River, no rites or gods' blessings for any of them."

"His name was Vincentus. I would honor him now if only in a silent prayer that his soul finds its way to the underworld."

Thick silence fell over us all, only the light trickle of the fountain making any sound. As for me, I did send a prayer to the gods for Vincentus and his wife. It was Horatius who spoke up first.

"What happened to his pregnant wife?"

I turned to him. "She took her own life with her husband's gladius."

Someone cursed and another hissed at the pity of it.

"Hear me now, gentlemen. This is only one instance, and I haven't even mentioned his increasing taxes he's enforced on nobles and merchants alike. If you believe his orgies and his carnivorous rites are all he is capable of, you are wrong. If you believe the laws he's enacted with his puppets, the consuls, have put Rome in a sad state, I promise you now they are only a prelude of what is to come. Stories like those of Vincentus will be commonplace by the time my uncle is done. But I for one would rather go the way of Vincentus than to watch us continue to be crushed and choked in the tyrant's fist."

For a solid minute, no one spoke as they let my decree sink in. Because I knew with all my heart that my uncle was just getting started. Debauchery and violence and degradation were what made him happiest. He wouldn't stop until he was crammed fat with it all. And Rome would be a hell on earth.

Appius was the first to speak. "Then we will be the liberators of Rome." He turned to look at his fellow senators, his deep voice resonating across the terrace. "We will take the risk and sacrifice our lives if necessary."

"Hear, hear!" called Horatius. Though a senator, he was built tall and strong, and I was glad to have him on our side.

Others joined in, nodding and agreeing with "hear, hear."

Gaius beamed at me with pride, and I was struck for a moment with a memory of my father when he would look at me that way. A maudlin thread tightened around my gut with my realization that I had no family left. Except Malina.

Malina. My heart ached and cracked at the thought of her now.

Gods, protect her.

Gaius raised his hand for quiet. "Then we are agreed. When Legatus Drussus returns from his campaign, we will strike immediately."

That caught my attention. "But Drussus could be gone for *weeks.*"

"Our intelligence has told us he is near an end," added Gaius. "Two weeks at the most. Possibly three."

"Three . . . *weeks?*" My voice had dropped deeper with the dragon.

Trajan stepped forward from where he'd been reclining. "Julian, you know that Drussus is the emperor's strongest general other than you, and possibly Sabinus, and with his blood of the Ignis line, he would certainly believe he has rights to the throne if we assassinate Igniculus while he's away. We can't allow him to live, and the assassinations must all be done at once, so no one can flee and hide and then return with an army."

All of this I knew. I wasn't a fool. But my dragon and my heart and my soul rebelled at the idea of Malina being in danger for three more weeks.

"Then Ciprian must fall to some untimely, accidental death," I added. "Immediately."

Ciprian was one of many on our targeted list who would all die in the same night. But I couldn't wait for Drussus to return before taking him out.

"The emperor will know it's you, Julian," said Trajan.

"Then we must devise a way that it couldn't possibly have been me who is responsible."

"I don't understand," said Horatius. "Why must Ciprian die now?"

Everyone here had heard, or most likely had witnessed, when the emperor handed over Malina into Ciprian's possession at the Colosseum. But none of them except Trajan understood her importance to me. And I wasn't going to bury or hide my love for Malina like a shame.

"Because Ciprian holds my dragon's mate in his home. *My* mate."

They froze and stared in shock, for it was rare a dragon would choose a human as a mate. Maybe it was my father's blood coursing through me. His dragon had also chosen a human as his god-given mate. Or perhaps it was simply the gods righting the wrongs, giving me a powerful, magnificent female to be my partner against the demons of this world. I didn't know. And I didn't care. All I knew was that it was right and true.

"Are you sure?" asked Gaius, unease etched into his brow.

"I am certain Malina has been anointed as mine by the gods. On Jupiter's stone, I swear it."

A cool breeze wafted over the terrace from the water. It should've calmed me, given me some relief on this hot and oppressive night. But nothing would ease me or my mind until I had Malina safely back in my arms.

"It's too risky," said Appius. "It could alarm Caesar."

"He's right," Gaius said to me. "How can we possibly do this when we're so close to success?"

Holding my temper while my dragon growled in my belly, I said, "I understand if none of you want part in this. But there is no way in this fucking world that I'm leaving her in Ciprian's home for three more weeks. My dragon won't stand for it. If you've had a mate, then you understand what I'm telling you."

Gaius flinched, for he had a long marriage with his true god-given mate and he understood. They all understood that when the dragon takes hold, there is no stopping him.

"My house is on the same street as his," said Horatius. "My slave girl goes to market with one of his every week. Perhaps we can slip him a poison."

"A poison would be too obvious," I said. "It needs to be something else."

"I could help," said Agrippa, a distinguished senator from the Media Nocte line. He was a somber dragon who wore a close-cropped beard and a scowl most of the time. "I hold no love for my cousin Ciprian. My son is his new prefect and might be able to get him where we need him for an untimely accident."

To my great relief, the conversation fell into the many accidents Ciprian might encounter in the city—a loaded cart of grain crushes him when a wheel breaks, an angry vendor shifts into half-skin as he passes by and accidentally claws his throat, or a street fight runs amok where he's caught in the mayhem and stabbed through the heart. The last was my favorite.

While the senators argued over what was best, I pulled Trajan to the side.

"I need one of your farthest homes to hide Malina once Ciprian is dead."

He nodded. "And you shall have it."

"Thank you, brother. When Ciprian is dead, I'll fly her there, then return to Rome."

"You can't both be missing when word reaches Igniculus that Ciprian is dead. He'll suspect you first."

"I know. Which is why when we do the deed, we'll have to keep Ciprian's death a secret for at least a day."

"I know plebs in the city who are loyal to me, one in particular," added Trajan thoughtfully. "We can have the 'accident' take place near her shop and hide the body there until the next day." Trajan eyed me. "You won't have time to linger with her. You'll have to return immediately."

I smiled for the first time since she'd been taken from my home. "Don't worry." I squeezed him on the shoulder. "If I can get her safely out of Rome, I will happily return to kill my uncle."

The night droned on with a little wine and food and more debate. We finally decided on the street fight run amok to do Ciprian in. Horatius said his two sons would gladly do the deed, while Agrippa's would be sure to get him at the right place at the right time. Horatio's sons would dress like plebs and blend into the crowd and take care of it quickly.

We knew Ciprian's route to the training yards every day, so we'd find the most secluded spot along the way. As long as Agrippa's son got him there when we needed him, it would work. And we'd do it in three days' time.

"Thank you," I said to them all before we began to break apart and ready ourselves to return to Rome.

"I'll return to the city tomorrow," Trajan told me on the terrace before I left. "Grandfather wants me to help solidify the details."

"Of course. I'll see you back in Rome."

I bid farewell to my fellow allies before I shifted on the lower terrace, then flew home. All of us planned to leave at staggered times to make it back to the city of Rome under the cover of night separately.

It wasn't uncommon for a dragon to fly out of his home at night in defiance of Igniculus's laws that no one but military men could shift inside the city. Sometimes, a dragon merely wanted out of the man, to soar the night skies. One would be overlooked. But a dozen of us flying back at the same time would certainly be noticed. As it was, we'd all planned ahead and would land and shift outside the city and make our way back on foot or horse.

My flight wasn't a relief as it usually was. Flying was often a soothing balm to my senses and my troubled spirit, but not tonight. By the time I landed in the field, found Volkan tied to the tree where I'd left him in the shadows, and returned home, I was more restless than ever.

My mind wouldn't stop repeating the horrific things that might be taking place back in Ciprian's home. But I promised Malina I would trust her, that she could take care of herself. It was only that I knew him for the true monster he was. He also wasn't an idiot. I worried that he might catch on to her.

When I trotted into the stable yard, Ivo was there and took Volkan for me.

"Thank you, Ivo."

I stalked through the quiet house and made my way to my bedroom. Without washing the dirt off my skin, I fell into my bed and groaned with deep grief. Her scent. It was everywhere from the night before.

The memory tortured me into a fitful sleep. Her silken skin, her soft mouth, her drugging scent, and sweet affection drowned me in agonizing ecstasy as I cried out her name over and over again. But she never answered.

XXXII

MALINA

"Mina . . ."

I awoke with a start, sweating through my tunic to the sheets. In that ethereal space between asleep and awake, I swear I heard my bunica whispering.

Heart pounding, I stared around the room, half expecting to see her standing in the doorway. But then nothing, only the faint feeling of dread, of foreboding.

Shoving off the covers, I hurried to the water basin and splashed water on my face.

"Are you all right?" asked Rhea, blinking her eyes sleepily.

The one consolation for the open doorway in a windowless room was that morning light filtered in and lit the room well enough to see.

"Rhea, would it be possible to visit a temple today? I know we'll have chores, but does Ciprian allow us to go out?"

She sat up, tucking her fine blond hair behind her ear. "It's market day so Cook will send us to fetch fruit and vegetables. I'm sure I can get Doro to let us." She shrugged. "He likes me."

I didn't know which one Doro was, but I trusted Rhea. Out of desperation, I had to trust someone.

"Which temple do you need to visit?" she asked.

My entire body trembled with the need and the knowing. "Minerva."

Her brows lifted as she stood from the bed and remade the covers neatly. "Minerva is a powerful goddess. What favor do you need of her?"

I bit my lip, then said, "I can't tell you."

I didn't trust her *that* much. But Rhea seemed to take no offense when she turned to me, wearing a soft expression. "Is it a serious favor?" She frowned when she caught sight of my trembling.

"Very," I admitted.

She stepped closer and eyed the doorway before she grabbed me by the shoulders and whispered, "Then we'll need dragon skin."

Blinking, I asked, "What?"

She hugged me tight and tried to calm me with a brush of her hand on my spine. "I can see that you need something more than a mere favor from the goddess. You need a miracle. So you'll need dragon skin."

I still didn't quite understand, so she explained it to me. I hugged her back and kissed her on the cheek, which made her laugh.

"Hurry! If we leave early, we can be done with our shopping and at the temple by noon."

Then she urged me to get changed into a fresh tunic to wear out of doors. Thankfully, Ciprian allowed his slave women to wear something more modest on the streets. Probably only to keep others from trying to touch or take his possessions. But I was glad of the small reprieve.

Doro wasn't one of the slaves who'd accosted me on the street with the bearded one that day with Stefanos and Ivo. I hadn't seen much of him or the others I'd cursed since I'd arrived. They were probably still terrified of me, witch that I was.

Doro was tall and wide as an ox, but he had a soft, tender look for Rhea. I noticed that she covertly touched her fingers to the back of his hand as she passed him with her basket. She said that Doro liked her, but I got a quick sense that she liked him as well. They obviously had to keep that a secret from their master.

"Time to go, Doro."

"Yes, Rhea."

"Watch them carefully," said Cook.

"I will." Doro followed us out onto the street.

When I turned toward the direction of the forum, Rhea looped her arm through mine and turned us in the opposite direction. "No, this way."

"Where are we going?"

"To the Aventine. That's where I get the best bargains." She glanced sweetly back at Doro, who walked in our wake. "Besides, that's where all the plebs live. The free folk. I like walking through their neighborhood and pretending I'm one of them."

"That is a nice fantasy."

She whispered, "One day, I want to live there and actually *be* one of them."

"How could that happen?"

She simply shrugged, but it seemed Rhea wasn't without a bit of plotting and dreams of her own. I couldn't imagine her planning to run away. The punishment if caught was torture and death. But I wasn't about to discourage Rhea or destroy whatever hopes she had for a happier future. After all, I knew for a fact that Ciprian would be dead soon.

"Well," I whispered back, "you never know what could happen."

She gave me a questioning look, then simply laughed. "Come on. I'm going to show you where to find the juiciest peaches in Rome."

"Peaches? That's quite a delicacy."

"There's an old lady whose son has an orchard in the country. He provides her the best fruit you could imagine. Doro and I always sneak one and share it on the way home."

We spent the next two hours popping into one shop, then another. I watched Rhea haggle with a toughness I didn't know was in her. She seemed at home among the streets of the Aventine where life was busy and bustling and loud.

Women laundered clothes at the public fountain while they fussed at young children not to stray too far. Men hauled carts of all kinds of wares—grain, carpets, clay oil lamps and pots. Two young boys herded five goats right down the middle of the street. The clatter of carts, the clopping of hooves, and the shouting of vendors filled the busy morning.

Finally, we finished. Doro carried the sack of leeks, turnips, parsnips, cabbage, and endives. Rhea and I each carried a satchel of fruit.

"This way," she told me as we took a narrow street off the wider one we'd been traveling most of the day.

Doro caught up to Rhea and pulled her to a stop by the arm. "Where are we going?"

"To Euphemia's. Malina needs something important," she said pleadingly. "Then a quick stop at the Temple of Minerva. It's on the way home anyway."

Doro peered down, frowning, then eyed me with skepticism.

"Doro." Rhea clutched a hand in his homespun tunic. "Please. It's for our new friend."

My heart cracked at her declaration. Not "the new slave girl" but "our friend." How Rhea could shine so bright and be so kind living in the devil's house, I'd never know. But I admired her for it.

Finally, Doro nodded, then we were off again. Rhea took two more turns down narrow alleys until we seemed far away from the hustle and bustle of the Aventine. We passed a brothel with giant phalluses painted over the door. A woman's laughter floated out of an open window.

Rhea stopped in front of a doorway next door to the brothel and told Doro, "Please wait here."

He nodded, then she led me up two steps into a shop with the word *pharmakopoles* painted beside the door framed by decorative green-painted palms. I didn't know the translation of the word in Dacian, but instantly realized this was an apothecary's shop.

Rows of herbs in jars and wrapped bundles dried along the wall. Potted plants lined three shelves on another wall and spiced incense burned on the counter and perfumed the air. The lamp oil flickering on the counter to my right seemed to give off a floral scent as well. A thin, gray-haired woman wearing kohl on her eyes entered from a back room and through a curtain made of strips of sparkly, sheer cloth.

"Rhea! So good to see you, my dear." She stepped behind her counter in front of us. "You aren't low on silphium already, are you?"

"Oh, no." Rhea blushed and cast me a sideways glance. "I have plenty of that for now."

I recognized the name of the drug. Women used it to keep from conceiving.

"Euphemia, this is my friend, Malina. She needs something special."

Euphemia narrowed her soot-lined eyes at me, staring down her long nose with severe calculation. She cocked one eyebrow.

"I am assuming you speak of my special collection, yes?"

"Yes. You can trust her. I promise."

"You vouch for her, do you?"

"I do."

Euphemia hadn't stopped staring at me the entire time. "Why do you need a precious prize like my special collection?"

I instantly bonded to her essence. It was warm and bright and welcoming, despite her dark and fragile physical appearance.

Wiping away the fear I'd felt when I woke this morning, I said, "Because I need Minerva's help. She can help me in my cause."

"What is this cause? To seduce a lover? Or to kill an enemy?"

"Neither. It is greater than that. Yes, I will ask for protection for the one I love, and to kill an enemy. But not just one enemy . . . *all* enemies to the downtrodden."

The three of us standing here were all certainly the downtrodden of Rome. A time was coming when the powerful would fall, I sensed it. But I couldn't say more to Euphemia or Rhea, too afraid to trust too much.

"I must beg a favor of the goddess," I pleaded. "Today."

She stepped from behind the counter to approach me. She was short and thin, but she exuded strength.

"Give me your hands, girl." She held out her own, palms up.

I placed mine into hers.

"I read auras, and I can tell if you're lying."

Wanting to smile at her threat to use a mystical ability on me, I nodded. "Ask me your question."

"Do you swear to tell no one where you obtained the dragon skin, if asked?"

"I swear." I pressed the emotions of trust and compassion into the bond.

She gasped and let go of my hands, staring wide-eyed. "You are a sister of the spirit world."

I didn't know what that meant exactly, only that she recognized I had a goddess-given gift.

I nodded. "I am."

She snapped her fingers. "Come." Then she turned and walked back through the curtain.

Rhea grinned, then we both followed. Behind the curtain was a short hallway with two rooms and a kitchen, her living quarters. She stalked quickly into the room at the end. By the time we got there, she was swiveling a bookshelf back into place, having removed something from a hidden space behind it.

"Here, this is what you need."

She handed me a folded cloth and hurried to a table where she opened a drawer. But it wasn't simply cloth. It was a square of the hide of a gray dragon.

"Who is it from?"

"A gladiator. His name was Livius."

She clattered things in her drawer while looking for something.

"He had never been defeated in over one hundred battles. He was beloved by all of Rome, patricians, plebs, and slaves alike. Then the emperor Igniculus demanded he execute a Vicus dragon, a priestess who had broken her vows of chastity. He was to slay both her and her lover as the finale of a day of games last year."

She picked up something.

"Ah, here it is."

She returned to stand before me, her expression grave.

"He refused to execute either of them and so Igniculus had his praetorians shift into dragon form and kill Livius instead. They lifted his body and dropped him in the Tiber like he was nothing but scum. Trash to be thrown away." She scoffed in disgust.

"I remember that day," said Rhea softly, sadly. "It was the one day there was no applause at the closing of the games."

"True, true," said Euphemia. "But the emperor got his point across clear enough. His orders are to be obeyed at all times." She opened my other hand and placed a small dagger in it. "Livius washed up on shore downriver. With Proserpina's blessing, I took some of his skin for only the most sacred bargains with the gods. Then my friends and I burned him in a pyre, with all the rites of the dead that he deserved."

"What is the dagger for?"

Euphemia scoffed and rolled her eyes. "You do not know how to properly ask the gods for help, I see. You must carve your request into the dragon skin, then you must seal it with a sacrifice. Blood of an animal. A goat is best. Here, you'll need to burn this candle afterward." She pulled a thick-stumped candle from a shelf and shoved it into my hand.

"Thank you," I told her. "I can't thank you enough. I don't have any denarii now, but I can get some and bring it back."

"No, no. I do not sell the sacred skin. It is given to those in need, and I decide who is most in need. The gods and I do."

"The gods tell you I am worthy."

"Of course. You have their magic." She winked. "Now you'd best get gone before Doro comes barreling into my home and tearing the place apart with his giant behemoth body."

Rhea giggled and led us back out through the curtain and into the main room. Doro was indeed peeking in from the steps outside, frowning until he saw us reappear. Rhea rushed and whispered something to him while I turned to Euphemia.

I couldn't help myself as I pulled her into an embrace. She stiffened and patted my back awkwardly. She smelled of willow bark tea and incense.

"Thank you again. Not just for this, but for what you did for Livius."

Euphemia was obviously not a dragon, and yet she'd shown the gladiator respect in death when his own people had not.

"There, there, child." She pushed out of my arms and smiled. "You go now and make that bargain with Minerva." She winked. "If any goddess can bring justice, it is our goddess of war."

Tucking the dagger, the dragon skin, and the candle into my satchel with the peaches, I met Rhea and Doro outside.

"Now to the temple. See, Doro. We won't be late at all."

"We best hurry," said Doro, looking up at the sky. "Rain is coming."

He was right. Gray clouds billowed low from over the hills, slowly creeping toward the city. I followed Rhea at a brisk pace, back through the narrow alleys and onto the main road through the Aventine. It was even busier now, thick with a crush of people.

A gusty wind began to blow, the sky growing darker, rolling with thunder. The wind whipped my hair and billowed the cloth canopies over the shops. Vendors rushed to get their wares indoors.

"Quickly, Gideon!" A mother holding a babe in one arm pressed the veil over her head with her other hand as the wind tried to rip it off. A boy ran alongside her, clutching onto her skirts.

By the time we reached the temple, the first drops of rain began to fall.

"Malina," called Rhea, taking Doro's hand and hauling him toward a taberna where the smell of roasted meats and vegetables wafted onto the street. "We will wait for you in there to keep out of the rain. Don't be too long!"

I nodded, then rushed into the temple, tucking the damp strands of hair that had come loose from my braid behind my ear. As soon as I was past the columns and inside the domed temple, there was that great hush of quiet that I loved about sacred spaces.

Lightning crashed outside, but I stepped farther into the atrium where two other worshippers knelt and whispered and prayed, lighting candles and leaving gifts of honey cakes and fruit and dead animals. I walked around them until I found a quiet spot to the left of the painted sculpture of Minerva close to the front altar.

Proserpina's statue was magnificent and awe-inspiring, but Minerva's likeness was horrifyingly beautiful.

Minerva was painted with mostly white wings, tipped with purple, the same shade as her eyes. Her black hair billowed in an unseen wind, which seemed to match the storm now pummeling the dome over our heads. Her breastplate was painted gold, a darker shade than her golden gown ending at her clawed feet. She held a sword high in her hand; her other hand was open, palm out, claws extended. The horns curling out of her skull were gold as well.

But it was her expression—fierce, determined, and confident—that held me most spellbound. I hoped this was what she actually looked like. A female goddess ready to do damage to her enemies. I needed a defender like Minerva on my side.

So I knelt quickly and pulled the square of dragon skin and the dagger from inside my bag. The other two worshippers were far away and wouldn't see, not that they were minding me anyway. They were deep in their own requests and prayers, whispering to the goddess with heads bowed.

The wind howled and the rain poured down outside as I flattened the dragon skin to the stone floor. The temple was dimly lit with torches circling the dome but I could see well enough.

I carved the words in my own language, tears springing to my eyes as I embedded the Dacian words, whispering them to Minerva.

"Minerva, divine goddess, I beg you to protect my love and destroy all of my enemies." I read what I'd written, then looked up at her and added, "You know who they are." For I could not take the chance and name them. Any of them. Then I began carving again. *"In exchange, and upon the final death of our oppressors, I give you back my magic. I return it entirely into your keeping for when it is needed again."*

I stared at the words, then lifted the dagger and sliced crossways where I'd been cut for the Rite of Skulls. How prophetic that I should overlap the same mark for their blasphemous rite with a righteous one. I cut deeper until my blood dripped freely upon the dragon skin, soaking in my sacrifice.

"Please, hear my prayer," I whispered to the goddess before I pressed my open palm, stamping the words one last time.

Folding the square several times, I wrapped it closed and ripped a strip of my tunic from the hem. Then I stared at it. I couldn't bind my prayer and my bargain with the goddess with a piece of cloth from

Ciprian, my chief enemy. It must be bound with something precious to me or she might not hear me.

I stared up at Minerva's fierce expression, thunder rumbling loud through the temple. Lightning flashed outside, brightening her face, her eyes, which seemed to be pinned on me. This was only a statue, and yet I felt her presence wafting and circling the room.

Tears streamed down my cheeks for I knew what was needed. With trembling fingers I reached behind my neck and unclasped the leather necklace. My papa had put the clasp on the soft hide rope and pierced a hole through the coin for me so that I could wear my talisman. And he'd never asked where I'd gotten it or why I'd kept it. He only knew that it made me smile.

Pulling the aureus into my palm, the gold coin minted with the face of Fortuna, the wedding gift of Julian's father to his mother, I pressed a kiss to the talisman. "Minerva, protect us," I whispered as I wound the chain around the dragon skin, binding the prayer with the possession I held most dear in all the world. "Loving spirits of the afterworld, protect us," I added.

Then I took the short, fat candle Euphemia had given me and lit it from the larger oil lamp on the altar at Minerva's clawed feet. I set the dragon skin, my sacrifice and prayer, underneath the candle, hoping the priestesses here would never remove it. Not until Minerva had granted my wish.

As if summoned, six priestesses draped in full white, veils covering their faces, slowly paraded out in a single line. They hummed in unison and then began singing a soft melody, a hymn to the goddess. I bowed my head and listened to the enchanting sound as they circled the altar, singing and praising her justice to protect the faithful, her mighty hand to destroy evildoers, and her wisdom in discerning who deserved her love. Their voices rose to the domed ceiling even as thunder rumbled louder.

Realizing I would be in their way when they circled to my side, I used the scrap of linen I'd pulled from my tunic and wrapped my cut, biting one end to pull the knot tight.

Reverently, I stood, taking one last look at my square of dragon skin, my gold coin, and the candle, then turned and hurried away, wiping my eyes as I went. I walked toward the exit down the corridor between the row of columns and the small curtained vestibules meant for private sacrifices of large animals to the goddess.

I pondered that only patricians would likely be allowed to use them when a shadow leaped from one of the chambers. I squealed as I was grabbed from behind, a large hand clamped over my mouth. I kicked and fought, but my attacker was too big and strong, dragging me bodily backward behind the curtain of the closest vestibule. My heart thudded a fearful beat in my chest until I recognized the scent and the feel of the man at my back. Pulling his hand free, I spun, tears springing anew.

"*Julian.*"

XXXIII

JULIAN

Malina leaped into my arms and wrapped her legs around my waist, weeping as she pressed her cheek to mine. I groaned as I kissed her soft face, then her sweet mouth, devouring her with insatiable, fevered nips and bites, skating my mouth along her jaw to her throat, pressing her body against the chamber wall, needing to *feel* her.

Then I confessed my heart. "By Dis, I'm dying inside, Malina. I *need* you." I pulled the strap of her thin black tunic to the side and nipped, growling angrily that she was wearing his cloth, his color. "*We* need you."

My dragon burned behind my eyes and in my blood as I pressed my forehead to hers, my skin prickling, wanting to stretch and shift and carry her away. Anger and lust and love combatted for dominance as I fell to kissing her again, scraping my teeth on her skin, pulling her strap down farther until her breast slipped free. On a groan, I lowered my mouth and sucked the tight peak, scraping with my sharp teeth that had elongated without my will, needing to mark her, embed my scent in her.

Rather than beat me off, my firebird fisted her fingers in my short hair and pressed me closer, moaning and grinding her cunny against my abdomen. Her scent had me reeling, groaning.

"Yes, yes," she crooned, "taste me, please, bite me, *yes.*"

My dragon purred at her desperate cries for more, my hands shoving up her tunic, my fingers finding her slick center before I slid a finger inside her.

"Gods!" she cried as lightning crashed and thunder boomed overhead.

"I need you. *Fuck,* I need you," I growled repeatedly like a mantra, a plea, a prayer.

"Shh," she whispered against my mouth, reaching down between us and pulling up my tunic until she could wrap her hand around my hard cock.

"Malina," I begged, my entire body trembling with desperate want. I thrust into her hand, pulling my finger from inside her to grip her bottom and lower her.

"Shh," she breathed softly again, her mouth sliding open as she notched the head of my cock at her quim.

With a feral grunt, I thrust deep to the hilt, shivering at the sweet tightness of her body taking me all the way in. "Yes, my love."

She gasped, dropping her head to the wall, baring her neck for me.

I kept still, the raging storm outside mimicking the one inside me, mocking the rage of emotions tearing me apart. I had her. In this moment, she was mine. But it was a fleeting, stinging moment, knowing I'd have to let her go again.

"Gods above and below," I rasped into the silken skin of her throat, "you are fucking *mine*, Malina."

I slid out to the tip and thrust deep inside her again, pounding her against the stone wall. She didn't seem to mind, whimpering with pleasure at my roughness.

"Mine," I growled again and licked her skin.

She kept her fingers fisted in my hair, her blunt nails scraping my skull as she lowered her chin and leveled those hauntingly beautiful green eyes at me.

"As you are mine," she breathed on a whisper. "Now show me that I am."

Squeezing her flesh, I pressed her against the wall and pumped deep, over and over, driving inside her sweet body, her slick cunny. She locked her ankles at my back and pulled my hair till it stung. We seemed to both need to mark each other, to remember and know this was real. No matter where we were when we parted, we belonged to each other and no one else.

I lifted one hand, my body pinning her to the wall, and sank my fingers into her hair, beneath her braid, gripping her skull in my palm.

"I feel you, my love," I grated against her lips, while tears slipped down her cheeks. "I feel all of you."

I pumped faster, my soul drifting into hers in an ecstasy of passion I had never known. Nor would I ever know again. My firebird was my end and beginning. No joy could surpass this belonging, this bond winding us into each other.

"Yes," she whispered on a sob, "I feel it too, Julian."

She moaned so sweetly, so exquisitely. Then she was coming, her cunny squeezing my cock. I groaned as she leaned forward and bit the bare skin above my collar, screaming into my flesh as she climaxed.

"Yes," I hissed, fucking her hard and deep, our flesh slapping. I couldn't stop as she shook and trembled in my arms, needing to bury my cock deeper and deeper.

The dragon roared inside me, his growl vibrating out of my belly as my cock swelled bigger. Then I speared her hard and spent my seed, rumbling my pleasure as I released inside her.

She unlatched her mouth from my shoulder, shuddering and panting, her sex still throbbing with her orgasm as she tilted her head to nuzzle her nose against mine. Her voice a pained whimper as she whispered, "I love you."

I kissed the tears that wet her cheeks, my heart bursting at her admission, the storm overhead seeming to diminish and drift away. "Don't cry, love," I begged, sliding my nose alongside hers, grinding my cock deeper while it still pulsed. "You're breaking my heart."

She smiled, and the sight gripped me with a wave of tenderness. "They are tears of joy," she promised, kissing me sweetly, tenderly.

I accepted her sweetness, her soft caress of lips and tongue, the beast inside me satiated for the moment. Gently, I pulled out of her body on a hiss. She made a soft noise of disappointment. I kept her in my arms and settled on a stone bench, pulling her legs across my lap and her head to my chest.

There was a mess between her legs, which I wiped with a fold of my tunic. Her soft, tender flesh made me stiffen with dread. When I'd tucked her close against me, I finally asked, "Has he touched you?"

"No," was her immediate reply. "As I told you, I'm able to protect myself."

But there was a catch in her voice.

"Is that why you've come to beg favors of the goddess Minerva?" I asked gently, tapping her cloth-wrapped hand where I'd watched her cut her palm.

She tilted her head back to look up at me, and I relished the sight.

Her affectionate, adoring gaze must've been mirrored in my own. She reached up and cupped my jaw.

"My darling Julian." She smiled again and I was her slave on the instant. But I always had been, since that moment I watched her dance beneath the moonlight in the Carpathian Mountains. "Do not worry. All is well in hand."

"I did not know Dacians worshipped Roman gods."

She pinched my chin to punish me, which made me chuckle. "Minerva knows me, a child of Dacia. It matters not I was born outside her favored patrons. Someone wise told me the gods know us whether we worship them or not."

"Mmm." I pressed a soft kiss to her forehead, inhaling her hypnotic scent. "So what have you asked of her?"

She paused, tracing her fingertips across my cheek and the bridge of my nose, seeming to memorize the planes she caressed. "For what we need."

She swallowed, and I began doing my own exploration, tracing a single finger down her throat.

"But I had to bind the bargain with a treasure," she admitted, her voice husky. "I had to give up the aureus." There was heartbreak in her eyes.

"You bound your prayer with your most precious treasure?"

"No," she answered quickly, gripping my jaw and brushing her thumb across my cheek. "I keep my most precious treasure with me always."

When I frowned, she said, "Your love." She dropped her hand from my face and pressed her palm to her chest. "I keep it here, well-guarded."

My entire soul wept as I pulled her tight against me and slanted my mouth over hers. We kissed tenderly and gently—mouths, cheeks, brows—pouring our affection into each other until I couldn't hear the rain or the storm at all anymore. The soft brush of lips and tongue eased my turmoil for the moment. Until we were interrupted.

"Malina," someone whispered nearby.

We broke the kiss and Malina jumped to sit upright on my lap. A slim blonde woman stood in the alcove leading into this vestibule where we'd blocked off the world for a few stolen moments.

She waved for her to come. "We must go." She looked back toward the exit. "Doro is anxious."

Instantly, I clutched her in my arms and pressed my forehead to the base of her neck, inhaling the scent of her hair. "No," I whispered.

"I'm coming, Rhea," she promised and shooed the woman away, then she stood between my legs, turned, and hugged me against her breast. "When will the deed take place?"

No need to explain what deed she meant. We'd discussed killing Ciprian the day she was taken from my home.

"In two or three nights. Can you come back to the temple tomorrow? I should have a definite answer then when all the plans are set."

She gripped my shoulders and pushed me back. With me sitting on the bench and her standing, we were face-to-face. "I'll find a way. Same time? I believe it's easier to get out of Ciprian's house during the morning hours."

My entire body locked with revulsion. "Promise me he hasn't hurt you." I'd already scanned her arms and legs for any sign of violence, of bruising, and had found none.

"I promise."

I stood and embraced her close. She pressed her cheek against my sternum. "Only a few days more," I whispered into the crown of her head. "Then we'll be gone and I can take you somewhere safe."

The dragon purred from within at the thought.

She hugged me tighter but asked, "Why would I have to leave if all goes well?"

She didn't know that I planned to kill Ciprian ahead of schedule, before my uncle and the others.

"There will be unrest after Ciprian is dead. No one should suspect me, but if they do, I don't want Caesar to target you to hurt me." I pressed her closer. "It would kill me, firebird."

She pressed a kiss to my chest. Even through my tunic, I felt the warmth of her mouth and affection. Then she gazed up at me, holding my heart in that look.

"I know the story of the firebird now."

"Do you? Who told you the tale?"

"Rhea." She nodded toward the doorway. "My friend." She tilted her head teasingly. "But I don't know if that's the right name for me. I'm not a golden dragon, Julian. Nor can I fly through the air and set men on fire."

"You think not?"

She laughed. "You know I can't."

"I know nothing of the sort." I cupped her face and pressed a hard kiss to her mouth. "Since that moment I saw you, flying across that stage, you have been burning inside me ever since. My entire soul is on fire for you, Malina." I pressed my forehead to hers. "And always will be."

"Malina," hissed the girl Rhea from outside. "We must go *now*."

Malina pressed one last kiss to my lips and tore from my arms. I felt the pain bodily, like something died inside me as I watched her leave. I couldn't keep from following.

I trailed at a distance, following her and the other slave girl out of the temple and into the rain-drenched streets. I followed as they met a large slave wearing Ciprian's collar, weaving through the sparse crowd of the Aventine. If anyone thought it strange for a Roman patrician to walk their streets, they made no note of it. None even seemed to recognize me as the famous Coldhearted Conqueror.

Perhaps because I didn't look much like him, slinking through the streets, trying to catch just one last glimpse of the black-haired beauty who owned my very soul. Stricken with the despair of her disappearing around a corner, I realized that there was nothing cold inside me now.

A furnace burned in the deep, darkest recesses of my being. In that place where my dragon slept and watched and waited, a fire had kindled when Malina had given me her love. Only taking her back to a lair where I could keep her safe would abate the beast. If she was hurt before I could I free her, I'd set the world on fire and gladly watch it burn.

XXXIV

MALINA

The house had been quiet upon our return. The cook whose name I still didn't know, nor did I care to know since I didn't plan on being here much longer, put us to work washing and cutting vegetables for the master's dinner.

There was a hubbub of noise when Ciprian returned home with his slaves, the bearded one and the others who'd attacked me that one day on the streets. They'd sequestered themselves in one of the parlors, then I heard Ciprian shouting orders for a bath and his dinner right after, but I kept away in the kitchens. As far away as I could.

I'd washed and changed my own tunic, afraid that he would somehow know I'd been with Julian. Rhea had been summoned to serve him dinner, but not me. I was both afraid for her and relieved for myself. While I was confident that I could tether him again and put him to sleep if necessary, that nightmare I'd had last night still lingered. A single thread of foreboding had followed me all day, especially after I'd left Julian's arms.

I waited in my bedchamber for Rhea to return when the bearded slave stepped into the open doorway. "Dominus commands you to come."

Stricken with alarm, I didn't show an ounce of it. I stood and followed him into the same dining hall where I'd made Ciprian spill his guts last night.

I paused when I first entered the room. It wasn't the fact that my attackers stood about the room or that Rhea was absent. It was the undeniably smug expression on Ciprian's face and the cloying sense of dread tapping on my magic.

His eyes weren't brown as usual. They glowed red with his dragon, which meant something had stirred his beast to the forefront. Something that excited him from that gleeful expression on his face. His bruises were already fading and he wore no bandages, his sutures visible. He didn't seem bothered at all by his injuries.

"Have a seat with me, Malina." He drew my name out in a long, sickening breath.

"I prefer to stand. What is it you need, dominus?"

"You will sit," he ordered with a hint of aggression, but that eerie smile remained.

So I sat upon the cushion opposite where he reclined on his chaise, his goblet of wine in hand, a platter of roasted meat and turnips I'd chopped today spread out before him.

"Eat." He gestured toward the platter.

I didn't want to raise his ire and refuse, so I picked up a cold turnip and nibbled, the bite cold as it went down. He seemed content that I obeyed, watching me over the rim of his wine goblet.

After a moment of silence, he said, "Drink with me."

That was when I noticed the second goblet. He leaned over and filled it himself with the decanter that had been left by Rhea.

I lifted the cup and took a small sip, then asked, "Do you often have your slaves dine with you?"

"Never," he admitted, red eyes gleaming.

"Why have I been singled out as special?" Yet again, I never could hold my tongue.

"Because you *are* special, Malina." He lifted his cup as in a toast to me. "Aren't you?"

My pulse pumped a little faster, sensing he knew something. I hid my reaction behind the goblet as I took another sip of wine and made no reply. He said nothing for a moment, the tension stretching. The bearded one and his two comrades stood at attention at the doorway, glaring at me, grim as always.

He swirled his wine cavalierly and said, "I know your secret."

I froze, cupping my goblet in my lap. "I have no secrets, dominus." All the while, visions of Julian thrusting inside me at the temple this morning ran through my mind.

"You have many, witch."

He sat up on the chaise, which put me on alert. But he simply placed his goblet carefully on the table and observed me. There was no malice in his gaze, at the moment. No, he was simply looking, as if trying to figure out a puzzle.

"And apparently, so does Julian."

When I couldn't keep my expression blank, knowing my eyes widened at his accusation, he tossed his head back on a bark of laughter. I remained completely still, my hands focusing on clutching the cup so I didn't panic.

"My former master?" I asked, wondering if he'd forced Doro or Rhea to tell him about my tryst today in the temple.

"Indeed, Malina. Your *former* master." He chuckled again, his canines sharp as he'd let the dragon slip a little more. "Seems he's been doing some extracurricular activities."

He knew. Gods, *he knew*.

"Sergius saw something very peculiar last night." He gestured back to the bearded slave, who still fixed his malicious glare on me. "Very strange indeed."

This wasn't about today. What was he talking about?

"Oh?" I asked innocently.

"The honorable Julianus Dakkia returning in dragon form by the cloak of night. Even stranger, he shifted outside of the city and rode his horse back to his home. Now, I may not be the strategist that he is, but I do know the laws. And I know what looks like covert maneuvers." He leaned forward, bracing his elbows on his knees and said in an intimate manner, "You know what's even more curious. He wasn't alone. Sergius, diligent spy that he is, watched the skies and saw two more senators return to the city in the same way."

My heart pounded in my throat while I remained as still as possible, listening to Ciprian tell me that he suspected Julian as some sort of conspirator. Which, of course, he was.

"Cunning, aren't you?" he whispered. "From your expression, I'd think you knew nothing at all. But by the tripling of your heart rate and the dilation of your eyes, I can feel the fear running through your body." He grinned wider. "It's delicious."

"I'm just a slave." My voice barely shook. "What would I know?"

"But you aren't just a slave to Julian, are you?" His brow rose in a mocking question. "You're his prized possession. I can fucking smell him on you," he growled, "and I know you know more."

"I don't know any—"

With unnatural speed, he reached across the table and backhanded me to the floor. My goblet clanged across the stone and my head buzzed at the shocking pain. There was a sudden, sharp stinging in my scalp as Ciprian crouched over me and curled a fist into my hair. With a sharp pull, he hauled me back onto my knees.

"Ah!" I cried out.

"That's right," he hissed in my ear, wrapping his other hand around my throat. "Get used to the pain."

I reached for my tether but it felt slippery and elusive, not tangible like it always did. Something was wrong.

Ciprian laughed in my ear, pulling me tighter against his chest where he knelt behind me. "You won't use your witchcraft on me again. Like you did last night. And at my own Rite of Skulls celebration, you fucking bitch."

My limbs felt lighter, looser, not my own as I slumped in his tight hold.

"That's right. The sedative won't kill you. It will simply cloud your mind and senses, but not enough you can't answer my questions." He firmed his grip on my throat. "And not enough you won't feel everything I'm doing to you tonight." He laughed and licked my cheek with his long tongue. "And we're going to have a lot of fun tonight, witch."

It dawned on me far too late that he'd drugged me. In my own arrogance, I sat and ate and drank at his table as if I were invincible. But I was not. Whatever it was he'd given me not only numbed my body and mind but it also dulled my connection to my magic. I tried again and again as he dragged me across the floor by my hair but I couldn't call upon my tether.

"Oh, I like that! Don't you, Sergius? She screams prettily."

"Yes, dominus," said Sergius.

I hadn't realized I was screaming, my mind drifting, when he hauled me roughly to the chaise and propped me up. I sat limply, my arms useless at my sides. He picked up his goblet of wine and gulped some down, then he winked at me.

"Would you like a sip?" he asked lightly. "Mine isn't drugged, so it's safe."

I simply stared, my heart beating so fast I was afraid it would pound right out of my chest. I'd never felt so helpless.

"Now, if you can scream, you can talk." His voice had darkened, his red eyes—slit like a serpent's—narrowed on me. "I want to know who Julian's plotting with. Tell me who he's been meeting with. Who's been coming to the house."

Thank the gods, he didn't know everything. He only suspected.

"Sergius has already delivered my message to the emperor tonight. I've listed Julian's suspicious behavior, along with the two senators', which only points to the fact that he's plotting against his uncle. But I'd like to bring a few more names to Igniculus, and you're going to give them to me." He lunged onto the chaise, straddling me and gripping my throat again. He didn't squeeze this time but my head fell to the sofa back, my entire being recoiling from his loathsome touch. "Come on now, Malina," he whispered, so close his lips brushed mine. "Give me what I want so we can really play."

There was only one defense I had at that moment, so I opened my mouth and bit his lip. He roared as he reared back, knocking me over. My body rolled halfway off the chaise until my cheek was planted on the seat cushion. I panted from the terror coursing through my veins, my limbs useless as I tried to right myself.

"Fucking witch," Ciprian hissed behind me, most probably wiping the blood from his lip for I tasted the foul tanginess of it. "On second thought, I like this view of her better. Maybe a good fucking will loosen her tongue."

"No," I mumbled and struggled, barely able to move my arms as I tried to scramble away.

"I enjoyed the taste of your blood too." I felt the tip of a cold blade against the back of my neck. "I think I'll have another taste."

Without another thought, I spoke through the one bond that never broke, the tether that had latched tight and never severed, the one to Julian.

JULIAN

I'd been restless all night. Seeing Malina today had only amplified my fear that something could go wrong. Perhaps it was simply that the house was so quiet that had me unsettled. I'd instructed Ruskus to prepare the others to pack. They'd soon be traveling to Trajan's distant home where they would be safe, where I'd take Malina as soon as it was all done.

Pacing the atrium, I still couldn't wipe away the dread that sat like a heavy stone in my stomach. I waited for Trajan, who said he'd visit tonight and give me the final details and timing for it all.

There was pounding on my outer door.

"Thank the gods."

I hurried through the foyer entrance and opened the door, expecting to find my friend on the other side. Instead, there were six armed praetorians, all of them in half-skin.

"Legatus Julianus," the first one said formally, "Emperor Igniculus commands that you come with us now to the palace."

There was a coldness in his voice and a flickering of his dragon in his gaze. He was on guard . . . against me.

My uncle knew. Somehow, he knew.

"Let me dress properly," I told them, as I was in my loose tunic for bed.

"That isn't necessary." He latched onto my forearm, something a praetorian had never done to me. "The emperor would like to see you *now*."

Instinct locked in. Without hesitation, I shifted into half-skin and swiped my claws across the first praetorian's throat. His eyes went wide as blood spurted from his neck. Then the others were on me, clawing and snarling.

Another fell into the melee from behind me. The flash of blue scales and a familiar growl buoyed me. Trajan had leaped into the fight. He must've arrived right after they did.

The praetorians had their swords drawn and sliced through the air at me.

"Your uncle wants you alive," snarled one of the praetorians in garbled speech.

"I'm sure he does," I snapped back, beating my wings and charging forward.

When he thrust his sword toward my gut, I deflected and bent his arm, driving his blade directly up through his chin and skull, blood spraying my face as I spun to fight the next one.

Trajan had killed another, then twisted again and decapitated a second with his gladius, his blue-spiked tail swiping one of the last two to the ground. Praetorians weren't as accustomed to battle as we were, and that was our advantage. Too many hours standing around on guard and doing nothing made them no match for us.

The sixth backed away, then flew off into the night toward the palace. Before the one rolling on the ground could get away, I raised an arm, holding my hand outstretched. "Trajan!"

He flipped his gladius through the air. I caught it and stabbed the praetorian on the ground through the heart, the blade crunching through to the paved stone beneath. Then I stood straight, pulling the blade free, panting hard and staring at Trajan.

"So he knows," said Trajan, his tail twitching behind him, his voice dangerous, eyes ice blue. "How?"

I shook my head. "Doesn't matter."

"I'll get the last one." Then Trajan was in the air, flying after the praetorian that got away.

Trajan was fast. The praetorian wouldn't reach the castle before Trajan caught him. I stared down at the mess of bodies, trying to figure out what to do next. If the emperor knew and his men didn't return, he'd send more or he'd come for me himself.

I turned for the door, needing my gladius, when Ruskus appeared suddenly, breathless and with a dagger in hand. Brave man.

"Dominus, are they all dead?"

"All dead."

"What do we do with them?"

A sharp jolt pinned me still, like a rope that constricted my chest, my entire body freezing at the jarring of my very soul.

Instantly, I heard her, *felt* her, *screaming* into my mind.

Julian! Help me!

"Get the others to Trajan's house," I growled.

"Tonight?"

"Now!"

Then my heart fell while my wings took flight.

Rage and terror dug their talons in deep, swelling my half-skin beast to gargantuan proportions. By the time I reached Ciprian's outer terrace, I was too large to fit through the archway made for dragons in half-skin.

I charged through the opening, my horns and wings crumbling stone. A bearded human jumped aside at the door. I grabbed his head and ripped it from his spine, then tossed it across the room, blood spraying. I barely noted the other men crying out in fear and fleeing, for my primal gaze was on Ciprian crouched over my mate, who was bent over a sofa, her tunic torn from her back, a trickle of blood sliding down her spine, and a knife in Ciprian's hand.

My roar shattered glass and shook the ceiling of the home I was about to destroy, along with its master. Ciprian leaped to his feet, bulging and rippling into half-skin. It wouldn't help him.

"I'm going to rip out your throat and bathe in your blood," I growled darkly as I stalked across the room.

His eyes widened as he took in my form. My horns scraped the ceiling with each step, crumbling plaster onto the floor. I was beyond half-skin, but not quite dragon—some terrible beast in between.

"So the traitor comes calling," he bellowed, planting his feet, flexing his muscles, and shedding his torn tunic.

It was him. He had been the one to tell the emperor. All the more reason to destroy him.

"That's right, Julianus." He spat my name with disgust, circling behind a table like a coward. "I know about your nightly errands out of the city. And so does the emperor now."

"I don't care." I continued straight for him. I wasn't going to parry or play games. "I'm going to kill you both."

"You finally figured it out, did you?"

Ignoring his ploy to distract me, I dug my claws into the table and threw it aside, the wood crashing and cracking against the wall. Ciprian scrambled toward the dining area and hauled Malina to her feet by her hair.

I lunged but he spun and pressed the tip of the blade to her throat. Her torn tunic slid off one shoulder.

She was listless, her eyes dilated, her expression scared and confused. Drugged. I could smell the taint of it on her.

Ciprian laughed while I stared at him, my tail lashing and flinging a chair across the room while I tried to figure out the best way to kill him before he hurt Malina.

"I wish I'd been there when you finally learned the truth."

I could barely hear his blathering through my intense focus on my mate. Her dazed expression and fumbling to stand distressed me. The dragon was edging hard for my skin. He wanted out.

My focus homed in on where Malina gripped his forearm, her gaze finally finding mine. She curled her fingers tight. I understood, so I entertained Ciprian's rambling. "The truth about what?"

He backed up, tightening his hold on her. "I suppose that would make any man go traitor."

I'd stopped stalking closer and locked in place, lengthening my claws, arms at my sides. "What are you talking about?"

"Fratricide, of course."

I froze, staring at him, trying to make sense of what he was saying. Slowly, slowly, dawning realization chilled my blood. My breathing became more labored.

While I wrapped my mind around what he was confessing, Ciprian belted out a loud, maniacal laugh.

"You didn't know!" His speech was barely discernible in half-skin, but I could understand well enough. "You didn't know that your uncle murdered your father. Well, he arranged for it anyway. Your mother too, and everyone in the house. He couldn't have a slave-loving brother while creating the empire he wanted." He shrugged, the gesture looking like a twitch in half-skin, his sharp blade still too close to Malina's throat. "Couldn't blame him. I'd have done the same."

My mind reeled and my gut churned while I held myself perfectly still. My uncle was the one to tell me they'd caught the perpetrators and executed them. I'd never questioned it. I'd never suspected him when it made perfect sense. Without my father—another Ignis of equally noble blood—protesting the emperor's every move, he could control Rome with unchecked dictatorial power. And he had. He'd even controlled me . . . until now.

"Who did the actual killing . . . of my family?" I asked, my timbre rumbling with danger.

He laughed again. "That's the fun part. Take a guess."

I already knew. It had never made sense, Ciprian's swift rise within the ranks, when his father had resigned from his legion too soon as a mediocre centurion of no high rank.

"Your father did it." I bent my neck till it cracked, my voice dropping deeper, my blood running hotter, scorching through my veins. "Your father killed mine."

"And he was happy to do it. My father was loyal to the new emperor. Unlike you." He let his blade drift away from her throat ever so slightly as he shifted in thought, distracted. "Why did you betray your own blood?"

"Now, Malina!"

She gripped his forearm and sank her teeth into his skin. Ciprian bellowed and jerked away on reflex. Before he could snatch her back, I was *on him*.

Malina fell to the side as I shoved Ciprian to the floor and straddled him, my clawed hands wrapping his throat. I bent forward and hissed, "May you rot in the deepest of hells."

For the first time since I'd known him, there was true fear shining in his demonic eyes, then he was fighting and snarling and growling . . . and growing.

"Malina!" I bellowed. "Run!"

He was shifting into his dragon. I glanced left to see her crawling to the outer terrace. She *couldn't* run.

Then it was too late. My beast wasn't about to let her go unprotected. He was tearing out of my skin, bones splintering, body and neck elongating, fire blazing deep within as I staggered onto the terrace and became the beast . . .

Vengeance.

The enemy opens his jaws and snaps. I crave his blood in my mouth, his flesh in my teeth. This demon shall go back to the netherworld. He belongs not on this earth. Not in our skies. He has no right to breathe air.

He hurt our treasure.

She crouches against a tree. Makes herself small and unseen. But I see her. I will protect her. I purr to let her know I am here. She is safe.

I slide my body in front of her and roar at the enemy, then slice my tail down upon the rubble of the enemy's lair. It crumbles beneath my might. He will do the same.

He roars. He leaps at me, jaws open.

Fool, this lowly demon.

I beat my wings and embed my claws deep into his flesh. The ripeness of blood. I relish the cracking of bones. He whips his head and curls his neck to clamp his jaws onto me.

Too late. I have my teeth in his throat. I rip it from his body, just as he belches fire. The flames burst from his mouth and the hole in his throat I have made. My scales protect me. I toss his head to the side and roar my rage to the skies. My voice shakes the trees and the earth with my power and rage.

I am death incarnate, and the world will know my wrath.

My enemy's demon spirit is already gone. But my rage needs more. I slice my claws down his body. It twitches in the final throes of death, his tail curling and shaking. Then he is still.

My fury is not sated. I summon the fire in my belly and pour it onto the carcass of the demon who thought to take my treasure. The stench of his burning corpse fills me with sweet pleasure.

Still, it is not enough. I inhale deep and blow a stream of fire into his lair, toppling the roof and incinerating everything within. There will be nothing left of him. Not a stone of his home, not an ash or a bone. I will devour all with my flames.

"Julian!"

My mate stands beside a tree, completely bare, her slender body lit by my firelight. She is weary. She is weak. She needs protection.

A whiff on the wind brings my attention to other dragons nearby. I should kill the uncle. I should not let him live for what he's done to me and mine.

"Julian." A low whisper, a soft plea.

My treasure. My mate.

I must protect her. We will go.

XXXVI

MALINA

Somehow, I summoned the strength to crawl out of Ciprian's home. I'd watched from the base of a tree in his side garden while Julian ripped him apart. His red dragon was a monumental beast with black horns and black-tipped wings. His golden eyes promised death to all who opposed him.

And yet, I did not fear him. He was my dragon, *my* protector.

Ciprian had sliced my tunic down the back and was entertaining himself with the blade and his foul taunts. I'd been falling into despair that I'd been outwitted by someone as despicable as Ciprian, but then Julian came. He'd heard my call.

"All is well," I whispered, stepping naked over stone debris from Ciprian's crumbled house toward my dragon, my beautiful beast. "I am well," I told him, raising a palm toward him.

He crouched his body to the blood-spattered terrace, Ciprian's headless corpse roasting in Julian's fire beside him. Julian purred deep as he lowered his head at my approach.

Nude and still dizzy from the drugged wine, I stumbled toward him and wrapped my arms around his giant snout, laying my cheek and torso against his warm, smooth scales.

"I'm all right now," I murmured.

Even as I felt listless and weak, there was a new strength inside me, and I knew instantly what it was. Our bond. Mine with Julian and his dragon. We were one, and we were mighty together.

He rumbled a growl, and I realized I was nearly asleep, resting against him.

"All right."

I lifted away and looked into one of his narrowed, golden eyes blinking slowly and contentedly at me, reminding me of a cat warm in the sunlight.

"Time to go, I know."

He kept very still while I managed to climb upon his clawed paw, slipping a little on his bloody scales, until I was finally atop, near the base of his neck, farther away from the spikes that lined his spine. I had nothing to tie myself to him this time, so I gripped the coarse hair that grew down the column of his neck.

"I'm ready," I murmured low, but somehow he heard me.

He beat his wings softly, swirling the fire and smoke that had engulfed Ciprian's home into a maelstrom, orange embers floating higher. Julian lifted off gently into the air, taking care not to jostle me, and circled over the conflagration he'd made. The flames licked and hopped through the boughs of trees to the next house, where the neighbors ran out onto the cobblestone street.

They looked up and pointed. It seemed as if this was a dragon's way of gloating, circling his destruction, making sure everyone knew it was his. Staring down, I could see dots of people all along Palatine Hill, some running toward the fire to see what had happened and some running away.

Of those running away, I noticed two figures—a slim one with blond hair holding the hand of a larger man—Rhea and Doro. I smiled as I watched them turn a corner toward the Aventine.

As Julian made a wider circle, drifting farther away from the fire-light, something caught my eye. A pull on my tether drew me to the faint outline of a transparent figure towering high as a mountain, looking down into the flames. My breath caught as she spread her nearly invisible dragon wings wide, gilded by the inferno's glow. Then she looked at me, her eyes nothing but lavender starlight and wonder. And she smiled.

Julian lifted higher into the night sky so that I had to twist around to look back. But the goddess Minerva was gone. Nothing but flames burning along the Palatine hillside of Rome and stars twinkling in the clear night sky.

Every person on the streets of Rome stopped where they were and looked up, watching us fly away. I wondered if they could see the naked woman flying atop the red dragon. I laughed, for I could hear my sister Lela saying to me now, *you're so reckless.*

I didn't feel reckless though. I felt mighty and strong . . . and free.

My red dragon roared up into the night, certainly proud of the destruction and death he'd left behind, before he turned away from Rome and flew west, the moonlight guiding our way.

JULIAN

She'd been sleeping for hours. I'd tended the cut Ciprian had made high at the base of her spine. He hadn't cut deep. Just deep enough to hurt and torment her.

I sighed with contentment yet again that he was dead by my hand and pulled Malina tighter into my arms. It was near morning, but I refused to wake her. We were safe here, far from Rome, in one of Trajan's many homes to the north.

We still had a long way to go across water to reach what would be our new home for a while. I'd have to send word to Trajan through his grandfather in Vulsinii to be sure all was safe for him.

If I knew anything about Trajan, he'd have slain that praetorian who fled my home last night. But I wasn't sure if he'd been seen and then had to go into hiding himself. I knew that Trajan would find a way to get Ruskus and the others to safety, to his secret property where he knew I'd take Malina.

I'd certainly ruined our plot to kill my uncle. But by my soul, we'd find another way.

My uncle had had my mother and father killed, and the rest of the house as well so there would be no witnesses. Kara had only survived because she had been delivering the babe of another patrician. How had I never come to the conclusion that he'd killed my family?

Once, in the beginning of my uncle's reign, I had suspected. But then my uncle showered me with what I knew now was false sympathy and another promotion in his army. He was on the rise, and I was foolish enough to be proud of my relation to him. However, that was short-lived. His laws and decrees took root, and I'd wrestled with my conflicting emotions until I decided my uncle must be killed. But I still hadn't imagined that he'd killed his own brother.

Perhaps it was because Igniculus had never shown any animosity toward my father, only a mild disappointment at his choices in life. My uncle only seemed to strike when his temper ran hot. But he was clever around me. Whatever hatred he held for my father, he never showed it to me.

That was because he would've lost my favor.

"You never had it," I whispered to the open window where the temperate night and cool, salty breeze wafted in.

"Who never had what?"

I rolled to my side so I could look at her. Her eyes were drowsy, her smile tender.

"How do you feel?" I asked.

"Wonderful." She stretched her naked body, wrapping an arm around my waist.

"Did he hurt you . . . other than here"—I slid my fingertips beneath her cheek where it was swollen and red—"and the cut here?" I then grazed my hand up her bare spine just beneath the cut on her back.

"No." She continued to smile.

"Why are you so happy? I allowed you to be taken away and harmed."

She lay back onto the pillow and laughed. "Silly man." She trailed a hand down my bare chest. "I am alive. I am with you. We are free." She glanced around and frowned. "Where are we, by the way?"

"In one of Trajan's homes. In Pisae." I glanced around. "It is one of his smaller ones. No one lives here regularly so I knew this would be safe for a night."

She inhaled deep. "I smell the ocean."

"Yes. The Tyrrhenian Sea. Sapphirus dragons love the water."

Malina practically leaped out of bed and hurried to the window. Then she looked over her shoulder and smiled. "Come look, Julian. It's beautiful."

"That it is," I agreed as I went to her.

Gods, she was divine. The moon gilded her in silvery light, the ocean breeze streaming through her dark, wavy hair. I wrapped my arms around her waist and nuzzled my face into her hair.

"You smell so good."

She laughed, then we grew quiet, staring out the window and down at the sea, waves glittering like glass. For a few moments, we said nothing at all, completely content in holding one another.

Then she pressed her head back against my sternum and I kissed her crown.

"So what happens now?" she asked, her arms crossed over mine at her waist.

"In a few hours, at dawn, we gather some provisions and leave for Britannia."

"Britannia?!"

"Yes. That's where Trajan has a home no one knows about."

"What about Stefanos, Ivo, and the others?"

"Trajan will get them there, if he can. Or he'll hide them somewhere safe."

"So we'll all be safe," she said contentedly.

"We will."

"Then what? What about everyone else?" Her concern was as much my own.

"We'll wait until my betrayal has died down, and we form a new plan."

"Died down?" she scoffed, trailing her hands over my chest. "You burned half of Palatine Hill."

"Not half," I argued. "A quarter, maybe."

Her smile returned as she arched a brow. "You were beautiful." She pressed a kiss to my sternum. "And fierce." Then she kissed me again before lowering to her knees.

"Malina," I warned. "You're still injured."

"I only need one thing to make me feel better."

She gripped me around the base of my cock, already hard at the first press of her lips on my skin.

"You shouldn't," I whispered, as I combed her hair away from her face.

"I decide what's best for me, and this is what I want." Then she wrapped her sweet mouth around the tip of my cock and my knees buckled.

"*Gods,*" I muttered, bracing a hand on the window frame, my other scooping beneath her hair to her neck.

She sucked me deep, loosening her jaw so I could slide even farther down her throat. I groaned as I fucked her mouth slowly, grazing my thumb to the edge of her mouth so I could feel where I slid inside her.

"Touch yourself," I commanded.

She did, her eyes rolling as she bobbed her head, her hand still gripping the base of my cock. Her other hand was busy between her legs, making slick sounds with her arousal.

"I can't." I slid my cock from her mouth on a moan. "I need to be inside you."

As I hauled her up, she turned and braced her hands on the windowsill, smiling over her shoulder. "Nice and slow."

"As you wish, firebird."

Gripping her hips, I sank inside her slowly. She exhaled a whimper and arched her back, thrusting her backside up.

"Yes," I groaned as I seated myself deep and ground inside her.

But I needed to feel more of her. I bent over her, bracing my hand on the sill next to hers, and slid my other hand between her legs into the slick she'd made.

"Love how wet you get for me," I whispered into her ear as I pumped nice and slow the way she wanted, the way she'd commanded.

"Always," she whispered breathily, grinding back against me as I gently pumped inside her. "I need you, Julian." Her whispered words were desperate and fearful.

"I'm here, my love." I removed my hand from between her legs and wrapped her waist tight so that her back was pressed entirely to my front. "Don't you feel me, firebird?"

"Yes. I want to feel all of you." She writhed back against me. "Forever, Julian."

"Yes." I fucked her faster, feeling her getting closer to climax. "Forever, love."

"Gods!" she screamed out the window toward the ocean as her sex squeezed and pulsed around my cock.

I groaned, biting her shoulder gently and thrusting twice more before I came inside her. She continued to squirm beneath me, wringing every drop from me.

When she went limp in my arms, I slid out of her, then carried her to bed, not bothering to wipe away my seed. I wanted it all over her. I wished I could remain in this bed with her for forever. But there was so much left to do.

She remained quiet, breathing heavily in my arms until I thought she was asleep. I'd let her doze until it was time to go.

But then she said, so softly I almost didn't hear her, "The goddess Minerva was there tonight."

I stroked my palm up and down her back, soothingly. "Indeed?"

"I asked her for something. And in exchange, I'd give up my magic."

"But you still have it." I felt her pull on me tonight louder than a waking scream. And it was still there now.

"I do."

"What did you ask of her?"

"To vanquish all of our enemies." She sat up and looked at me in earnest.

I cupped her face. "Then we still have work to do before she'll take your magic from you."

"Yes." She smiled and laid her cheek to my chest. "We still do." She curled her arm tighter around my waist. "I love you, Julian."

"As I love you, firebird." I pressed another kiss into her hair. "Now get some sleep before our journey."

EPILOGUE

Four months later . . .

MALINA

Stefanos and his dog, Amica, chased the sheep back into the pen. We'd told him a thousand times that Amica could do it by herself, but he refused to let her do it alone. So here I was at the top of the hill above our new home, sitting on the green grass, watching a gangly boy and his dog herd sheep.

"What's that smile for?" Julian lowered himself behind me, straddling his legs on either side.

I placed my hands on his woolen pants as he wrapped his arms around my waist and bent forward to kiss the side of my neck. There was an unsealed scroll in his left hand.

"Word from Trajan?"

"Yes. What's that smile for?"

"Stefanos."

"Not for me?" He curled his fingers into my ribs and tickled.

I laughed and squirmed until he stopped and buried his face in my hair as he always did. He practically commanded that I leave it down all the time, which was ridiculous because it was a hassle and in the way. Nevertheless, I left it down more often than not.

"I love how happy and carefree he is here," I finally told him.

Julian watched with me, seeming to see what I did. When I turned my head to look at him, he wasn't smiling. He was frowning.

"What is it?"

"It's a shame is all." His timbre dipped, his expression thoughtful. "He should be able to be this way anywhere. Not just in Britannia, a foreign land so far from his home."

This weighed hard on Julian. He accepted full responsibility for the failure of their plot to overthrow the emperor and his followers. Even though he said none of the allies directly blamed him—or that's what Trajan told us—the fact was that it would be more difficult to get to the emperor now. We both knew that. Ciprian had given us little choice, but it didn't make the current state of affairs any better.

"What of Rome?" I asked soberly.

He heaved a sigh. "The consul Valerius just pushed a new law through the senate."

"And?"

"No Roman may leave the city without direct permission from the emperor."

I scoffed and half turned in his arms. "How could he enforce such a law?"

"He's enlarged his praetorian guard. Special recruits from Legatus Drussus's legions."

"What does that mean?"

He swiveled his amber-gold gaze from down the hill to me. "Drussus is as cruel as they come. He's given orders to kill any Roman trying to fly out of the city at night. He's also assigned deathriders to guard the skies."

"But they never discovered any of your allies, have they?"

"No more than Marcus and Phillius." Those were the two senators who had been seen by Ciprian's slave and named in the report to the emperor. They'd been killed when they refused to give any other conspirators' names before the praetorian guards had then gone to Julian's home the night we fled.

"Thank the gods Trajan's quick thinking saved himself that night."

"Indeed."

After Trajan had killed the final praetorian guard, he'd watched us fly away, then rushed to the emperor's palace. But he waited in the shadows until we'd had enough time to flee beyond anyone following us and until the shouts of alarm could be heard at the top of the hill. That was when Trajan rushed into the palace, covered in blood, still in half-skin—knowing it was against the law.

When the praetorian guard shifted into half-skin and captured him, the clamor of noise bringing the emperor to the entrance, he told the emperor that Julian was a traitor. That he knew he was going to Ciprian's to take back his slave girl, and when Trajan went after Julian to stop him, he'd attacked Trajan.

That explained why he was in half-skin and bruised and battered. Trajan had declared angrily that Julian was a traitor. Somehow, being the first one to bring the emperor the news made him more believable. Igniculus didn't suspect Trajan as part of Julian's alliance, as far as we knew. If he did, Trajan wouldn't be sending us messages through our connection in Londinium.

He'd taken up speaking out against Julianus Dakkia in the forum, that it was a heinous betrayal that a general killed another general for a mere slave girl. Interestingly enough, Trajan said he could see who agreed with him and who did not by the looks in their eyes when he spoke out against us. He'd already rallied more allies to their cause that way.

Julian lifted the scroll. "Do you know they actually elected him tribune of the senate?"

"Really?"

"All his talk against me"—he gestured to himself—"the traitor Julianus, bought him sympathy with the Romans following Igniculus." He smiled. "And of course, his own grandfather and our allies fell right in line, cheering him on as he blackened my name on the forum pulpit."

I laughed, imagining Trajan putting on quite a show in the forum. "He must be a superb actor."

"Apparently so."

"We should've brought him on tour with our troupe." A maudlin memory of me and my sisters dancing whispered across my mind.

"No," said Julian gravely, "then he'd be flirting with you and your pretty sisters incessantly and I'd have to beat him for it."

I leaned back against him and let him take my weight—physically and emotionally—for a moment. That was what was most fascinating about the tether I'd created between us. There were times when the memories were too much, and he was able to lift that burden from me, to comfort me with his love. And the promise that we would right the wrongs. That we would create a new Rome.

"Look at that," he said, holding me close, pointing toward the garden behind the farmhouse we all shared.

Ruskus followed Agatha along a line of squash in the garden, holding her basket while she pulled the ripe vegetables from the vines. Agatha was the older, widowed daughter of a local blacksmith who was one of Trajan's contacts here in Britannia. We'd hired Agatha to aid us in getting settled here in our new home, and she'd been paramount in helping us.

"I know," I sighed. "Who would've thought? A Thracian and a Saxon."

He nuzzled my cheek and kissed my jaw. "A Roman dragon and a dancing Dacian."

Laughing, I turned my head for a kiss. He obliged as always.

"And did Trajan deliver our wedding gift to the emperor?"

Julian smiled against my mouth. "He said he'd deliver it whenever he had a way of not getting caught."

"Of course. We don't want Trajan's head on the Wall of Traitors."

"I wish I could be there to see the bastard's face when he opens it."

"No more talk of Rome," I said, turning and pushing him to his back. I sprawled across his chest, admiring him in his non-Roman clothes. He wore the same shirts and pants as local Saxons. I liked seeing him out of a toga. "Right now, your new bride wants your un-divided attention."

"Whatever my wife wants, she gets."

Then he pulled me down for a deep kiss. We stayed there until the sun began to set. And until Stefanos called up the hill that it was time for dinner.

Back in Rome . . .

"Sir, we found this box on the palace doorstep."

Igniculus looked up from the dinner he was having alone. "Who delivered it?"

"We don't know. No one knows. It is addressed to you."

The emperor waved for the praetorian to bring the box to him. It was an ornate wooden box carved with Roman gilding and the god-dess Minerva on the top. He unlatched and opened the box to find a single gold coin in the bottom. An aureus.

Igniculus frowned. It wasn't minted with his likeness, but it appeared shiny and new.

He lifted and flipped it over, recognizing his family symbol of the Dakkian dragon flying upward and blowing flame. On the other side was the profile of a woman. He didn't understand. Who had minted gold with his own seal and a strange woman's face?

Some of the older generation had the custom of doing this for weddings. But he hadn't authorized any weddings of the aristocracy, and certainly not of his—

He made a sound of distress.

"Emperor?" His praetorian stepped forward, then saw the emperor's face and stepped back as Igniculus seemed to understand who had sent him the gift in Minerva's box.

The emperor's furious roar could be heard all the way down Palatine Hill to the forum, where Trajan was meeting with a group of senators. He looked up at the sound and smiled.

But in one home farther up Palatine Hill, where Consul Valerius lived, a slave woman who'd been in the herb garden startled at the deafening sound. She froze and stared up, waiting to see if the beast who'd made that cry would soar overhead.

"What was that?" called the new young girl, coming up beside her.

"I don't know."

"Perhaps the dragons will all kill each other soon," whispered the new girl.

"We can only hope so," said Lela, staring up at the noonday sky, wishing it were so.

ACKNOWLEDGMENTS

First and foremost, I'd like to thank Monique Patterson and my agent, Rachel Brooks, for wholeheartedly believing in and supporting this idea I had sitting in my "one-day-I'll-write-this" vault for nearly a decade. Your vision for Malina and her sisters equals mine, and I couldn't be happier sharing their journey with Tor Bramble. Much appreciation also to my editor, Erika Tsang, who exceeded my lofty expectations in helping me make *Firebird* the best she could possibly be.

To Alexandra Roncea, I am so grateful to you for providing careful feedback on the Romanian language used in the text and ensuring its authenticity. To my niece, Jessen Judice, who is the best sounding board and brainstormer in the world, I can't thank you enough.

Finally, and most importantly, to my husband, Kevin, and my family, who tirelessly support me through all of the stressful moments and the exciting celebrations. I couldn't do it without you.

Read on for exclusive content for FairyLoot readers.
This bonus chapter takes place following Chapter XXVII.

MALINA

I awoke with a start and jolted upright. I couldn't remember my dream, but Kizzy's laughter echoed in my mind.

I felt beside me in the dark—the curtains around the bed drawn—but Julian wasn't there. That was when I noticed a tug on the tether I kept tied to him.

Rubbing my palm over my heart, I realized that was what had woken me.

I rose, wrapping the wool blanket around my naked shoulders, and padded in the darkness to find him. He was stood on the terrace beneath the half-moon, staring out into the night. Silvery moonlight caressed the masculine curves of his naked body. I shivered, but didn't make a sound. Still, he knew I was there.

"You should get your sleep while you can. Dawn is a few hours yet."

I continued across the terrace and stepped in front of him to look out at sleeping Rome. No oil lamps lit the windows. No noise came from taverns or brothels. She was a slumbering beast, resting easily in her bower. No worries that an enemy might strike her in the night. For who would dare to strike at the heart of the gods' anointed?

Julian wrapped his arms around me from behind, holding me close in the warmth of his embrace.

"You should sleep," he rumbled against my temple.

"Like you are?"

A soothing growl vibrated in his chest, then he hugged me closer against him.

"What worries you?" I asked. "The combat against Ciprian tomorrow?"

"No."

He went quiet again so I persisted. "Then what?"

"Tell me about your mother, Malina."

Surprised at the request, I thought a moment. "She was strict with us girls. Demanding. Kizzy often said, 'Mama, you fuss too much.' Then Mama would reply, 'That's because your father fusses too little.'"

His quiet chuckle vibrated against my back. I smiled.

"Your father was the softer one then."

"He was," I agreed. "He loved to jest and make us laugh. But especially Mama. If she was in one of her foul moods, he'd tease her until she smiled." I blinked away the emotion that brimmed tears in my eyes. "But they both loved us fiercely," I added softly.

"Your mother sounds a lot like mine."

"Really? I can't believe she was hard on her precious only son Julianus."

He laughed lightly. "You would if you'd met her."

There was a wistful longing in his voice. I could even feel it tremble along the ethereal cord that connected us.

"Tell me one story that would make me believe such a thing."

He heaved out a sigh. "One time, when I was about as old as Stefanos, my mother was preparing to host a party. I don't remember what it was for, but my parents rarely did such things. I didn't realize until later that it was because of my mother's birth and caste as a freed slave. They had a very small social circle."

He paused, and I waited, trying to imagine what his mother's life might have been like.

"She'd warned me to stay out of the house because everyone was cleaning for their party. But I didn't listen. I'd been playing soldiers, sword fighting with sticks with Memio, our cook's son."

"Kara wasn't your cook then?"

"She was my mother's body slave at that time."

Before she was murdered, he didn't say. I turned in his arms, still keeping the blanket wrapped around me, and pressed my cheek to his chest.

He didn't have to explain the achingly sweet sort of pain I felt singing along our bond. I knew exactly what it was like to recall the good memories of loved ones who were violently taken from you.

"You can probably imagine what I did," he continued quietly, sliding a hand up and down my spine. "I got myself covered in mud and trampled right through the gathering hall where the feast was to take place."

"Oh, no." I laughed.

"Oh, yes."

"So you got a good scolding, I'm sure."

"Much worse than that. I had to scrub and clean the floors all by myself, then help Memio with his chores of cleaning out the stables

387

since that was what he was supposed to be doing when we ran off into the field."

"You're right. That sounds a lot like my mother."

"Who knows," he slid a hand beneath my fall of hair and clasped the nape of my neck gently. "They might've even been friends. In a different world."

I didn't contradict such a fantasy, but I couldn't see any possible reality where that would've happened.

"That's what keeps me up at night," he said gruffly. "That's what I want."

I stepped back and looked up at him. "What do you mean?"

"A whole new world, Malina." He cupped my face with both hands. "And I'm going to make it happen."

There was such determination in his voice, but I couldn't keep silent at that.

"Julian, I understand why you want this, but do you realize what you want seems . . ." I shook my head, trying to find the right words before finally whispering, "You dream the impossible."

His brow pinched into a frown while he brushed his thumbs along the swell of my cheeks. "I do not. I will make it happen."

"You sound so sure."

"That's because I am."

I scoffed. "Spoken like a dragon who has always gotten his way." Sliding one arm out of the fold of my blanket, I pressed my palm to the center of his broad chest. "Just because you are touched by the gods, it does not mean you are one of them, Julian. You are not invincible."

He arched a brow with that superior gleam in his eyes. "I will make the world right. I will make *Rome* right again. It is my destiny."

"You do realize that killing your uncle isn't enough? Even killing all of his men isn't enough. You'd have to change society's way of thinking." I blew out a breath of frustration. "For that, you'd have to burn the whole city and start over. Even then, it might not be enough."

"Well, then," he lowered his head and brushed a soft kiss against my lips, "I suppose I'll have to burn Rome and start over then." He swept his lips against mine again, whispering, "For I won't live in a world where I can't have you by my side, Malina. Not as my slave, but as my wife."

I soaked in his tender words along with his kisses. The very thought of being his wife elevated my heart rate. How could that ever happen in the world we lived in?

"And you plan to take your uncle's throne?" I asked as he slid his mouth along my jaw to my throat. "That I would become . . ."

"My empress? Yes. That is what I plan to do."

He nipped and licked that tender place below my ear, one of his hands sliding through the folds of the blanket I still held around me.

"My firebird will burn bright," he murmured into my skin, sliding his warm palm around my bare waist and pulling me closer, curling his body over mine.

"Am I your destiny too?" I asked, a vulnerable wobble in my voice. "Would the gods do such a thing?"

He lifted his head and stood straight, staring down, his expression grave as the dragon flickered behind his golden eyes. Without a word, he scooped me into his arms and turned for the bedchamber. I buried my face into his neck, inhaling the hypnotic scent of him.

He lay me onto the bed and pulled the curtains closed, blotting out the rest of the world. He hovered over me before pressing another kiss to my lips and opening the blanket I'd wrapped around myself.

It was too dark to see, except for the flicker of his dragon eyes as he trailed his fingers over my collarbone, down between my breasts and over my belly. I squirmed and whimpered when he wrapped his fingers around my thigh and spread me open.

"I know you're sore," he said, his voice farther away as he shifted down the bed. "But we'll have no more talk tonight. And no more doubts about your place with me." His voice dipped deeper as he pressed a kiss to my inner thigh.

I jumped. "Julian," I protested, reaching down and threading my fingers into his hair.

"Let me worship you, love," he whispered before he opened his mouth on my core and licked inside.

I jolted again, but this time my hips lifted toward his mouth rather than away, my body knowing what to do even if I felt tender—both in my body and my soul. I let my knees fall wider, and he groaned while licking and kissing my sex.

Throwing my other arm over my eyes, I arched my neck and gave in to the sensation, letting Julian do what he wanted, what I wanted. My pleasure seemed to be his, for as I moaned louder, so did he.

He scooped his hands under my buttocks and teased my swollen bud, coaxing my body to respond. While I was hotly aroused, my head spun with all the worries we had discussed, all the impossibilities that Julian planned to bring to fruition.

I curled my fingers in his hair, scraping my blunt nails along his scalp. He groaned, stroking his tongue inside me.

Again, I felt a climax swim closer then fade away.

"I can't," I whispered into the dark.

He continued his relentless, gentle sucking and flicking of his tongue. He'd surely heard me, but he didn't care. If he was anything, Julian was persistent.

I reached down with my other hand, attempting to push him away. "*I can't*," I said louder.

He grabbed my wrist and guided my other hand to his head. I could see nothing, but could only imagine what I might look like, both hands pressing my master's head down between my legs while he pleasured me with his tongue. The vision in my mind, and his panting and constant attention where I needed it, had my body suddenly climbing faster toward climax.

Then I heard it, the rumbling growl of his dragon. I lifted my head and stared down into the dark, the golden slits of his eyes watching me as he licked me to orgasm. As he and his dragon made me come.

"Ah!" I cried out with sudden sharpness, but he didn't relent, licking me tenderly while my hips rocked against his mouth.

When I was finally done, completely limp and spent, he crawled up my body. I thought he would enter me, wanting his own satisfaction. But no, he curled me onto my side and pulled me into the warm curve of his body. He pressed a kiss to the crown of my head as he pulled a blanket over us.

"Julian, I'm sorry if I—"

"No apologies."

I sighed, sliding my arm over the one he had around my waist, curling my fingers around his thick wrist.

"Sleep, my sweet." He pressed another kiss to my temple. "I simply want to hold you a while longer. Until dawn comes. Until day takes this away from me."

We snuggled closer in the warm darkness of his bed, behind the curtains that hid us away from the world. Though we tried to forget, tangled in each other's arms, I knew that the gods saw us. And I worried what punishment they might cast upon me for doing the forbidden; a human girl falling in love with a dragon.

I wasn't as sure as Julian. I wasn't born with a divine beast living inside me.

But you were born with magic, whispered the witch within me.

Sighing, I tugged on the tether as I burrowed deeper into Julian's arms, pulling him tighter to me in every way. I hoped that if I pulled tight enough, I could keep him from being severed from me.

As I finally drifted into dreams, I thought I heard my sister Kizzy again. This time, she wasn't laughing . . . she was crying.

Turn the page for a sneak peek at the second book
in the Fires That Bind series

BLOODSINGER

Available Winter 2o26

LELA

Masculine laughter rumbled up to the domed ceiling of the great hall. The lilting flute music grated my nerves, but I remained still and mute as always in the corner, waiting to be summoned by my master, Consul Valerius.

Sometimes I thought—hoped—he might forget about my quiet presence at these revelries. But he never did. He liked to flaunt all of his pretty possessions.

For the moment, the new slave girl, Roza, danced and twirled, her sheer green skirt lifting to reveal her naked body beneath. Her breasts were bare, painted with green and gold paint in the pattern of dragon scales.

Valerius's three guests—senators of Rome—were enraptured by Roza's seductive display. All but one, whose gaze moved about the room with a slow, calculating sweep.

I'd never seen him before. He was younger than the other senators Valerius usually invited into his home and far more attractive. His black wavy hair was short as most Roman nobles'. He wore a close-cropped beard that didn't hide the sharp-cut edges of his jaw and chin. His blue toga denoted him of the Sapphirus House—one of the higher-ranking dragon houses. Higher than Valerius. No wonder he'd hired the more expensive musicians and had prepared such an extravagant feast.

I'd spent several minutes observing my master's new guest, who didn't seem to quite fit in with the others. Distracted by his unusual demeanor, I hadn't noticed him noticing me, his arresting blue eyes fixed and intense.

I immediately averted my gaze to the floor, disliking the skitter of my pulse. Rarely did anything make my heart race anymore, not even Master's visits in the night.

I managed to become numb to everything—easily able to let my mind drift to a safer place when my body was being used.

"Valerius," called the stranger. "I did not know you took a wife."

Kaius laughed, chilling my blood to ice. The first time I had heard that laugh was when I screamed and cried for mercy the night he and other Romans in half-skin form attacked our village—my wedding night. That laugh had burned into my bones and my very soul as he killed my beloved Jardani. Kaius was the one who'd sold me to Valerius. Not for money, but for a high seat in the senate.

"I don't have a wife. Lela is my favored slave," he answered the stranger before calling louder, "Lela! Come forward."

I stepped toward the lounging, feasting demons in human form, ready to play my part as his walking sculpture, his muzzled pet. Valerius waved his hand for Roza to move to the side. She sauntered to the left and continued dancing, her concerned gaze catching mine as she swept past me.

Valerius lounged on his side on the highest cushioned chaise facing forward within the atrium that opened up to the dome's oculus, giving his guests a view of the starry night. Corinthian columns encircled the intimate salon. Green velvet chaise sofas and golden silk cushions filled the intimate space. It was a pile of luxury for Valerius's most important guests.

Leto, his closest ally in the senate, stretched out on his side to Valerius's left, filling his gullet as usual. Kaius lounged on the floor of cushions to his right. And the new, handsome stranger sat up on the rug beneath, his back propped against one of the pillars that enclosed the atrium. He sat with them, but also somehow seemed apart.

"What is that thing on her neck and mouth?" asked the dark-haired stranger, his expression grim and tight.

His attention to my ornate gold-plated bridle instantly dragged my own to the coldness of it against my skin and the plate in my mouth pressing down on my tongue. The metal collar was wrapped around my throat with the muzzle sculpting over my chin, jaw, and mouth.

The bridle had been specifically designed for me. Valerius had wanted one that was elegant but still completely covered my mouth. Thin golden chains anchored it over my head so that I could still wear my hair down the way he preferred. The mechanism locked at the base of my neck beneath my hair. He kept the key in his bedchamber. Only he and his body slave had access to it. So he thought.

Valerius had paid a high price to the sculptor. Not only for the crafting of it but also for the emeralds encrusted in a straight line where my mouth should be.

But I had no mouth in this house, no voice at all. Not even when the bridle was off.

I walked to the center of the room, my dark wavy hair brushing my hips. The picture of caged beauty. I turned and faced them, my demeanor cool. My mind blank and my heart invisible. As always.

"That's right," said Kaius to the younger senator. "This is your first visit to Valerius's lair, isn't it?" He chuckled, but I refused to look at him. "You've never seen the pretty viper he keeps in his home."

"What do you mean?" asked the stranger.

I kept my eyes straight while all of theirs were on me, looking their fill, gorging themselves on my state of torture.

Lego, a rotund man, chimed in while chewing on his roasted lamb. "She's a witch."

The stranger huffed in disbelief. "There's no such thing."

"How can you even say that?" snarled Kaius. "When your own general was beguiled by one. They say that Celtic witch caused mayhem for our armies until Julianus took over. Then he fell spellbound by her as well."

"You witnessed Legatus Julianus's downfall by the woman," added Leto, narrowing his beady eyes on the younger senator. "You had to know she was a witch. Used her powers to make him betray the emperor, his own blood."

"Julianus was insane," added my master, watching me intently. "To kill another general, burn his corpse and half of Palatine Hill, then flee Rome. For a woman?" Valerius chuckled, plucking a plump peach from a bowl at his elbow. "Fool."

"Yes," agreed the handsome stranger. "General Julianus was indeed ensnared by the woman. But she was no witch. Just a woman who seduced her master and made him into a traitor."

I absorbed the story I'd heard more than once by now. The once famous Roman general known as the Coldhearted Conqueror, nephew to Caesar, had shifted into his giant red dragon, killed and burned another Roman patrician who'd hurt his slave woman, then flew away with her on his back away from Rome, somewhere across the ocean. I wished I'd seen it. The beautiful fantasy of it kept me awake some nights, a dream that would never come true for me.

Refocusing on my reality, I let the cold settle in again. It was dangerous to wish for more, to wish for escape. I'd tried. And it had gotten this golden muzzle on my face and made my master maniacal and obsessive of me.

"You never said why you still keep her after what she did," added Kaius. His gaze always devoured me, but I refused to ever look him in the eye. The day I did, I would kill him.

"What did she do?" asked the stranger.

Valerius fingered the scar on his throat. The one I'd given him. "You may not believe that your general was charmed by a sorceress, but these witches do exist. You're looking at one."

His voice dropped deep, his eyes glinting an otherworldly green. His dragon loved to tell this story. The one where he nearly died at my hands and survived to cage me so well.

"Kaius didn't know what she was either until after he'd sold Lela to me. One night, when I took her to my bed, she bit me so hard that I bled."

I stared at my master, loving to hear this story of how I almost regained my freedom. His eerie, glittering gaze bore into mine.

"I thought it strange when she sucked the blood from the bite mark. But then I felt it, the kind of magic I feel in transformation."

The men were riveted by his story. So was I. It had been the first time I felt the magic surge up inside of me. My bunica had always told me it would come, that I would know when to use it. And I had. It was the first night Valerius forced me into his bed. And the mystical powers that lived in my blood instantly awoke, fed by my rage.

"Then what happened?" asked the younger one.

"She spoke and told me to pick up my dagger and slit my own throat." Valerius grinned, his fangs extending. "And I immediately did as she ordered." He laughed. "Thank the gods, my body slave stopped me, or I'd be dead."

"She's god-touched," said the stranger with such awe that I turned my attention to him.

His eyes lit with something more than curiosity or wonder. It was almost like recognition. But that couldn't be. We'd never met.

"A child of Minerva, it seems." Valerius tilted his head, still staring at me while he ate his peach, the juice dribbling down his chin.

"That cunt of a goddess should never have defied her betters," grunted Kaius, guzzling his goblet of wine.

Bunica had told me and my sisters the story of Medusa and her own sisters, who'd been given special gifts by the goddess Minerva. I'd never believed it until the night I'd almost killed Valerius, the night I felt the magic living inside me.

"Fascinating," said the stranger, his expression pinched with concern.

"But why keep her?" demanded Kaius. "Now that you know she's so deadly. She's a coiled serpent, waiting to strike. Look at her. Even now, she stares as if she's plotting against us. Her pulse is steady, her heart as cold as ice."

Valerius's grin widened. "Oh, she can get hot enough."

Kaius chuckled. "I bet she can."

Valerius tossed the half-eaten peach on the platter and wiped his fingers on a fold of his green toga. "Besides, I like the reminder to be wary. When death lives in your home, you never let your guard down."

His eyes glinted with menace and a promise that he would never give me a second chance to kill him. In that first fit of rage, I'd ruined my opportunity. Rather than plan it out and find the right moment, I'd reacted to the fear and dread of being raped. I'd given my heart and body and soul to Jardani and couldn't allow another man to take what wasn't his. I'd reacted like a free woman, not the slave I'd become.

And so now, it was hopeless. This was my life, unless I ended it.

I longed for the coolness of the temple in the back of Valerius's home. My only place of solace. For when I was within its quiet, chilled walls, I could imagine that I was in fact in my own crypt. I welcomed this stillness like death.

"Good thing you don't need her mouth to make good use of her," added Kaius.

They all laughed at my expense, except for the younger senator. His blue eyes flared bright for a fleeting second.

"Beware, Consul Valerius."

His voice had dropped deep, his dragon present. A prickle of power skated across my skin, raising gooseflesh. The other three stopped laughing and looked at him.

"Death lurks everywhere in Rome. We should all heed caution. None of us suspected Legatus Julianus of being a traitor and yet he was. Legatus Ciprian didn't suspect him, and now he's dead. Julianus even fooled me, his own second-in-command. Best be mindful, senators, or death will find you sooner than you think."

The handsome senator in blue of the House of Sapphirus spoke in a low, rumbling timbre, his dominance radiating across the room, pressing these smaller men down with only a few words. Again, my pulse quickened and not out of fear for once. But because I knew there was a power greater than my master, greater than my misery.

"You're quite right, Trajan," conceded Valerius, clearing his throat nervously.

Trajan.

I let the name sift through my mind as the man himself picked up his own cup and drank, his gaze flicking to me, the piercing blue of his dragon brightening before he looked away again.

With a warning that put my master and his foul comrades in their place, Trajan had given me something I never dared dream to let flicker inside my heart again. . . . Hope.